I0572976

FALL WHEREVER THEY MAY

ELYSIA WAGES

CONTENT WARNING

Your mental health is important. Content warnings are on the next page. If you would prefer to go into this book blind, please skip to the dedication pages . . . you won't be sorry.

TRIGGER WARNINGS CONTAIN:

This is a romance with dark undertones. This book includes graphic depictions of sexually explicit scenes. If any of this content is triggering for you, please do not read this book.

Suicide (not in detail)

Abandonment

Miscarriage

Postpartum Depression

Postpartum Psychosis

Domestic Abuse (not in detail)

Homelessness

Child Neglect (not in detail)

Grief and Loss

Trauma

Physical Violence

Parental Loss

Alcohol Use

Cancer (not in detail)

Teenage Pregnancy

PTSD

Drug Reference

Workplace Sexual Harassment

Detailed sexual content include but are not limited to:

Dom/Sub Interactions

Praise Kink

Rough Sex

Bondage

Whipping

Spanking

Degradation

Choking

Breath Play

Mask Play

Public Sex

Edging

Sensory Deprivation

Gagging/Inappropriate Use of a Hockey Puck

Mouth Fucking

Sex Toys

Flogger

Restraints

Fear Play

Reader discretion is advised. If you find any of these topics to be distressing, please proceed with caution, or find a different book. Your mental health matters.

Playlist

"Trevi" - Holly Beth
"Gravity" - John Mayer
"Promises" - Calvin Harris & Sam Smith
"Million Dollar Baby" - Tommy Richman
"I Love This Bar" - Toby Keith
"No" - Meghan Trainor
"I Want You to Want Me" - Cheap Trick
"Walk" - Pantera
"Big Dawgs" - Humankind
"You Put a Spell on Me" - Austin Giorgio
"Breathe" - Kansh
"Sheets" - Kansh
"Cravin'" - Stileto & Kendyle Paige
"Mine" - Bazzi
"That's What I Like" - Bruno Mars
"You Make it Easy" - Jason Aldean
"Middle of the Night" - Elley Duhe
"Love on the Brain" - Rihanna
"Worship" - Ari Abdul
"Die for You" - The Weekend
"Pain" - Three Days Grace
"Love Me Harder" - Steven Rodriguez

This book is dedicated to my readers who have experienced abandonment: You are worthy, and you are loveable. Never allow someone's choice of walking out of your life to depict your self-worth.

To my self-proclaimed good girl,

When your eyes flick to each word in this book, imagine mine exploring your entire body. When your fingers glide down these pages, think of mine caressing your skin. Now, spread those pages like a good fucking girl.

~Your book boyfriend,

Callan Miles

That's my good girl . . .

Prologue

You could call me philosophical. I've always thought of life as a road with a million different turns along the way. Every single decision made is a turn in the road, which is met with obstacles and more decisions that lead to your destiny. You could also call me a dreamer, because a part of me wants to believe in events so random and so incredibly coincidental it couldn't possibly be anything other than fate.

You don't have to believe in fate; you can control your own destiny. But what if fate is real? What if fate and destiny collide? What if the stars align just right and the universe delivers exactly what you need at the precise moment you need it, and what if that alignment led to your destiny? Do you seize it with both hands, or do you disregard it because it's certainly "too good to be true"? You only live one life; you can choose to live it in joy or live it in misery.

One life to make the absolute most of. I knew the moment I got the phone call, I would be moving to New York. It didn't matter what took me there, fate or circumstances. The only thing that mattered to me was that the life I was living wasn't the life that I wanted. My past was continuing to dictate my future. My choice was simple.

Chapter One

Cal

All I'm saying is you need to stop sitting here in your godforsaken house, dwelling on your miserable past, and playing with your lonely ass dick! Get out and start living life!" Carter scolds, opening the grill and checking the meat. "Do you need some assistance? I'm sure I have someone in my contacts I can call for you."

As the smoke billows, I inhale, relishing in the smell of the savory meat cooking on the grill. I tip my beer back; the cold, crisp liquid glides down my throat. Staying silent, I avert my eyes. Avoidance is something I've mastered over the years, especially when it's concerning something I don't want to talk about. It's a character flaw, but I couldn't care less. I don't have the mental capacity nor the patience to deal with this shit right now, and I don't know if I ever will.

Carter is one of the right-wingers on my team, our enforcer. He's also my best friend. Of all my teammates, he's the outspoken one. The man with the pep talks. The guy who has his life together. He meets every challenge head-on and confronts his obstacles, taking them to the next level, even off the ice. I know he means well, but he doesn't understand because he's never been in my shoes. God, I wouldn't wish that on anybody.

"What?" He cuts into my thoughts, "You're just going to stand there and look at me but not say anything? Avoid the topic?" He points the spatula, dripping grease onto my patio. His eyes squint as he scrutinizes me. "If evasion were a career, you would make more money than you do in hockey." The antagonizing asshole presses as he flips the burgers. Okay . . . so . . . he's about to be my ex-best friend.

"I don't need anyone to . . ." I pause, chewing on my words, searching for the best way to articulate what's on my mind. ". . . assist with my dick. And I'll have you know I am living life right now. The team is coming over, and we're going to have a nice little barbecue. What more do you want from me? I'm doing my best here." Exhaling slowly, I crane my neck to glance at the side of the house, wishing for one of the other guys to appear and save me from this asshole.

Mediocrity is my best right now, even if that's all I've been doing for the past four years, but I don't need to give him that validation.

He releases a drawn-out sigh and sets the spatula down, then picks up the tongs. With the precision of a chef, he turns over the chicken and ribs, making sure the grill marks are perfect. "Are you? I'll have *you* know that fulfilling an obligation is not living. This little barbecue is a team-building event; it's your job. Yes, the team is important, and so are our teammates, but there's more to life than hockey."

Maybe for him there is, but he's already won two Stanley Cups. He didn't have his world turned upside down during game seven of the playoffs when his team was in a wild card spot, causing them to lose it all. He actually has something to show for his sacrifices. As for myself, I made the biggest sacrifice of all, and it cost me my fucking wife and baby. They were my life, and I lost them. I would give up everything to have them back. *Everything.*

My soul was crushed. I was completely broken, and my world had just imploded around me. There was no hope in sight. And what little support system I did have vanished in the blink of an eye. I was at rock bottom when the Colorado Wolves completely blindsided me by trading me off in a fire sale. One person didn't give up on me; there was a whole conglomerate.

In order to keep my sanity, I decided it was best to leave that life in the past, along with everyone in it. Now, winning the Stanley Cup before I fall to an injury or am forced into retirement is my main focus. Failure isn't an option. And I'll be damned if I'll leave this league giving my wife and son the middle finger, and that's exactly what I would be doing if I left without that trophy before I retired. Now all I have left are my new teammates and the game. There is no room for anyone or anything else.

I don't have the time, tolerance, or the drive to experience anything outside of hockey. At thirty-one years old—on the brink of thirty-two—my time in the pros is dwindling. I live, eat, and breathe my career. It's the only thing that keeps me going.

Carter picks up his beer and tips it my way. "It's time you get out there and start dating again."

"Not a fucking chance in hell . . ." I scoff, shaking my head at him.

All my prayers are answered when I spot someone's head peeking around the corner as they stroll along the side of my house.

"Yo, Smiley! What's happenin', my man?" Jerome Johnson, one of our defensemen, calls out.

I mosey his way, smiling at him like the saving grace he is. He reaches out to shake my hand as his arm wraps me up in a man hug.

"You didn't tell me there was a total smoke show moving in across the street! I might have to go introduce myself to the new, hot neighbor girl." He bites his bottom lip while rubbing his palms together. His head turns toward the house across the street. Inadvertently, my eyes follow the direction he's looking. In my line of sight, I find a woman with short, toned legs, cut-off shorts, and a red halter top. Long, blonde hair cascades down her back. She's facing the trunk of her black car, so I can't see her face, but objectively, I can see where he would think she's hot—if you're into the Malibu Barbie type. With a garment bag placed over her arm, she hoists a box out of the car, using her elbow to close the trunk.

"Shit!" She curses loudly.

Malibu Barbie sets down the box, and the garment bag slides down her arm before haphazardly falling to the ground. She rubs her elbow, inspecting the spot where I'm sure there will be a bruise tomorrow, based on how loud she cursed. The wind whips the long golden waves around her face, masking her profile.

"Maybe you should go help her, Smiley," Carter calls out.

I turn to find a smug expression resting on his face.

"Or . . . maybe *I* should go help her," Jerome counters.

Carter and Jerome lean to the side as they watch her make her way into the house. Without a word, I turn around and walk back to the outdoor kitchen. Gripping the island countertop with both hands, I hang my head in defeat, trying to collect myself.

I've gone out with my friend Nate on several different occasions in an attempt to hook up with a woman, but I never could follow through. I want to erase the pain and the emptiness that comes with the loss of my marriage—to heal and get past it—but it feels like cheating. Even the thought of kissing another woman leaves me with a sick feeling in the pit of my stomach and the urge to vomit.

I rub my chest where the dull ache still resides. You would think after all these years, I would be on a path to healing, but I'm not. Healing means therapy, therapy means talking and talking means reliving those memories. Even though a constant void lingers, and every day is a struggle to roll out of bed, avoiding all discussions concerning my wife seems like a better option than the alternative. Uncomfortable with the direction the conversation is going, I change the subject.

The bottle hisses as I pop the top and hand the beer to Jerome. "Where is everyone else?"

Just as I ask, the rest of my teammates come milling around the corner of my house. They greet me with handshakes, back slaps, and man-hugs as I direct them to a cooler filled with beer.

Ivan Lukov, our goalie, and his wife, Evie, make their way to greet me with a casserole dish in tow. Ivan shakes my hand with his free one. My eyes shift to Evie and the dish she holds in her hand. I know whatever is underneath that foil is a treat.

"Evie, you're glowing!" I wrap her in a side hug.

A genuine smile spreads across my face as she places a hand on her growing belly. Her luminous, ebony skin is radiant and glowing. A mess of chestnut, corkscrew curls fall to her shoulders. Her yellow sundress catches in the wind and ripples around her. Evelyn Lukov is elegance personified.

"Thanks, friend," she says with a beaming white smile.

Ivan and Evie are older than me by a few years and have a ten-year-old son named Elija. They weren't trying for this one. I chuckle at the memory of Ivan calling to tell me that life as he knew it was over. He was so dramatic about the situation. The reason for his despair: Their son, Elija, will graduate before this one is even out of elementary school. I guess I would be a little out of my head about that situation as well. However, planned or not, now it appears the two of them couldn't be happier with the new addition.

"I'll take that," I offer, relieving Evie of the dish. An unexpected moan escapes my lips, and my eyes close at the sweet aroma escaping from under the foil.

"This woman." I turn my head to look at Ivan. "It's no wonder you went and wifed her up. She is the best damn cook. What is this?" I hold up the dish, focusing my attention back on Evie.

"That, my friend, is an apricot galette with almond cream."

"Well, it smells delicious."

Taking the dessert to the outdoor kitchen island with Ivan and Evie trailing behind me, I look around and my brows furrow. "Where's Elija?" I ask.

"He's at our neighbor's house playing Fortnite," Ivan responds.

Evie pulls a water bottle out of the ice chest. "Who's the designated driver tonight?" She takes a drink, then places the cap back on the plastic bottle.

"I think it's Drew," I say, nodding my head in his direction.

Drew is one of our left-wingers and lightning fast. He lost a bet with our defenseman, Trevor Williams, making him the designated driver for the night.

"Perfect! I thought I would pop in and say hi before I headed to the boutique."

I give Evie one last hug before she leaves. "Thank you for the dessert. It was great to see you."

Ivan wraps his wife in his arms and gives her a kiss that would be considered almost inappropriate for company. Even though I told Carter I would never date again, I secretly crave to have a relationship that resembles what these two have. My wife and I were only twenty-one when we married. We loved each other, but we didn't have the kind of connection you read about in novels. We couldn't read each other's thoughts like these two can by just a mere look or expression. Paisley and I never experienced that, and maybe the reason is because she and I were too young and naive to understand ourselves, let alone each other.

"We got him, Mama. I'll have him home by curfew." Drew chuckles and takes a drink of his water as she leaves with a wave.

Casting a glance across the street, my eyes narrow on the two-story house where the Malibu Barbie resides. Parked cars litter the road, my driveway is jam-packed, and the music thumps throughout the neighborhood. My teammates loiter in the yard; their laughter and loud voices can be heard over the blaring music. This get-together reminds me of the frat parties I attended back in my college days. A whole fucking lot has changed since then. One of them being hospitality; it doesn't suit me very well. I hope like hell the neighbor doesn't find my party as an invitation to pop in and introduce herself. The thought makes me groan.

I take a seat beside Ivan and lean back in my chair, for once enjoying the company. The warm sun beats down on my face and causes sweat to ripple down my temple.

As I stretch out my aching joints, Ivan hits me in the chest while he looks down at his phone. "Whoa. Whoa. Whoa. What is this? And since when did you get social media?"

I tip my beer back, taking a sip before replying. "Since Teagan made me sign up for it about a month ago."

I loathe social media. Let's go back to the days before technology, when visiting someone's house or dialing a landline phone was how we communicated. I guess I'm kind of old school. Teagan, our PR manager, says it's good for my image, especially since as of late I've been labeled a broody asshole, but I hate being so accessible. And the thirst traps she makes me do! For the love of all that is holy, is it really necessary?

I do what Teagan tells me because she is the best. But sometimes, I think she makes me post stuff to make me uncomfortable on purpose. She gets a kick out of it. And I know this because she cackles as she tells me what to do. She insists being in front of people on social media makes me look like a real person to my fans. I don't understand how people can think that because I'm a professional athlete, I'm not just like them—that I'm not a real person with genuine problems and feelings.

This month, my social media following was insane, and my phone was constantly dinging with notifications from my DMs until I finally figured out how to mute them. The number of women begging for my attention by sending me nudes is completely insane. The whole reason for me not having social media was so I could focus on hockey. But here I am on all platforms, making sure I show the world I'm a "real person" and not a "broody asshole."

"Why didn't you follow me?" Ivan asks with a frown, seeming completely butt hurt.

"He apparently hasn't followed anyone," Carter placates, patting him on the back. "Don't get your feelings hurt. See?" He points to Ivan's phone: "Zero following."

I don't follow anyone. Like I said, I have enough to worry about in my life than to worry about someone other than myself. If I had it my way, Teagan would handle all my social media shit, and I wouldn't have access to it at all.

"So," Trevor looks at each of us, "any word on the new team owner?" He casually changes the subject as if we all aren't worried about what's going to happen to our team when the new owner takes over.

"There's been a lot of speculation in the media about a family member taking over. I hope he's not a complete dick and trades all our asses." Drew pauses with a contemplative frown before he continues, "I don't recall seeing a single family member at his funeral."

"There wasn't," Trevor responds. "Outside of all of us, the reserved seating for family was empty."

Carter gives me a pointed look. "I guess that's what happens when your career becomes your life."

Since Mr. West's death, I haven't thought about the repercussions of a new team owner. He may let us stay where we are; then again, there's the possibility he'll want to rebuild.

Three hours later, I'm ten beers in with red solo cups lined up on either side of the table. When we have team-building dinners, we always accompany them with an activity or a game, but we rarely drink like this. Most of the time, the guys bring their family, but since it's just the boys today, we let loose. Everyone is watching us, yelling and cheering. Jerome and Trevor have two cups left on our side, and Ivan and I have only one cup left on theirs. Not a peep rings out as Trevor throws the ping-pong ball . . . it misses his cup.

"It's down to this shot, gentlemen. The pressure is on. Callan 'Smiley' Miles pulled a hat trick in the last play, but can the center of The New York Blaze pull off the win for this year's Beer Pong Championship? We know Smiley's ego has a lot riding on this win. Will he do it?" Drew commentates, drawing laughs out of everyone.

I throw the ping-pong ball . . . it sinks into the very last cup on the opposing team's side. Everyone cheers and makes a ruckus as they jump up and down. In Trevor's inebriated state, he goes to chug the beer in his red solo cup, but the beer completely misses his mouth and pours down his chin.

"Oh no! That's a party foul! Now you have to chug an entire bottle!" Drew yells out. He produces a bottle of beer out of thin air, pops the top, then hands it over to Trevor.

"Those aren't the rules," Trevor throws his hands up in complaint, looking at Drew and the rest of the guys surrounding him in confusion.

"They are now," someone in the back retorts as everyone chants, "Chug! Chug! Chug! Chug!"

Trevor raises his bottle up. "Cheers," he shouts out, then downs the beer in one swift go, making sure not to spill a single drop from his lips. He thrusts the empty bottle into the air.

Everyone is yelling and cheering. When the crowd breaks apart, and my eyes snag on a kid wearing a ball cap. With a basketball tucked under his arm, he stops Aiden Brodie, one of our right-wingers, who stepped away to take a call from his agent. I can't see the kid or hear their conversation, but I see Aiden shake his head.

A feminine voice with a slight southern drawl cuts into their conversation. She speaks loud enough for me to understand her clearly. "Get back to the house, Buddy. I told you to stay in our driveway if you're going to play basketball."

Out of curiosity, I crane my neck to see what's going on, but my view is blocked by my teammate's big ass body.

"I was just trying to make new friends, Mom," he counters.

"We don't know these people. You can't go walkin' into someone else's yard; it's rude . . ." She trails off. Although I can no longer understand her words, the southern drawl of her voice still reaches me, and if I were a man with a voice fetish, I could sit and listen to her speak all day.

I plop down on the outdoor sectional and bend to grab another beer out of the cooler stationed by my feet. I close the lid and stretch out, propping a foot on top of the Yeti. I lounge back alone in my seat, basking in dopamine and serotonin from the alcohol coursing through my system, while watching my teammates wrestle around near the pool. Before he even knows what's happening, Carter is pushed in, clothes and all. I choke in a fit of laughter. It's nice. It feels good to laugh for once. And now that I have a few drinks in me, I can admit to myself that I've kind of missed hanging out with people. Aiden snags my attention as he ambles toward me.

"You want another one?" I nod toward the cooler.

"Yeah, man. Last one, then I'm out." Aiden parks himself in the chair across from me.

I reach into the Yeti and grab him a cold one. "You got a ride home?" I ask, since Drew just left with a car full of people.

Aiden reaches over and plucks the bottle from my hand. "Sure do," he says as he twists the top. With the cap between his middle finger and thumb, he snaps his fingers, sending the cap flying into my chest. I chuckle and tip my beer back to take a long pull from the bottle.

"Someone has party tricks, I see." I toss the cap back at him, hitting his chin.

Aiden snickers. "Stick with me, and I'll teach you a hundred more."

I breathe out a short laugh. Resting my head back against the cushions, I stare at the Edison lights hanging above us. That woman's sexy-as-sin voice plays out in my head. "So, what was up with the kid?"

"I have no idea." He leans back in the chair, removes his ball cap, and tosses it onto the small patio table. "Some kid looking for someone to play ball with, but did you see his mom?"

"Nope." I pop the p.

"Fuck me." His eyes roll to the back of his head as he clutches his chest dramatically. "Listen, dude." He sits back up with the most serious expression on his face. "She's so fucking hot, I would drink her bath water one sip at a time and simultaneously try to guess what part of her body it touched."

"Where the hell do you come up with this shit?" I laugh, picking the label from my beer bottle. Aiden is from Dallas, Texas, and he is as country as they come.

"I don't know. What I do know is she's hotter than a tweaker's spoon in a trap house on payday."

A deep, wheezing laugh burst out of me. I cough into my fist as I try to breathe through the laughter. I'm doubled over, my face heated, trying to catch a breath.

The guys and I hung out well into Sunday morning. I nursed a hangover from hell all day Sunday. Fuck, I haven't been that hungover since my early college days. Of course, I don't really drink, so it's no surprise I spent the day lying around with the worst headache known to man. Once you hit thirty, your body changes, and I realized yesterday that I'm no spring chicken. After spending Monday morning running my usual errands, I hit the gym at the hockey facility.

When I'm in the gym, I lose myself. I shed my concerns and focus solely on releasing frustrations. There's no media circus, no facade to put on, and if I get here early enough, there's no best friend breathing down my neck to "live life." Mondays are my days to mentally prepare for the week, so I do light weights and forego someone here to spot me. Despite the off-season, the facility remains busy. New professional league draft picks make it necessary for all of the veterans, like me, to maintain top shape. That means extra workouts, ice time, and clean eating. I may look like I have the body of a twenty-year-old, but my joints say otherwise. That's why I stretch daily and do yoga to keep myself flexible.

Pantera's "Walk" blares through my iPod as I pull my chin to the bar for the very last time. I drop down to my feet and bend over with my hands on my knees, taking in deep breaths. Sweat streams in rivulets down my exhausted body and drips onto the floor. I chug down a bottle of water then toss the bottle into the trash as I make my way to the showers.

Drew walks into the locker room while I'm lacing up my shoes. "What's up? Great party Saturday." He gives me a fist bump. "It was nice to see you let loose for once, man."

"Yeah. Hey, I was thinking about getting in some ice time tomorrow. You down?"

I used to be the center of attention—the fun friend who liked crowds and parties. Drew reminds me a lot of myself from before . . . well before everything. Everyone knows I'm not the type to "let loose," and I have absolutely no desire to hear how nice it was for my teammates to see me have a good time. Those words remind me of the person I used to be, and fuck if I don't wish I could be that person again. The presence of others can be excruciating. I prefer solo drills; actually, I prefer to do everything on my own—if for no other reason than to avoid awkward conversations like this. Yet, I find myself here, striving to make an effort, to take the advice Carter shelled out to me on Saturday and connect with my teammate. I pull on my charcoal henley, ready to flee, and then sling my gym bag over my shoulder.

Drew throws his bag into his stall and removes his shirt, tossing it onto the bag. "What time?" He asks.

"I'll be here around ten thirty."

"Sorry, dude. No can do. I take Gran to lunch on Tuesdays."

Well, at least I can say that I tried.

"Don't forget about the team meeting tomorrow at two." I give a wave and head out the door. "See you tomorrow."

I've been following the little, black, beat-up Honda in front of me since the exit about five miles back. I'm a mile or two from my house, and I cannot wait to plop my ass on my couch, watch some sports with a beer in my hand, and do nothing for the rest of the night. Except this person is driving so slowly it will be a fucking miracle if it's not tomorrow before I have that luxury. *Come on. Come on. Come on.* I could go around them. Just as I'm about to pass them, the car swerves a little, then corrects. I go for a second attempt at passing them; the car swerves again to the left, then overcorrects to the right, before straightening.

Fuck, this person either cannot drive or they're drunk off their ass. *Shit or get off the pot, asshole. Better yet, learn how to fucking drive.* I lay on my horn, lift my hand to flip them the bird, then remember who the fuck I am and put my hand back on the steering wheel where it belongs. I can't be driving around with road rage, flipping people off. Man, Teagan would just love me to death if I created a PR nightmare for her to clean up. Suddenly, the person in the car slams on their brakes. Though neither one of us is going over thirty miles per hour, it's at the very moment when

I stomp my foot to the brake pedal that I realize I don't have enough time or space to stop my vehicle from hitting theirs.

I only have a few seconds to brace myself. My head jerks forward as the front end of my car smashes into the back of the Honda. Theres a bang and a crunch, followed by a pop. My bumper is surely fucked.

What the ever-loving . . .

Fuming with anger, I practically fly out of my car and slam the door. The woman jumps out of her car, races to the front, and bends down. What the fuck is she doing? If this woman is under the influence, I swear to all that's holy that I'll . . . well, I don't know what I'll do, but I know I'd rather not call the police. The media circus would eat me alive, even though this woman obviously has no business behind the wheel of a car.

I try to get a look at her face to see if she's maybe high or drunk, but all I can see is a mass of waist-length, thick, black hair whipping around her face from the wind and a puppy in her arms.

"What are you doing in the middle of the road? I could have run you over," she coos at the pup while scratching its head.

That voice. Holy shit, that fucking voice. Sexy as hell with a slight southern drawl. All I can think about right now is self-preservation because I know without a doubt this is the woman I heard during the party. Which means she lives not too far from me. Which also means I'm more than likely going to see her again. Her voice played on repeat in my head all Saturday night: a low, sultry tone. The way she drew out her vowels. That alone had me wanting to seek her out, even after I had told Carter and myself that I wasn't interested in dating. But a woman with a voice like that can't be anything other than fucking gorgeous.

I haven't even seen her yet, and my fight-or-flight reflexes have kicked in. Nevertheless, I can't keep my eyes from traveling all the way down her long, toned, tanned legs in a pair of denim shorts that are short enough to make any man salivate. My eyes roam back up her body, taking in the wide curve of her hips. A white tank top is stretched tight across her chest. Her body is sexy as hell. I've always been a man for curves. Wide hips and big tits; that was my motto back in the day. I cast my eyes down to stop myself from eye-fucking the woman who just caused me to fuck up the frontend of my car with her inept driving skills.

"What you did was very dangerous. Yes, it was." She scolds the puppy.

My attention shifts back to her as she lifts the brown fur ball to her face. He wiggles his tiny body in her hands, then relaxes before stretching out his neck to lick her face. I saunter closer to her—like a moth to a flame—just to get a better look. Or rather, to see if she's drunk or high. That's what I tell myself anyway. I'm still pissed. Beyond furious. It's going to take a whole hell of a lot more than a rockin' body and a sexy ass voice to get her out of the clusterfuck of a mess she's made with me. The wind blows her long, raven locks out of her face and back behind her.

Fuck me!

I'll need to use all my resolve to avoid this woman regardless of my current anger towards her. She is insanely beautiful, just like Aiden said. I don't even know if beautiful is even the correct adjective to describe her, because she is beyond that.

I don't have time for this shit, is my last thought before stunning, teary, green eyes lock with mine.

Chapter Two

Aspen

I plop down into the driver's seat of my black Honda Accord. It was bought for me brand new as a high school graduation present nine years ago. A graduation present that I thought came from my mom, but now that the lies and secrets have come tumbling out, I'm beginning to believe this car is yet another gift she didn't pay for. It seems as though most of the luxuries in my life actually came from the man who I thought was a "deadbeat dad." I bet this car was bought and paid for in cash by that man too. Releasing a deep breath, I decide it's time to adjust my perspective and attitude toward the turn my life has unexpectedly taken. *This is a new beginning, Aspen. Try to make the most of it.*

I glance at my cute little house that we just moved into last week. White planters hang from under the windows waiting to be decorated with pretty flowers. The morning sun beams against the second-story window, causing a glare to hit my eyes and me to squint. We're renting this place temporarily until everything is sorted and settled, but it's ours for now. Plus, it's the nicest home we've ever lived in.

When I called the property management company, the realtor told me this little house had just become available to rent for the next nine months, which should be long enough for me to sort out my affairs and find a permanent place. I say little because it's the smallest one in the neighborhood. Even so, the house is still generous in size. With it being a two-story home with four bedrooms, not to mention the addition of it being fully furnished and in a gated community with a security booth, the rent was almost too good to be true. It's not as though we've ever lived in a dump or an old run-down shack at any point in our lives. Back home was just . . . different . . . simple. This new life is certainly going to take time to adjust to after living on a farm back in Oklahoma.

I start my car, round the driveway and admire the houses in the neighborhood. Our new home looks so out of place compared to the rest of these. It's one of the oldest in the estate, but I think it possesses a unique charm because of its age. As I focus on the enormous house in front of me, I think back to Saturday.

My plan was to meet the neighbor across the street once I was done introducing myself to the little old lady next door, Ms. Tillman. But, when people started showing up and lingering in the yard, it became evident they were throwing a huge party. So, I decided not to impose. That didn't stop Tucker from being a little party crasher. I should probably drop by this evening and apologize for my son's intrusion. Pulling up the notes app on my phone, I add a few things to my grocery list so we can make cookies for them as an apology, then head out of the estate.

I'm pulling out of the store's parking lot and making my way back home when fumes from the exhaust begin to permeate the air and fill the cabin of my car. I scrunch my nose. Leaning forward, I sniff the air vent and groan. *No. No. No. No. No.* I slam my hand against the steering wheel, then roll down the window. This damn car is falling apart. Nine years of driving on gravel and dirt roads will do that to you, I guess. The never-ending list of car repairs continues to grow: new belts, air conditioning, tires, brake pads, and now possibly an exhaust leak. It's time to retire this old thing and trade it in for something new.

I'm doing everything within my power to avoid relying on my father's money, but my resolve and bank account are dwindling. I can't very well drive my ten-year-old son around in a car that has an exhaust problem. Thoughts about my to-do list are interrupted by the ringing of my cell phone. I pluck the device from the top of my purse and cast a glance at the screen to find my mom calling again. That's call number one hundred and thirty-seven since I've been in New York the past week.

It's totally out of character for us to be at odds. She's always been a wonderful mom. However, that doesn't mean she isn't flawed, no matter how perfect she is on paper. Up until a month ago we were extremely close. I would even say as I became an adult, we've become best friends. As a single mom, I've always wondered how she took care of my needs and our finances while working a part-time job; now I know.

Just as I thought I knew her better than anyone, the skeletons in her closet came tumbling out, leaving my life in utter chaos. I was pissed to learn that my deadbeat dad wasn't a deadbeat after all. Feeling abandoned by him my entire life made it damn near impossible for me to connect with men. His absence fucked with my head. I've always felt as though I wasn't good enough for someone to stick around. I mean, if the person who had a hand in creating me didn't want me, why would anyone else? A point my ex-boyfriend certainly drove home. So, since that breakup, I just never really gave anyone else a chance. I spent my time focusing on improving my life and taking care of my son.

I don't believe my parents considered the ramifications of their choices. The lies and major secrets they've kept hidden from me my entire life now have an impact on Tucker. I'm not one to easily forgive, and hell, even if I were, this would still be too much. If it's forgiveness she wants for her and my father, I'm going to need time . . . a lot of time.

Turning down the radio, I take several deep, calming breaths of not-so-fresh air to attempt centering myself before answering her call. Before shit hit the fan, she and I wouldn't go even one day without speaking. Now I can't even stand the thought of her. I'm beyond livid.

With a huff, I pressed the green button to accept her call.

Mom speaks before I have a chance to say anything. "Hello? Hello? Aspen?"

"Yup. I'm here."

"Oh, thank God! I've been trying to call you for a week. I've been worried sick."

"Mom, there's no need for dramatics. I overheard River talking on the phone with you the other day; she gave you an update on our well-being."

I roll up my window so we can hear each other, praying I don't pass out from the fumes coming through my vent.

"I'm so sorry, Aspen. You were absolutely right. I should have told you everything a long time ago."

I put my turn signal on and look over my shoulder before moving into the right lane to turn. "Yes, you should have," I snap.

"We wanted to protect you . . ." Mom blathers on, but I'm barely listening—still entirely too upset to have this conversation.

"So, let me make sure I have this straight . . ." I take a right onto the street leading to my neighborhood. "Y'all thought it would be a good idea to throw Tucker into the exact same situation you were protecting me from all these years? Warning me at some point would have been nice, you know. Now, I'm thrust into this new life that I wasn't even prepared for, with a child no less. This is complete bullshit, Mom. That's my kid's life you two have messed with." My voice cracks, and I sniff. My nose burns as my eyes fill with tears. The weight of everything coming down on me is too overwhelming. I'm so angry that the only outlet I have at this point is crying, and I hate it. There is only so much a person can take, and after a month, I'm finally breaking down.

"I think he will be—" She is cut off when my phone tumbles out of my hand.

"Shit! Hold on, Mom. I dropped my phone." Reaching for it, I bend over; my fingertips brush the screen. I swerve—look up—swerve again—then reach for my phone in one last-ditch effort. Feeling the sides of the protective case with my fingertips, I glance down for a brief second and snatch up the device. When my eyes focus back on the road, all the blood rushes to my head, tingles shoot up my body, and it's possible my heart literally stops beating.

"Oh my God!" I shriek. Swerving to the correct side of the road, I overcorrect before straightening up. No cars were approaching, thank God, but if they had been, that could have been a disaster.

"Are you okay?" There's panic in her voice.

"Give me a minute. I need to collect my heart from the floor." I take a deep breath, trying to regain control of my breathing. A lone tear trickles down my cheek. I swipe it away with the back of my hand before another one falls. *Fuck!*

"Maybe you should call me back when you're home. I would really like to talk this out with no distractions."

"Actually, I need you to respect my boundaries and back off a little. Please, just let me sort through these emotions. Okay? I appreciate your apology—and I'm not trying to hurt your feelings—but this mess you both have created for us is too much."

"Aspen, please," she begs.

"Mom," I choke out. "I'll call you when I'm ready." I glance down, then press the red end button.

Just as I look up, a ball of fur runs directly in my path, causing me to slam on my brakes.

My head and body jerk as my car jolts forward. My heart accelerates. I'm stunned, and for a brief second, I'm also confused why I stopped. Remembering the animal I almost hit, I put the car in park, jump out, and run to the front of my car. I look down into a pair of pleading blue eyes staring up at me. Bending down, I pick up the little guy.

"Oh my goodness, what are you doing in the middle of the road? You could have been run over," I coo.

He's so tiny, and I can't imagine that someone isn't missing him. I cuddle him up to my chest and pet his sweet little head. "What you did was very dangerous. Yes, it was," I scold, then hold him up at eye level. He licks my face, and my nose scrunches up in response. Movement catches my eyes when I bring him back to my chest.

An extremely attractive man stands beside my car. Our eyes lock. My heart beats rapidly, my cheeks heat, and my stomach dips as if I were on a roller coaster. Muscular forearms are crossed tight against his chest. His charcoal henley taut—the fabric straining around his big muscular biceps. My eyes map the sleeve tattoo on his left arm, then travel up to his pretty hazel eyes as I take him in. His dark brown hair is mussed and sexy, short on the sides, a little longer on top. I wonder what it would be like to run my finger through it. I'm momentarily mute, at a complete loss for words as I stand in the middle of the road taking in the sight of this gorgeous man in front of me.

A car slows down and moves around us, shaking me from my lust-filled haze. I realize I've been staring at him as we stand in the street, blocking traffic. I wipe the lingering tears from my face and take a deep, calming breath, then stride to the back of my car to assess the damage. As if it matters at this point. He moves closer to assess the damage to his own car. Tingles shoot through my body at his close proximity.

"Has anyone ever told you that you can't drive for shit?" He barks out in a clipped tone.

My head rears back from the man's rudeness. Welcome to New York. I'm quickly learning that people aren't quite like they are back home. If someone were to rear-end me in Oklahoma, they'd probably be fussin' all over me to make sure I was alright, but this man is making it appear as if I'm at fault.

"Well, isn't he just a ray of sunshine?" I say to the pup as I cuddle him closer in my arms, as if he—all two pounds of him—could become a barrier to protect me from all these foreign feelings this man is conjuring up within me.

I don't know what to feel right now: attraction or disdain. The man steps into my space; his head bends down close to mine, so close, in fact, that we are almost nose to nose. Based on my rapid breathing and the butterflies taking flight in my stomach, it's definitely attraction that I feel.

"Do you know how many times you swerved?"

In a trance-like state, I look down at his lips as he speaks. They're full. Perfect for kissing. I imagine giving him a reason for those lips to be moving, and it has nothing to do with any words coming out of his mouth.

What the fuck am I thinking? I was just in a wreck! This asshole hit my car, and I nearly hit a puppy for Pete's sake. Yet here I am standing in the middle of the street salivating over this . . . this beautiful man. Something is very wrong with me. My eyes flick back up to his.

His fingers snap in my face. "Are you drunk?" He leans in and sniffs me. "God, you reek of fumes. Have you been huffing something?"

And now I'm back to disdain.

I break out of my wordless stupor. "What the fuck is wrong with you?" I jerk back, swatting him away with one hand. "Look . . ." I blow out a breath of exhaustion. "It's been a terrible week. A terrible month, actually—"

"Did I ask about your terrible week or month? No. Now, answer the question. Are. You. Drunk?" Hazel eyes lock on mine, gauging whether the next few words out of my mouth are true or not.

"No," I say, shaking my head. "I'm not drunk."

"Are you high?"

"God, no!" Ugh, this guy is insufferable. "I was talking to my mom, and the phone slipped from my hand. Like I said, it's been—"

"So, not only can you not drive for shit, but you're irresponsible too."

I point my pretty, pink-manicured fingernail in his face and scoff. "Oh, like you never talk on the phone while you're driving."

"Of course I do. But I do it hands-free. I pay attention to the road. You could have gotten yourself or someone else killed."

"Mr.—" I trail off, waiting for a name that never comes. Rude ass! I pinch the bridge of my nose, then drop my hand and focus back on him. "Whatever your name is . . . we can't very well stand here in the middle of the street arguing." His jaw ticks in response, but he stays silent.

"You know what? Maybe we should call the police." I thrust the puppy into his arms. He cradles the pup with confusion marring his brows as he stalks behind me. I lean into my car, grab my phone off the seat, and pick up my purse. Riffling through the old worn-out thing, I grab my insurance card and license. I toss my purse back into the seat, focus on the screen, and unlock my device. I hit the phone icon to type in the number.

"No police!" His tone is in a panic as I forcefully punch 9-1-1 into my phone.

Long, strong fingers wrap around my small, delicate hand. I tilt my head up and raise a brow at him in question. His grip is strong, his touch rough, and his palms calloused as though maybe he works with his hands. My eyes land back on his hand engulfing mine. Big, prominent veins trail their way from his hand up to his muscled forearm. I allow my eyes to map the green lines. Tingles shoot through my entire body. He jerks his hand away.

"Okay. Let's just get this out of the way then. I'm going to need your license, insurance card, and your phone number."

"What do you need my phone number for?" He frowns.

"In case my insurance agent or I need to get in touch with you. You know? Ask you questions."

"If anyone is getting a number here, it's me."

"Well, Hotshot, if you wanted my number, you could have asked for it; you didn't have to hit my car." Okay, so I know that was lame and completely cliché, but at this point it's either I make a joke or I cry, and I refuse to shed another damn tear today.

"Of course, I would have to go and hit a puck bunny's car," he mumbles under his breath.

"Excuse me? A what bunny?"

He doesn't respond, and I'm left questioning what the hell this guy is talking about. Maybe he's the one who's drunk. He is the one who hit my car, not the other way around. Also, he's rambling nonsense like a crazy person. Shaking my head, I hand him my license and insurance verification, then take his. I look at his picture, then back at him, making sure it's the same person, then glance at his name and take a picture of both items. Callan Miles, such a nice name for a pretentious asshole. I realize he's still holding the puppy and fumbling to get pictures of my information, so I take the little guy out of his arms.

He inspects my license. "Aspen R. Taylor, from . . . Stroud, Oklahoma. You're a long way from home, aren't you?" He reaches out a hand to give my items back.

I pluck them from his hand, a little more forceful than necessary, then toss the items into my purse. When I turn around, I find him staring at my legs. I smirk. His jaw ticks. I raise a brow. He frowns. Finally, I answer his question. "This is my home now . . . new home, new job, new life."

"It was a rhetorical question."

"This is exhausting," I snap, massaging my forehead before peering back up at him. "I want to be an asshole right now because clearly you're being one to me. I wasn't raised to be rude and hateful, but you're quickly pushing me to the point of showing a side of myself that not even I have seen. You're the one who hit me! Remember?" I point my finger at him. "If you weren't being a bumper humper, then maybe you would've had plenty of time to stop."

He runs a hand through his hair. "Just give me your number so we can get out of the street."

I roll my eyes. "Nope. I'm good, Hotshot!"

"Why not?" He asks.

I place a hand on my hip. "Because you don't need it. You have my insurance agent's number. File a claim or don't. I really don't give a shit. Do whatever you feel you need to do for yourself—that's on you. I've decided I'm not filing a claim. I'm getting rid of this beat-up thing anyway."

"Why is it beat up? Oh, that's right, because you drive like shit?" He smirks.

"No, that's not why it's beat up, you fucking moron. And just so you know, not that you're entitled to shit, but I changed my mind on filing a claim because the less I have to deal with you, the better. You know, people live frugal lives and drive old cars. I don't think I've ever met a single fucking person who needed a Lamborghini to overcompensate for anything they may be lacking . . . well . . . until I met you." I glance down at his crotch, then back at him and smirk. He lets out a grunt, then smirks right back. *Ugh!* He's excruciating. "I don't have to stand here and explain my decisions to anyone, least of all to you."

I turn around and throw one arm up in the air in exasperation. Spinning back around to face him, I point my finger at his face. "You really bring out the worst in people. You know that?"

Turning back to my Honda, I lean in and place the puppy on the passenger seat. I close my eyes and let air fill my lungs in a futile attempt to calm down.

Before I leave him stranded in the middle of the road, I should at least try to be the bigger person and do the right thing. "If you have everything, I'm going to head home. Do you need me to call you a tow truck?"

I tilt my head at his silence as he raises one eyebrow at me like I'm stupid. "Oh right, you have your phone that you use with 'hands-free calling.'" I use air quotes and mimic him like an immature teenage girl.

I can't help it! He has seriously turned me into a fucking psycho.

"Alright, are we good here then?"

He nods with a smirk, obviously enjoying my tantrum. *Prick!*

"Okay, well, thanks . . . I mean . . . you know what I fucking mean." I wave my hand around in the air. He chuckles, and the sound of it would be like music to my ears if he didn't just turn me into Satan. Also, did I just thank him for hitting my car? Yes. Yes, I fucking did. I just made myself look like a complete idiot!

My head bangs twice against the steering wheel. I start my engine and take off, leaving the asshole behind. A few minutes later, I glance in the rearview mirror, finding Callan's car following mine. I turn into my neighborhood and stop at the security booth. The jerk-face pulls in behind me. Of course he would live in my neighborhood. That just seems to be the luck I have today. The security guard on duty, who appears to be in his mid-thirties, approaches my car; his brown eyes assessing.

"Hi. You have your driver's license on you?"

Smiling politely, I take a quick peek at his name. "I sure do, Leo."

I grab my purse out of the passenger seat, place the bag on my lap, and rummage through it. Where the fuck did my license go? If I had just put the damn thing back in my wallet instead of carelessly throwing it into my purse, I wouldn't be sitting here . . . holding up the asshole behind me. Glancing up into my rearview mirror, I find Callan impatiently tapping his thumb against the steering wheel. I spot my license at the bottom of my purse, but I'm not handing it over quite yet. I chuckle to myself and glance up at Leo. "Sorry. Just one more second. I know it's in here somewhere."

Callan bangs the back of his head against his headrest a few times. I snort. *Hope you have somewhere you need to be, fucker.*

I internally—and very slowly—count to thirty.

"Aha!" I mock surprise. "Here you go, sir." I hand over my license.

Leo looks at his clipboard. "Oh, you're the new girl over on Bennett." His left forearm rests on top of my car as he leans in to talk to me.

"Yep, that's me."

Leo nods his head to the passenger seat, where the puppy is resting comfortably. "And who is this little guy?"

"Oh, I found him in the middle of the road about a mile back. If anyone is looking for him, please let them know I have him."

"Will do." He hands my license back to me with a bright white smile; his dimples make an appearance. "It's nice to meet you, Aspen," he says to me with a wink, then taps the top of my car. "You have a good day."

"You too," I call out.

Leo opens the gate for me. Then, to my annoyance, he waves Callan on through without stopping him. I know it's bitchy, but I was hoping for him to be further inconvenienced. *I should have counted to one hundred.*

I round the curvy road throughout the beautifully landscaped neighborhood leading to my house. Peeking in the rearview mirror, I see Callan still following behind me. Finally, my sight sets on my house up ahead. Relief that I'm home settles over me. Maybe I'll never have to see this asshole's face again. *One could only hope.*

I pull into my driveway.

He pulls into the driveway across the street.

I turn off my car, grab the pup, and step out.

He steps out.

Chapter Three

Aspen

My brows tug into a frown of confusion as I face the driveway across the street with my hip leaning against the side of my car. "Are you a creeper?"

"I beg your pardon?" He questions with a smile so big and knowing, his cheeks may hurt.

I throw my free arm out in exasperation. "I asked if you're a creeper. Are you following me?"

"I know what you asked, but I thought you were being facetious. No, I live here." He points to the massive house across the street. "Hi, neighbor." He gives me an exaggerated wave.

No. No. No. This cannot be happening to me. Fuck. My. Life. I'll tell you one thing: those cookies I was going to bake . . . yeah, I'm not baking them for this asshole!

"So, you're the infamous frat boy."

He huffs a laugh. "Yup, guess that would be me," he says with a shrug, his smile still on display. Why does his smile have to be pretty too? It's like a weapon of mass destruction.

"You see . . . there, I was being facetious. I know better. You're too . . ." I wrinkle my nose. "Old." Is the word I settle with. "But you were acting like one the other day. Mature. Truly." I roll my eyes. "Anyway, see you around, Hotshot. Guess you didn't need my number after all." I toss up a middle finger as I walk into the house with the puppy in tow.

"Wait!" He calls out, stopping me in my tracks.

I turn around and stare him down. "What?"

"So, you know who I am?"

I step back outside with an incredulous expression. Who does this guy think he is? Jesus? I bet he even thinks he walks on water.

"You called me Hotshot not once, but twice now."

"And?" My hand rests on my doorknob, ready to make an escape.

"And . . . I'm just saying you wouldn't have called me that if you didn't know who I was." Callan leans against the side of his now beat-up midnight black sports car, with his body facing mine and legs crossed at the ankle. He casually runs his fingers through his hair and scratches the back of his neck.

I study him for a beat, feigning surprise. "Oh. My. God. You're Callan Fucking Miles! Wow! I can't believe it!" I exaggerate a gasp and bring one hand up to cover my mouth. He nods his head with a smug smile on his face. He seriously thinks I should know who he is, doesn't he? I know he's not an actor. If that's the case, he's definitely not a good one or one with the big name he thinks he has. "I know exactly who you are!" I bring my hand up to my chest, mocking excitement with a huge smile. "You're the Callan Miles!" The smile and mock surprised expression fall from my face as I drop my hand. "A self-absorbed, egotistical, pompous prick who just hit my fucking car then treated me like complete shit!" I yell.

Letting out a chuckle, then a sigh, his head tilts back contemplatively. He crosses his arms tight against his chest, giving me another spectacular view of his huge biceps. Blowing out a big puff of air, he lowers his head, and his hazel eyes lock with mine.

"We got off on the wrong foot. Now that I know we are neighbors, maybe we should just, you know, start over. Be cordial . . . I don't want things to be awkward when we see each other in passing." He waves his hand back and forth between us.

"Oh, no! No way! You had your chance to shoot your shot, and you missed . . . completely." I keep my eyes on Callan and pet the pup's head when he starts to lick my hand for attention.

"I fucking knew it!" He points at me with eyes squinting.

My eyes roll. "You don't know jack shit. Now, if you'll excuse me, I have more important things to do than stand here and bicker with you." This guy truly is as frustrating and annoying as he is sinfully hot.

"Shoot your shot. Really?" He throws his hands out at his sides.

I shrug, truly not understanding what the fuck he's talking about. "It's a common figure of speech."

"Yeah. We can go with that," he says sarcastically.

"Or we can go with this . . . go screw yourself!" I flip him the bird, then turn and waltz into the house.

The door slams behind me as I drop my keys in the bowl resting on the entry table. I take a gander around the living room looking for Tucker. Not seeing him, I focus on River sitting on the living room floor, back against the couch. Her short legs are stretched out in front of her, and she has one of my romance novels in her hand. She swipes her long blond locks out of her face and peers up at me over the top of the book with her big brown, almond-shaped eyes.

River and I have been inseparable since birth. Our mothers are best friends, and they've joked our entire lives that she and I were best friends even when we were in the womb. She's my sister, not biologically, obviously, but I believe you can choose your family. Especially when they are the only family you have. I've always referenced and introduced her as my sister. There isn't a secret, vacation, heartbreak, or milestone of our life that we haven't shared together. With her going through her own issues, she couldn't run away from Oklahoma fast enough. That, and she wasn't going to let me move to start a whole new career and life in a huge city on my own.

I take a deep, calming breath and steady my tone before speaking. "Well, I just met the dickhead who lives across the street. The fucker hit my car."

With a shocked expression, she bookmarks the page, then sets the book down beside her as she gives me a questioning look. She brings her knees up and wraps her arms around them. "The frat boy? Wait. Hold that thought. One thing at a time. Can we talk about the puppy you have in your arms right now?" She points to the fur ball.

Tucker bounds down the stairs with excitement on his face. "You got us a puppy?"

My son is the spitting image of me, with black hair and green eyes. Our dark hair comes from our Native American heritage on my mother's side. I think the only attributes he inherited from his father were his athletic ability, nose, freckles, and wavy hair. Tucker is the absolute best thing to ever happen to me, even if we did basically raise each other.

With how adorable this puppy is, I worry he will become attached, resulting in heartbreak. I set the puppy down, and he immediately runs to Tucker, wagging his tail and licking him all over his face as he bends down to pick him up.

Tucker stands up, holding the puppy in his arms. I squat down in front of him. "I'm sorry, Buddy. He doesn't belong to us, but we can keep him for a couple of days while we find his owner."

"Oh! We can make flyers!"

"That, we can do." I throw my thumb over my shoulder. "Can you put the puppy in the utility room, so we can unload the car?"

Tucker takes the puppy and makes his way through the kitchen as I stand up. "I promise I won't leave you in here long . . ." His voice trails off as he coos at the pup.

When he returns, he's the first to run outside. River and I trail behind him.

"Did you talk to your mom?" River questions.

"Yup."

"And?"

I stop at the trunk, pop it open, then face her, resting my hip against the back of my car. "And . . . I'm not ready."

River pulls a few grocery bags from the trunk. I do the same, then we head inside. "Everything they did was done for your own good, and you damn well know it." She doesn't pull any punches. We set the groceries on the counter, then head back outside.

"Maybe their heart was in the right place, but it doesn't mean they didn't betray me." We both grab more bags from the trunk. "It's like they didn't think about what would happen to their grandchildren one day. You know?"

River closes the trunk and follows behind me. "We're all the family we have, Aspen. Maybe try to have a little grace."

"Grace would have been someone giving me a heads up before throwing me to the wolves. Look, I get what you're saying. I'll work on it." I walk to the island, where Tucker is unbagging the groceries, and set more bags down.

"Ooh! You got stuff for pizza! Can we have that for dinner?" Tucker licks his lips, bouncing on the balls of his feet.

I kiss the top of his head and ruffle his hair. "How can I say no to that?"

The rest of my day is spent working up an appetite as I attempt to unpack my clothes and organize my room, and most importantly right now my closet. Tomorrow is my first day of a new career, and I have so damn much to prove. Although my outfit alone can't prove anything, I do understand the importance of making a good impression. Finding something unwrinkled to wear with clothes still packed in boxes is futile, and I don't have time to dry clean anything. With my legs crossed, I sit on the floor of my closet, nibbling on my lip, as I try to come up with a plan.

There's shuffling in my room, then River's smiling face appears in the doorway to my closet with a glass of wine in each hand. "What are you doing sitting on the floor all alone? Did you put yourself in timeout again?"

I huff a laugh. "While I wish I could say that's the case, it's not. No, I can't find anything to wear tomorrow that's not wrinkled, so I thought I'd just sit here until something suitable to wear tomorrow magically appeared before my eyes. Think a fairy godmother might rescue me?"

River saunters into the closet, passing a glass to me. "Well, I'm no fairy godmother, but I do have wine, and . . . remember that black dress you let me borrow for my interview last week?"

"Don't tell me . . ."

"I picked it up from the cleaners on Saturday, and it's hanging in my closet. You're welcome." She giggles. "Now, move your ass. I'm hungry, and the pizzas aren't going to make themselves."

Ingredients rest on the center island in our kitchen; a mess of flour covers every inch of the surface. The windows are open, and the fresh night breeze flows through the house, cooling down the rising temperature from the preheating oven. Long gray curtains in the living room ripple and whip from the wind, creating a bit of nostalgia of my childhood back when the nights were cool, and Mom would open up all the windows. Music streams through the surround sound, enveloping the kitchen with our favorite songs from the playlist set on random shuffle.

"Am I doing it right, Momma?" Tucker kneads the dough, his head bobbing to Tommy Richman's "Million Dollar Baby."

"That's exactly right, buddy. Except you're missing something." I chuckle.

Tucker's brows furrow as he looks around trying to figure out what he missed. "Did I forget to mix something in?" He asks in confusion. I take a finger and run it down the length of the island.

"Nope . . . Boop." I dot flour on his freckled nose. "That's what's missing." A burst of laughter flies from my mouth.

"Oh, I know she didn't!" River laughs as she reaches a hand into the bag of flour.

One after the other, they grab a handful of flour out of the sack, and I already know I have started an all-out war. I run around the counter, first turning one way, then the other, trying to evade them. Flour is being thrown in all directions, and it's no use; I already resemble the Pillsbury Dough Boy.

"Why must you both always team up on me?" I chuckle, finding myself in a pickle between the two.

"Because he's my favorite nephew. Don't start no shit; there won't be no shit." She calls out with both hands full of flour.

"That's five dollars in the swear jar, Aunt River." Tucker laughs.

"Add it to my tab. Now, let's get her!"

River comes at me from the right and Tucker from the left. As soon as they both raise their arms to throw, I jump back out of the line of fire, leaving them to hit each other with the flour. I'm bent over laughing so hard that I don't realize someone is behind me until I feel something wet hit the top of my head. Red tomato sauce drips down, painting my hair, clothes, and the laminate wood floor. I hear the slaps of River's and Tucker's hands as they high-five.

"Okay! Okay! You win! I'm going to jump in the shower." Laughing, I point at River. "You are so lucky I'm wearing ratty clothes right now."

"We'll clean this mess up and finish the pizzas," she says as I make an awkward shuffle up to my room.

After I'm showered and changed, I make my way downstairs with a laundry basket. Through the expansive living room, you can see the dining room to the right of the front door. A large oak table with seating for twelve is centered in the middle of the room. There's a sideboard that rests along the wall opposite the bay window, which overlooks the neighborhood. Tucker sets out plates and napkins as River takes the pizzas out of the oven. The aroma of garlic wafts in the air as River walks past with our dinner. She sets the pizzas down at the end of the table. After I'm finished in the laundry room, I grab drinks for us and join them with the dog trailing at my heels; he lays down at my feet. Dinner with my family every night is one of the things I'm going to miss when I start my new job.

I turn to address Tucker, "Tomorrow, Aunt River has a job interview, so you'll be going to work with me."

Tucker thrusts his fist in the air. "YES! Do you think I'll get to meet any of the players?"

"We have a team meeting, and the entire team will be there." I shrug, then nod. "So yes, I'm sure you will run into one of them at some point. But I need you to remember this is their job, as well as mine. I will be working, and so will they, so you need to be on your best behavior."

"Yes, ma'am." He salutes.

River turns to face me. "I'm so sorry, Aspen. I know it's your first day, and it probably looks bad on you to bring your son with you to work, especially when you have a meeting."

"No worries. Hannah and I were going over things this past week, and she told me that sometimes staff and players bring their kids with them to the facility during the offseason. Actually, with it being summer break and school being out, everyone expects to see kids there." I smile reassuringly and continue. "River, you came to New York to restart your life, not be my live-in babysitter. I appreciate your help; I really do, but I can't form a dependency on you. I need to learn to juggle this new life on my own."

"Babysitter?" Tucker cuts in incredulously, then adds, "I'm not a baby. I'll be in fifth grade; I'm practically grown." River and I both laugh in unison.

My eyes land on Tucker, and I pat his hand, placatingly. "Buddy, I know you're not a baby anymore; in a few more weeks you will have your last first day of elementary school. Before you know it, you'll be an adult wishing to return to the carefree days of being a baby. So, enjoy it while it lasts."

I take a bite of my pizza and chew carefully before I address River. "If you want, you can watch Tucker some when I travel with the team—at least until I can secure other arrangements—but other than that, maybe you could just keep an eye on him for a few minutes if I need to run somewhere close by. I'm serious, River, this is your chance to make your life whatever you want to make it. You have to stop feeling obligated to help me."

"I can't wait to meet the hockey team!" Tucker cuts in around a mouthful of pizza with sauce dribbling down his chin.

"Same." River giggles.

"What's your job, anyway?"

"Well, Buddy," I hand him a napkin and continue. "I have a lot of jobs. My most important job is to make sure the players are taken care of." He nods his head in understanding.

"I would like to take care of a few of those players." River mumbles then laughs as I give her a pointed look.

"You are so full of it. I haven't seen you look another guy's way in almost a year."

"Yeah, well, I guess that goes with the territory when you've dealt with what I have, you know? Anyway, you are going to be amazing." River stands up with her empty plate and ruffles my wet head.

Tucker nods his head. "Yeah, Mom, you're going to be great." He leaves to take his plate to the kitchen but stops to give me a kiss on the cheek on his way out.

When I was going to college, I had a goal in mind, and working with professional athletes was not one of them. I guess sometimes things just don't end up going according to plan. Now, my career has catapulted on a whole other trajectory.

After we finish dinner and wash the dishes, I decide to wind down for some much-needed sleep so I can be refreshed for my new job tomorrow. I make sure Tucker is showered and settled into bed before I head to my room. Even after the conversation with my mom and the encounter with the asshole across the street, this day hasn't been so bad.

Rounding my bed, I turn on my bedside lamp and fluff my pillows. I glance across the street to notice all the lights are off. I don't know why I looked over there or what I was even looking for. I guess curiosity. God, he was such a jerk, but damn, was he a gorgeous one. The way his jeans fit over his thick thighs, and yes, I did notice his firm ass too. I sigh, lay down, and pick up the new romance novel I'm in the middle of reading.

I admit, I'm a smut slut, but I can't help it. I like what I like. Brooding, sexy, possessive, and dominating male main characters who say things like, "You're mine," are my weakness. Thinking of brooding males has me thinking about Callan and the way my body reacted to him. It was the pheromones. That's all it was. This is real life, and if I've learned anything in the past two years, it's that broody and possessive men are usually psycho. Since dating hasn't been in the cards for me since my teens,

I just live vicariously through the female main characters while simultaneously wishing the ultimate book boyfriend did in fact exist.

I keep thinking of those hazel eyes. Ugh. Unable to focus on my book, I huff, turn off my lamp, and plop my head back on my pillow. I try to sleep, but my mind is racing, and I'm so nervous about tomorrow. What if I don't make a good impression? What if they don't like me? What if I do a horrible job or make a terrible mistake? All the "what ifs" boggle my mind. I toss and turn for hours, and the last thought before sleep finds me is that it doesn't matter whether or not I think I can do this; what matters is I have to.

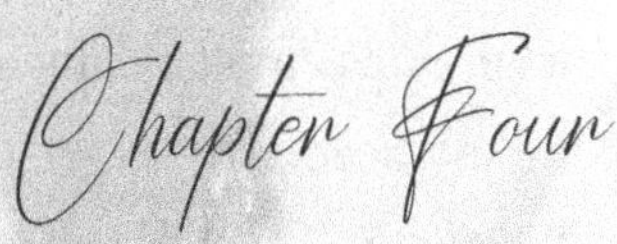

Chapter Four

Aspen

We arrive at the facility fifteen minutes till eight and are buzzed in at security. A black focal wall stands directly in front of us; the other walls are painted in a very light muted gray. Situated in the center of the reception area is a round platform, topped by a huge glass flame that's lit up with a dim red light. The Blaze logo is on display. To the right, a screen taking up an entire wall is replaying highlight reels from previous seasons in high definition. Two black leather couches face each other. An unoccupied, neatly organized glass reception desk sits on the left. White floors, with very tiny sporadic sparkled flecks of red, black, and silver, tie everything together to give a high-end aesthetic.

A woman who appears to be in her mid-twenties, maybe even around my age, rounds the corner. Her auburn hair is in a tight, high ponytail. Light freckles decorate her alabaster skin, and a pair of kind brown eyes sit behind chic red glasses. A form-fitting pair of black slacks complements her curvy figure, and her black polo shirt with a red Blaze logo sits snug across her chest.

She smiles kindly at us in greeting, "Hello. I'm Hannah Jenkins."

"Hi, Hannah, I'm Aspen Taylor, and this . . ." I place my hand on top of my son's head. ". . . is Tucker, my son."

She strolls over to shake my hand. "It's a pleasure to finally meet you both. Are you ready for the grand tour?"

"Absolutely!" Tucker exclaims as he bounces on the balls of his feet in excitement. "I really hope I get to meet Carter Graham today; he's my favorite." He turns his attention to me, "Mom, you have to see him. His brawls are epic."

"Oh. You're a hockey fan?" She chuckles and looks at me.

"Yes, Ma'am." Tucker nods emphatically as I say, "Not really," at the same time while shaking my head.

Tucker recovers, "Actually, I watch hockey; Mom doesn't." His brows furrow. "Well, I guess she will now," he shrugs.

"Oh, she will." Hannah giggles. "We have a team meeting today, so all the guys will be here," Hannah says to Tucker as we walk along the expansive hallway leading to the executive offices.

She turns to me and waves a hand toward the entry of an office, "You can just set your purse down in here if you want."

Taking her up on the offer, I walk into the stranger's office, tossing my purse onto the office chair before rejoining her in the hallway.

"Be prepared to have your mind blown. This place is unbelievable," she says, smiling at me in excitement.

Hannah continues to lead us down the hallway. Floor-to-ceiling, metal action-shot portraits of the players line the walls. We come to a stop and enter a game room that overlooks the ice rink; it has a glass window taking up the entire expanse of the wall. There are six gaming chairs, each with their own individual screens. An enormous, black leather sectional couch faces a cluster of small screens that form into one massive screen. Four different types of gaming consoles sit on a shelf to the right side of the screens. Arcade games line a wall behind the couch and are stationed right next to a beverage and snack bar. An air hockey table resides on the far side of the room with a pool table next to it. She wasn't wrong; I'm already mind blown.

"Whooooaaaa," Tucker says with his eyes wide. "This is sick!"

"This is where the kids your age hang out while their parents are working," she says to Tucker, then she directs her attention to me and gives me a wink. I've expressed my concern to her over bringing him with me, but this puts my mind at ease.

With a chuckle, Hannah adds, "You can also find a man-child or two in here from time to time."

"Mom, can I stay here?"

"That's fine. Just don't run around." I look to Hannah.

Hannah sets up the big screen for Tucker and shows him how to switch to different gaming consoles and games. With him situated, we continue our tour. She first takes me to the ice, then we take a path through another hallway to a corridor housing several offices. A man walks out of a door and locks it behind him. Hannah turns to introduce us.

"Coach, this is Aspen Taylor. Aspen, this is the head coach, Luke Jenkins."

"Aspen. It's so nice to meet you." He shakes my hand.

"You too, Coach Jenkins." As I say his name, it registers that their last names are the same.

"You can call me Luke . . ."

"Jenkins?" My brows furrow, and I look between them.

"Yep. He's my dad," Hannah says, chuckling nervously and clasping her hands together.

Now that she's mentioned it, I see the resemblance. Luke Jenkins doesn't look old enough to be a head coach of a pro hockey team, though his eyes crinkle at the corners when he smiles. He has brown hair with an auburn tint and brown eyes that are the same as hers, but this guy doesn't look like a father of a woman in her twenties. He's built, like muscles so big that maybe even those muscles have muscles. *Aren't coaches supposed to be old and have potbellies or something?*

My fingers twist together, my nerves getting the best of me. Even though I feel like an idiot with what I'm about to tell him, I might as well let him know the truth. He's going to figure it out eventually. "You know, I'll be honest with you, Coach. I'm extremely nervous and out of my depth here. I don't know anything about hockey."

"No need to feel nervous," he reassures me. "We have a great team and staff willing to help you with whatever you need." He winks at his daughter.

"I'm going to take her to meet Dr. Winslet; I know he's been waiting."

"It was nice meeting you, and I'm looking forward to the team meeting this afternoon." I shake his hand again.

"You too, Miss Taylor. I'm glad you're finally here," he says, taking my hand in his and shaking it again.

On our way to the team doctor's office, we pass floor-to-ceiling windows that allow a complete view of the incredibly large weight room. Hannah leads us inside. Televisions are strategically placed on every wall. A sound system is mounted to the ceiling. As we travel the length of the weight room, my vision snags on what looks to be four hot tubs.

"The two in the back are hot tubs, and the two in the front are the cold tubs," she informs me.

We exit the weight room and enter into . . . well, I don't know exactly what this room is. If the red file cabinets tightly pressed together were anything to go by, I would guess it's a file room, but the location doesn't make sense. Hannah crosses the room and comes to a stop in front of a keypad mounted next to a door, where she types in a series of numbers and special characters.

"Voilà!" She says, as shelves begin to electronically shift and glide along the tracks on the floor.

As they widen, we are given access to rows upon rows of hockey equipment. *Um, what now?* My mouth is literally hanging open.

"Pick up your jaw, Aspen." She laughs, "I warned you that you would be mind blown. These storage units contain custom, individualized hockey equipment for each player. See the bin numbers?" I nod. "When they need something, they type in their code, press pound, then type in the bin number containing what they need and press star. When they're ready to exit, they type their code into the keypad and press the pound button. The units then move back together and lock."

Hannah opens the door next to the keypad, and we stroll into the adjoining locker room. In the center of the room, attached to the ceiling, hangs a large Blaze logo. Hockey uniforms are clean and hung in stalls. Designated places inside and outside the stalls hold equipment.

Something catches my attention, and I stop in front of the nearest stall, brushing my bottom lip with my thumb as I study the open cubicle. My eyes trail up to a gold nameplate above. Lukov C. My eyes travel back to what originally caught my attention. I point. "Are those air vents in the stalls?"

"After the uniforms are washed, they're hung to dry in each of the players stalls. Every stall has a heat source drying vent. That's not all." She tilts her head to the stall. "Go smell his jersey."

I point to said jersey with raised brows. "You . . . you want me to stick my nose in a stranger's uniform? That's just . . . weird," I release a nervous laugh.

"Oh, just do it," she goads.

I stand statue-still in my place, refusing to budge.

"Fine." She rolls her eyes. "I'll go first to demonstrate Lukov's cootie-free status." She giggles.

I like Hannah. You know when you meet someone, and you can just feel the positive vibes radiating off them? I could tell she was a genuinely good person the moment I met her. The more I'm around her, the more relaxed I become in this unfamiliar territory. She's not only sweet; she also seems real.

She saunters over, sticks her nose to the jersey, and inhales deeply with much exaggeration. Her eyes are still closed when she leans back, as if she's savoring the scent. Her eyes pop open expectantly. "See? Now it's your turn." She chuckles, holding out her hand toward the red jersey.

I glance at her nervously. Craning my neck. I check to make sure no one is going to sneak up on us and accuse me of being a creep. She lets out a snort.

"No one is coming; just do it," she whispers as she rolls her eyes.

Steeling myself, I tilt my head from side to side, cracking my neck as I build up courage and succumb to her playful peer pressure. I lean in, place my nose to the jersey, and take a small whiff. The scent is intoxicating, and my eyes roll into the back of my head. I inhale the scent once more and realize she wasn't exaggerating anything—the smell is just so damn good; you can't help but take it in deeply.

"Nice, huh?" She raises one brow.

I lean back and point to the jersey. "What is that? It smells like cologne. That could honestly be an aphrodisiac."

She giggles, "That fresh, woodsy scent comes from an all-natural, hypoallergenic solution that is placed within the air filtration system of the heat vents."

"Wow." Both of my eyebrows raise in surprise.

"I know, right? Technology is insane. Before we started using that solution, the guys were always complaining about their jerseys holding a sour smell. So, the system was installed, and all new uniforms were bought." She beams.

I guess that's why this locker room doesn't smell like soured socks.

"This is just . . ." I shake my head, ". . . insane."

We exit out of the locker room and begin to trek down the hallway, I'm assuming toward the team doctor's office.

"So much has changed over the years." She smiles and looks around as if she's taking in how the facility has transformed. "When I was a little girl, I would run up and down these halls while my dad was at practice. That was long before my dad even considered retiring or becoming a coach."

I stop walking. "Wait. Your dad played professional hockey before he was a coach?"

"Yep, he played hockey for The Blaze most of his career. When I was nine, my mom passed away. My dad sat down with Mr. West and told him he was going to hang up his skates because there was no way he was leaving me for someone else to take care of."

I smile. "Sounds like you were blessed with a great dad."

"The best." She beams. "So, Mr. West made a deal with my dad to finish out the last two years of his contract. He allowed me to practically live here during the off season. During the season, Mr. West hired the best nannies to travel with me to my dad's away games. It took some adjusting to a new norm, but it wasn't long before I was thriving—despite my mom's passing."

"How did you do that and go to school?"

"I was homeschooled." We stop in another corridor next to the restrooms. "Do you need to go?" She points in the direction of the ladies room. I shake my head. We continue on our way. "When my dad's contract ended, Mr. West asked him to stay on as one of the assistant coaches. My dad worked his way up to head coach."

I turn my head toward her, giving her my attention as we carry on our stroll I turn my head toward her, giving her my attention as we carry on our stroll around the facility. She stops every so often to show me something new. I realize we've almost come full circle. Hannah looks around with nostalgia. "This facility has pretty much been my home away from home." Her smile is so wide and bright as she recounts her time growing up in this place alongside her dad.

A pang spears right through my heart at her words. She continues speaking—not realizing the impact she's making on my battered soul.

"Watching this place transform from what it was when I was a little girl to what it is today . . ." she shakes her head. "Well, it's a feeling I can't even describe. About three years ago, Mr. West upgraded our dining room and kitchen. So, we now have an onsite chef and nutritionist year-round. A lot of the players come around during the off season. The meals are completely free, so whenever you or Tucker are hungry, just pop in there, tell Emilio, and he will fix you right up. It's just upstairs on the other side of the conference room. Oh, I almost forgot!" She stops in her tracks and gives one little bounce on the balls of her feet as she turns to me.

She points toward the second floor. "There's a door in the dining room that leads out onto a covered patio with a spectacular view if you ever want to eat outside. In the winter, we just roll down the wind blockers and turn on the heaters; it stays surprisingly warm. It's one of my favorite places to have lunch."

Hannah continues walking, and I follow. She points to a door as we pass by, "That is our workshop. Mr. Markovic takes most of the summer off, but come September, he'll be here from sunup to sundown. He does all of our skate repairs."

We make it to the team doc's office. Dr. August Winslet is etched on a gold nameplate next to the door.

"Dr. Winslet?" Hannah peeks her head into his doorway. "I have Aspen Taylor here to meet you."

"Ah. I've been waiting for you." He comes through the door and shakes my hand.

Dr. Winslet is older, maybe in his early sixties, and has a mild English accent. He's dressed casually today, but I guess with it being the off season, he has no reason to wear the white coat I see hanging up through the open doorway.

"I figured you might be a little overwhelmed. Here's an extra tablet that we use in physiotherapy. You'll find information on each player," he says, tapping on the little device, causing the screen to light up. He pulls up one of the players. "This tablet stores their name, picture, stats, and injuries. I'll need that back before preseason training starts, but this information should help you learn more about who the players are and what we're working with."

"Oh, my goodness. This is so helpful. Thank you so much!" I take the tablet in one hand and shake his hand with the other.

Hannah looks between the two of us with an excited smile. "Ready to go to your office?"

"Ready as I'll ever be," I state nervously. "I'm looking forward to working with you, Dr. Winslet." I shake his hand again.

"The feeling is mutual."

Hannah continues upstairs to give me the rest of the tour before leading me to my office, where I find a mess of stacked papers on my desk. My eyes widen in response.

"Yeah, sorry about that. We didn't really know what to do with everything, so we didn't clear it out. I'll give you time to organize everything to your liking, and then we can talk more." Hannah gives me a sympathetic smile and turns to leave.

"Hey, Hannah?" She turns back around. "Thank you . . . for everything."

Hannah nods her head and walks out the door.

Sorting through the mess, I categorize what I think needs to take priority. I clean and box up someone else's old memories left behind. Time flies, and by noon I'm starving, so I decide to leave the tablet as an after-lunch project. I trek down the never-ending hallway towards the game room, but when I get there, it's empty. Looking around in a panic, I catch movement through the glass and make my way over to peer down at the ice. Tucker is on the ice, skating with a hockey player. *Damn it. What the hell is he doing?* Releasing a huff, I make my way down to the rink. I'm halfway down the stairs when my eyes widen, and my face drains of color. I quickly recover, putting on a mask of indifference.

Chapter Five

Cal

Rain pelts down on the windshield, setting the mood for the day as I head to the practice facility. Of course, every day has been like a dark cloud hanging over my head for the past four years, so what else is new? I park at the back entrance and make the trek into the facility. Due to the wet clothes and shoes, the cold air from the air conditioner slices through me, causing an involuntary shiver to course through my body. Goosebumps pebble my tanned skin.

I arrive at the locker room, strip out of my wet clothes, change into my practice gear, and make my way onto the ice with my gloves in hand. As I go to put the glove on my left hand, I flex my fingers, looking down where my wedding ring resided. Shaking my head to clear the thoughts of my doomed marriage, my hand enters the glove, and a new memory pops up out of nowhere. A foreign electric current shoots through my body at the thought. The deep green eyes. The pointed and disgusted looks. That smart fucking mouth. Her long, black hair blowing into her face.

I've been a professional athlete for almost a decade, and women usually throw themselves at me, giving me unwanted attention. Not that girl. In fact, I'm pretty sure she hates me. And, though the feeling is completely mutual, the way she met me toe-to-toe was something I have never experienced.

Shaking myself of the thoughts of that infuriating raven-haired woman, I skate laps around the ice to warm up. I grab a basket of pucks, dump them onto the center of the ice, and take shot after shot after shot. Rounding the crease and stopping quickly, my blades shoot ice across the goal line as I take yet another slap shot. Over and over, my drills continue.

A water bottle sits on the boards. I snatch it up and squirt the cold liquid into my mouth, then skate over to grab the pylons when movement catches my eyes. I look up and notice a boy standing in the window of the game room upstairs. Focusing back on the drills, I disregard him and lay out the equipment. I'm on the last drill when echoes of someone running down the stairs catches my attention.

The kid looks familiar, but I can't quite place him; he's definitely not a teammate's kid—I know all of them. He's sporting a baseball cap with our team logo on the front, and his green eyes are wide. His mouth is open in awe, but he quickly recovers. The boy takes his hat off, runs his fingers through his hair, then puts the cap on backwards. Taking a step down, he casually leans against a handrail, arms crossed tight across his chest and feet crossed at the ankle. I can't help but chuckle at how much his body language resembles my usual stance.

"Excuse me, sir, are you Callan Miles?" He calls out. Shaking his head, then tilting it up, he says to no one in particular, "Shoot. That's stupid. Of course he is."

I give him a nod and carry on with my deke drills. Slapping the puck against the boards, I let it bounce back before cradling it with my stick. I skate around the ice, pivoting my skates left-right-left through the pylons, deking again. Coming to a sudden stop, ice flies into the crease. I rear my stick back, take a slapshot to send the puck flying into the net. When I turn around, the kid is standing on the ice. I close my eyes tight. *What the fuck?*

"Can you please teach me how to do that?" He looks up at me timidly. And shit, something about the expression on this kid's face just won't allow me to tell him no.

"Uh . . . yeah. Sure. Do you skate, kid?"

"I rollerblade sometimes, but my mom takes me ice skating at Christmas every year. I'm not as good as you, though."

I scratch the back of my neck. I didn't sign up for this shit, but I can't be an asshole to a kid. My mind battles with itself over how I want to play this until I finally decide. "Come with me," I give a reluctant sigh.

We walk to the supply room where Ivan's son, Elija, usually keeps his skates. I find them sitting right next to a little girl's pink skates and hand them to him, "Here, try these on."

Making our way back to the rink, the kid sits on the bench right outside the ice, pulls off his shoes, and slides the skates on.

"Do they fit?" I push around on the toe and the sides to make sure. *They seem to fit.*

"Yes, sir. It feels like it." He ties them, but they're too loose.

"Lesson number one: make sure your skates are always tight." I look at him, "What's your name?"

"Tucker, sir." He holds out his hand to shake mine. I can't help but notice how polite he is, and the grip this kid has when he shakes my hand is firm and confident.

"Hi, Tucker, you can just call me Cal." I squat down, tighten the laces, then tie them. Steadying him by his elbow, I help him out onto the ice. "So, who are you here with?"

"My mom. It's her first day. My Aunt River had an interview and couldn't watch me. I told them I'm almost grown now and don't need a babysitter, but that didn't go over well. Now, I'm here, but that's okay because this . . ." He looks up, spreads his arms out wide, looking around as he twists his body from one side to the other to show me the arena. ". . . is fire."

I laugh as Tucker talks in rapid excitement.

I lean my elbow on the boards, watching him as he balances on the ice without slipping. "Oh yeah? What does your mom do?" I ask curiously.

"She helps the players."

Ah, the new physiotherapist.

He grabs my stick resting against the boards and takes off in a sprint with the sound of laughter trailing behind him. The kid was full of shit when he said he wasn't that good. He only skates at Christmas time, and he skates like that? I don't buy it. He cradles a puck and goes for a slap shot, making it into the unattended goal. My mouth hangs open.

"You only skate during the holidays?" I ask to confirm.

"Yes, sir. Well, ice skate, anyways."

"You've never played hockey before?"

Tucker shakes his head, "No, sir. We don't have hockey leagues for kids where I'm from; we play football. My buddy's dad always has hockey on the TV, though. I would watch it when I was at his house. And sometimes, his dad would take us to watch the semi-pro team in Tulsa. That was cool. But Brent, that's Rich's dad . . . you know? My friend? His name is Rich. Anyway, Brent would say they fight like sissies in the semis; the pro teams are more hardcore. Their favorite team is Colorado, no offense," he rambles, pulling another laugh from me.

This kid needs to be on a little league hockey team; he's a natural. I run him through drills trying to teach him how to deke like he asked. He fumbles and falls during several attempts. We spend about an hour practicing, goofing off, joking, and giving fist bumps every time he gets something right. I haven't had this much fun in a long time.

From the corner of my eye, I see someone watching us. I look up to find a tall woman with long black hair, standing in the exact same spot and in the same way Tucker did earlier. My eyes widen in surprise to see Aspen here at the facility. What the fuck is she doing here? But I look at the boy and realize she must be his mom; he's a spitting image of her. Anyone with a brain can look at these two and tell they're related. Same black hair, tan skin, green eyes; he even has the same smile, though I've only seen her smile appear twice when she was petting that puppy. The rest of the time, she was scowling at me. The only difference between their features is his nose; it's a little more upturned, and he has a smattering of freckles where she has none.

"Are you a creeper?" I ask her.

The way I seem to fire her up and agitate her every fiber makes me feel more alive than I have in years. I have to admit, I enjoyed riling her up in the driveway yesterday.

"Excuse me?" Her brows pull down, and she gives me a puzzled look.

I throw the words at her that she threw at me yesterday, "Are you following me?"

Tucker laughs, making his way over to the boards, "No way, Cal. That's my mom."

She shakes her head. "To answer your question, Mr. Miles, I am not following you . . ." She pauses, looking me dead in the eyes, and says, "I own you."

What? What does she mean she owns me? Nobody fucking owns me. Just because she had the last words yesterday doesn't mean jack shit. I squint my eyes at her, and she returns the glare with a satisfied smile. It takes a minute for her words to sink in, and I feel like I've been slapped in the damn face.

Holy fuck! No fucking way. She's the new team owner? *She's* the daughter of Ryan West? This can't be real. This has to be a fucking joke. She gives me a smug smile, and I. Don't. Fucking. Like. It. It's bad enough that I have to live across the street from this crazy ass woman, but now I have to share a workplace with her too?

"Never thought I'd render you speechless. Looks good on you. I'll see you at the team meeting this afternoon, Hotshot," she says to me, then directs her attention to Tucker, "Come on, Buddy, it's time for lunch."

"Mooooommm. Please don't do this to me. Do you know who he is? He's Callan Miles! The best center in professional hockey." He puts his hands together in a plea.

I smirk thinking back to yesterday when I asked if she knew who I was and she was a snarky little shit. I mean, how could she not know who I am? She obviously owns the fucking team. My eyes catch her fierce green ones, and I would almost swear she is plotting my demise. I see the hesitancy in her expression; she doesn't want to tell him no, but she doesn't much like me either. Well, the feeling is mutual.

Hell, I don't really want her to tell him no either, which is a strange feeling, but we were having fun. She's as beautiful as she is infuriating. My stomach flips when her emerald eyes connect with mine.

She looks between us, nibbling on her bottom lip. Her expression softens towards her son. "Tell your friend bye. We have to go." She turns around, not giving him another chance to argue. A black dress hugs her body, and her ass sways as she makes her way up the steps in her black strappy heels.

Tucker skates back over to me and holds out his hand. I place mine in his, and he shakes it with a firm grip. "It was really nice to meet you, Cal. Thank you for teaching me today." He exits the ice, takes off the skates, and starts toward the supply room.

"I'll take care of it, Tucker." I call to him. "Go on with your mom."

"Thanks." Tucker gives a quick wave before running up the stairs. That girl drives me absolutely fucking crazy. She HATES me! Now she's my boss? Shit! I need to talk to Carter before everyone rolls in for the team meeting. Skating over to the bench, I pick up my phone and shoot him a text.

Me: I'm so fucked!
Carter: A little dramatic, don't you think?
Me: I'm serious. I'm pretty sure my ass is about to be traded.
I plop down to rest, waiting for his reply.

Carter: Why? What happened?
Me: Remember that woman I ran into the other day?
Carter: You mean the woman whose car you smashed into? Yeah, what about her?
Me: That's the new owner.
Carter: You mean the woman you accused of being drunk and high?
Me: In my defense, I thought she was drunk or high.
Me: She was driving like a fucking idiot.
Carter: The same woman who lives across the street?
Me: Don't fucking remind me.
Carter: The same woman you said had an accent so sexy and hypnotizing that you could listen to her voice for hours.

Me: I didn't say that.

Carter: Eh, I'm pretty sure you said that.

Carter: She was the same woman who got that kid from the party, right? The one you and Aiden were talking about?

Me: Yeah . . . why?

Carter: You said what you said.

Me: Whatever, dude. Would you stop?

Carter: Truth hurts.

Me: She came down to the ice and said, "I own you."

Carter: LMAO. She came down there just to tell you that she owned your ass?

Me: No. She came down to get her kid. I was teaching him how to deke. Dude, I gotta tell you, this kid is talented. Like God-gifted natural talent.

Carter: Be there in a few.

I head to the locker room, take a shower, and dress for the team meeting. We always dress up when we have meetings like this. I pair navy Armani pants with a white button-up shirt and a silver tie. It's a little after one o'clock when Carter walks into the locker room. One hand is in the pocket of his black dress pants, while the other smooths down his tie. Facing me, he casually leans his shoulder against the doorway. "So, are we going to talk about it?"

"Talk about what?" I grab my keys and make my way out of the locker room, passing him. The conference room is on the second floor, so I trek up the stairs, passing the red stadium benches, with Carter trailing behind me.

"Oh, I don't know . . . maybe the fact you took time out of your solo practice to play hockey with a kid you don't even know. That's not like you."

"It's not a big deal. And the kid was cool," I shrug.

"The kid was cool?" He looks at me incredulously.

He's making a mountain out of a molehill with this. It's not that I don't like kids; I actually love kids. I mean, look at Elija; I love that kid as if he were my own. If he were to ask me to skate with him, I would. Tucker asked me if I would teach him something, so I took a little time out of my practice; it isn't something I would normally do, but I'm not a complete dick.

"Yeah, the kid was cool," I say nonchalantly, shrugging one shoulder.

Carter hums and catches up with me; our steps are in sequence with each other as we walk down the hallway. We're almost to the game room when a small body comes barreling out of the room and plows right into Carter. Tucker almost falls on his rear, but my hand snaps out to grab him. His head slowly moves up-up-up, and then his face takes on an expression of surprise.

"No way." He breathes out, squares his shoulders, and straightens up to his full height. "Hi, Mr. Graham. Sorry for bumping into you like that. I just whipped around that doorway—" His hands close, then pop back open. "BAM. There you were." Tucker holds out his hand to shake Carter's. "It's nice to meet you; I'm Tucker Taylor, sir." Carter looks from him to me, then back to him. He tilts his head back and bursts into laughter, his shoulders shaking uncontrollably. When he recovers, he shakes Tucker's hand.

"Hi, Tucker Taylor. I'm Carter. It's nice to meet you."

As if life couldn't fuck me any more than it already has, Aspen comes around the corner. Our eyes connect. She gives a polite smile, though I know it's not directed toward me. Sure, I assumed after her little performance—when she told me that she owned my ass—that she would probably be the one to conduct the meeting. But I was hoping I would beat her to the conference room so I could hide back in the corner and not make eye contact with her.

"Tucker." She calls out. "You're going the wrong way, Buddy. We're in here." She nods her head to the conference room by her dad's office—well, her office now.

She's an entirely different person with Tucker. Her demeanor is patient, kind, and gentle. With me, her voice is full of sharp tones, and her face is filled with exasperated expressions, but I guess I did piss her off; I can't really expect anything less.

"Alright boys," Tucker claps and rubs his hands together, "let's get this shindig started." He turns around, leading us toward the conference room.

Carter laughs, "Oh yeah, I can see this from a mile away—you're S-C-R-E-W-E-D."

Tucker takes off his ball cap, runs his hand through his hair to straighten it up, and holds the cap to his side, tapping it against his leg. "Umm . . . Mr.? You . . . you do know I can spell, right? That's five dollars for the swear jar." He holds out his hand.

Carter chuckles, shaking his head. He pulls out his wallet and slaps a twenty into Tucker's hand. "You are going to be one rich kid by the time this season is over."

Carter sports a shit-eating grin as we follow Tucker to the conference room, but before we make it through the door, he places a hand on my chest, stopping me in my tracks. He turns to face me, keeping his voice low. "She's hot. She is smoking fucking hot. I don't care what you say about her; this little bickering thing you both have going on . . . yeah, that's called foreplay. I'm calling it now. You're fucked." With that, he turns around with me trailing behind.

My now ex-best friend, Carter, and I sit beside each other in a corner at the back of the room. I'm slumped down behind the bodies of a few big, burly players, actively trying to avoid Aspen's attention. The rest of the players begin to trickle in, one after another, filling the seats around us. I know what this meeting is about, and I don't want to be here. I don't want to see her smug face. This is a waste of my time.

"Holy shit, who's that?" I hear Jerome whisper.

"I don't know, but she is a smoke show," Fletcher Wilson, a new rookie, whispers back.

A scoff burst out of me. I roll my eyes. Yeah, she's gorgeous, but that woman has an attitude problem, a smart mouth, and she is irritating as hell.

"Good afternoon, gentlemen," Coach Jenkins addresses us. He turns his head towards Aspen and Hannah. "And ladies, let's get this meeting underway. First, I would like to introduce you to Mr. West's daughter and our new team owner; this is Aspen Taylor." Aspen and Tucker stand beside Coach at front of the conference room. "And this . . ." He puts a hand on each one of Tucker's shoulders. ". . . is her son Tucker. I asked Miss Taylor to allow me to introduce him because he's now a part of the family, and you will be seeing a lot of him."

"This is unreal," he whispers with eyes blown wide.

Aspen leans down to whisper something in his ear; he looks up at her, nods with a big smile, stands up straight, then addresses the room. "It's a pleasure; I'm looking forward to seeing y'all around, but for now, I have a video game calling my name." He throws his thumb over his shoulder before walking out the door. The room fills with laughter. The kid is fucking hilarious.

"So, I'm going to go ahead and hand the floor over to Miss Taylor."

"Good afternoon, everyone." Aspen smiles cheerfully while she makes eye contact with the people in the room. With her slight southern drawl, not to mention her killer body and gorgeous face, she holds everyone's stares with rapt attention. Our new team owner is stunning, even if she is a grade-a-pain-in-the-ass. I saw the little hearts in the eyes of some of my teammates' faces when they saw Aspen; they looked intoxicated by her. As murmurs begin to grow silent, she continues.

"Though the circumstances that brought me here are tragic, I feel honored to be here, fulfilling my father's legacy. My father believed in my potential, so I guess that has to be enough for all of us." She drops her head toward the floor, inhales a deep breath, and exhales slowly. It takes her a minute to gather herself. She raises her head back up and meets my eyes before casting them around the room to my other teammates. I slide down further in my chair. Carter elbows me in the ribs for being rude, and I let out a grunt.

"I'm going to allow myself to be very vulnerable here for a moment. I'm not only new to this position and organization, but I'm also new to hockey. Given who my father is, I know that may come as a shock to all of you, but without going into detail, those are the facts. My degree is in business, but it's not in sports business, so I'm not going to pretend to have all the answers. And I'm not going to stand here, lie to your face, and tell you I'm a huge hockey fan. I'm not. But I can promise you one thing: I will be.

'I will be your biggest cheerleader. I will work hard to learn about this team and the sport my father loved more than anything else. I will grow to know each one of you and your families personally. And I will have your backs day in and day out. I hope, in return, that you will have mine." She smooths her dress and continues.

"My door is always open, and if there is something you need, you can call or text; Coach is sending out a mass text with my cell number." She turns and looks at Coach, giving him a soft smile, then turns back to all of us. "And please, just call me Aspen; I'm not big on formalities. If any of you have any questions, please feel free to stay behind and ask. Let's have a great season."

"Thank you, Aspen, we're glad to have you," Coach says, then turns his attention to me. "Cal, can you hang back a minute?"

"Yeah, Coach."

Players start making their way out, but some linger to shake Aspen's hand and ask her questions. Thirty minutes later, the conference room is emptied out, and I'm alone with Coach and Aspen. I don't know what he wants, but I have a suspicion he knows something about the dynamics between Aspen and me, and I'm about to get my ass chewed for it.

"Aspen, this is Cal. He's a veteran player with the team and has been in the pros for a decade." He turns to me, pausing, waiting . . . and I stand there, looking between the two of them, not knowing how she wants to play this because we have already met. Do I tell him we've met? Do I shake her hand? Do I tell him she's a pain in the ass? I don't know what to do; this is awkward as fuck. What I do know is we don't like each other.

Before I can say anything, she reaches out her hand to shake mine. Ah, so this is how we're going to play this. Okay, I'll bite.

"Actually, Cal and I have already met. He was showing Tucker some things down on the ice earlier today." She gives me a saccharine smile. I shake her hand, and the minute our hands touch, that foreign energy runs through my body again.

"Pleasure," I'm trying my damnedest to be polite in front of my coach, but my jaw takes on an involuntary tick. I can literally feel my molars cracking. It's anything but a pleasure to be standing here with her.

"Oh, well, good. I'm glad you two are familiar; that will make this less awkward for you both. Cal, I am putting you on an assignment to help Aspen learn the ins and outs of the game before pre-season starts."

I don't want to help her. I don't want to be anywhere near her. I'm pretty sure our expressions match as both of our brows hit our hairline, but I quickly recover.

"Oh, that won't be necessary." She says at the same time I say, "I think she can handle it."

Coach looks between the two of us, and his eyes narrow on me. "I don't doubt her capabilities, Cal; I know she can handle it, but this team doesn't leave anyone out on a limb to flail and struggle. You of all people should know that, after everything you've been through. Mr. West was there for you in your worst times; I think the least you can do is help his daughter." Coach's tone is sharp, and his eyes hold a look of disappointment.

I was in the midst of my darkest time when I first arrived in New York. Mr. West took me in and treated me as his own son. He was there for me. Which leads me to question, why wasn't Aspen there for him? Ryan West was one of the best men I've ever known. When you joined the team, you became his family. He knew everyone on a personal level, even the player's kids. Hell, that game room was built so the employees could bring their kids to work and would have somewhere to play. I heard him say on several occasions that the one thing he didn't want anyone to miss out on was time. So, tell me, how could someone dip out on a man like that?

She was wrong when she said her dad loved the game more than anything else. He was a good man who cared about his players and their families far more than he cared about the game. Just when I thought she couldn't make me dislike her more, she proved me wrong. She doesn't deserve this team, and she sure as hell never deserved her dad.

I stay silent. I respect the hell out of Coach, but I'm not agreeing to shit.

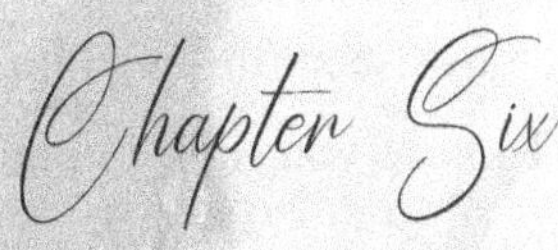

Chapter Six

Aspen

Somehow, I've managed to survive these past few weeks without the help of Callan Miles. Shocking, I know. He hasn't made any effort to help me, which is fine because I don't need him or his assholery. We see each other in passing, but no words are ever exchanged. I guess what bothers me more than anything is his lack of respect for me as his boss. Then again, what Cal lacks when it comes to me, he makes up for with the way he treats Tucker.

The two are inseparable. Every day they skate and hang out in the game room. They have a bond, and that scares the shit out of me. What happens to my son when this man leaves him high and dry? Especially since his contract is up at the end of the season. It's not like I'm going to trade him or prevent his contract from being renewed based on our personal issues; I'm a professional after all, but that doesn't mean he won't want to leave the team. I suppose as long as he's good to my kid, I can't ask for anything else.

As I sit in my office and work, a video of last season's game plays on my laptop. A knock sounds at the door. I click the red x to close out of the window on my computer and look up to find Luke standing in the doorway.

"Come on in, Luke. I'm glad you caught me. I was about to grab Tucker and leave early for the day."

"Oh? Big plans today?" He smiles. He really does have a beautiful smile, not that I look at him in a romantic way; he's old enough to be my dad.

"I'm just registering Tucker for school, then we're going shopping. I thought I would make it a long weekend."

"He's a hoot. The guys seem to love him."

"That he is. But I know you didn't come here to talk about my kid. What's up?" I ask curiously.

Luke scratches the back of his neck nervously. He walks in and sits down in a chair in front of my desk. Resting his elbows on his knees, he leans forward. "I didn't want to put this on you when you first started, but we're going to need to hire a new general manager."

"Umm . . . Okay?" I frown. I don't have a clue how this stuff works. I thought the owner was pretty much the same as a GM. I wait for him to elaborate.

"Hannah can help you, but our old GM retired right before your father's sudden passing, and I was left as interim GM. Mr. West was in the middle of the hiring process but hadn't made a final decision. My daughter has the notes on the prospects, and if you need help, I don't mind sitting in on a few interviews. I hate to put this on you right now, but my focus needs to be on the team I have, and the GM will focus on building the future team."

"Oh! I'm so sorry, Luke! I had no idea."

That makes sense; though, I thought the coach did the team building. I have to keep reminding myself that I'm learning, and I really shouldn't beat myself up too much over this.

"It's no big deal. I was just hoping you might be able to hire someone before the season starts."

"Absolutely. I'll start on that first thing Monday morning."

Luke picks up a baby picture of Tucker that my father had left on his desk. Dusting it off, he beams. "He really is a great kid. I know your dad was proud." He sets the picture back down in its place and knocks on my desk. "Well, now that my business is concluded, I guess I'll let you have at it."

We both stand up as I gather my things, then make our way out the door.

"Thanks, Luke. If there is anything else you need, please don't hesitate. Like I said, this is all very new to me, and I'm going to need guidance. I really want everything to run smoothly without too many hiccups."

"Thank you for being so receptive," he says.

I poke my head into the game room to tell Tucker we're leaving, but it's empty. "Where's Tucker?" I say to no one in particular. I roll my eyes because I know exactly where I'll find him this time of day if he's not in the game room.

"I saw him down on the ice with Cal on my way up here." Luke puts his hands in his pockets as we both stroll down to the rink together.

He and I watch Tucker try to fake out Cal , but of course, Cal can see it from a mile away and steals the puck from him.

"Alright, Tuck, listen, the guys you play against are going to study you. They're going to pick apart your weaknesses on the ice. You're right-handed, and guys will pay attention to that. The best way to fake someone out is to skate up the left, wind up—almost like you're going to shoot, but instead you need to slice the puck to the backhand, then slice back to the forehand. Like this," Cal demonstrates. "When you do that, make sure to include your body and your head. You're going to cut across, wind up, and shoot. Now, let's go."

Tucker takes off skating to the left, then does a series of moves too fast and complicated for my eyes to follow. When he's inches within reach of the goal, he winds up, shooting the puck into the net.

Cal skates over to Tucker, picks him up, and spins him around.

"You did it, Tuck! Did you see that? You did it exactly right that time!"

Shrieks of laughter spill from Tucker, and my heart stops. I don't know if it's from seeing Tucker so happy, seeing a man with him in this way, or from the pure terror that Cal might drop him.

"Now, try it out on me," Cal says, setting him back down.

Tucker handles the stick with quick movements, alternating the puck between the back of his stick and the front. Cal closes in on him. Tucker shoots the puck between Cal's legs. He dekes, recovers, then takes a shot that sends the puck flying into the goal again. *What just happened?*

"Nice wrist shot," Cal calls out.

"Who's the man?" Tucker yells, nodding his head and putting his arms in the air. "Better watch out, dude." He points the hockey stick at Cal. "I might take your job." They fist bump, laughing.

"No doubt! I can see it now: you playing in the pros for your mom." Cal looks up, and a huge smile lights up his entire face when his eyes meet mine. I know that smile isn't for me, but God, with him smiling like that, I can't help my body's reaction. My heart skips a beat, and butterflies take flight in my stomach. Cal is beautiful. Okay, he's not just beautiful; he's insanely hot, especially when he's with my kid . . . and not scowling . . . or talking. Luke clears his throat, and the connection breaks. I try to curtain my face with my hair, so Luke won't see how Cal is affecting me. I cast my sight on Tucker. His smile drops in disappointment.

"Mom. Please don't; not today." He begs.

"Sorry, Bud. We need to register you for school."

Tucker drops his head and begins to skate to the boards but quickly turns back around and skates towards Cal. He throws his arms around Cal's waist to hug him and mumbles something. Cal squats down and talks to him for a second. Standing back up, he pats Tucker's back and sends him to me.

Luke whispers under his breath, "Well, I'll be damned," before shaking his head, turning around, and walking to the hallway leading to his office.

Tucker takes off the skates and heads into a storage room, slipping inside. He's been wearing someone else's skates for weeks. I never even thought to buy him his own. What kind of a mother am I? He slips out of the room and sits down on the bench to put on his shoes.

"While we're out today, we can buy you a pair of skates. Okay, Buddy?" I know he is bummed out, so hopefully that will cheer him up.

"Those are my skates." I frown in confusion, and he continues, "They used to belong to Elija, but he outgrew them, so Ivan told me that I could have them."

"Oh, that was nice," I say, as Cal exits the ice.

"Actually," Cal cuts in. "Those are regular skates; if you want to keep training for hockey, you will need a different pair. Elija joined a little league hockey team this year and retired them. Those are considered figure skates, and they're easier to balance on. Hockey skates are made for speed and agility. Since you're getting the hang of things, and your skating technique is good, I don't think it would be a bad idea to switch."

I had no idea there was even a difference. I look down at the ones Cal has on. I can't even tell you what the skates Tucker just took off look like, but now I have an idea of what to buy for him.

Several hours and a ton of paperwork later, Tucker is registered for school. We shop from place to place, gathering school clothes and supplies.

He stops in his tracks and pulls on my arm. "Mom! Can we stop here, please? There's a chapter book I want."

I turn around and follow him into the bookstore. The chime rings out above the door, announcing our entrance.

"Hi, welcome in!" A young college-aged guy greets us. "If you need any help, just let me know."

"Thanks."

The children's section has a guest reader, so I leave Tucker to listen to the story with the other children. There are a few books that I've been anxious to add to my shelf. Finding the romance section, I skim through, finding four books that I have been dying to read. Strolling back to the children's section, I round an endcap. Umph. I slam right into a very tall, firm, muscled, brick wall of a man.

"Oh, I'm—"

I look up, and standing there is Callan freaking Miles.

"I'm . . . I'm sorry," I stammer.

The way Cal was with Tucker today shifted something in me. I've had several hours to reflect on our unique situation and concluded our little spats are just stupid. Not only does this man work for me, but he also takes time out of his solo practice to teach my kid hockey. Maybe it's time I break the ice—no pun intended.

"Are you creeping on me again? Ooooh, what do we have here?" I joke.

I cast my eyes down at his books to see what he's into. He tries to hide them behind his back, but I've already read part of the title for one of them. His eyes find the smut material in my hands, and he gives me one raised eyebrow. I give him one back as he responds, "It's nothing."

"Did that title say self-help for the recovering pretentious asshole?" I ask in jest, chuckling.

His hazel eyes flick from my books up to my eyes. "It's sad that you read romance novels to live vicariously through your fictional characters. Fuck, it must be a lonely life living in a real world where nobody wants you."

My head rears back as if he slapped me. Actually, I wish he would have slapped me because at least that sting would go away quicker, where this one will linger. All the blood drains from my face, and my eyelids burn. I deserved that. If he was looking to hit a mark, he just hit the bullseye with that one. I was only kidding around, but given our history, I shouldn't have said it. Plus, I'm his boss, so what I said was unprofessional and uncalled for.

Sometimes I get carried away and my mouth just pops off. Cal hasn't said anything to me in weeks, and I go and ruin everything by running my mouth. Why? I turn my head trying to fight off the tears and mask my hurt feelings.

"Asp—"

"Cal!" Tucker runs down the aisle, bypassing me. "What are you doing here?" They give fist bumps.

Quickly, I avert my eyes towards the bookshelf and pretend to look for a book, so neither one of them can see the unshed tears burning in my eyes.

"What up, Tuck? I was out and about and thought I would grab a couple of books that would help you. This one is on mental strength for young athletes, and this one is just some hockey stories for kids your age. And this one is for me."

"Oh cool! Thank you, Cal."

"Yes," I mutter, "Thank you, Cal."

I want to turn my head; to watch their interaction and see the way Tucker's face lights up, but I don't. I trace my fingertips along the spine of the books in front of me as I slowly make my way down an aisle, giving them a little time and space to talk. Okay, so that's total bullshit. My nose is running, and I need to sniff, and if I do, Cal will know that I'm crying, so I'm trying to distance myself. As I move further away from them, I sniff and swipe at my tears.

"Aspen," Cal pleads. "Can we talk, please?"

"Come on, Tucker, we still need to buy your hockey skates." I call over my shoulder.

"Aspen, wait."

I make my way to the register. I can't let him see me cry. No man will ever see me cry . . . well, except the guy ringing up our books who's giving me a concerned look. Tucker joins me at the counter, and I throw on my sunglasses and grab our bag of books. Cal is behind me, ready to check out. I don't want to face him, but I know I need to. With no one else in line behind us and the sunglasses in place, acting as a shield between him and my emotions, it's a little easier to face him.

"Tucker, I forgot you're going to need a bookmark for your books; go ahead and pick one out."

"Yes! Thanks, Mom."

"Cal," And fuck it; I'm not a coward, so I take off my glasses and look him in the eyes like an adult. "I'm truly sorry for what I said to you. I was honestly kidding, but with our history, I can see how you wouldn't take it that way—"

"Asp—" I hold up my hand to stop him.

"Please, let me finish. I was unprofessional, and my comment was uncalled for. You are nothing but good to Tucker, and I'm so grateful for that. I thought I was lightening up the mood when really, I was setting the tone for what you said to me." With a bookmark in hand, Tucker reaches us. I hand over a ten-dollar bill so he can check out. "Anyway, I hope you can forgive me. Enjoy the rest of your weekend."

I put my sunglasses on, place the books in my oversized purse, and put a hand on Tucker's shoulder to guide him out the door. With my thoughts in the clouds, I'm not paying attention to what's going on around us. A crowd gathers around Tucker and me. I'm shoved in all directions. Cameras flash. One minute Tucker is standing beside me with confusion mirroring mine, and the next, he's on the ground crying. I'm in a state of shock. Before I can bend down to pick Tucker up from the ground, he's lifted into the air, then strong arms wrap around my waist, pulling me in close and away from the crowd.

<h1 style="text-align:center; font-family:cursive;">Chapter Seven</h1>

Cal

Have you ever heard the phrase: *"If you can't say something nice, don't say anything at all?"* Yeah, we've all heard it. For the past few weeks, it's a motto I've lived by, and that's why I've stayed away from Aspen, even though I was supposed to help her. I gave Tuck information to pass on to her and have been pretty well mute. That is, until she said something about me being a pretentious asshole. I was instantly fired up, but the moment the words flew out of my mouth, the stricken look on her face and tears in her eyes made me want to take those words back.

When we're bantering, I don't think about what I'm saying, but her defeated expression did something to me I didn't like, and it will haunt me. In that moment, I didn't like myself. And after her heartfelt apology and the realization that she was only kidding, I felt sickened by my words and actions.

Standing at the counter, ready to check out, I hear a cacophony of shouts and voices. I drop the books onto the counter and run out of the store. Everything is utter chaos; people are shoving, lights are flashing, and shouting voices fill the air. Someone pushes Aspen, and I see red. All the blood rushes to my head, and everything goes dark for a split second. I'm sprinting towards them when Tuck is knocked to the ground.

I don't think; I just jump into action. Picking up Tucker, I cradle him in my arms with his face buried into my neck, grab Aspen around the waist, and guide her into the back seat of my black Chevy Silverado. She scoots over to the middle and puts on her seatbelt while I strap Tuck in, all the while, my truck is being surrounded by the paparazzi.

Quickly, I hop in the drivers seat. With one hand on the passenger's side headrest, I turn my head, look behind me, and make sure I don't run over the invading assholes while I reverse. Once we make it onto the main road, I drive for about ten minutes to put space between them and us. Pulling into a burger joint, I put the truck in park, jump out, and open the rear passenger door. Tears stream down Aspen's cheeks.

"Hey, are you okay?" I ask them.

They both nod their heads in response, but I'm not picking up what they're putting down.

"While we are here, are you hungry?"

Tuck nods his head, and Aspen shakes hers no. Well, that's too damn bad; she's getting something anyway, whether she eats it or not.

"Okay, you two stay in here, and I'll go grab you something to eat. I'll leave the truck running, but when I get out, I want you to lean over the seats and lock the doors."

Aspen nods, and I hop out, leaving my keys in the truck in case they need to make a getaway. When I walk back outside with their food, everything is still calm.

I slide back into the truck, start driving, and press the hands-free button on my steering wheel. "Call Teagan Price," I say into the speaker when it makes a beep. The phone rings a few times before she picks up.

"This is Teagan."

"Teagan, it's Cal. Listen, I don't have a lot of time, and I don't really want to explain right now, but I need you to be aware the paparazzi know about Aspen somehow, and they swarmed her and her son at the bookstore. I have them with me, but you're going to have to work your PR magic."

"Shit."

"Kid in the truck, Teag. You're on speaker."

"Shiiiiiiooooot."

She pulls a laugh out of Tuck. "That's five dollars in the swear jar, ma'am. Carter was right! I'll be rich by the end of the season," he says.

Teagan laughs. "Yes, sir."

I can't help but love the girl for making Tuck laugh when he's clearly not okay.

"Alright, I have another call to make," I tell her.

"Miss Taylor, I'm sorry about this. I'll do my best to clean it up, but I have to warn you, I can only do so much."

"You have my authorization; try to outbid the paparazzi to keep my son out of the tabloids. Just text or call to keep me informed. I'm not worried about me, but I am worried about Tucker."

"Will do, Miss Taylor."

"Thank you," Aspen says as Teagan hangs up.

I press the hands-free button again. "Call," I pause and try to keep my voice down to a whisper so Tuck can't hear me.

"Fuck Face," I whisper.

I renamed Carter in my phone after he spouted off about me being fucked. Now look at me; I realize he might not be wrong.

"I'm sorry, who would you like to call?" The AI voice responds.

I try again and whisper. "Call Fuck Face." I hear chuckles from the back seat.

"I'm sorry, who would you like to call?"

I sigh, then say loud enough so I don't have to repeat myself. "Call Fuck Face."

"That's fifteen dollars, Cal!" Tuck says loudly.

"Calling Fuck Face." The AI voice says, and boisterous laughter fills the back seat.

Carter picks up on the first ring. "Yo, Smiley . . . Do I hear laughter? Where are you?"

"Hey, umm . . . yes, you hear laughter. And you're on speaker."

The laughter is so contagious, I start laughing too. We bust up and don't stop. I'm wheezing, tears are flowing, and I'm trying to talk between laughing, but it's no use. After several minutes of my now best friend again being patient, I finally collect myself.

"Okay, I'm good now. Uh, paparazzi got wind of who Aspen is and got rough with her and Tuck outside of the bookstore. I have them, but I'm going to need you to meet us at her house to pick up keys and ride with me to grab her car."

He's silent for a moment. "Hi Aspen. Hi Tucker. Are you both okay?"

"They are okay. Just meet us there."

"I'll be there," Carter says.

"Thanks, man." I end the call.

Releasing a deep sigh, I shake my head in disbelief. "I'm sorry this happened to you guys."

As we come closer to our neighborhood, a large crowd, gathered around our security gate, comes into view. What the fuck? As we pull in, cameras are flashing, there's shouting, and people are pounding on my truck. Anything to get a damn buck. I swear these guys are leeches. Several armed security guards stand at the gate, forcing the crowd back so we can drive through.

We pull into Aspen's driveway, and a blonde is standing outside, bouncing from foot to foot. She runs to the back of my truck and flings open the door. "Oh my gosh, Aspen! Are you both okay?"

He nods his head, and Aspen answers as they climb out of the truck. "Yeah. It just scared us . . . wait, how did you know?"

"It's all over the local news! Someone was recording the paparazzi with their phone from a window. I saw your profile, then I saw Tucker go down, and then The Hulk over here swooped y'all up. I tried texting and calling, but you didn't answer. I've been so worried!" She says with a southern drawl.

Aspen is explaining to the girl about her phone being buried in her purse when Carter pulls into the drive. He gets out and strolls over to us. He pulls a twenty-dollar bill out of his wallet and slaps it in Tuck's hand.

"The gate is a shit show. Security almost didn't let me in." He eyes the blonde.

"Oh! This is my sister, River. River, this is Callan Miles, the one you call 'Frat Boy,' and Carter Graham, the one you call 'Fight Club.'"

I bust up laughing. I then realize River is the girl Jerome and Carter were going on about at my barbecue. Aspen introduced her as her sister, but the two don't look anything alike. She could be her stepsister. She shakes my hand, then turns her attention to Carter. River raises a brow as he stands in a wordless stupor staring at her. He reaches out his hand to shake hers. She's reluctant but returns the handshake. As the three of them stand there talking about the events that went down today, I squat down to Tuck's height.

"Hey, Tuck," I say in a low voice. "Are you hurt anywhere?"

"My arm is scraped, but it's okay." He shrugs, then shows me the scrape on his left arm.

I check him for other injuries. Seeing he's okay, I stand and address Aspen.

"Can I talk to you for a minute?"

"Yeah, sure." She saunters over to me, and I send Tuck to his aunt.

"I know I have no right to say anything . . . I mean, I have no place here . . ." I stumble over my words and run a hand through my hair, pacing back and forth. Today was stressful and terrifying. Seeing Tuck on the ground like that scared the fuck out of me. "What I'm trying to say is, I know I'm not his dad, and I'm not sure what he thinks about—"

"His dad isn't in the picture at all," she cuts me of.

"Tuck never talks about him, but I wasn't sure. Either way, I think with all that's happened, if he's not in private school, he probably should be."

She casts a glance at Tuck, nibbling on her bottom lip. "Yeah, you're probably right. I'll take off next Tuesday." She nods. Then a huge smile lights up her face. "Look at us, Hotshot, finally agreeing on something."

Aspen hands me her car keys, then ushers her family into the house. Carter and I take off, making the drive to the bookstore. He's abnormally quiet as I drive. Usually, I avoid talking about things, but today the silence in the truck is smothering. I need to get this off my chest.

My thumb taps the steering wheel as I contemplate how I want to start this conversation.

"I want to talk."

He turns his head. His expression, shocked. I exhale a deep sigh, continuing, "I feel terrible, dude. I said something to Aspen before all this shit went down with the paparazzi, and her reaction didn't sit well with me.

Before, we just said whatever the fuck was on our mind, and no one's feelings got hurt. But today, what I said hit her differently. I feel like the biggest asshole. The things I said to her were far worse than what I usually spout off when we have our little tête-à-tête. Now, I don't know how to make it right. She just . . . she gets under my damn skin, and it's like I can't help it. You know me; I'm a man of few words, but when she's around, years' worth of built-up shit comes spewing out of my mouth." Nervously, I run my fingers through my hair while resting one hand on the wheel. "Spit it out. I know you have something to say."

"For once, I'm speechless." He chuckles, unwrapping a piece of gum, then popping it into his mouth. "What did you say to her that you feel guilty about?"

"Something to the effect of her living vicariously through romance characters because no one wants her in real life."

His expression is incredulous. "Harsh. Did you ever think that maybe she stirs up feelings you haven't felt and that's why you're so quick to go to war with her? Maybe you do the same to her?" He shrugs one shoulder.

I chew on that thought and let it settle before speaking. "She's a pain in the ass. But God, I never want to see that look on her face again. It was like I punched her in the gut."

"She makes you feel."

"Yeah, pissed off is what she makes me feel."

"Because she makes you feel. It's been four years, Cal. I don't want to . . . you know what? I do want to push you because it's time to move on. Not necessarily romantically per se, if that's not what you want, but just live your life and do it unabashedly. When you're around her, I think you feel alive, and that scares you. I also see the way you are with Tucker; when you're around him, you're living. Which leads me to believe you think he's safe, but you don't think she is."

"You've met that kid. He's something else."

"There are a lot of kids who are something else." He puts up quotations. "But that kid, you have a bond with. And don't spout your bullshit on me; it goes way beyond the bond you have with Elija or any of the other kids that come around us. You let loose with him; you're happy when he's around. You laugh more than I've ever seen you laugh. And I'm going out on a limb here when I say you let loose with her too. You may not laugh, but you do talk, and you show your emotions with her, even if it's anger. Granted, it's not the most positive emotion, but it's still more than you give anyone else. Maybe she isn't as bad as you've been forcing yourself to believe."

"I don't know about all that. I don't need any distractions. My contract is up this season, and you know how I feel about my career. I don't have the time or the room in my life for—."

"Yeah, yeah, yeah. I've heard this spiel before."

I roll my eyes and continue, "Not to mention she's my boss, and she could send my ass packing at any time." I turn into the parking lot, park next to Aspen's car, and hop out.

Carter hums, then slides out of the truck. Rounding the hood, his eyes lock with mine. "I don't know, man. Maybe just start with an apology and let the chips fall wherever they may. But in all seriousness, stop blocking your blessings."

With that, he hops into the driver's seat and takes off back to my house, while I pop back into the store and purchase the books I left on the counter

It's been a couple of days since the incident, and I'm still not feeling great about the things I said to Aspen. I toss and turn, unable to sleep. When I look out my bedroom window, I find the lights still on at Aspen's house. With the decision made, I pull on my gray sweatpants and throw on a Blaze t-shirt, then I make my way to her house.

Chapter Eight

Aspen

In need of space and some peace and quiet, I lay down on one of my old quilts in the backyard, staring at the starless night sky. It's late, and the dew is starting to settle on the grass, making my quilt damp. The cadences of the crickets and locusts that I would hear in Oklahoma are replaced by cars driving down the road outside our estate here in New York. There's rustling in the yard. I sit up, looking around. A tall, dark figure stalks towards me. Unable to see the face of the trespasser, I'm frozen in fear until I hear his voice.

"I hope I didn't startle you. The lights were on, so I knocked on your door. River said you were back here looking at the stars. I think I woke her up."

I stay silent and peer up at him.

"You know there's too much light pollution to actually see the stars here?" He kicks the toe of his shoe against the ground.

I look up at the sky, then lay back down. "I know, but I can pretend." I sigh.

Cal sits down beside me on the blanket. Silence surrounds us, but it's not uncomfortable.

"I came to apologize."

"Hmm. About what?"

"The media, the wreck, my attitude…I've not been the most pleasant person to deal with." He looks up into the black abyss.

"Are you apologizing because you truly feel bad or because I'm your boss and you're scared shitless to be traded?"

He scratches the back of his neck and chuckles under his breath. "Both?"

"Hmm."

I wouldn't trade him. I wouldn't abuse my power like that. I hope he knows I was teasing. I'm pretty sure that he does . . .

He laughs. "I'm the best center in the league." Then he adds, as if he were reading my mind, "I'm not worried about you trading me."

"Humble too," I volley back.

Maybe I'm a masochist, or maybe I need validation, but I ask anyway.

"I don't know why I'm asking you this. I guess I just really need to know. Did you mean what you said in the bookstore the other day about no one wanting me?"

His brows furrow. "What? Jesus, no Aspen! That's what we do. We talk shit. We get under each other's skin and piss each other off . . ." He trails off and lies down next to me. We turn our heads to face each other. Our eyes meet, and mine burn with unshed tears.

"When I was a little girl, I would lie in the pasture alone, sometimes for so long I would fall asleep there. God, I was so stupid . . ." I huff a breath.

"What? Why would you think that?"

"Because I would lie there and try to wish on every single star in the sky that my dad would come find me. That he would want to know me . . ." I whisper as his eyes map my face. I turn my head back to the sky, not wanting him to see my tears, and continue, "You probably don't know this, but I didn't even know who he was or that he owned a pro hockey team until the attorney called me to tell me my father passed away from a massive heart attack. How messed up is that? Of course, then I found out he had been supporting me with his money all my life, and my mom never said a word. She acted as if she took care of me on her own. I just wanted his time, Cal. He gave his time to everyone but me. My entire life I thought he was a dead-beat dad, but in reality he and my mom kept this big secret. They kept me a secret."

He runs his fingers through his hair, then tucks his hand behind his head. "Did you ever find out why?"

"My mom said they did it to give me a sense of normalcy. After Friday, I could possibly understand why, but that doesn't erase the abandonment I've felt my entire life. What's worse is the abandonment didn't stop there . . . oh no, I had to pass that little generational bondage down to my kid . . ." He waits for me to gather myself to continue. "Tucker is my whole life. I don't ever want him to feel how I've felt: unwanted and unloved."

"I don't think he feels that way, Aspen. I mean, look at him; he's happy and thriving." Cal laughs, "I don't think I've ever met a kid with such a big personality."

"He does have that." I chuckle, then sigh, playing with the ends of my hair, "No thanks to his father. Jason and I started dating right after I turned sixteen." I release a self-deprecating laugh. God, how freaking naïve was I?

"The whole thing was so cliché. I was a cheerleader; Jason was the quarterback and team captain. We dated almost a year, and I held out for a long time, but he was about to go off to college, and I thought I loved him; I thought he loved me. I had no idea he was about to break up with me. I found out the summer after my sophomore year, right before he left, that I was pregnant. He said he wasn't ready to be a dad, and didn't want to be tied down to me when he was about to start his new life. We broke up, and once Tucker was born and the DNA test came back, he just signed over his rights. Like, it was so fucking easy."

"Fucker," he breathes.

"When he moved back to town three months ago, with his sweet new family, I might add, I knew it would only be a matter of time before Tucker found out who his biological father was. I didn't want him to feel the abandonment on that level. Can you imagine watching your dad play with his other kids while you're sitting on the sidelines or watching from the window of your own home—the rejection and self-esteem issues that come along with that?" I shake my head. "So, when I got the phone call from the attorney, I didn't waste any time moving to here."

"You're a good mom."

I smile thinking of Tucker. "I try to be."

I turn my head back to him. "I haven't dated since Jason. I've been too busy being a mom and working on my master's degree. I had to grow up fast. When I was twenty and in college, the guys my age weren't looking for the same things I was. Sure, they would be glad to sleep with me, but to connect on a deeper level? No. They were all about hitting it and quitting it. That's not what I want. That's not me. Men who are worth a damn just don't pursue me. So, as you can imagine, your comment cut deep, but you weren't wrong. I mean, if my own father left me, and my kid's father left him so he didn't have to deal with me, then who else would want to stick around? Not to mention, most men don't want a single mom, and now that I'm getting older . . . you know, I don't even know why I'm telling you all of this."

Of all the people I could unload on, why am I unloading on the one person who can use it as ammunition against me? I'm a glutton for punishment, I guess. When he looks at me, I can see the remorse in his expression.

"I . . ." He hesitates before finally speaking, "I'm really sorry I said that. I was just being an ass. But you have to know, I don't think that you're undesirable or that no one wants you. And about the single mom thing: boys don't want a single mom, but a man will look at Tucker and see him as a bonus. The right man will want you, Aspen, and the right man will want him. That kid is so incredible, and so is his mom."

"Yeah?"

"Yeah. I just think you haven't met a man who can handle your ass yet." He chuckles. "He's going to have his hands full, whoever he is, that's for damn sure. But yeah, anyone who single-handedly raises a kid to be as great as him," he points to the house, "is pretty spectacular."

I sniff as tears trail down my face. Cal sits up and hesitantly places his hand on my cheek and brushes the tears away with his thumb.

"Thank you." I sniff.

"He doesn't deserve your tears," he says, as his calloused thumb wipes away yet another tear.

"Who? My dad or Jason?"

He exhales slowly. "Both? I'm not going to sit here and try to understand what was going on in your dad's head, Aspen. It's possible he was protecting you, but I don't have any real answers there; I can only speculate. I found it odd that you were thrust into this position, and no one knew who you were. Hell, from what you just told me, you didn't even know who you were until two months ago. Now that I know your dad was absent from your entire life, I'm baffled. What I do know is that man has been in my life for three years, and throughout those three years, he was always about family." He bends his knees, resting his elbows on them. "The game room? He didn't build that for the players; he built that for the kids. Hannah was hired to be his assistant, so she could be close to her dad. He allowed children to come to work with their parents. Maybe that was because he was missing out on you. But Jason? Yeah, that guy's a dick. He didn't deserve you, and he sure the fuck doesn't deserve Tuck." He lays back down beside me, both of us focusing on the cloudless dark sky. "Can I ask you a question?"

"Yeah?"

"Why weren't you at your dad's funeral?"

I frown. "I was. I sat in the back." I'm confused, but then it dawns on me. "If you're referring to me not sitting in the front row, it's because I didn't feel like I belonged in the family section."

"That's understandable. I have another question."

"Shoot."

"River . . . um . . . she's your sister? I'm sorry if I'm being forward, but I'm curious; she doesn't look anything like you."

I giggle, "That's because she isn't my biological sister. We've been best friends since we were babies. She is the only family I have, aside from my mom, so yeah, we chose each other. We look at each other as sisters even though we aren't blood-related."

"So, she moved up here to help you?"

I run my hands through my hair, then adjust my shirt, stopping it from riding further up my stomach. "Yeah, um . . . she had some stuff going on and wanted to get away."

The heaviness of our conversation wafts in the air as we lay in silence once more, looking up at the night sky.

I turn my head back to him, studying his profile. He's beautiful. His right arm is bent with his hand tucked behind his head, and his other one is flat between us. Long lashes that are just not fair for a guy to possess fan around his hazel eyes. Eyes so alluring and beautiful that when you look close enough, you can even see the gold flecks in them. His lips are plump and perfect. I imagine their softness; what they might feel like on mine. "I don't know if I said it earlier, but I'm sorry for everything as well."

"Apology accepted," he tells me, then adds, "Truce?"

"Truce. Thank you for taking care of us on Friday."

It's an odd feeling; I don't think I have ever had a man take care of me or Tucker. It felt . . . nice. His pinky slightly grazes the side of my hand. I don't know if it's intentional or if it's because we're lying so close to one another, but an unfamiliar tingling sensation runs through me.

"You know, I was thinking . . ." His eyes trace my face when I turn my head back to him. My heart picks up speed.

I laugh. "Don't go thinking we're friends now because we had a moment, Hotshot."

"Oh, I wouldn't dream of it, Firecracker." He chuckles.

Chapter Nine

Aspen

Projections analysis need to be completed, contracts need to be reviewed, I have resumes for the GM position to go through. Not to mention, my meeting with the commissioner in less than a week that I must prepare for. There are a million other things I need to be doing instead of thinking about Callan Miles. I can't concentrate. Memories of Sunday night keep distracting me: the way Cal looked at me, his hand on my cheek wiping away my tears, the way his lips moved when he spoke—all keep popping into my head at the most random moments.

He listened, allowed me to unload on him, and validated my feelings in the process. What I half expected him to say was, "See, I told you no one wanted you," but he didn't. What he said was far more dangerous: words that I never thought would escape his mouth, words no man has ever said to me before, words of affirmation.

"You're desirable . . . You're incredible . . . You're a good mom."

The compassion he showed when I was having a very vulnerable moment was beyond my comprehension. Not to mention the way he gently wiped away my tears. I'm not going to lie and say my body didn't react to that—it totally did. I don't understand why I felt so comfortable sharing such deep, personal traumas with a person who could very well have used them against me. The only thing I can come up with is that maybe there is more to him than the broody asshole persona he puts off. I also know if I keep thinking about him, I'm not going to accomplish a damn thing today.

Contracts are strewn across my desk, and I'm up to my eyeballs in decisions that need to be made for the organization. Even after hours of studying each possible candidate for the GM position, there's still no clarity in sight. I'm just thankful Hannah will be here in an hour to help me decide. She had a doctor's appointment this morning, and honestly, I'm so thankful because the last thing I want is for one of my employees to bear witness to this shit show.

I'm a woman in a male-dominant position. I know I'm being scrutinized, which leads me back to why I shouldn't be sitting here thinking about Callan Fucking Miles, never mind the fact that I'm his boss.

"Mom?"

"Yeah, Buddy?" I say, still filtering through resumes.

I massage my temples, feeling a headache coming on. It's not like I'm making progress, and I never want to make my son feel second to my job, no matter how busy I am. So, I look up, giving him my full attention. Tucker stands in my office with Elija.

I smile brightly, surprised to see him with Tucker. "Hi Elija! How's the new hockey team?"

"Good. It would be better if Tucker were on it, though," he says.

I'll have to look into that. Maybe I can talk to River and see if she can help when I'm out of town.

I give Tucker my attention. "Whatcha got?"

"Can we go down on the ice?"

A couple of weeks ago Ivan brought Elija to skate with Tucker and Cal. Since then, the boys have been inseparable. There are two things those two undoubtedly have in common: Fortnite and hockey. River and I have been to their house a couple of times since the boys met. We both clicked with Evie and are becoming fast friends.

I chuckle and shake my head. "In the past month, when have you ever asked me for permission to go down on the ice?"

"Never." He laughs. "But there was always an adult there. Cal's not here today, and Ivan is in the weight room. He said he wasn't skating today, but he didn't care if Elija did as long as you said that I could too.

He doesn't want him on the ice by himself in case he gets hurt. So, if I can't skate, neither can he. Please, Mom, can we?"

"Oh. Yeah. That's fine."

"Cool! Thanks, Mom!" He says, as they turn around and run out of my office excitedly.

An hour later, I've narrowed down the candidates for the GM position from five to three. Hannah was supposed to be here thirty minutes ago. Just when I reach for my cell to call her, she comes barreling into my office with disheveled hair and breathing hard. She bends over with her hands on her knees, trying to catch her breath.

She wheezes and holds up one finger. "Give me a second." Once she's composed, she throws her cell on my desk—screen up—and says, "Have you seen this yet?"

My eyes widen in disbelief at the grainy picture of Cal leaning over me with his hand on my cheek. The headline makes my blood turn to ice. How the fuck did they get this?

THINGS HEAT UP WITH THE NEW YORK BLAZE'S CENTER AND HIS NEW BOSS

Everyone knows the broody hockey player from the New York Blaze, Callan Miles, but who's the girl? Pictured above with Callan Miles is none other than the twenty-seven-year-old heiress and new team owner, Aspen Ryan Taylor. The couple was spotted Friday outside a bookstore in an embrace with Miss Taylor's ten-year-old son. Since then, there have been rumors of their relationship. However, nothing was confirmed until a cozy secret moment was caught on camera late Sunday night. Miss Taylor is the illegitimate daughter of New York Blaze's late owner, Mr. Ryan Allan West

. . .

I scroll down, skimming the trashy tabloid. My eyes land on words like: **"teen mom," "fraternization,"** and finally, **"unqualified."** They made me look like the team whore, brought up my teen pregnancy, and said that I was unqualified to run this organization. Disgusted and feeling sick, I hand the cell back to Hannah. My entire body feels like it's on fire as my blood pressure spikes, and tears burn the back of my eyes.

"It's a media circus outside. That's what took me so long. Teagan said Cal has already called her and is on his way down here. She wants us in the conference room as soon as he arrives."

I'm so embarrassed. I can't bear to look at Hannah. God, what she must think of me. "Excuse me, please."

Storming out of my office, I burst into the ladies room. This was bound to happen, right? I knew eventually someone would look me up, air out my dirty laundry, make me feel inferior, and make up lies. I grip the sink and stare into the mirror. Come on, Aspen, get your shit together. Grabbing a handful of tissues, I wipe under my eyes—careful not to smear my mascara. Finally, I collect myself before trekking down to the weight room.

"Hey, Ivan?"

He pushes up from his squat and carefully sets the bar back in the rack. "Yeah, boss?"

"I have an important meeting. Is there any way you can keep an eye on Tucker and make sure he stays down here? I don't want him near the conference room right now."

He picks up a towel from a weight bench and wipes his sweaty face. "I got you. Don't worry."

"Thanks."

It isn't long until we're all seated in the conference room. Teagan walks in and studies us carefully.

"Explain."

We go into detail about our fight in the bookstore, the paparazzi, and Sunday evening.

"This is a PR nightmare. You're being honest when you say nothing is going on between you two? Because that," she points to her blank cell phone screen. "Didn't look like nothing."

"Nothing is going on between us," we say in unison.

"Well, we can play this a couple of different ways," Teagan says. "You can say nothing at all and let the media frenzy die down. But I must warn you, that will leave you vulnerable to being further scrutinized. Another option would be to roll with it. Pretend to be dating. Make the media believe that you're in a committed relationship."

I nibble on my bottom lip and contemplate the best course of action. "I'll go with the first option." There is no way I'm faking a relationship with this guy. We've just come to a point where we can co-exist.

"Is there an option between the two?" Cal interjects. I squint my eyes at him, trying to figure out where he is going with this.

He rubs his hands down his face and releases an exaggerated sigh. "Faking a relationship isn't something either one of us wants to do, and staying silent isn't a good idea either. Maybe there's a way the media will back off and Tucker won't be so affected. You don't need any more scrutiny, Aspen. It's hard enough for you to focus on learning your role while having intrusions."

Putting out fires is Teagan's job; she must have another option.

"Whatever you want to do is up to you, and I will respect your decision. Can I just say one thing?"

I flourish my hand for her to proceed.

"You're trying to hire a GM. No one is going to want to work for an owner that has a crumbling reputation and looks as though she is jumping in the sack with one of her hockey players. That kind of reputation reflects on the rest of the team. You're a beautiful woman in a male-dominant position. The tabloids are going to pick you apart and make you look like the team whore," she pauses, "Sorry, that was crass, but also the truth. If an owner gives any reason for pause, or the team has a bad reputation, it's going to be a challenging time finding a GM replacement. Well, a good one anyway . . ." She trails off.

"Fuck! All I was doing was consoling her when she was upset. Why do they have to make things into something they're not?" He spins a pen with a contemplative expression.

I direct my attention back to Teagan. "I'm not a liar, and I'm not going to put Tucker in a situation where he thinks Cal is my boyfriend only to get his heart broken when we have to fake a breakup. Tucker adores Cal and I don't want ideas to get stuck in his head. I don't give two shit's what those leeches have to say. I'm going to continue to live my life unashamedly, but I understand your point about the impact it will make with hiring a new GM."

"She right. I wasn't thinking of it like that. So, give her something else to work with," Cal agrees.

Teagan taps her chin with a red manicured nail. "We can put out a crisis release. We'll let the media know you underwent a traumatic experience with the paparazzi, and with Cal being your neighbor, he came to check on you. We can give them the truth without disclosing the details of your life. I don't know if people will believe it, but I guess it's worth a shot. But if this doesn't work . . ." She trails off.

"That option I can deal with. I'll take my chances."

Cal stands, making his way to the door. "Okay, well since I'm here, I'm going to find Tuck and get some ice time with him."

"He and Elija were down on the ice earlier. If they aren't in the game room, you will probably find them down there," I say to him.

I look to Hannah, who's been silently watching us the whole time. I forgot she was even here.

"Are you ready to help me find our new GM?"

"Let's do this!" She says.

"Before you two leave," Teagan addresses me. "You've been here a month, and we can't hold off any longer. I've set you up with a live interview with T.T.S.N. The Total Sports Network, for Wednesday of next week at six p.m., so you'll need to find arrangements for Tucker. They may ask you questions about your relationship with Mr. Miles after all of this, but I'm going to tell them you will have no comment on that particular subject. I'll prepare you in the meantime."

As if things weren't bad enough, let's just douse the flame in kerosene. I don't want to face the media, but I guess I have no choice in the matter. "Okay. Thank you, Teagan."

Hannah and I head back to my office. We go through the candidates, eliminating one more from my list. The afternoon goes by rather quickly. As soon as we conclude our business, and she walks out the door, Cal strolls into my office with Tucker hot on his heels.

"Mom!" Tucker says excitedly and runs around Cal to stand beside me. "You will never guess what Cal did!"

I look at Cal curiously as they both stand beside my desk.

"What, Buddy?"

Tucker pulls skates from behind his back. "Hockey skates! I'm so pumped!" He shows me his brand-new skates, and I look between him and Cal.

This man. He keeps showing up and doing things that surprise me. "Thank you. You really didn't have to do that. I was going to get to it this week."

"Can I join the little league team?" Tucker fires off rapidly.

"Uh . . ." I look between the two again.

The question isn't unexpected, but the dynamics of how I'm going to get him to practice and games while working and traveling isn't something I've worked out yet.

"I spoke to Ivan and Evie already. Evie said she can help. If your sister can help too, do you think it's doable with your schedule?" Cal interjects.

I mull it over for a few minutes, trying to mentally scan through my schedule of events, games, and meetings. "I'll tell you what, Tucker, let me shoot a text to Evie and River, I'll get more details, and if Aunt River agrees to help, then I'll say yes."

With Cal and Tucker standing beside my desk, I unlock my phone and enter the group chat. A booming laugh escapes from Cal's mouth.

"What are you laughing at?"

Frowning, I look down at my blouse to make sure I don't have anything on it.

"Did . . . did you . . ." He wheezes a laugh, trying to collect himself. "Oh fuck, this is too good. You really named the group 'Chamber of Secrets'?" Cal asks. I can barely understand him because he's laughing so hard.

I deadpan and roll my eyes. "It was a collective . . . you know what? I don't have to explain it to you." I laugh.

"Never took you for a *Harry Potter* nerd," he says, raising one eyebrow curiously.

"Mom loves *Harry Potter*!" Tucker pipes in.

I glare, letting him know to zip his dang lips, then look back to Cal.

"Well, I've always taken you for a creeper, and you just keep proving me right. Looking over my shoulder at my text thread. What kind of person does that, anyway?"

I rapidly fire off several texts to Evie and River. Immediately Evie sends a schedule. I look it over. River responds to us that she has all the time in the world to help. She's been looking for a job in marketing. You would think in a place as big as New York City, a job wouldn't be so hard to find, but she hasn't had any luck—just a slew of denials for lack of experience.

Tucker looks at me with pleading eyes. I look at Cal, then back to Tucker, and close out of my text thread. "It looks like we have a new little hockey player."

"What?!" Tucker all but yells.

"See, Tuck. What did I tell you? I told you it would all work out." Cal ruffles his hair. Then gives him a high five.

"I want to be a center just like you!" Tucker says. Cal smiles down at him.

"Alright. I'm heading out. You're going to look at private schools tomorrow, right?"

"That's the plan. Will I find you following me around like a creeper?"

He shrugs and chuckles. "Maybe."

Tucker's face lights up, and a bright, toothy smile pulls at his lips. "Yes! I didn't know Cal was coming, but why does he have to follow us? Why can't we just ride together?" My eyes widen, and Cal looks confused.

I shake my head. "Oh, no. He's not—"

"I'm not following; you guys are riding with me." Cal cuts me off mid-sentence. *Wait, what? Did he just railroad me?*

"Do you think it's a good idea, with all of the . . ." I trail off and wave my hand through the air. ". . . you know, stuff going on?"

"Do you think it's a good idea to go by yourself with all of the stuff going on?"

"River can go with us. You probably have other things to do."

"Is River six-foot-two and two hundred ten pounds of pure muscle?" I roll my eyes. *Oh my God!* Can he be any more full of himself? Though, he's not wrong. Cal continues, "Can she protect you both from events like what happened Friday? No. That girl is the size of a pixie and can barely swat off a gnat. I got this."

"Fine!" I relent.

"See you both at eight a.m."

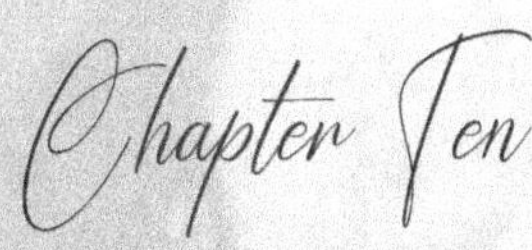

Aspen

River and I sit on the couch, relaxing as John Mayer's "Gravity" plays low through the speaker. Well, I'm stretched out, and River is sitting at the end petting Puck as he lies comfortably in her lap. I'm surprised no one claimed the little Teacup Yorkie. I swore I wouldn't let him stay, but then Tucker named him and became attached. Love the name; sometimes it saves me from having to contribute to the swear jar. I can just play it off as though I was misheard. Shh. Don't tell anyone.

It's late, Tucker's in bed, and after today, I just wanted to relax. And damn, am I relaxed after my second glass of wine and now working on my third.

"Have you ever paid attention to the lyrics of this song?" I ask, pointing to the speaker.

She tilts her head and listens, squinting her eyes in thought.

I laugh. "God, it is fucking depressing, River. I love some John Mayer, but this . . ." I shake my head and take a sip of wine. "Alexa, play 'Promises' by Calvin Harris and Sam Smith."

An upbeat tempo begins to play.

"There, so much better." I sit up to face her, cross my legs under me, and prop my elbow on the back of the couch. "I had a thought today." I skim my finger around the rim of my glass making it sing. "How would you like to come work for me? I can put you in the marketing department: you can learn from the best and gain the experience you need."

She sputters, which sends her descending into a coughing fit. "Are you serious?" She beams. "Isn't that, like, nepotism or something?"

"Pfft. I can do whatever I want." I giggle. "Seriously though. No, I don't feel that way. I'm not starting you in a director's position. You'll have to work your way up. With your degree, you're more than qualified for an entry-level position. Plus, if you hadn't moved here with me, you would still have a job. So let me just do this for you."

"Yes!" She sets Puck down on the floor and hops up, then leans over to hug me. "Thank you so much, Aspen."

I pat her back. "Well, I'm sorry I didn't think of it sooner. You can start next Monday." I release her. "Also, I have a very teeny, tiny, tincy, wincey favor to ask of you."

"Anything," she insists, sitting back down.

Taking a deep breath, I recount today's events. I tell her how Tucker took me literally when I asked Cal if he was going to follow me. "So now, Cal is determined to take us. And I just don't know how I feel about that. Will you please go with us?"

"I retract my statement. I'm not playing fourth wheel."

"What do you mean 'playing fourth wheel?' You can't leave me with him by myself."

"You won't be by yourself. Tucker will be there too."

"Yeah, but it'll be awkward. We've just started speaking to each other without ripping each other's heads off. I've been in a vehicle with him one time, and that was during a traumatic event. It's going to be uncomfortable." I trace my finger around the rim of my glass.

"Fine! I'll go." She acquiesces. "But I think someone might have a little crush."

I gasp in horror. "I do not!"

"Oh, look at those little red cheeks." She pokes her finger into said cheek. "I bet he makes your heart go pitter patter." She baby talks with a giggle, then stands back up. "You know it's true."

Grabbing the bottle of wine from the kitchen island, she stumbles her way over, tops off my glass, and fills her empty one.

"I know he makes me feel something. At first it was annoyed and exasperated, but now it's . . . I don't know what it is."

"I saw him with Tucker when he brought you both home. He was hovering over him like a helicopter dad. That even made *my* ovaries go into overdrive, and I'm not even the kid's mother. I also noticed you glancing over at them when you thought I wasn't paying attention. Don't even get me started on how fine he is—the guy's a total snack."

I chug the entire contents of my glass. It scares me how rapidly I went from loathing him to actually liking him. He has softened up, and I think it has to do with the sweet little ten-year-old boy sleeping upstairs.

"Okay, it's time I go to bed. I'm going to take Puck out, then take a PartySmart and call it a night."

"Goodnight." River singsongs and strolls over to the kitchen to put her glass in the sink, then heads upstairs, tripping on a step on the way up. Her giggle fades out as she makes her way into her bedroom, and then I hear the click of her bedroom door.

Grabbing the leash, I pick up Puck and head out. I descend the steps and start to make my way into the backyard, but before I get there, I hear footsteps slapping the pavement behind me. "Aspen!" Cal calls out.

"Yeah?" I turn around. "What are you doing here?"

I'm not dressed appropriately. I have on short sleep shorts and a tank top, sans a bra. I cross my arms over my chest. My cheeks heat. It's eleven o'clock at night, and I wasn't expecting to run into anyone.

"I couldn't sleep, so I went for a run and saw you out here." He pauses, catching his breath. "Um . . . I inserted myself into your business and made a decision without talking to you about it."

"That you did."

He just ran with Tucker's assumption. He didn't even give me a chance to correct my son. Like he said, he literally inserted himself into my business as if this is a fiduciary relationship. I don't know what to think or feel about that. Confusion? A week ago we couldn't stand each other, and now . . . well, I don't hate him anymore.

Cal swallows hard, and when he does, his Adam's apple bobs. He runs a hand through his hair, then paces back and forth. "I'm not sorry about that." He looks at me, then continues pacing. Suddenly, he stops, tilts his head to the sky, and rubs his hands up and down his face, then whispers. "Fuck! I don't know why I feel like this. I don't know how to do this."

He places his hands on his hips and sighs. "The thought of you both being in the middle of New York City by yourselves and something happening to you, like what happened on Friday, and me not being there to protect you, terrifies me. When you were shoved and then Tuck was knocked down . . ." His jaw ticks as he turns his head back to look at me. "It pissed me off, but more than that, it scared the hell out of me. So, I'm not going to ask your permission to protect you both, and I'm not going to say I'm sorry if I'm not. Because, as traumatic as that was for you, it was traumatic for me too. I will, however, ask you to have a little grace. I've tried to concentrate on hockey and nothing but hockey. I don't make time for other people, and I haven't cared about anyone but myself in a long time. Well, except for Carter. So, I don't know how to channel what I'm feeling right now. But fuck, I love the hell out of Tuck and the thought of someone hurting him like that again because I'm not there to protect him." He pauses and shakes his head. "I can't do it. So please, don't ask me to."

"Okay." I whisper. It's then I realize I do feel something for this man, even if I don't know what it is. Even if he has been infuriating. This man. God, this man. He makes me feel things I've never felt before: anger, lust, happiness, butterflies. The way he is with my son and the softer side I've seen of him with me in the past few days, I could easily fall in love with that side of him, and that scares me to death.

"Alright, well, take your ass to bed; we have an early start tomorrow."

"So bossy!" I laugh and begin to make my way to the front door. "Oh, and Hotshot?"

"Yeah?"

"You can love Tucker all you want. He needs you, and I think you really need him, but if you break his heart, Callan Miles, I will break your damn neck."

"Duly noted . . . you know, I was thinking . . ."

"Don't go hurting yourself."

"Har-har." He takes the steps up quickly and stands in front of me on the porch. "Seriously, I was thinking." His eyes lock with mine; the porch light catches the golden flecks in them.

"Okay?" I frown. He studies my lips for a beat, then quickly averts his gaze. His eyes slowly make their way back to mine.

"Uh . . . you know I said I haven't cared about anyone but myself for a long time. I've been really fucking selfish until Tuck came blowing through my life like a goddamned tornado." I giggle because that's Tucker; his joy is contagious, and he kind of just attaches to you and doesn't let you go. Cal continues, "God, this is so stupid, but . . . um . . ." He stops talking and rubs the back of his neck, the vulnerability showing on his face. I give him a reassuring smile to continue. "Carter knows a little bit about my past, and some of his advice from the last couple of months is kind of starting to settle with me." I give him a confused look. "I guess what I'm trying to do is turn over a new leaf, and I don't know how to do that, so I'm just going to spit it out. I want to try this friendship thing . . . with you."

A smile lights up my face. "We can be friends on one condition. Well, actually two."

"What's that?"

"I don't take friendships lightly, so if you're going to be my friend, you have to stay my friend. None of the back-and-forth shit. That doesn't sit well with me. You're either in or you're out. Capisce? I'll probably push your buttons and piss you off, but you can't just stop being friends with me."

"And the other condition?"

"You can't go catching feelings for me."

"I wouldn't dream of it, Firecracker." He turns around swiftly and skips down the steps. "Goodnight, *friend.*"

I watch him until he makes it back to his house.

"Go inside!" He yells from across the street.

I roll my eyes and step across the threshold. Tomorrow is going to be interesting.

The sound of my alarm is blaring in my ears, yelling at me to start the day. My head feels like someone is taking a pickaxe to it. Wine always does that to me—guaranteed headache. I groan and slap at my alarm clock. Peeking through squinty eyes, I see the time. Shit! It's seven forty-five! Jumping out of bed, I race to the shower, take the fastest shower in the history of showers, and wash my hair. I throw on a long, light blue, floral, sleeveless dress with a high neck, put my hair in a quick bun, and accessorize with a pair of pearl earrings. Forgoing a full face of makeup and only using a few swipes of mascara and lip gloss, I decide this is as good as it's going to get today. I send up a silent thank you to the universe for clear skin and sprint out of my bedroom to coax Tucker out of bed.

When I waltz into his room, his bed is made, so I turn and run downstairs. I find him sitting on a stool at the kitchen island, completely dressed, reading a book, and eating a bowl of cereal.

"Thank God! Did Aunt River get you ready?" I kiss the top of his head.

"No. She's still in bed."

Of course she is! Wine was a terrible idea. I'm surprised to see Tucker remembered dress clothes and a tie.

"Okay, we don't have time to wait. We have three minutes to be outside. Did you eat enough?"

"Yes ma'am." He rinses out his bowl and leaves it on the counter.

"Dishwasher, Bud." I direct a pointed look at him. "Then go brush your teeth, please."

As I'm sorting through papers, making sure we have everything for enrollment should we decide on a school today, the doorbell rings. I start to shove the papers back into the envelope when River appears at the bottom of the stairs, her hair a mess, and clad in pajamas. She stumbles over a pair of Tucker's shoes in the entryway, kicks them off to the side, and opens the door. Cal is standing there with a cup carrier holding what I'm guessing is three coffees and a hot chocolate, looking every bit of a GQ magazine model. *Goddamn.*

My eyes travel the length of him when he walks through the door sporting a pair of navy slacks, a white t-shirt, and a navy blazer. Short stubble enhances his sharp jawline. The way he is standing at the door with the left corner of his lips popping into a smirk tells me I've been caught checking him out. Damn it! I avert my eyes. I'm his boss; I really need to stop ogling him. Way to play it cool, Aspen. I shake my head and place my concentration back on the papers.

"Good morning, Frat Boy. Are you going to continue to make a habit of pulling me out of my slumber?" River grumbles, rubbing her eyes. "She's in here." She thumbs over her shoulder in my direction while I continue sorting through all of the ridiculous items needing to be submitted: birth certificate, immunization records, letters of recommendation . . . what ten-year-old needs a letter of recommendation?

"You should have been out of bed already! I guess I can assume you're not going with us today?" I raise one eyebrow at her.

She groans at me in response and plops face down onto the couch. Her response is muffled. I'm taking that as a no. I roll my eyes. The freaking traitor!

"Morning, Cal!" Tucker casually walks down the stairs and across the entryway to Cal and gives him a fist bump. "You ready to do this thang?" Tucker asks Cal.

"Yep. Are you?"

Tucker looks down at himself and straightens out his clip-on tie. "Do I look good?"

"Yeah, man. Fit is drip." He hands Tucker what I assume is hot chocolate. "Did I say that right?"

"You're catching on." Tucker pats Cal's back.

I chuckle under my breath and watch their interaction while I place everything back into the folder, then stroll over to join the boys at the door. Before we leave, he walks over to the coffee table and sets down the coffee for River, then rejoins us outside. Cal hurries around me and opens the front passenger door of the truck.

"Callan Miles." I scold and whisper. "Friends don't open doors for each other." I frown at him in confusion when he offers his hand, then bypass his offer and boost myself up into his truck.

His face lights up; I wish he would smile like this more often. "Friends who have little boys around that need to be taught how to treat a lady do." He retorts.

Callan closes my door, then makes sure Tucker is buckled in. Once everyone is situated and we've started driving, Tucker calls for my attention. I turn in my seat to look at him.

"You look really pretty today, Momma." My lips contort into a smile, and my heart soars at his sweet words. When I turn back around in my seat, I catch Cal wink at Tucker.

"Thank you."

We sit in front of the headmistress' long walnut desk in her office as she shuffles through the documents I've brought with me. It smells of the old, musty books lining the bookcase behind her desk. The clock on the wall to the right gives a click, click, click, click, like it's counting down our doom as she looks over Tucker's entrance exam that he completed fifteen minutes ago. Ms. Kadence, the headmistress, is beautiful and polished. Her rich, dark brown hair is cut into a cute bob that complements her high cheekbones and big blue eyes.

"Mr. & Mrs. Taylor." Ms. Kadence begins.

"Oh, this isn't . . ." I shake my head. "It's Mr. Miles. He's a friend of ours." I say, and her lips spread into a wide smile showing off her perfectly straight teeth.

"My apologies." She turns her head from me and addresses Cal. "Everything looks good here; would you like a tour of the school?" I'm not good at masking my facial expressions. My brows pull down in confusion. Quickly, I mask my irritation and smile. It's not hard to tell that Tucker is my son; we look just alike. I told her Cal was a friend of ours. I mean, if Cal was his father, wouldn't I have introduced him as such? Why is she addressing him instead of me? Passing it off as a misunderstanding, I let it go.

After she hands me my documents, we begin our tour. I can't help but notice she seems to put a little more sway in her hips when she walks. Well, more than what I would consider to be normal. Her red dress is fitting—sexy yet still classy. She's certainly alluring.

She shows us the computer lab, library, and music room—addressing Cal the entire time and ignoring me. Me . . . Tucker's mother. She keeps placing her hand on Cal's forearm or grazing her hand across his shoulder and giggling like a little fucking schoolgirl, and I. Don't. Like. It. I don't know why I don't like it, but it's starting to really piss me off. I can't explain it. Maybe because she is doing it in front of Tucker? I don't know. Cal is beginning to look uncomfortable by the time we pass the art room. Finally, I've had enough.

"Ms. Kadence, Mr. Miles is my friend, not Tucker's father, so if you don't mind, I would appreciate it if you would address me."

Cal's eyebrows meet his hairline. I'm sure he can tell I'm at my wits end with this lady. She is completely unprofessional, not that I have any room to talk after checking him out this morning, but still . . .

"Yes, ma'am." She nods.

Ten minutes later, it's as if she didn't hear me at all, because contradictory to her acknowledgment, she carries on in the exact same manner and disregards what I just told her. We're on the playground when I see her slip him her business card from my periphery; I lose it. I completely lose my mind.

I turn and waltz up to her. "This meeting is concluded. I don't really think we have anything left in this institution that we need to see further. May I make a suggestion?" I don't wait for a response. "Maybe next time someone comes to look at your facility, you keep your hands, your eyes, and any other objects to yourself. You know? Something I'm sure you teach here in the kindergarten classrooms." I pluck the card from Cal's fingers, grab her hand, and shove it into her palm. "We won't be needing this; Tucker won't be attending here."

"Tucker! Let's go." My voice booms, coming out a little louder than intended. Tucker races down from the jungle gym and catches up with us.

"On to the next place, Bud." I make sure to correct my tone to be sweet and my voice low. I just made an ass out of myself in front of Cal. His face is beaming. I want to slap that smile off of his stupid, handsome face.

When we're back at the truck, he opens my door once again and makes a repeat of settling Tucker in the back.

"So." He scratches his neck and starts the truck. "That was . . . interesting. Care to share what that was about?"

"Not particularly, but I will if you insist."

And he laughs. He fucking laughs! With his head tilted back, he gives a full-on belly laugh. I look out of the window stewing with my elbow propped on the door and my cheek resting on my fist. Tucker begins to laugh. I try like hell to fight my smile. My lips are tugging hard, and I'm forcing them back into a thin line, but then a laugh bursts out of me.

"I kind of missed you there for a minute, Firecracker."

Chapter Eleven

Cal

I don't know what got into Aspen today, but I have to say, being on her side of things and watching her unleash on someone other than me was entertaining. She's been nice to me the past few days, and honestly, I was starting to miss her smart mouth. The headmistress was obviously flirting with me, and the way she kept touching me and giving me all her attention was making me very uncomfortable. Something about Aspen's protectiveness, made me feel a way I can't describe. I'm not Tuck's father, but even if I were, Ms. Kadence should have been addressing both of us. Aspen doesn't mask her emotions very well, and I could tell she was upset about being disregarded, so by the time we were on the playground, I was already about to call the tour off before she stepped in.

The laughter in the truck was contagious, pulling her out of her foul mood; it was good to finally see her laugh. I turn on the radio low enough where we can talk and hear each other over the music. Bruno Mars "That's What I Like" plays through the Bose speakers as we drive down the highway to the next school.

"Ooh, this slaps! Can you turn it up?" Tuck asks. I reach over and turn up the volume.

Tuck begins singing, so I join him. Before I know it, we're all singing at the top of our lungs. From the rearview mirror, I see Tucker bobbing his head as he sings out loud. Aspen and I look at each other while singing the chorus in unison. She shakes her shoulders, pointing to me then herself.

She tilts her head back and belts out the bridge of the song. With the music playing, I can barely hear her. I back off singing, so I can hear her voice better. Knowing it's a dick move, but doing it anyway, when the bridge hits the high note, I press the mute button on my steering wheel. What? Don't judge me. I want to hear her sing. I catch two words before she stops abruptly: like a record scratching. Her eyes widen in embarrassment and she covers her face. Tuck snickers from the back seat. Aspen turns to me and smacks me on the arm, then turns the radio back on. "Ass!" She mouths, so Tucker can't hear her, coaxing a chuckle from my lips.

When we pull into the parking lot, I face her, putting on my most serious face. We lock eyes. "Okay, Firecracker. I'm going to need you to be on your best behavior in here."

A laugh spills out of her. "Hey! She was being highly unprofessional."

"That, she was." I shake my head.

When I look up at the private school through my windshield, a deep foreboding feeling settles over me. The school is two stories and made of stone with a concrete archway. It looks more like an old orphanage you would see in movies than a school. We stroll through the front door with Tuck walking between us, chatting about the robotics class at Elija's school. The hallway is long and narrow. A glass case of student accolades resides on the left, and the main office is situated on the right. The air is cold and smothering. No sounds come from the hallways or classrooms. No laughter. No talking.

"Good morning, I'm Mrs. Winston." The headmistress greets us and shakes our hand at the entrance to the main office. Her handshake is soft, her hand cold and unwelcoming.

"Pleasure, I'm Mr. Miles and this is Miss Taylor, and this is Tucker Taylor."

She purses her lips and looks between Aspen and Tuck. "The pleasure is mine." She says, but it doesn't sound like it's a pleasure at all.

Maybe she is one of those no-nonsense-straight-to-the-point people. She leads us on the tour of the classrooms, followed by the gym, and then the cafeteria. Where the other institution appeared to have fun activities and felt welcoming, there doesn't seem to be anything fun about this place. This school seems uninviting. Mrs. Winston reminds me of someone, but I can't quite place it. She's a thicker woman, her face mars fine lines, and she appears to be in her late forties, if I had to guess. Her hair is brown, peppered with streaks of gray, and is slicked back into a bun. She doesn't seem pleasant or show any kindness towards Tuck. Actually, when he speaks, she seems put out. Once we are done with the tour, Aspen begins to ask questions.

Tuck turns to me and gestures for me to bend down. He whispers in my ear. "I've been looking for the chokey around every corner." He wraps one hand around his neck like he's choking himself. I frown at first, not understanding what he's talking about, but then remember he and Elija were watching the movie *Matilda* in the game room a couple of weeks ago. They roped me into watching the last half of it before we went skating. It's then I realize that's who this lady reminds me of. Mrs. Winston gives us a stern look when we begin to snicker.

"Do you have a PTA or PTO?" Aspen asks curiously.

"Yes. However, there is an impressive age gap between you and the other parents, so I am uncertain to how much you will have in common with them."

"Excuse me?" I frown. "Can you explain to me what you just said to her?"

She's hesitant at first then she addresses me with directness. "Mr. Miles. You cannot fault me. The PTA acts as a liaison between the teacher, parents and community. Miss Taylor is young, and her lack of experience will most certainly cause discord."

My molars creak and I'm sure I just cracked one of my teeth with how hard my jaw is grinding. My vision darkens as anger consumes me, but I take a deep breath to reel it in. I don't know why her words are affecting me so strongly. All I know is, I'm not giving this woman a second chance to offend Aspen, especially in front of Tuck. We're done here.

"Aspen here are my keys, take Tuck to the truck, please. I would like to have a word with Ms. Trunchbull."

Tuck snickers at the Matilda reference; though I'm sure he doesn't understand the back handed comment this lady just made to his mother. It's taking all my self-control to reign in my anger and not lose my shit in front of him.

"It's fine, Cal. I'm used to it," Aspen retorts.

It's not fine. It shouldn't be fine. Right now, I don't want her on her best behavior. I want her to stand up for herself. The Aspen I know isn't apprehensive when it comes to releasing her quick wit and smart-ass mouth. I'm sure she is used to the condescending comments from other people because she was a teen mom at one time. I'm also sure it's probably an insecurity for her—she feels self-conscious about it.

Dangling my keys in front of her face, I say, "Truck. Now. Please." She rolls her eyes and snatches the keys from my fingers.

"Come on, Buddy." Aspen puts a hand on Tuck's shoulder and guides him away.

"Thank God. I don't like this place. It was giving me the heebie-jeebies," Tuck says mirroring my thoughts.

I watch them walk down the hallway to make sure they're both out of earshot before I speak. "I don't need to explain anything to you, but your comment was asinine." My jaw ticks. "I want you to understand your mistake so you can absolve yourself from making it again in the future. That woman you just spoke down to for being a young mother, is the sole owner of a multi-billion-dollar empire. She runs that organization like a tight ship, and very successfully, I might add. With a mere phone call, she can add this institution to her investment portfolio and fire your ass. So maybe you should think twice before you make the wrong assumption about someone." I raise an eyebrow.

She nods. "My apologies, Mr. Miles."

"I'm sure it goes without saying, but Tucker will not be attending this school." I turn around and make my way through the corridor and out to the truck.

Once I'm in the truck, I turn in my seat to face Aspen. "Hi."

"Hi." She smiles.

"You okay?"

She sighs and plays with one of her pearl earrings. "I'm good. Listen, what I told you the other night . . ." She turns in the seat to face me and begins intertwining her fingers nervously, "I didn't tell you that so you would feel sorry for me. I told you so you would understand my boundaries. I saw a different side of you, and it made me feel safe in sharing. But I don't want you to feel sorry for me or feel the need to protect me every time someone makes a backhanded comment about my age. I'm not a teenager anymore, and I've made peace with that judgment." Her green eyes collide with mine.

I reach over and tuck a strand of hair behind her ear. "I don't feel sorry for you, but you can't ask me to stand by and let someone talk to you that way, especially in front of Tuck. Now, you ready? I think we have one more stop."

"These are the only two appointments I had scheduled for today." She turns in her seat to address Tuck in the back. "You good, Buddy?"

"I'm happy as a tick on a fat dog if I don't have to go to that place."

The things that come out of this kid's mouth . . . I shake my head and wheeze a laugh. I don't think I have ever laughed as much in my life as I have with these two. We pull out onto the road. I call Ivan to find out where Elija goes to school, then I call the school. I'm relieved they can fit us in immediately.

We take the tour of Elija's school. It's . . . normal. Thank fuck. We meet several teachers who seem to be friendly. A sense of relief fills me knowing Tuck will be okay; that he will thrive here. We have him enrolled within an hour and are out the door and on our way to lunch.

During lunch, Aspen told me she and Tuck had never been to Central Park and asked if we could go. I can't tell her no, and even if I could, I wouldn't want to. As we walk around the park mindlessly, we come to the entrance of Bethesda Fountain. Aspen reaches into her purse and pulls out all of her change. She hands a few coins to Tuck, then takes my hand and dumps a few into my palm. Her eyes slowly move up to mine. My heart races at her touch.

"What are we doing?" I ask her.

"Making wishes. What does it look like?" She eyes me curiously before coasting her way to the fountain.

We close the distance to the fountain and stand in front of the angel. With her eyes shut for a few long moments, Aspen's head tilts up toward the sky. A smile plays on her lips as she mouths her wishes wordlessly, then she tosses her coins into the fountain. Tuck does the same, so I guess it's my turn.

I'm not really sure what to wish for. I've never done this before, and I don't know if I even believe in wishes coming true. Playing along to make them happy, and on the off chance that something will come of it, I make several wishes, then toss my coins in with theirs. Aspen gives me a bright smile.

She is the definition of joy. I know all too well how mad she can become and how mouthy she can be, but she doesn't seem to let her anger simmer too long. Well, unless you were Callan Miles pre our heart-to-heart discussion. I guess I just knew what buttons to push. What I've noticed is even then, nothing—not past, present, or possible outcomes of the future—stands in the way of her happiness. She has every right to be mad at God or the universe, but she's not. I admire her for that. I crave her joy. I don't want to be broken anymore. I don't want to feel like waking up every day is a chore. I want to be more like her . . . resilient.

"This is beautiful," she whispers, staring at the fountain.

I cast my eyes on her profile, and for the first time she takes my breath away. I've always thought she was beautiful, but with a broad smile on her lips and the way her hair and skin glow from the sun, making her look like an angel, in this moment she is truly breathtaking. I want to touch her so badly, but we're friends, and that's all we can ever be. So, like I did the night we were lying under the sky in her backyard, I let my pinky slightly graze her hand—just to get a fix. You can call me a coward for the not-so-accidental touches, but I don't care. The need to touch her in some way consumes me.

"Yeah, it is," I say, not taking my eyes off her. She turns to face me, her beautiful green eyes sparkling in the sunlight. She has a graceful smile, and I can't help but smile back.

Tuck bumps into us while chasing pigeons just as I ask her, "What did you wish for?"

He opens his mouth to speak, but Aspen covers his mouth with her hand to stop him from talking. Giggling, she says, "You can't say! It won't come true!" She ruffles his head, then turns towards the entrance of the fountain, ready to leave.

People are standing still as statues in various places while music begins to play. Suddenly group of people begins to dance. She spins around in a circle watching all of them dance to a mix of pop songs.

"What is this?" She yells over the music.

"It's a flash mob." I yell back. She and Tuck turn their heads, watching and laughing over the music. I swear it's the sweetest sound I've heard. A woman and young boy stand in the middle of the dancers. In front of her is a man down on one knee. I don't miss the longing on Aspen's face as the man proposes to the woman. She watches with a sweet smile. The woman nods her head and throws her arms around the man. When the music stops and everyone begins to walk away, going about their lives like they didn't just put on an incredible performance, we stroll out of the fountain area.

"That was amazing!" She beams.

We make our way through The Mall and Literary Walk, and then we take Tuck to sail remote control model sailboats. After two rides on the carousel, everything starts to shut down. One of the things I learned about Aspen today is that she likes a little spontaneity. We spent the entire day together laughing and enjoying each other's company. For the first time in four years, I lived.

Chapter Twelve

Aspen

"Has anyone seen Coach?" I ask, as I round the doorway to the weight room. I stop dead in my tracks. I'm completely stunned into silence as my eyes land on a shirtless Cal doing pull-ups. With his arms, back, and core muscles straining, every single divot and predominant cut is on display for me. I have never in my life found forearms fucking sexy—until now. He's so strong. His back muscles flex with each pull; the movement involuntarily draws my tongue out to lick my lips. My mind wanders to visions of me running my hands down his bare back, caressing as his muscles flex under my fingertips while he's hovering over me. Considering it's been years since I've been intimate with anyone, he would completely wreck me. But you know what? I would be wrecked with a satisfied smile on my face. Damn, he's beautiful.

A reflection in the mirror catches my attention from my periphery, and draws me to his reflection. Gym shorts sit low on his waist, showing off his Adonis belt—the sexy V makes my thighs clench together. Holy shit. My brain is seriously short-circuiting as I watch rivulets of sweat drop down his rock-hard abs. My eyes trace up his torso to his shoulders, to his sharp jaw, before landing on his hazel eyes. They lock with mine. Heat flames my cheek.

I clear my throat, then quickly turn my head to find a shirtless Carter looking at me with a smirk and one raised brow.

"Holy fuck!" I nearly jump out of my skin. I certainly didn't see him standing there. "Jesus! Do either of you wear clothes?" I snap. "Where's coach?"

"Haven't seen him." Carter puts down the barbell.

I need to talk to Luke about our interview this afternoon. But what I need more than that is to get the fuck out of this weight room before I lose any more brain cells. I turn to leave.

"Hold up." Cal releases the bar, and his feet—clad in white shoes—bounce on the ground once before he stalks over to me. "What are you and Tucker doing for lunch today?"

I can't even make eye contact with Cal at this point. "I have to stick around here, but I am having pizza delivered if you two want to join us in the conference room."

"What time?" Cal asks, his chest right in my face.

I avert my eyes. "Noon," I say, and walk out the door. I've had enough embarrassment for one day. The last thing I need to do is stand there and gawk at him any longer.

A few hours later, River and I sit in the conference room with several pizza boxes between us when Hannah breezes in. "Hey boss, the stylist picked out your wardrobe for tonight's interview with T.T.S.N. it's hanging in your office. Also, don't forget you have a three o'clock interview for the GM position. I peeked at your calendar, and you have . . ." I hold up my hand to silence her.

"Hannah, I'm at lunch right now, and that's exactly where you should be. Now, come sit, eat pizza with us, and let's talk about *anything* except work." I pause, thinking about how my words just came out as a direct order. "That is, if you would like to, we would love for you to join us, but I don't want you to feel obligated," I amend.

"Girl. Me? Turn down free pizza? Hell no." She laughs.

I push the box to her as she sits down beside me. Teagan strolls in. "Miss Taylor?"

I wave my hand in for her to sit. "Please eat with us if you're hungry; we have plenty as long as you eat before the boys arrive, but we have a new rule: Lunch time is our time to regroup for the rest of the day, so no talk of work. Everything can wait until we're done with our timeout."

"Timeout?" Hannah questions.

"Yeah. It's a mom thing, I guess. Any time she needs a break, she puts herself in timeout." River laughs, grabbing another slice of pizza and stuffing a bite into her mouth. She shoves the box towards Teagan as she chews. Grabbing a slice, Teagan makes her way around the table and sits down next to River, but not before grabbing a water out of the mini fridge.

"What?" I laugh and shrug my shoulders. Pointing between the three of them, I add, "Wait until y'all have kids; then you will understand the importance of putting yourself in timeout."

Teagan wipes her mouth. "Your kid is adorable. He seems to really love Cal."

River covers her mouth and swallows. "Yeah, those boys seem to be inseparable. I don't know who is going to be more distraught when school starts, Cal or Tucker."

"My bet is on Cal. I've never seen him as happy as he is when he's on the ice or in the game room with that kid," Hannah pipes in just as Cal, Carter, and Tucker waltz through the door.

"Did I hear my name? Are you talking about me?" Cal winks and takes a seat next to me. I feel like a fucking teenage girl right now. I've never had this reaction to anyone before.

Carter pulls out the chair next to River and sits down. She ignores him. "Yep. We're talking mad shit about you," she says to Cal before directing her attention to Tucker. "Put it on my tab, Sport."

"Your tab is probably at a hundred thousand dollars by now." Tucker rolls his eyes and grabs a slice of pizza, plopping down next to Cal.

"We were just talking about who is going to suffer more when Tucker goes to school," I inform him.

"Oh, me. Definitely me." Cal ruffles Tucker's head.

Before Tucker stuffs a bite into his mouth, he leans on the table with his forearms, peering around Cal to get my attention. "Mom, I need hockey gear. Can you take me?"

I don't even know what he would possibly need. I glance at Cal nervously. "Umm, is that something you can help me with?"

Cal nods, "Sure thing." Then he grabs a slice of pizza and directs his attention to Tucker, "I got you, my dude."

Carter lifts his cap, runs a hand through his sandy blonde hair, then puts his cap back on backwards. He lays his arm over the back of River's chair and lifts his chin. Her spine goes rigid as he says, "So, what are you doing here?"

River's face flushes. "I, umm . . ." She clears her throat. "I work here now." She says, a little caught off guard. "What are you doing here? Training doesn't start until next week."

He waves her off. "Eh, I thought I would spend some ice time with Cal beforehand. I haven't been as dedicated as he has, but don't tell the boss." He winks at me. *Charming.*

Carter's dimples pop, and his blue eyes sparkle in mischief as he turns his attention back to River. A small bump sits at the bridge of his nose where it's been broken, but it's not terribly noticeable. He's hot, but he doesn't make my heart race; he's exactly River's type, though. Standing at over six-foot-three, the man towers over River, who is only five-foot-two. And his muscles . . . good lord. Her ex has about the same build, but the comparison ends there.

I'm more of a tall, dark, and handsome type of girl. Now, I find myself envisioning a sweaty, shirtless Cal—ripped, lean muscles, his sexy ass tattoo that snakes up his arm, around his bulging bicep, and travels all the way up his shoulder and over his pecs. I can still imagine the smirk resting on his kissable lips. Oh God, not to mention his tight, muscled ass that looks so fucking perfect and round, I can't help but wonder how those glutes would flex when he's thrusting his . . .

"What position?" Carter asks. I nearly choke. I sputter and cough. Cal pats my back to try and help, but the effort is futile. I take a drink of my water to help clear my airways.

River rolls her eyes, even though he's only making friendly conversation. Her mind must have been with mine.

"Marketing."

Once I can finally breathe again. I cut their conversation off when I notice River on the verge of fleeing. "No more work talk. I'm done with work for the next twenty minutes."

Carter rocks back in his seat with his intent still set on River. "Want to grab a coffee or lunch this week?"

I groan, knowing where this is going. Placing my head in my hands, I massage my temples. River is about to bolt. Her fight-or-flight response is set on get-the-fuck-out-of-Dodge. She stands up and throws her food in the trash. "I'm good, Fight Club. Thanks for lunch, sis." She saunters over to Tucker and places a kiss on his forehead before walking out. "Love you, Sport," she says as he quickly wipes the kiss away.

Once she is gone, I hone in on Carter. "Yeah, I think you're wasting your time, honestly."

He shakes his head. "Nah, she'll come around."

I'm not going to argue with the guy. It's not like I've known her my entire life, or anything, so I change the subject. "Please eat the pizza. Whatever is left, someone can take home." I stand.

Cal grabs my arm. "Are you leaving? We just got here."

In response, I throw a thumb over my shoulder to let him know I'm going after River without saying it out loud. I say goodbye to everyone and ask Hannah to meet me in my office at one o'clock.

I find River in her office and knock on the door before I enter. "Hey, you okay?"

"Yep."

"Not all men are like Jaxson, you know?"

"And not all men are like Jason, but here you are acting like every man you meet is going to walk out on you," she counters, and my eyes widen. I know she's a little triggered, but damn, that was a low blow. I nod and turn to leave.

"Aspen, wait. I'm sorry."

"River, you know how I pop off, and I'm trying hard to rein it in. Cal and I are just now becoming friends. Plus, I'm his boss. It's not like that with us. For *once* in Tucker's life, he *finally* has a man who gives a shit about him. Cal is a good man who Tucker looks up to. I'm not trying to jump into a relationship and mess that up for him. No man sticks around for me, but at least there's one who I think might stick around for him and be a mentor or whatever . . ." I take a breath trying to rein in my temper. "Maybe I said the wrong thing when I walked in. I'm sorry." I laugh at myself. I'm being a hypocrite and a fucking liar. "You're right. I think you and I both have some things to sort through inside here." I point to my temple. "And here." I pat my heart.

"I'm really sorry I snapped at you, Aspen. There's just something about Carter. Sure, he's hot, but you see how he is on the ice."

"I do see how he is on the ice; he's protective and aggressive. He does his job, and he does it well," I cross my arms tight against my chest. "I also see how he is off the ice; he's playful, but at the same time he can be very levelheaded and serious. Carter is a nice guy. Be nice to him. Be professional and friendly."

"Pfft, he's nice and levelheaded? He beats the shit out of people." She counters, shaking her head. "I just can't."

I lean against the doorway of her office and take a deep breath in understanding. "He fights because that's his job. It changes the momentum of the game, River. He also holds his opponents accountable for dangerous plays. He's protective. He's not . . . look, if you're not interested, be direct and stop running away. But if by some miracle you decide to go on a date with him, sign something with HR."

"There will be no date, but I suppose I can try to be nice to him," she says, rolling her eyes.

I can deal with that. I nod and walk over to give her a hug before heading to my office. As I leave, River mumbles, "Maybe you're the one who needs to speak to HR."

I snicker and leave without argument.

Yes, Cal makes me feel things I've never felt before. And yes, he is hotter than the damn devil on doomsday, but that man is just my friend . . . fuck me, who am I kidding? I'm only lying to myself. I like him. I really freaking like him.

It's been a long, yet productive day. We hired our new GM, Trey Miller. He and his wife were looking to make a move from L.A. to New York, and with the contract we just offered him, he was eager to accept. Teagan and I shot through a number of questions T.T.S.N. was set on asking me tonight. She requested all questions be sent in advance and told them I would not be addressing any tabloid rumors during the interview. Thankfully, they stuck to every question submitted to us and didn't veer off script.

It's ten o'clock at night, and I'm dead-ass tired. I take my weary ass up to my room, and as I pass by the window, I see Cal walking over. I watch him as he makes it halfway through my yard, then he seems to think better of it and turns to walk away. Remembering what River said to me earlier and the promise I made, I quickly throw on a robe, dash down the stairs, and make a quick but quiet exit out the door, closing it lightly behind me.

"Cal," I call out, "What are you doing?"

Turning around, he runs a hand through his hair and blows out a puff of air. "I have no idea. I was up and wanted to see how the interview went."

"Oh. It went well."

"Okay." He nods. "That's good."

That's it? That's all he was coming over for? Wanting a little more time with him, I ask before he can leave, "Do you want to sit outside and chat?" I close my robe tighter around me.

"Sure. Yeah."

We saunter to my backyard and sit across from each other on the patio furniture. I'm exhausted, but I start a small fire in the fire pit. "Back home, River and I loved to make fires and roast marshmallows with Tucker on the weekends." I picture our quiet farmhouse and all of the memories we built there. Everything is different here. Bigger. Louder. More populated.

"While our friends were off partying and living their best lives in high school and college, we were living our best lives creating memories with Tucker. You know, I wouldn't trade a single minute." I chuckle, thinking back to when Tucker was six years old.

Cal listens intently, as if he's mesmerized by my voice. "Tucker loved to stick the marshmallows into the fire, but as soon as the darn thing caught fire, he would drop the damn stick into the pit and run." I shake my head. "Do you know how many marshmallows that boy wasted?" A laugh escapes my lips, and he lets out a chuckle. Then I think about how I've been living my life. "What's ironic is, in life, I do the same thing. I've squandered so many opportunities out of fear, dropping that damn metaphorical stick, and running like hell." I shake my head.

I remember what I said about not being pursued, and I wonder if that's even true. Maybe men did pursue me, but I was too scared. Maybe I chose to ignore them even if it were subconsciously. Or maybe not, who knows? But what I do know is I'm tired of running. Remembering how River acted today towards Carter, I wonder if I've been doing the same thing since Jason.

"You know, you're not the only one who runs. I can admit I do it too. But look at you now. Something big and scary came along, and you met it head-on. You're not giving yourself enough credit." He looks me in the eyes intently, and I avert mine. The sound of his voice and his sincere expression makes my heart race. If it were daylight, he would be able to see the blush creeping up my neck and into my face.

"I made a promise to myself today that I would try to sort out my shit." I whisper. I clear my throat. "But you didn't come here for philosophical backyard confessions," I chuckle.

He's so damn easy to talk to. When it's just us, I word vomit. He doesn't want to hear about my problems. Why do I keep doing this?

"I like listening to you speak. I'll admit your accent is hypnotizing." He rests his hands behind his head, and fuck me, his rock-hard biceps bulge, making my mouth water.

"What? This backwoods hillbilly accent?" I exaggerate my accent and place a hand over my heart like a southern belle. I laugh, trying like hell to draw attention from the fact that I'm sitting here checking him out. "What was it like where you grew up?"

He leans forward, resting his elbows on his knees while his eyes roam over my face. "Eh, it was cold," is all he gives me. What the fuck? It was cold? That's it? "I don't really miss it much. I like it here in New York."

"But New York is cold," I counter.

"Not that cold," he says vaguely.

I cover my mouth and let out a yawn.

"You've had a long day. Why don't you head on inside, and I'll put this out." He looks around, then stands from his chair.

"Water hose is over there," I point to the right side of my sliding glass door.

"Look at your calendar tomorrow and let me know when you have free time; I'll take you to buy Tuck's equipment."

I nod. "Thank you. Goodnight. Thank you for putting out the fire."

"Sleep well," he says, turning on the spigot.

Once I'm in the house, I trail up to my room and fall into bed, foregoing my latest romance novel. The only thing, or person rather, I can think of before I go to sleep is Callan Miles.

Chapter Thirteen

Cal

God. This place smells like a grandma's attic. The musty smell invades my senses as Aspen and I stand inside a thrift store. Racks upon racks of used clothing fill the store. Shelves and glass cases display old Halloween knickknacks and decorations as the holiday quickly approaches. I have no idea what we are doing here; this woman has more money than she could ever know what to do with, yet she chose to come here.

It's morning, and the store is empty, sans the little old lady who looks to be in her eighties. I hand her a few hundred-dollar bills to lock the doors to the shop behind us until we're finished with whatever this is.

"Why did we stop here again?"

As we pass a glass case, I tap a bobblehead black cat wearing a witch's hat; the head wiggles and wobbles around. I look around, and a chill visibly runs through me as I take in all the used clothes. Aspen rolls her eyes, grabs my hand, and pulls me towards the men's section.

"Don't be such a name brand whore, Hotshot. We're here because I want to be, and you're going to be a good sport about this. We're playing a game. Capisce?" She laughs. "Okay. Now, close your eyes. And don't peek!" She warns.

I didn't come shopping with her to play games; I came with her today to help pick out Tuck's hockey gear, since his first practice is this evening. For the past few weeks, since agreeing to sign him up for hockey, Aspen has been busy with work, and I've been in grueling practices. Our time to buy him gear has run out. When she gives me a pleading look and pouts her bottom lip, I relent with a sigh and close my eyes. Air hits my face, and I can only assume she is waving her hand in front of it.

"I'm going to guide you through the store, and you're going to feel and grab." She giggles.

"Feel and grab sounds like an interesting game, Firecracker." I chuckle.

"Shut up," she laughs. "Okay, start here; just run your hands along the clothes and pick out something."

Aspen goes on to explain her ridiculous rules, then with my hand in hers, she leads me through the store. My fingers fumble along the racks of shirts, feeling the textures; I'm only allowed to touch the upper part of the sleeves. I can't see the color or print, but I come across one that has the texture of a dress shirt and snatch it up. We do the same thing with the pants; the same rule applying. I feel for texture and pluck the hanger from the rack, handing it to her. When we get to the ties, I'm not allowed to do anything except touch the top part; it feels silky, so I point, and she removes the tie from the hook.

Throughout our game, her laughter plays on like a melody. I'm only allowed to feel the top of the shoes and the rim of the hats. I have a suspicion she is making these rules up as she goes because these weren't the ones we started with. I'm being a good sport, doing as the boss woman says. We come to a dead stop. Slowly, I peel my eyes open. As I glance at everything in her hand, my eyes spring wide. A booming laugh escapes my mouth.

"Now, go put all of this on." She shoves the clothes at me haphazardly.

I look down at the them. I don't know what I thought was going to happen once I picked everything out, but there is no fucking way I'm putting this shit on. She's out of her ever-loving mind. It's not that I'm stuck up; it's just the thought of putting on someone else's clothes makes my skin crawl. Probably because that's all I was afforded as a child. With one raised brow, she gestures her hand toward the dressing room. I want to put up a fight, but I know it would be useless.

I give her a scathing glare. "Fine, but you're next!" I point at her.

My gaze lingers on the clothes hanging on the hook and the hat laying on the dressing room chair; I hesitate. The shoes aren't that bad; they're stylish, though they're way too small. I'm going to look like a complete idiot; my hesitation isn't about that. But, to hear her laugh, I would do just about anything. A long inhale fills my lungs.

Am I fucking doing this? Reluctant, I stand with my hands on my hips, making no move to change.

"Just put it on, Hotshot, and don't look in the mirror," she calls out on the other side of the dressing room door.

"You're still making up rules as we go, I see."

I change into the atrocious get-up. This is stupid; I don't need to look in the mirror to know how ridiculous I look.

When I step out of the dressing room, Aspen immediately bursts out laughing. She's bent over, one hand on the arm of a chair, holding herself up. She pauses; her face is red with tears streaking down. Then, she burst into more uncontrollable laughter. I know it's bad, but damn, how bad can it be? I face the mirror, catching sight of myself. I try to hold it in, but a laugh flies out of my mouth. I look completely unhinged, sporting a purple blazer with faux fur on the lapels, Hawaiian shirt with flamingos, neon green golf shorts, and a silk scarf decorated with tiny snowmen and Christmas trees tied around my neck. The brown leather dress shoes don't fit at all, so I wear them as slides with my feet resting on the heels. An ugly black hat topped with big purple peonies rests on my head. She snaps a picture with her phone.

My eyes widen, and she laughs. Reaching for her, I try to grab the menacing device from her hand, but she pulls away—twisting her body one direction, then the other. I wrap her in my arms, swinging her around, as I try to pluck the phone from her hand. She squeals and shoves her device into her pants.

"Oh, you laugh now, little missy, but paybacks a bitch. You better not send that picture to *anyone*." I set her to her feet.

"Only if you wear that the entire time I pick," she volleys.

Taking the scarf from around my neck, I turn her around. I lean in as I place the silk fabric over her eyes and whisper in her ear, "I don't trust you not to peek." I tie the silk around her head.

When I turn her back around, she's biting her lip. I wonder what her lips would feel like.

Shaking the thought, I guide her to the most hideous items I can find, making up my own rules as we go. Aspen comes out of the dressing room, looking utterly ridiculous. She's in a white, nineteen-nineties, poofy-sleeved, mid-length, floral dress, a pair of baggy khakis, a green boa draped over her arms, and resting on top of her head is a vintage red beret with a red veil and feathers. The heels are sexy, though. I take picture after picture of her posing ridiculously. My body is shaking in laughter, so half of these are probably going to be blurry. I feel life breathed into me.

"Hold on," she says, plucking the phone from my hand.

Aspen asks the store clerk to take our picture. The old lady chuckles as she takes several of us together. Aspen retrieves her phone and angles it above us. I bend down to her height and she takes a selfie of us cheek to cheek.

"You two are just adorable together," the little old lady says.

Both of our eyes widen. We burst out laughing again. We put back all the items, and I slip the little old lady another one-hundred-dollar bill for her time. Then race Aspen to her new Range Rover, plucking the keys out of her hand on the way. Rounding the SUV, I open the passenger side door for her, holding out my hand to help her in. She hates it when I do this because she says it's not a "friend" thing to do. Whatever. I'm doing it anyways; I guess I'm old-fashioned.

"I can drive, you know?"

"Pfft. Tell that to the front end of my car," I counter.

"So, tell me more about you."

I hesitate, "I grew up in Washington and went to college in Seattle, where I was drafted into the NHL. My rookie year, until about three and a half years ago, was spent playing for Colorado. Then, I was sold in a fire sale to your dad. I've been in New York ever since." I keep it brief, not wanting to relive the depressing details of my life. It's just not something I share with anyone. "So, what we did back there, you've done that before?"

"The game we just played?" She asks chuckling, and I nod my head. "Oh yes. Where I'm from . . . well, you see, it's a very small town. There are literally two stoplights . . . wait, no, three actually, but one of them is a blinking red and yellow light that doesn't work anymore. Anyways, there's really nothing to do close by, so when River and I were bored, we would go to this old consignment store on Main Street and play that game; we'd use the pictures as blackmail." She laughs. "So, you lived in Washington and in Colorado. What was it like in Colorado?"

I immediately want to shut down. Seeing the perfect opportunity to keep her out of my past, I pull into her favorite coffee shop. "What's your favorite coffee?" I ask, jumping out of the car to avoid any more questions about my life.

"White chocolate mocha latte." Her face lights up.

We stroll into the coffee shop, and once we've ordered, I hand my black Amex card to the barista. While we wait for our drinks, I open my cell to make sure the store I'm looking for is within walking distance. With our coffees in hand, we head out the door.

"I have a treat for you." I steer her down the sidewalk to the store at the corner of Broadway and twenty-second street. "Close your eyes."

She rolls her eyes, then closes them. As I guide her through the entrance, someone greets us, "Welcome to the Harry Potter Store."

Her eyes pop open as she looks up and turns around to take in our surroundings. She faces me, and her smile is enough to knock me on my ass.

"Wow," she whispers. "This is amazing."

As we roam around the store, Aspen takes me by the hand, dragging me along with her from one thing to another. Toward the back of the store, we find a bar. Her text notification pings at the same time as mine.

Aspen takes out her phone and barks a laugh that catches me off guard. I peer over at her questioningly. I pull out my phone to find a text from Carter; I type out a quick response, then shove the device back into my pocket.

"I just got a text from River." She flashes the phone for me to look at her text.

River: Can I run Carter over with the Zamboni?!?
River: Never mind; that's too messy. Could you just trade him?

I laugh, pulling my phone from my pocket and handing it to her.

Carter: This girl does know I'm up for a challenge, right?
Me: What girl?
Carter: River. I asked her again if she wanted to have a drink with me, and you know what her response was?
Carter: That if I asked her again, she was going to run me over with the Zamboni.
Carter: She hates me for no damn reason, but that's okay, hate sex is great sex.

"They will never happen," Aspen says.

She doesn't know Carter very well. That guy doesn't back down from shit.

The bartender moseys over and interrupts us, "One for you both?" He questions in an English accent while slinging a white towel over his shoulder.

I hand him my card. "Please."

Turning back to Aspen, I say, "Eh. I'll take you up on that bet. I'll put one hundred dollars on them hooking up within six months." I hold my hand out to shake hers with no intention of ever making her pay if I win.

"Bet, Hotshot." She shakes my hand.

I pluck my phone from Aspen's other hand and stuff it back in my pocket to give her my full attention. Once the bartender places our butterbeers in front of us, we talk about her childhood with River, then we touch on mine a bit, but still, I try to steer away from too many details. We finish our drinks; Aspen only drank half due to being full from the coffee, then we're off to find the sorting hat. We both end up in Slytherin.

"You know, I'm Gryffindor all the way, but I'm sidled up next to your rotten ass, and you know the saying . . . 'You're the company you keep.'" She giggles. I pinch her side.

She picks out wands for Tuck and Elija, and then we browse through other interactive experiences. I'm stopped several times to sign autographs while Aspen watches patiently with a sweet smile. She gladly takes pictures when my fans ask and hand over their phones. Several bags in hand, and three hours later, we stroll out of the store.

"Thank you," she breathes and surprises me with a hug. I hesitate for a second but wrap my arms tight around her and breathe in the intoxicating floral scent of her perfume. Her body feels so right next to mine.

"This day has been incredible. Nobody has ever done anything this nice for me," she adds, looking up into my eyes with a bright smile. I want to bend down and place my lips on hers, only to see if they are as soft as they look.

When we're seated in the SUV, she turns her body towards mine and pulls a box of jellybeans out of the bag.

Shaking the box, she asks, "Want to try one?"

"I haven't had a jellybean in forever. Hit me." I hold out my hand. "Greedy girl. You're only giving me one?" I shake my head and pop the jellybean into my mouth. The minute I bite down, I damn near throw up. Fumbling with the door handle, I fling the door open, jump out, and spit out the jellybean.

"Good God, Aspen. What the fuck was that?" It's taking all I have not to hurl. I reach into her glovebox and pull out a napkin, trying to wipe the taste off my tongue.

Aspen laughs; it's a full-on, uncontrollable, body-shaking, tears-rolling-down-your-cheek kind of laugh.

"Oh! I have an idea!" She wipes her eyes. "Let's pop them one at a time into our mouths and see who makes a face first."

"You and your ideas, let me see that." I snatch the box out of her hand and look over the flavors: earwax, rotten egg, vomit. I shake my head vigorously. "Nope! No way." I pass the box of jellybeans back to her.

"Oh, come on, Callan Miles, live a little. Don't be such a wuss." She giggles as she dumps the jellybeans into her hand. She holds out a fistful of them and bats her gorgeous green eyes. *Fuck! For some reason I can't say no to her.*

I relent, holding out my hand. "Fine! Ugh . . . you are the worst; you know that woman?"

"On the count of three . . . One. Two. Three," she says and pops a jellybean into her mouth, and I do the same. Mine tastes like black pepper. The flavor isn't terrible, though a little strong. I can see her eyes watering, but she is trying like hell to keep a straight face.

"Wait!" I hold up a hand after the first one. "What do we get if we win?"

"Winner's choice. But just so you know, if I win, you have to come over and do my laundry . . . for a whole week," she says, coaxing a chuckle out of me.

We repeat the process on the count of three, two more times, before she jumps out of the car and heaves. I feel kind of bad, but karma is a . . . well, you know, and she did trick me with the first jellybean and she also made me wear that ridiculous outfit today.

Aspen slides back into the car and reaches into her purse before popping a stick of gum in her mouth.

"Do I even want to know what flavor that was?" I ask curiously.

She laughs at her expense and runs her hand through her hair. "Probably not."

The way her face lights up causes my heart rate to spike, and for the second time today, I feel a little more alive. She's brought out a playful side of me that I never knew I had.

Once we've completed our shopping at the hockey store, I drive us to pick up Tuck. I pull up behind the long line of cars parked in front of the school, and we wait for classes to be released. Kids begin to filter outside of the building, then Tuck bursts out the glass doors with a group of boys. Finding Aspen's SUV, he says goodbye to his friends and makes his way across the crosswalk to the passenger door. As he sees me in the driver's seat, he becomes visibly excited and moves to the rear door of the SUV.

I push the button to unlock the doors, and he hops into the back seat. While putting on his seatbelt, he begins to chatter about his day. Leaning forward, with both hands on each of our seats, he asks, "Cal, are you coming to watch me practice?"

I look at him through the rearview mirror. "I wouldn't miss it."

Tuck turns his head toward Aspen. "Mom, did you get my gear?"

"Sure did, Bud. Everything is in the trunk."

The relief that takes over his expressions sends a pang to my heart. It takes me back to my childhood when I didn't know if or when I would be able to get the things I needed. I know he will never have to worry about anything, but I still understand his concern. With the schedule we've been dealing with, finding time has made shopping for him difficult, and we were down to the wire.

We opt to stop by their house first so we can make dinner and then head over to the practice facility. When we walk down to the ice and the kids see us, their chatter immediately stops.

"Wow. That's Callan Miles!" A kid with blonde hair states. Elija runs over and gives Tuck a fist bump before they take off to the locker room to change. Aspen and I sit with Ivan and Evie, and I can't help but notice the side glances Ivan is throwing my way.

"What?" I shrug.

"Nothing." He smirks.

The boys filter onto the ice, and the coach rounds them up, and begins practice. He asks them questions, then begins breakout drills. Tuck is a natural. Spending this past summer training him and then watching him implement what he's learned on the ice fills me with pride. He dekes on several of the boys once they've moved into the team scrimmage. The puck is passed back and forth between other players before coming back to Tuck, where he drives it down the ice and makes a wrist shot into the goal. The scrimmage continues with Tuck gaining most of the possessions and sending the puck into the goal. The coach makes notes on his clipboard, then blows a few puffs on his whistle to stop practice.

The kids gather in a circle around the coach as he reads from his clipboard to call out names and the positions they will play. When he says, "Tucker Taylor, you'll be our center." I nearly come out of my seat. I want to jump in the air and fist pump. Fuck yes! An overwhelming sense of pride consumes me, and I can't fight the smile beaming on my face. Aspen looks at me and gives a knowing wink, and damn, every time I look at her, my heart begins racing at an unbelievable speed.

Once practice is over and I've taken Aspen and Tuck back home, I head across the street. It's dark, and the streetlights illuminate the road. Aspen stops me halfway to my house.

"Hey, Cal?" She calls out, and I turn around in the middle of the road. Fuck, with the way the moon is beaming down on her, she's breathtaking.

"Thank you for today. It was one of the best days I've had in a really long time."

I want to trot back over there and wrap her in my arms like I did earlier today, but I stop myself and shake my head. "I should be thanking you. Goodnight, Firecracker."

After finally making it inside my house, I lean my back against the front door. My eyes close as an ache builds inside my chest. I press my fist to it, trying to alleviate the pain, but it's no use. No matter what I do, there will always be a dull ache there. My thoughts begin to circle around my day with Aspen. She brings so much light into the darkness that has become my life. Every day, I live just a little bit more, but with that also comes guilt. Even as the guilt eats at me, when my head hits the pillow, it's Aspen's face I fall asleep to.

Chapter Fourteen

Cal

As days turn into weeks, my feelings for Aspen grow deeper, and I don't know what to do with that. I should stay away from her, but I can't. An array of emotions swirls through me, ranging from lust, guilt, happiness, sadness, confusion, and anger—a daily battle between my mind and my heart. I know I shouldn't, but still, I can't help but find reasons to touch her in subtle ways. Even if it is just a graze, a little hit to get me by for a little while. She lives rent-free in my head, and many nights she takes residence in my dreams. Several times a week, we take walks together in the cool night air. Sometimes we sneak over to each other's houses late at night and sit in the backyard wrapped in a blanket and talk about everything or nothing at all. It's when I return home that I always feel conflicted.

I try to shake her from my thoughts as I skate around the ice, warming up for my game. For some reason unbeknownst to me, I'm nervous—I feel off. Something just doesn't sit right. This isn't normal for me. My eyes continue to find their way to the owner's box, looking for Aspen. Why do I keep looking up there, and why does it feel like I miss her? I shouldn't be feeling this way. My hands shake. My mind doesn't want to cooperate with my body—I'm sweating, even though I haven't worked up a sweat. I don't understand why.

I'm scowling when Aiden yells out, "Yo, Smiley! What's wrong, man?"

I shake my head, conveying I don't want to talk about it. I don't tell anyone anything, but even if I did, it isn't like I would talk my shit out on the ice in front of everyone and especially right before a game. I don't even fully understand what I'm feeling myself; I'm sure as hell not going to gain clarity from a teammate.

Trying to clear my head and my nerves, I take one last lap around the ice. When it's time to face off, and the puck is dropped, I'm quick to pass the puck back to Jerome. He skates up the right, fighting for the puck against the boards with Toronto. Jerome passes to Trevor, but Trevor misses the pass, sending the puck into Toronto's possession. Toronto passes back and forth, dodging our guys, before their player rounds the crease to shoot for a goal. Ivan makes the block.

I don't know what's wrong with me, but my head isn't clear, and I just let these assholes by me. I take a deep breath and try to center myself between plays.

The puck is passed to me. I pass to Trevor; he passes to Drew, then it comes back to me. I skate up the left side, over the red line to circle the crease, then I'm slammed into the boards. Before I know what's happening, Carter slams into someone beside me and begins throwing punches. He's booted from the ice, mouthing off while skating to the sin bin.

We alternate taking possession of the puck. Our opponent is playing to win. Aiden has the puck; he makes it over the blue line and passes to me. I cut, skate up the left, deke around Toronto, cut to the right, wind up for a wrist shot, sending the puck to the goal—it hits the post and bounces off. *Fuck!*

We recover the puck; Jerome passes to Trevor, he winds up, takes the shot, the red light spins, and the siren blares. Fuck yes! We're in the lead, zero to one.

We end up winning four to three, but Toronto handed us our asses for a minute. Everyone jumps around shouting. There are rounds of backslaps, hugs, and fist bumping. The locker room is loud in celebration with Humankind's "Big Dawgs" blaring through the speakers. I hit the showers, letting the hot water soothe my aching muscles as I wash away my sweat. That uneasy feeling still doesn't settle, but after our win I'm in a much better mood. While I dress in the black Armani suit I arrived in, the guys are talking shit and popping each other with towels.

I'm standing at my locker, spraying cologne on my neck, when Carter sidles up next to me. "You want to go out with us to The Sapphire Lounge?"

The Sapphire Lounge is an exclusive club for the elite down in the lower east side of New York City.

"No, I think I'm going to call it a night."

It's an instinctive habit to say no right away. I've never wanted to do anything with them outside of hockey, and he knows what my response will be, but to be polite, he continues to ask me anyway. I just wonder when the invitations will stop completely because it's expected of me to decline them. Do I want to go to the club with everyone and celebrate? Thinking of how much fun I've been having lately by spending time with Aspen has me second-guessing my original response. I don't know if it's just her or the fact that I don't want to be trapped in my lonely ass house anymore. Life is becoming just a little bit easier to manage, and I do have fun when I'm out.

"You know what? I've changed my mind." I wrap Carter in a headlock. "Let's do this!" I give a broad smile.

"No shit?" He asks, smiling back.

Jerome, Carter, Drew, and I bypass the long line for the club and head straight in. We ascend up the stairs to the VIP section reserved for us. Standing at our private bar are Aspen, Hannah, and River, along with a few other teammates. I walk toward the bar to greet the girls, but Aspen must sense me approaching because she spins around to face me.

"God!" She groans, tilts her head back, and puffs out an exhale. She tips her martini glass at me. "You are such a damn creeper!"

"Oh, I'll just . . ." I throw my thumb over my shoulder and turn around like I'm going to leave.

She quickly grabs my hand, and a current of energy travels through me. Every time she touches me, my stomach flips. I've never felt that before her.

"No. No. No. No. Don't you dare," she says, turning us and pulling me toward the bar. "I'm glad you're here. By the way, good game tonight. I'm proud of you guys!"

I don't know when Aspen had time to change after the game, but she has on a tight red mini dress that hugs her round ass. Her perfect tits are not completely on display, but her dress is tight across her chest, and even with the modest neckline, I have to avert my eyes. Don't look at her tits. Don't look at her tits. Don't look at her fucking tits. I repeat the mantra in my head. She looks hot as fuck. My hands are clammy. My heart beats a little faster, and all of the blood rushes south to my cock, where it begins to strain against my pants.

A busty blonde bartender is working behind the sleek black bar. Underneath the bar, glows a cool blue light, showing off the upscale vibe. There are a few stools, but all of us stand at the bar. The bartender sports a tight, haltered, tuxedo top, cut low enough to show off her tits. She's paired it with a black miniskirt. Her name tag reads, *Gina*. Gina leans on the bar, and her boobs squeeze together. "What can I getcha, Hotshot?"

Aspen's head rears back like she's been backhanded, and she frowns. Even though I'm pretty sure it's a common nickname, I can see the annoyance on Aspen's face. Gina's friendliness is obviously saturated in motivation. I could be mistaken, but I'm almost certain I see a little jealousy in Aspen's eyes as she glares at the bartender. The left side of my mouth lifts into a knowing smirk. I place my hand on Aspen's lower back. Her lips part with a gasp.

"Macallan, neat." I say and toss a twenty into Gina's tip jar. "And here's another twenty if you call me by my name all night; it's Callan. Hotshot is off-limits." I look to the side and throw a wink at Aspen.

River leans over to whisper in Aspen's ear. Aspen shakes her head no in response, and River quirks an eyebrow. I hear Aspen murmur to River to "leave it," over the loud music as Carter finds us at the bar. He coasts his way over to River like a sly fox. "Look who it is! How are you, gorgeous?" His eyes roam over her face.

"Thirsty," she retorts.

"Well, let me buy you a drink then." He turns to the bar to get Gina's attention, but River's words stop him in his tracks.

"No, I was talking about you, not to you." She pushes at his shoulder and walks over to the round booth.

"Ooooooh," Drew goads, as we all laugh at Carter's expense.

Aspen sits beside me in the booth River snagged; everyone else in our group is seated all around us as we play speed quarters. We all take shot after shot, joking, laughing, and having a good time. The two shot glasses have caught up with me. With a quarter in my hand, I bounce it on the table and miss. I have one more chance to bounce another quarter; I shoot again and miss. I quickly take both shot glasses and down them. I've never been good at quarters, and it shows. I'm certain we played the entire game wrong, but we're all drunk by the end of the round, so either way, mission accomplished.

River grabs Hannah and Aspen's hands, dragging them down the stairs and onto the dance floor. The guys stand with me at the railing of the loft upstairs, which overlooks them. There are cages in every corner with women dancing, but are my eyes on them? No, they are on the raven-haired beauty that has seemed to gain all of my attention. We watch the girls dance, arms in the air, swaying their hips to the music.

"So, are you going to finally admit you got a thing for the boss lady?" Carter asks with his elbows resting on the banister.

I scoff. "I don't have a thing for Aspen. We're just friends."

The moment I say that, my eyes narrow on three guys making their way over to the girls. One of them begins dancing with Aspen. He runs the back of his hand from her shoulder down to her hand, intertwining them as his other hand goes to her waist. He grinds his crotch on her ass, but she immediately moves to put space between them. He leans down to whisper in her ear. My blood begins to boil, and I become dizzy. I don't want him near her. I would probably label this feeling as jealousy, but I don't want to be jealous. We're friends, and that's it, but I sure the fuck don't like his hands on her. My jaw ticks, and my teeth literally crack as I stand by idly and watch them. When she turns around and wraps her arms around his neck, I can't take it anymore. I swiftly turn and breeze my way down the stairs, cutting through the crowd, maneuvering people out of my way until I'm standing in front of them.

"Move." I say to the guy.

"No. Aspen . . . It's Aspen, right?" He asks her, and she nods. "Aspen and I are talking. You can wait." He pushes me back.

He has one hand on her waist and one on my chest, and all I see is red. "Get your fucking hand off of her," I say.

"Cal!" She scolds, then steps back from the asshole.

"Fucking make me," the douche says with his fist flexing at his side. He still has his hand on my chest. My fist flies.

"Cal! Stop!" Aspen screams as I punch him two times in the face, feeling his nose crunch. "Stop it now!" She goes to grab my arm, but I jerk back from her touch and turn to walk away. Bouncers are hot on my heels as they follow me to the door. The cell phones in my face don't escape my attention as I dash out of the club. *FUCK!* Once outside, I jog down the sidewalk, trying to put distance between myself and anyone who might want more pictures to sell to the tabloids. Aspen is running after me, her heels clacking loudly.

"Cal! Stop!"

My feet meet the pavement in fast strides. I can't talk; I'm too pissed off, and fuck, I'm drunk. And something has been stirring within me all day. I'm confused as to what. I'm trying so hard to keep everything locked up tight, but Aspen makes me feel. She's always made me feel. From the moment I heard her voice, before I even saw her beautiful face, she's been embedded so deep in me. The guilt assaults me again. My conscience tells me I shouldn't have these feelings for Aspen; it's wrong for my heart to race when she's near me. As if I have any control over how she makes me feel. It's right then that I realize why I've been feeling like I have today. It's my wife's birthday. *Fuck my life*. It's my wife's fucking birthday, and here I am out with another woman. Wanting another woman. I can't do this.

"Cal, stop fucking walking!" She yells.

I stop abruptly and turn around. "Are you telling me that as my boss or my friend?"

She rears back and looks at me incredulously. "Cal, I'm your friend. I mean . . . yes, I'm your boss, and what just happened is going to be a fun time to clean up with Teagan, but I'm asking you to please stop walking and talk to me—as your friend."

"I don't want to be your fucking friend!" All my emotions spill out of me. Her face immediately drains.

I rub my hands up and down my face trying to collect myself. Pulling her into the dark alley, I back her up against the brick wall. One hand goes to gently cradle her throat, and the other grabs her hip as I push our bodies close together—I rest my forehead on hers. I close my eyes and whisper the lie I've been telling myself, "I don't want to be your fucking friend. I don't want you." The lie tastes bitter on my tongue as it leaves my mouth.

She gasps. My mouth is so close to hers I can taste the Patrón from all the shots we had. I want to kiss her, but I know if I do, there will be no turning back for me, and I'm not ready. I'm such an asshole.

My hand slides from her neck and traces across her collarbone and down her arm, erasing that bastard's touch. Our fingers intertwine, and our foreheads break apart. I just want to be close to her. I'm tormented. I'm tired of being sad. I'm tired of being broken. I'm tired of wanting her and feeling awful about it. I'm just fucking tired. Our eyes clash. "You come into my life and turn it upside down. I thought I could do this."

"You promised." She says softly, tears marring her emerald eyes. "You said you wouldn't do this to me. You know my history—and you say you don't want me? Fine! I told you not to catch feelings. But if that's the case, Cal, if you really don't want me, then what was that bullshit back there with the guy I was dancing with? Huh?"

"Well, what was that shit with the bartender? Huh? What was that?" I point in the direction of the club. "You're being a fucking hypocrite, Aspen."

"Me?" She pats her chest, then digs into mine with every poke of her pointy red-polished nail. "You're the one who takes all my secrets, all my confessions, and hoards them, but you give me nothing in return! You're locked up like Fort Knox. When I ask about your life, you give me nothing. Nothing! You redirect or change the subject. I asked you what it was like where you grew up, and your answer was, 'It was cold.' Like, what kind of fucking answer is that? What does that even mean? So yeah, I might be a hypocrite, but so are you . . . and what's more is you're a fucking coward too." She swipes a finger under her eye to wipe away a stray tear, shakes our hands apart, then she pushes me off her.

"It was cold because I was fucking homeless, Aspen! Okay?" I yell. I rub my palms over my face, gathering myself. "Nights wherever I could lay my head on a bench were fucking cold. Trying to make sure I was safe and in a well-lit place where some creep wouldn't try to violate me in my sleep was terrifying. I was a homeless child with a cracked-out mother. Is that what you want to hear? Because it sure the fuck isn't what I want to discuss. It's not something I'm proud of. I don't go around sharing that tidbit of information in casual conversation."

With her fingertips spread over her lips, she gasps, her eyes wide with the realization I presented her. "Cal, I'm sor—"

"I just need to go home. We can talk this out when we are both sober. I'm getting a ride." I say softly as I cut her off. I don't want her pity. I pull up the app on my phone and order a ride for us.

"Well, that's not surprising, Callan Miles. A man's back is something I'm used to," she cries, brushing away her tears. "Go on! Leave! It should be easy for you. It's been easy for everyone else," she yells.

I exhale a long breath. "I've ordered *us* a ride. You seriously think I would leave you here by yourself? We both have far too much alcohol in our systems. We can have a conversation tomorrow when we're both sober."

The hurt expression on her face causes a discomfort in my chest. Knowing that I did this to her, that I caused her pain by telling her I didn't want her or her friendship, I can't bear it. I try to pull her into a hug, but she fights me off. So, I try again. "I'm sorry. I'm so sorry. I didn't mean it. I don't want to hurt you." Finally, she relents and curls into me; her tears soak my shirt.

We wait in the alley until our ride pulls up. I usher her into the car. The ride is eerily silent the whole way home. She stares out the window and wipes the errant tears from her face as she silently cries. I scoot over and pull her against me, holding her the rest of the way home. When we make it home, I walk her to her door and give her another hug. I place a kiss on her forehead and mumble, "I'm so sorry, Firecracker. I truly didn't mean what I said. Let's talk tomorrow. Okay?"

She nods, and without a word, she steps into her house. I turn around and walk back to my lonely house. Once I make it up the stairs and plop into my bed, regret slams into me. Fuck! Fuck! Fuck! Fuck! My fist comes down on my pillow over and over. Something in me has to change. I can't keep doing this to myself or to her.

Chapter Fifteen

Aspen

I feel a tongue lapping at my face and crack an eye open. Groaning, I roll my face into the pillow trying to stop the assault. Puck sniffs around my neck, tickling me, and I realize I'm never going back to sleep. Reluctantly, I roll over and check the time—it's ten in the morning. I drag myself out of bed and trudge downstairs to feed Puck. My phone pings. When I check the screen, I see a text from Evie telling me the boys are playing and not to rush—to pick up Tucker whenever I'm ready.

I fire off a text thanking her, then spend the morning lounging around and trying like hell to get rid of this god-awful hangover. I'm still camped out on the couch watching a trash reality show when River finally emerges from her room.

"Rough night, huh?"

"Understatement of the century. Remind me never to drink like that again," I state, shifting my focus from her back to the TV.

"Want to talk about it?" She settles in at the end of the couch, then grabs a throw blanket from the back, resting it over her lap as she tucks her feet underneath her.

I shift my focus back to her. "Not particularly, no." Then I amend with a puff of air, "Cal and I got into a huge fight."

She hums but waits for me. I don't want to go into the confusing details. "Ugh. I don't know what is going on with us, to be honest." I'm not in the headspace to deep dive into my complicated relationship with Cal, so I change the subject. "I'm sorry I left you like that. It was inexcusable."

She waves a hand in the air like it's no big deal. "I made it home okay. Plus, I had Hannah and the guys with me. When I saw you run after

Cal, I knew you wouldn't be coming back. But hey, thanks for leaving me with Carter." She laughs, but I still feel like a shit friend.

By three o'clock we both finally feel alive enough to make it to Evie and Ivan's house to pick up Tucker. Evie opens the door to greet us. Her beautiful brown skin simply glows, and her baby bump is a bit bigger than when I met her. Curly chestnut hair is pulled into a mess on top of her head, and she's wearing red Adidas joggers. Evelyn Lukov is stunning. Even if this woman showed up to a gala in a trash bag, she would still hold the attention of every person in the room. Brown, calculated eyes stare back at me as we sit across from each other on her couch.

"The boys are playing in the game room. I put on a pot of coffee; it looks like you could really use it. What did you get into last night?" She asks me, but River cuts in with her big fat mouth.

"Let's see, after the hockey game, we went to The Sapphire Lounge, where she got possessive over Cal because the bartender called him Hotshot. Then he got possessive over her because she was dancing with another guy. He went batshit crazy on the guy, and I'm pretty sure he broke the dude's nose. Then she and Cal had their first fight. Well, first fight as 'friends.'" She uses quotations. "That pretty well sums it up, right?" She giggles at my expense.

"Oh, my . . . want to talk about it?" Evie asks me with both brows raised.

Taking my hair down, I retie it back into a tighter ponytail. I curl my feet underneath me on the couch, and get comfortable, knowing this is going to be a long conversation. I'm recounting in detail what happened when Ivan walks through the living room. He makes everyone a cup of coffee, then hands one to each of us.

"The guy is in love with you. He may not know it yet, but that doesn't make it false." Evie tells me while Ivan sits down quietly, keeping his thoughts to himself.

I shake my head in denial. "He's not."

"Either you're blind or dense . . ." River trails off seeing my annoyance. "I'm just saying." She holds her hands up defensively.

Evie stands, moving to sit beside me, and places her tiny hand on my knee. "Did you know that Ivan and I hated each other for the longest time?" A laugh lurches from her chest as I look at her incredulously. These two are the epitome of a perfect couple. There's no way they ever hated each other. "It's true. He was my brother's best friend in high school. I thought he was a pompous shithead, and he thought I was . . ."

Ivan cuts her off. "Don't go assuming you know what I thought, Sparrow . . . I always thought you were perfect."

My brows draw in confusion. "Sparrow?"

Evie rolls her eyes. "He used to say I was loud and annoying; he said that I squawked like a bird. He's been calling me Sparrow since my junior year in high school."

Ivan shakes his head. "That's not why. It's because a sparrow is a type of spiritual symbolism, and Baby, being 'round you makes me feel closer to heaven." He chuckles.

She barks a laugh. "Damn right. Do you know how many times you came close to heaven in high school? Every time you pulled a prank on me, you were on the verge of death." She raises one eyebrow at him, and we all bust up laughing. "This one time, I had just showered and washed my hair. I have type three-b hair; let's just say it can get nappy. Well, when I tried to use a wide-tooth comb, it wouldn't easily move through my hair like normal. I couldn't figure out why. I finally went to the shower, grabbed the co-wash bottle, and smelled the contents. This asshole had replaced my co-wash with some white girl shit that doesn't mesh well with my hair type. I think it was Suave or something cheap like that. I was already late for school, so I had to go to school with an afro. I rocked that shit, though. But I was so mad; I could've choked him out." She laughs.

"Eventually, you did . . ." Then I catch him mouthing to her: *with your thighs.* The way they are with each other, seeing a true connection like theirs, makes me want the same thing for myself more so than I ever have.

Evie giggles and rolls her eyes, then directs her attention back to us before clearing her throat, "Anyways," she exaggerates the word. "We drove each other up the wall. We were always bickering, and pulling pretty shitty pranks on each other . . ."

Ivan interupts. "Yeah, like that time you retaliated for the shampoo prank. It was about a week later, and I should have known to sleep with one eye open. This woman . . ." He points a finger at Evie. "Took a set of her dad's clippers right up the middle of my head while I was sleeping. She gave me a reverse mohawk."

I imagine Ivan with a two-inch-wide bald strip down the center of his white head and bark out a laugh.

Evie stands up, walks to Ivan, and sits on his lap, running her fingers through his long, wavy hair. "He had to completely shave those beautiful brown locks right off. Went to school with a bald head that Monday. He was so traumatized, that to this day he still hates getting his hair cut." She giggles. "Somewhere along the way our feelings morphed from hate into love. It took five years of rivalry for us to admit we'd always had a thing for each other. I guess his pranks were his way of flirting. We were in college by the time we called a truce. Now, I'm not comparing you and Cal to us; your situation is completely different. I will say there was a lot of tension. You two really went at each other when you first met; so much so, I'm not sure which surprises me most: that you're both still alive or that you haven't jumped in the sack with each other." They all laugh in unison.

Ivan points at me. "For the first time since I've known him, he's happy, and he gets out of the house. Granted, it's only for hockey or for you and Tucker, but I see a significant difference in him. Six months ago, you would've never caught him in a club. Aspen, you and Tucker have changed him."

"I think Tucker has more to do with it than me," I counter.

Evie shakes her head. "Tucker may have been a conductor, but you were the catalyst."

I thought I was losing him, but I don't want to voice that to my friends. "He acted more like a jealous boyfriend than my friend last night, and I don't know what to make of that."

River rolls her eyes and makes a pfft sound at me. "Oh puhleez. What was that little performance at the bar? You don't own the nickname Hotshot, you know? Like you weren't acting like a jealous girlfriend."

I let her words wash over me. I *was* jealous over that blonde bartender. She's insanely gorgeous, and it hit me wrong when she called him by the nickname I gave him. A possessive feeling I don't understand consumes me at the thought. Ugh. I pinch the bridge of my nose.

"Just go talk to him. Maybe you will understand each other better." Ivan pipes in.

Evie pulls me into a hug that feels so motherly. "It will all work out how it's supposed to."

After we arrive home, have dinner, and watch recaps of last night's hockey game on T.T.S.N., I help Tucker into bed. I call Teagan to fill her in on last night's debacle—in case she needs to do damage control. Knowing it's probably time to clear the air, I make the decision to walk over to Cal's house so we can talk. I haven't heard from him at all today, but if he is feeling like I've been feeling, it's unsurprising.

"Hey." I knock on River's door and crack it. "I'm going to Cal's. Are you okay to watch Tucker?"

"Go get your man." She giggles, and I roll my eyes at her.

"You know that isn't what this is." I shoot her a pointed look. Though I want it to be, but the thought of putting my trust in another man and allowing him the chance to walk away from me—from Tucker—is terrifying.

Once I cross the street and make my way to Cal's house, I knock on the door, but there's no answer. The lights are on, and his car is in the driveway. I ring the doorbell and wait for a few minutes before knocking again. Still nothing. I jiggle the door handle, and it's unlocked, so I peek in.

"Cal?" I call out. No answer.

Looking around the house, I make my way inside and call again, "Cal?" Still no answer.

I pluck my phone out of my back pocket to call him but catch movement in the backyard as he plops down in a lounger by the pool. I grab a blanket from the blanket rack beside his couch, open the French door, then close it behind me with a soft click.

Cal

"What are you doing out here? It's freezing."

I startle in surprise at the sound of Aspen's voice. I didn't hear anyone walk up. I crane my neck to find her walking towards me with one of my blankets wrapped around her shoulders.

"It's not freezing; it's fifty degrees out here. Actually, it's really warm for an October night."

She invades my space, drops her ass down next to me in my oversized lounger, and stares up at the sky. "Look, I'm from Oklahoma, where the temperature is set on hell from May to November. Seventy degrees is freezing to me." Aspen wraps herself tighter in the blanket as we sit in silence for a few long minutes. She looks into the night sky. "Do you believe in extraterrestrials?" She finally asks, breaking the silence.

The question is so out there, no pun intended, that it forces a laugh out of me. "That's a random question. Are you trying to say I must be an alien because I like sitting outside when it's fifty degrees?"

She chuckles. "Maybe." She sighs. "No. I'm genuinely curious."

I think about the question. "Which kind of extraterrestrials are we talking about? The kind from *ET, Men in Black, Alien,* or *X-Files*?" I ask with my head tilted back, staring out into the dark sky. From my periphery,

I can see the pool lights reflect a turquoise glow on her skin. I turn my head in her direction, awaiting her answer.

"I guess more like *X-Files* or, oh, maybe even *Roswell*." A smile lights up her face. The sight of her causes my stomach to dip in a weird way, and tingles shoot through my body.

I turn back, staring into the endless night. "I mean, part of me is a realist. I don't know if I believe there are aliens walking around on earth in skin suits. But then again, I think about all the galaxies in space, and it's kind of hard to believe we are the only living beings in the entire universe."

"Same." Aspen shifts her body to face me, lying on her side. I turn my body to mirror her. Her emerald eyes dance across my face. My eyes fall to her lips as they move; I want to know what they would taste like.

"Sometimes I wonder what the purpose of all of this is, you know? Like, why are we here? Why do bad things happen to us? But then I look at my son, and realize I don't need all the answers; I'm just glad to be here and to simply have him. Perhaps my purpose here is to be his mom, or maybe it's just to be, who knows? Or, maybe, just maybe, the reason for everything crappy that happens in our lives is a juxtaposition—it's there so we can find joy. It's like yin and yang. How would you know peace if there was no chaos?"

This woman amazes me every time she opens her mouth. She can be so playful one minute, then philosophical and deep the next. Every moment spent together, I find myself falling a little deeper.

"Perhaps," I say, truly meaning it. "Who knows? And whatever the universe has in store for us, I have to believe there's a reason for it; otherwise, what's the point, right?"

The conversation has me reflecting on my own life and the things that have happened to me. What was the purpose of it all? Everything is too painful to even think about, and it makes me wonder why life is so cruel. Like, why hand me something just to snatch it away? Aspen's voice pulls me from my thoughts before they spiral and put me in a somber mood.

She sits up and pulls the blanket from around her shoulders, then covers us both up with it. Placing both hands under her cheek, she settles back in, lying sideways to face me again. "I don't know what happened between us last night, but Cal, you're quickly becoming one of my closest friends. I'm sorry I acted like a jealous girlfriend. I don't want to lose your friendship because I was being an idiot."

I tuck a piece of loose hair behind her ear. "Me too. I don't know what got into me. Well, I do know . . . it was the alcohol, but that's no excuse. I made an ass out of myself. I don't want to lose you either."

I was a complete jerk, I know. All these feelings are so new to me; I don't know how to act or what to say. She makes me feel, and it's fucking terrifying, but the thought of Aspen and Tuck not being in my life is unfathomable. "I want you to know I'm not going anywhere. I know those are just words to you right now, but it's something I will prove to you and to Tuck."

I awake with Aspen wrapped tight in my arms; the crisp autumn morning air kisses our skin. The emotional weekend must have drained our bodies because we crashed on the lounger together. I haven't slept that well in what seems like forever. My arm is numb as hell; the lounger is cutting into my hip, and even though there's a chill in the air, the sun beats down on one of my legs sticking out from the blanket. But that's not what wakes me. No, it's the shadow looming over my face. I crack open an eye to find River standing directly above us, her heart-shaped face peering down into mine, and her long blonde hair tickling my nose. Laughter spills from her lips as she straightens up and allows sunlight to hit me right in the face. The bright, beaming rays of light feel like a fire has been set to my retinas, and it causes me to squint. I quickly jerk my hand up to shield my eyes.

With one quirked eyebrow, River greets me, "Good morning, Frat Boy. Don't you have a practice to get to? It's already seven thirty in the morning, and the boss lady is going to be late for work."

I reach over and cover my watch with my hand to check the time as Aspen stirs. "Time to get up, Firecracker," I whisper in her ear as I gently run the back of my hand down her arm.

"Mmm. No! You're so comfy and warm," she muffles, burrowing deeper into my chest, drawing a chuckle out of me.

"Come on, we have work," I try again, nudging her.

Aspen springs up, almost knocking me in the face. She looks around for a few seconds. "Oh my god! Tucker!" She panics, but then she spots River and plops her head back down on my arm, sending thousands of needles prickling down it. She groans and covers her eyes with the crook of her elbow.

River gives Aspen's foot a hard shake. "Tucker is dressed and fed. I'll run him to school, but you need to get up, Sweet Cheeks. The boss is going to be mad if we're late."

Aspen sits up and swings her legs over the side of the oversized lounger. "I am the boss, but fine!" She huffs and stands, holding out a hand to help me up. I grab her hand and playfully pull her back down, causing a giggle to burst out of her. She makes another attempt, successfully making it back to her feet.

"Can you give us a sec?" She asks River.

River turns around and moseys her way toward the side of the house, throwing up a peace sign. "Deuces," she calls out, "Oh, coffee is made, grumpy ass. I'll see you at work."

Aspen tries to help me up again. "Not much of a morning person, I see," I say to her.

Without a word, she gives an exaggerated shrug of one shoulder, then trails after me into the house.

Once we're inside, I wrap her up in a tight hug, resting my cheek on the top of her head; the scent of her floral perfume fills my senses. She smells incredible. I press my lips to her hair. I want to go back and tell her that she's been taking over my thoughts. I want to tell her that I want to be with her. But I can't, so instead I settle on, "Thank you for last night."

She squeezes me. And God, does her body feel right against mine.

"That's what friends are for." She releases me. "You know . . . I was thinking," she adds, opening the front door and looking back at me.

I cast her a smirk.

She looks at me with so much vulnerability. "I never in a million years thought I would say this, but I think we're best friends now."

I place my hands in my pockets. "Yeah, we're the best of friends." My voice is thick with emotion. I've never felt this way about anyone. How can I feel so deeply about someone other than my wife? Shame washes over me, but I smile at her to mask the emotion.

"Thank you for last night. See you at work, *bestie*." She responds, walking out, letting the door close softly behind her.

I groan and rub my hands down my face. I'm truly and utterly fucked.

Chapter Sixteen

Aspen

Two weeks until Christmas and I have yet to do any Christmas shopping. Procrastination isn't my thing. I usually tackle my shopping in November, but between Tucker's practices and games, work, and pro games, finding time to do anything for myself is fleeting. I consider ordering presents online, but there's just something about browsing the little shops and finding personal gifts while sipping on a coffee that feeds my soul. I want to experience the spirit of Christmas in New York; not doing so seems like such a shame. There's something so nostalgic about the smell of Christmas: roasted pecan booths, cinnamon wafting through the air, and fresh-cut Christmas trees.

I think of Cal and wonder what his plans are. My thoughts seem to constantly revolve around him lately. I wonder who he will spend Christmas with or if he will be alone. We all spent Thanksgiving at my house, and not once did he bring up his family. I can just envision Cal sitting alone on his comfy, cream-colored couch, with a football game playing on the television. No tree. No presents. No family. No joy. The vision of him not celebrating with anyone is sad and pulls on my heartstrings.

Hannah strolls into my office with her laptop in hand, breaking me out of the depressing thought. "Are you ready for the meeting?"

I close my laptop. "Yes. After the meeting, please clear my schedule for the rest of the day. I have some things I need to take care of." I stand from my chair and follow her to the conference room.

Teagan, Trey, Luke, and the assistant coaches are already seated at the conference table. I find an empty chair next to one of the assistant coaches, Michael Gallagher, and take a seat while Hannah sits at the other end of the table beside Teagan. Trey's laptop is connected to the big screen at the front of the room. A brooding hockey player's picture is plastered on the screen.

"Most of you may know this face." Trey begins. "But for those of you who don't, this is the goalie for Boston, Sean 'Mac' Mackenzie. I called this meeting to go over some prospects and trade deals, but also because Ivan has come to share in confidence that he will be announcing his retirement at the end of the season."

I had no idea he was considering retirement, though he is in his late thirties, so I guess that makes sense.

"I'm not a fan," Luke says, resting his elbows on the conference table. He levels Trey with a pointed look. "I don't have time to babysit a player who flaunts around his revolving door of women and bad boy reputation. We don't need that kind of distraction in this organization."

Trey rubs his hand along his jaw. "That's why I'm coming to you all. If Teagan can work with him on the PR side of things and whip him into shape, I think he could be an asset to the team. Not to mention, Boston is looking to trade him."

"Why do they want to trade him if he is so good?" I frown in curiosity.

"For the exact reason I said. The guy is a PR nightmare and causes distractions for his team. Look, I will coach whoever you put in front of me, but I'm warning you against making this deal. Ultimately, the decision is yours and Aspen's," Luke says.

Trey levels with Luke. "I want him. He may have a reputation, but he's also one of the best goalies in the league. He will also boost ticket sales. He's good . . . really good." Trey directs his attention to me. "Aspen, what are your thoughts? If Teagan can work with him, would you be willing to give him a shot?"

I mull it over, then look to Teagan. "Is this something you can handle?"

Teagan nods her head. "Yes, I've been looking into him for the past month. He just needs some good coaching on the PR side of things."

Silently thinking, I look to Trey. "How much is his contract with Boston right now?"

"He's at 8 million annually. There are rumors of offers coming in at 9.25 million with a three-year contract."

My nails tap on the conference table. I don't know much about purchasing or trading players, so I'm pulling this out of my ass. The only reason I'm here is because I'm the one with the money, and I have to sign off on the contract. "How much of our budget would he use up if we bought out his contract?"

"Not much."

I direct my attention to Luke. "Ultimately, you are the one who has to deal with him day in and day out. Get with Trey and work out whatever you two want. You know this isn't my wheelhouse." I focus on Trey. "If this guy is as good as you say he is, and Luke agrees, offer no more than ten million annually. You can go with a three-year contract; it's up to you both to decide. Is that reasonable?"

Trey and Luke nod their heads. "That's more than reasonable. Now, moving on." Trey changes the picture on the screen to Callan in his hockey jersey. A million tiny tingles shoot up my spine and to my head. Even in this picture, with no expression marring his face, he's gorgeous: olive skin tone, one tiny frown line that rests right beside his left eyebrow. His brown hair is dark, cut the same as always: short on the sides and faded into a little length on the top—messy, how he wears it most days. My nails itch to scratch the stubbles that shadow his sharp jawline. I always thought he was beautiful, but the more I've grown to know him and his heart, the more he lights my soul on fire and the more attractive I find him.

And I swear, every time he looks at me like he does with those pretty hazel eyes, I'm left craving to suck and bite his plump, fucking kissable lips. I bet he's a fantastic kisser. I mean, with lips like his, how could he not be?

Trey pulls me from my thoughts when he says, "Callan Miles. Thirty-one years old. Best center in the NHL right now. His contract is up at the end of this season, and his agent says—"

I cut Trey off. "No."

Everyone whips their head around to look at me. I fumble to recover. I know I'm acting on my own selfish agenda, but I don't want him to go anywhere. "Like you said, he's the best in the league." I shrug. "Do what you need to do to renew his contract. Next."

Trey nods as I take a sip of the water in front of me. "The thing is: his contract right now is at 42 million. The way his agent is talking, we would have to offer him at least a 49-million-dollar extension for three years, and there's a possibility we would have to offer him even more just to compete with the offers coming in from other teams in the league. Whatever we do, we can't go over our salary cap. He could choose to retire or leave the team on his own accord once his contract is up."

I sputter my drink and begin to cough.

After I recover, I say, "Do it. Make the offer; just don't go over the salary cap." I don't care how much it costs me to keep Callan on my team.

I hope he wants to stay. What if he decides he doesn't want to be here anymore? Oh God, how will Tucker deal with his leaving if he decides to go? His heart will be broken. Fuck, my heart will be broken.

Luke nods in agreement with me. Luke's voice saves me from freefalling further into a pit of spiraling thoughts. "I agree. Don't let Miles go. He's worth every penny. I know he's close to reaching retirement, but I say give him three more years at fifty-two million. That puts him retiring with us around the age of thirty-five."

"If he wants more than that, I'll sign off on it, and we can renegotiate other contracts to stay below the salary cap," I add.

The last thing I need is to be assessed extra taxes or to face any fines from the NHL.

With that settled, other faces appear on the screen as we discuss who we are sending back down to the farm team and which college players we are looking at drafting. We wrap up the meeting, and as we filter out of the conference room, Hannah catches up with me. "Nice recovery there, boss lady."

I chuckle.

"You know you need to talk to HR soon."

"Look, nothing is going on with us, but if that changes, HR will be the first to know. I'm not above my own rules. I'll be the first to sign the contract, but as it stands right now, we're just friends."

We have a policy in place here for fraternization. Everyone has to sign contracts with HR if they enter into a workplace relationship. Mine is just a little more extensive with me being in a position of power. There are clauses about abuse of power and so on. Teagan presented the stack to me after the incident with the paparazzi. She didn't believe with one hundred percent certainty that nothing was going on between Cal and me. The papers are still sitting on my desk four months later.

"Mmhmm. I saw the way you got lost in that picture of him, but whatever you need to tell yourself to make you feel better. Look, everyone knows how close you two are, and not a single person in this organization would think anything of it if you two were officially together," she says, as she saunters away to her office.

I collect my belongings from my desk, then make the jaunt through the snow-covered parking lot to my SUV. I'm just ready to get away from work and lose myself to shopping in peace. I pull my cell from my purse and text Cal.

Me: What are your plans for Christmas?

Without waiting for a response, I toss the device back into my purse. Thirty minutes later, I'm pulling into a parking spot near the shops in the city. My phone chimes, and I retrieve it out of my purse to find a message from Cal.

Cal: I don't have plans.

Me: Want to spend Christmas with us?

Cal: I can't think of anything better.

Christmas is truly magical in New York: the hustle and bustle of people shopping, the decorations, the smells, the Christmas music pouring over the streets. Sleigh bells ring on a horse-drawn carriage, carrying a couple wrapped in each other's arms. The woman giggles as the man buries his nose in her hair. I feel like an intruder; I can't help but watch their sweet moment. A longing aches within me to have someone look at me the way he's looking at her. Once they pass, the spell is broken. A woman stands on the street corner swinging a bell, so I grab a bill and drop it into her tin as I pass by.

"Merry Christmas," the lady calls out.

I toss her a smile. "Merry Christmas."

I've been mulling things over lately, deciding that now is as good of a time as any; I pull my phone from my purse to call my mom.

"Aspen, I'm so glad you called. Marcy and I both received the plane tickets yesterday. We can't wait to see y'all."

"That's why I was calling, actually. I wanted to make sure everything was set."

My mom and I have been talking since the whole paparazzi incident; it gave me a different perspective. I can relate to her. I would move Heaven and Earth to protect my child. I still don't agree with their methods, but no one can go back and change the past, so I chose to forgive her and move on.

"I'm already packing. One whole week with my babies. I can't wait," she laughs.

"I'm excited too. Listen . . . I now have several investment properties; why don't we look at them while you're here? I would love for you to be closer."

Mom stays silent for what feels like a few minutes, and I look at my phone to make sure it's still connected. "Mom?" My brows furrow.

"Yes. I'm still here. That was just an unexpected question. Those are yours now, Honey. Why don't you move into one of them yourself, or you could sell them off?"

"I don't know. It doesn't feel right to sell them, but I don't want to live there either. I just want you close by, and I know Tucker misses his Mamaw. Our lease is up at the end of April, so I will have to make a move soon. I still haven't been able to bring myself to look at them yet, but once you get here, we could look at them all and figure it out together."

"Sounds great, Baby. Whatever you need. I have nothing tying me down here."

"Perfect. I can't wait to see you, Mom. I miss you so much."

Mom's voice cracks. "Me too, sweetheart. I love you. Give River and Tucker my love."

I enter a little boutique and glance around. "I will. I love you too. See you soon."

I hang up the call and toss my phone back into my purse. Now, what do you buy for a man who has everything?

I'm pulling a ham from the oven and chatting with my mom and Marcy, River's mom, when the front door opens. I hear the clear sound of boots stomping on the mat as the door closes. My lips curl into a smile.

"Merry Christmas!" Cal calls out.

I circle the kitchen island to greet him and introduce him to my mother, but Tucker comes barreling down the stairs with Puck hot on his heels, stopping me in my tracks.

"Merry Christmas!" Tucker says, plowing into Cal.

I watch their interaction. Cal and Tucker do the whole bro hug thing, then bump fists. Cal is looking too sexy for his own good. A red Santa hat rests on his head. He has on a red henley to match, which sculpts his big biceps and clings to his washboard abs. The jeans he's wearing hug his muscular thighs and perfect ass. In his hand is a Santa bag full of gifts. I can't control my body's reaction to him. Heat pools in my abdomen. My mom is right behind me with Marcy at her side. I turn my head to look at them, and my mom raises one eyebrow while Marcy blatantly ogles Cal.

"Hot," Marcy whispers, fanning her face, and I chuckle. Yeah, he is.

Tucker follows Cal as he walks over to the Christmas tree and begins strategically placing the presents underneath, talking a mile a minute. Cal picks up Puck, cuddling him and cooing at the little feller, while talking to Tucker.

Tucker notices me standing there and draws attention to me. "Oh, look! My mom is standing under the mistletoe!" He calls out excitedly with a conspiratorial smile, forcing Cal's attention on us.

I look up and blush, then quickly jump back. The retreat causes me to bump into Mom. *Damn it, River!* I know she did this on purpose and put Tucker up to playing matchmaker.

Cal strides over and places a kiss on my cheek. "Merry Christmas," he says in a low, sexy voice, causing goosebumps to pebble on my flesh under my cream sweater.

I clear my throat and turn towards my mom and Marcy as I try to mask how he's affecting me. "Merry Christmas, Cal. This is my mom, Katherine, and River's mom, Marcy. Mom, Marcy, this is Callan Miles."

My mom gives him a hug. "Cal, it's so nice to finally meet you. Tucker and Aspen talk so much about you; I feel like I know you already."

He receives a hug and warm welcome from Marcy too, then follows me into the kitchen. "Need any help?"

"No. Y'all can go relax in the living room. I just need to throw the rolls in the oven to heat up, then we can eat. Do you want a glass of wine?"

"That would be great," he says, heading for the living room with Mom and Marcy trailing after him. Marcy has her eyes trained on his spectacular ass, and I chuckle again.

I pour a glass of wine, take it to Cal, then go back in the kitchen to finish up. I hear everyone talking in the other room. Peeking around the corner, I find River and toss a glare her way. She smirks, then joins me in the kitchen.

"Is there anything I can do?"

I slap the kitchen towel in my hand onto the counter and say, "Yep! You can stop meddling, you hussy. What is that?" I nod up towards the mistletoe. She doubles over laughing. I squint my eyes at her again. "Go set the table." I laugh. "You know what they say about payback."

With a devious chuckle, River takes plates out of the cabinet and heads to the dining room. When the rolls are ready, I plate them and take them to the table. Someone has placed me right next to Cal. Tucker and River seem to be in on a covert operative mission to set us up, and it's blatantly obvious. Mom and Marcy's snickers prove all of them are up to something. I ignore their antics and sit between Mom and Cal. Cal says the prayer before we dig in. We aren't a religious family, but we do always give thanks for our blessings during the holidays.

After dinner, Mom and I relax on the couch and catch up. River and Marcy separate gifts into piles, while the boys are left to wash the dishes. Once the dishes are washed and the food is put away, everyone takes a place in front of their pile of gifts. Tucker unwraps all his presents with excitement, showing them off with enthusiasm, while Cal and I snap pictures on our phones. When Tucker has unwrapped his last present, I focus on Cal.

He's sitting on the floor next to Tucker with the box from me in his lap. Unwrapping the red foil, he curls over in laughter. In the box is a picture of us from the thrift store, wrapped in the Christmas scarf he wore that day. I thought the scarf would be a funny little gag gift, so I revisited the store last week and was surprised to find it still on the hook.

Everyone has finished opening presents when Mom reminds me that I still need to open mine.

I grab the one from Tucker first: a homemade clay ornament that he made in class before school released for break. I give him a hug and kiss him on his cheek. "Thank you, this means so much to me, Tucker."

He hugs me back. "You're welcome," he says, then adds like an infomercial guru, "But wait, there's more."

I laugh. Tucker picks up a beautifully wrapped present from my stack and hands it to me. "It's actually from me and Cal. Go on, open it," he encourages, with a big smile.

I unravel the gold bow and carefully open the black wrapping paper, revealing a black, velvet jewelry box. I flip open the box—resting inside is a gold bracelet with charms: a puck, a hockey stick, one round flat charm with the words *Hockey Mom* engraved, a heart, and a charm with the number eighty-five. I rub the number with my finger.

"It's Tuck's jersey number," Cal points out.

Tucker laughs. "It's your number too, Cal."

"Thank you, both. It's beautiful." I study the bracelet again.

Cal takes the box from my hand and removes the bracelet. I watch his face as he takes my wrist in his hand, bringing it toward him. Carefully he clasps the bracelet around my wrist. His thumb caresses my pulse point, and his gaze locks with mine as I'm sure he feels my pulse racing a million beats per minute. His eyes flick down to my lips, then back up to my eyes.

"All set," he whispers softly, licking his lips.

I'm lost in him when my mom interrupts the connection. "That's so pretty," she croons.

We finish unwrapping presents, then spend the rest of the evening playing games. It's after eleven when everyone has snuck off to bed. Cal and I relax by the fire alone, drinking wine and talking.

Cal

Aspen's long black waves tumble between her shoulder blades as she leans back on her elbows on the rug in front of the fire. The orange glow of the fire flickers across her face. One word describes her in this moment: stunning.

She sits up and takes a drink from her wine glass, then spins the glass back and forth between her thumb and forefinger by the stem. "What do you usually do for the holidays?"

I shrug. "Stay at home. Enjoy the time off."

"You mean to tell me that Mr. Overachiever actually takes a break?"

I playfully poke her in the side, pulling a giggle out of her.

Aspen sets her glass down on the hardwood floor, stands up, and casually walks over to the tree. "I bought you another present, but it's personal, so I didn't want to give it to you in front of everyone."

Curiosity gnaws at me as she retrieves a small box from behind the tree.

Aspen sits back down beside me, handing over the gift. "I hope you like it."

I take the gift from her, then carefully unwrap it. I flip open the box; inside sits a Rolex. I take the watch out and toy with the links.

"The back is engraved." She taps the face of the watch.

I flip the watch over. "Live today like there's no tomorrow," I read out loud.

I choke up, but I somehow stifle down my emotions, forcing them to stay in check. I don't have to tell Aspen anything; she just gets me. I swivel my head to look at her in awe. Her emerald eyes shine when our eyes lock. She's so fucking perfect. I lean in closer, and between my fingers, I take a stray strand of silky black hair, brushing it back behind her ear. My hand continues to trail down her arm. "Thank you." I intertwine our fingers together.

My eyes move to her full, soft lips. I slowly lift my other hand to cup her cheek and allow myself to caress it with my thumb. Her skin is so damn soft. If I take this leap, there will be no turning back, and if I don't, I'll miss this opportunity. With my mind made up, I lean in closer, our lips just a breath apart. I can already taste the sweet wine on her lips, and I haven't closed in yet. She takes unsteady breaths, closing her eyes in anticipation.

My lips barely graze hers when a clank from a glass makes me jump. I let out a soft groan and place my forehead on her shoulders. Half relieved and half annoyed by the interruption.

"Shit!" Aspen's mom whispers to herself. When I look up, she's standing at the sink with her back turned to us. "Sorry, y'all! I was just getting a drink of water. I forgot to take my pills," she says as she turns on the tap water to fill her glass.

"It's okay, Katherine. I was just about to leave."

I stand, holding out a hand to help Aspen up from the floor. She grabs ahold of it, and I pull her up into a hug. "Thank you again for inviting me tonight . . . and for the presents; they're perfect." I whisper. Her hair smells of something floral, but I can't quite place it. I take another inconspicuous inhale through my nose to breathe her in.

"You're welcome," she squeezes me a little tighter. Then peers up at me with a sweet smile. "Thank you for mine."

I release her, then collect my gifts and stroll to the door. "Merry Christmas. Goodnight, *y'all*."

Katherine throws her head back and howls in laughter, then points her finger at me. "Don't you go mockin' me, young man."

I wink at her as I walk out the door. The icy road causes me to slip and slide as I cross the street. You would think with me being a hockey player, I would be able to handle a little bit of ice, but I barely make it back home in one piece. I laugh at myself as I walk through my front door.

I carry my gifts into my room and place them on my nightstand. After I've completed my nightly routine, I tumble into bed and envision Aspen's beautiful face. The curve of her hips. The feel of her skin. Fuck me—those pouty lips. The guilt for kissing her slams into me like a ton of bricks. I don't understand this. Why can't I just move the fuck on? I feel fine when I'm with her, but the moment I leave her side, I'm right back where I started. I feel myself constantly slipping right back into a very dark place; it's a never-ending cycle. Which is why I don't want her to ever leave my side. I like the way I feel when I'm with her.

Picking up the box from my nightstand, I take the watch out, flipping it over to read the inscription again; I'm trying like hell to grab onto the joy she brings out of me. I want to live today like there's no tomorrow. I shoot her a text.

Me: Are you still up?

A few minutes later my phone rings. "Hi."

"Hey," she breathes. "Miss me already?"

I give a noncommittal laugh.

"Because I'm standing at your door. Let me in; it's freezing out here."

My eyes widen in surprise. I don't know what I was expecting from texting her, but it wasn't for her to show up at my door. I jump up from my bed and throw on a pair of gray sweatpants, then race down the stairs to open the door. Aspen stands gawking at me for a few seconds, her tongue licking those beautiful lips before she can fully mask her expression. The frosty air hits my bare chest, causing goosebumps to pebble on my flesh. I grab her hand and pull her inside. My throat moves in a hard swallow at our close proximity. God, she's everything. *Everything.* Aspen is silent for a few moments as she peers up at me. There's an ache in my chest for her.

"You left without finishing something."

Chapter Seventeen

Aspen

Cal stands at his open door with a bare chest, looking every bit the demigod, and it causes my mouth to water. I drink him in as he towers over me. His pecs and abs are cut and defined. I just want to run my hands and tongue all over every dip of his taut muscles. Is this guy even real? Sweatpants rest low on his hips, showing off that sexy V. My core heats at the sight of him, and my thighs involuntarily squeeze together. He grabs my hand and pulls me inside, shutting the door behind us.

My body trembles with nerves. I worked up the courage to come over here, so I'm not chickening out now. I peer up at him. His hazel eyes lock with mine, and a small frown of curiosity hangs on his expression.

"You left without finishing something."

My heart is galloping as I close the distance between us. With shaky fingers, I tentatively touch the bare skin of his rock-hard chest, trailing them to the back of his neck. He moves closer, his rough palm cupping my cheek. We're merely inches away. I peer up into his gorgeous eyes in anticipation. He roughly grabs my hips, slamming my back against the wall. His fingers tangle in my hair, tilting my head back, then his lips crash to mine. Grazing my bottom lip with his teeth, he sucks it into his mouth. His lips trail from my mouth across my jaw and down my neck, where he places light, open-mouthed kisses. My breathing accelerates. I become desperate for him. I pull his hair with one hand, digging my fingers into his back with the other, trying to bring him closer. I need relief. I need to feel him. His hand grabs my ass, pulling me closer, as I grind on his thigh, seeking some sort of friction. His warm breath skims up my neck, coaxing a moan from my lips. He presses his hard length into my hip. We're feral and panting. I want more. I need more. He breaks our kiss, pressing forehead against mine.

"Aspen," he whispers. My eyes pop open. His breaths are short and brisk.

He swallows hard again and licks his lips. "I . . . I can't." He exhales a sigh.

My heart completely stops and obliterates right there in his entryway. All the blood rushes to my head. I'm stunned. Tears of rejection sting behind my eyelids. He kissed me, right? I didn't imagine that, did I? Fuck. Fuck. Fuck. He was into it, right? I don't understand why the sudden shift. What I do understand is that I need to get the fuck out of here.

My hand slides from around his neck and falls to my side. He takes a step back. Maybe I came on too strong, but fuck, I thought . . . I guess it doesn't matter what I thought. He was obviously caught up in the moment. He doesn't want me.

"Okay." I turn my head; not wanting him to see the embarrassment on my face. My voice is thick when I speak. "I'll . . . umm . . . I'm just going to go." I don't give him time to speak; I turn around and dash out of his house, slamming the door behind me.

His door quickly opens. "Aspen, wait!"

I don't stop. I'm too fucking embarrassed and hurt. I keep walking. The ice on the road has been long forgotten, but I'm soon reminded when my feet fly out from under me, and I land on my back. *Umph.* The wind is knocked out of me for a second.

"Fuck!" Cal yells, running to me.

I'm disoriented. It takes me a minute to recover as I lay on the freezing asphalt. Groaning, I roll over. Cal is at my side trying to help me up.

"Please, Cal. I can't do this. Just . . . please." I try to shake him off.

"Let me at least help you up." He grabs my elbow, lifting me off the ground, steadying me. "I'm sorry, Aspen."

I jerk out of his hold. "Please, just go home."

I'm a mess, and I hate that he's seeing my embarrassment right now. I turn, walking toward my house, careful to avoid slipping again.

Cal stands in the street, waiting until I get to my door. I finally make it inside without any more mishaps. The second my door closes, I lean against it, and the dam breaks—I sob. Deep, guttural, body-wracking sobs from both rejection and embarrassment.

"Want to talk about it?"

Fuck! I let out a gasp and jump at the sound of my mom's voice. My hand flies to my chest. I don't know how long I was standing there crying, but it looks like she just witnessed it all. Mom sits at the kitchen island. The only light illuminating the house is the one directly above the stove. She uses her foot to pull out the stool next to hers, waving me over.

"Come sit," she orders.

I huff a sigh, unsuccessfully trying to dry my tears with the back of my hand—they just keep flowing. I take off my coat, hang it on the hook, then stroll over and plop my ass down on the stool. Mom reaches up and wipes my tears with her thumbs.

She rubs my back. "Want to tell me what just happened that brought you home in tears?"

I shake my head, then nod. I give myself a minute to cry, burying my face in my hands as I sob. "He rejected me," I cry. "I've imagined so many possibilities for Cal and me, thinking that we were becoming more and . . . I just . . ."

"Oh, honey. I don't know what's going on with Cal, but I will say, I can tell that man has been deeply hurt."

I twist my fingers together and bite my bottom lip. "What?" I ask in confusion, a frown marring my face. I wipe my eyes again. "What makes you say that?"

She sighs and runs her hand through her hair. "I guess I can see myself in him. I saw so many conflicting emotions cross his face this evening: love, joy, pain, longing, confusion. I recognize it."

I sigh, and my mom wraps her arms around me.

"He won't let me in, Mom. I don't know what happened to him because he won't freaking open up. He's so closed off about his life. When I first came here, Tucker was the only person who could draw him out of his shell. Everyone says he pretty much stayed to himself; he didn't go out or talk to anyone." I bury my head in my hands, then pull them away to look at her. "When we're together, he laughs, and seems so alive. His friends tell me that's a rarity, but I think I misread everything. Maybe he doesn't see me the way I see him."

"Oh, I don't think that's the case, sweetheart. I witnessed how he looked at you all night."

I turn my head and study her. "Yeah? And how is that? Because I just went over to his house and made a complete fool of myself."

She moves my hair from my face, "Like you're his whole world."

"That can't be the look you saw because he flat-out rejected me just now. Well, he kissed me then rejected me." I groan, embarrassment still at the surface of my emotions. "I'm falling for him. I've never felt this way about anyone."

"If you spend all of your time with him and nothing else comes of your relationship other than friendship, will you regret the time you've invested or your feelings for him?"

"No, Mom. Of course not. He's my best friend."

"I really like Cal, and I think he is good for you and Tucker. I can tell he has feelings for you. If he is who you want, then you have to let him set the pace; don't push him. Though, there may come a point where you will have to decide not to let *your* life pass you by. You can't wait forever for someone who isn't willing to push through their own barriers for you. Okay?"

"Okay." I wipe the mascara from under my eyes with my fingers. Mom kisses my temple, squeezes me tight, then releases me. I'm thinking about what she just said when she cuts off my train of thought by changing the subject.

"Just give him a little more time. Now about tomorrow. Are we still going to look at houses?"

"Yes. I'm nervous about how I'll feel when I walk through one of my father's properties for the first time. Part of me is anxious to get it out of the way, and the other part is downright dreading it."

"I think you need this closure. I've decided I'm not moving into one of his properties, though. Even with him gone, I would feel like an intruder."

"You shouldn't. But, if it's too hard for you, I'll buy you a house nearby."

"I don't want you spending your money on me. I can just sell my house and see where I'm at. I've been smart with my money; I can figure it out myself. How about I call the realtor back home tomorrow and have my house listed, and then we can call your realtor here and tour some houses on the market? I can still go with you to look at your father's properties, though."

"Sounds like a plan." I scoot the stool back and stand. "It's late, and we have to be up early." I place a kiss on Mom's cheek. "Night, Mama."

"Night, sweetheart. Don't beat yourself up."

I mosey up to my room and fall into bed. My chest aches, but I try to remember what my mom said. Did he really look at me like that, or was Mom imagining things?

Music plays softly through my speakers as we drive through the city.

Mom is in the passenger seat; River and Tucker are nestled in the back.

"When is your lease up?" My mom asks.

"The owners will be back May first, so I have to make some decisions quickly."

We snag a ground-level parking spot in the private, secure parking garage two blocks from Central Park. As we walk to the tower, Tucker cranes his head all the way up.

"Whoa," Tucker says in awe, "That building is taller than the clouds."

I look up, and my head spins; the height of the building makes me dizzy. I can only imagine what it feels like from the top floors looking down. With ninety-eight stories, the building is the second tallest building in New York City. Glass encases the entire structure.

We make our way to the residential lobby, and when we walk in the glass doors, I'm stunned by the beauty this building inhabits: black, sleek walls with gold trim, a gold and crystal waterfall chandelier hangs over a grey velvet seating area. Facing the seating area is a backlit white wall with gold geometric shapes. I turn to my right and find a white marble concierge desk inside a golden nook. I'm in awe. This building is extremely upscale. I don't know what I expected, but this wasn't it. We're greeted by the concierge, Nigel, a short older man in his late sixties with kind eyes and a welcoming smile.

I hand him my identification and explain who I am and what we are doing here. He begins talking about my father, and of course, like everyone else, he only has good things to say about him. He has a bit of a New York accent, but every now and then, a British one slips through.

Nigel informs me of an app to download on my phone for the property guide. I download the app; then he walks me through it. He shows me the amenities: a fitness lounge, basketball court, billiard room, theater room, children's play area, indoor pool, and a spa. There's also a terrace with a swimming pool, sundeck, and cabanas. I'm just a small-town girl from Oklahoma; this place is fancy as hell. He tells me where to find the property map and contact information for building maintenance and for him. We thank him for his help and saunter to the elevators, taking it up to the seventy-eighth floor.

I open the apartment door, step inside, and look around in awe and wonder at the beautiful living area. The luxurious apartment is massive and gorgeous. I have mixed emotions while standing here. According to my father's attorney, this is a place where he spent a lot of his time during the season. There are no traces of his life here—pictures or mementos. I want to gain insight as to who this man was.

White walls and white marble floors reflect the natural light, creating a bright and airy atmosphere. White furniture, various lamps, end tables, plants, and other décor are strategically placed and tied together beautifully with a massive area rug. With eight thousand square feet of space, the apartment has two levels: five bedrooms, six bathrooms, and floor-to-ceiling windows that wrap around the entire front of the penthouse, showcasing the most magnificent view overlooking the city and Central Park. A glass staircase winds up from the first level to the second. So, while this apartment is amazing and filled with beautiful furniture, it also seems lonely and empty. Why did my father need a place so big?

Tucker runs over to the window and looks down below. "Look, Mom, the cars are so tiny."

Nope. Nope. Nope. I'm good on that. "I think I'm okay right here, Buddy."

"I don't know about you, but I wouldn't mind living here," River says thoughtfully.

River looks around the expansive apartment, and I notice the expression of awe on her face as she runs her hand along the back of the couch. "Yeah? You can live here if you want." I shrug one shoulder. River needs her own space, I know she doesn't want to live with me forever. Does she need such a big apartment? No, but that girl has been my rock my entire life, and gifting this apartment to her for as long as she needs it seems like a small drop in the hat compared to what she's done for me over the past decade.

Her eyebrows hit her hairline. "Are you serious?"

"Yep. Just pay the utilities, and it's yours as long as you want it. Otherwise, it will just sit here empty."

Mom runs her hand along the marble island and cuts into our conversation. "That's a pretty sweet deal, River."

She squeals and jumps up and down. "Are you sure? Because if you're not, that's too bad. No take backs."

I laugh. "Yes. I'm sure. Merry Christmas, Sis."

"Oh my gosh. I can't believe I get to live here! When can I move in?" She claps.

I beam a smile, reveling in her happiness. "You can move in whenever you're ready." River runs over and nearly knocks me down with a hug. I rub her back as we embrace. I'll be sad to see her move out, but River needs her own place to call home. She's been dealt a shitty hand; her whole life was torn into shambles before we moved to New York.

"This will be good for you," Mom says to River as she looks around the room, then she pulls me into a hug. "I'm proud of the woman you've become," she whispers. Tears sting my eyes.

After River has inspected every inch of her new apartment, we make our way back down to the concierge. Mom takes Tucker to the lounge to wait for us while I inform Nigel that River will be moving into the apartment soon. He goes through the same routine of downloading the app and walking her through it, then puts her information into the system. She hands him her driver's license, and he scans it into his computer so other employees will know she belongs there. I love the setup and security of this place. Especially with River's past. It gives me comfort to know she can live somewhere she feels safe.

He hands her license back to her. "You will have a different code from Miss Taylor. Each person receives a unique code to enter the building for security purposes. Miss Taylor will continue to keep a code for herself, since she is the property owner. What would you like your six-digit code to be?" Nigel peers up at River through his black-rimmed glasses as he pushes them further up the bridge of his nose. "I would suggest it not be your birthday." River rattles off a code as he puts it into the system.

Once she is completely set up in the system, Nigel extends a hand to River. "It will be lovely to have you here, my dear."

We thank him, collect Mom and Tucker, and make our way to my SUV. There are a few more properties we need to look at, but I really don't want to view the next few properties. Especially with one of them being about an hour away. Last night took a toll on me. I'm exhausted and emotionally tapped out. All I want to do is go home and relax. I expel a heavy sigh and begin to put the address into my GPS.

My mom must notice my reluctance because she takes my hand in hers and gives it a gentle pat. "Let's not do this today, Honey. It's my last day here; we can figure out a living situation and visit the rest of the properties in a few weeks when I come back. I just want to spend the day with my babies."

I couldn't be more relieved. I'm sure this is hard on my mom too. From our conversations, I've gathered that my dad was the love of her life. She's never married, and I never saw her date while I was growing up. It's almost like she put her life on hold for something that was never going to happen. I realize that last night she must have been speaking from experience last night.

I start the car and wind through the maze of this garage to the exit, then take a right onto the road.

Lost in thought, I reflect on all that happened last night with Cal and what Mom said. Maybe his heart's been broken, and that's why he's keeping me at arm's length. Now that I think about it, I haven't seen him with anyone. I mean, I guess it isn't out of the realm of possibility that he's hooking up with someone and I don't know about it. That thought makes me sick to my stomach.

"Oh my gosh!" River's unexpected outburst causes me to slam on my brakes. A car zooms past me blaring its horn. The driver reaches his hand out the window, flipping me off.

"Jesus, River," I scold and accelerate back to the speed limit.

"Sorry. Yikes! That was close." She gives a nervous giggle, then leans between the seats. "I was just excited. I found this little tavern online. It's on the outskirts of Chicago. The place looks so cool, and wait for it . . . they are having open mic night the night we land. We should go."

I turn on my blinker to exit the highway. "Yeah. Well, I'm pretty sure they don't allow ten-year-olds in a bar." I laugh.

She sighs, "Ask Evie to watch him. When was the last time you just let your hair down and did something for yourself?"

I quickly glance at her over my shoulder. "The Sapphire Lounge. Remember what happened there?"

"Oh, I remember, but Cal won't be there." She glances towards Tucker, then whispers. "Maybe what you need is a good hookup. Get Frat Boy out of your system since he doesn't realize what's right in front of him."

Mom snorts a laugh as I think about it. Maybe I do need to put myself out there more. I mean, isn't that what I've been telling myself? I'm not a casual hookup type of girl, but I'm all for letting my hair down as River puts it. If I don't do something, I'm going to end up an old maid full of fucking cobwebs. I bet my hymen has already grown back together, if that's even possible. But then I think about Cal. He's the one I really want to be with, not anyone else. I can't even think about being with anyone else, but I could just go and have a good time.

"Let's do it!" I say.

Chapter Eighteen

Cal

It's been a couple of weeks since Christmas, and aside from the day Aspen came back from her father's apartment, she's pretty much avoided me. That night Tuck called and told me he could hear Aspen crying through her closed bedroom door, but he didn't understand what was going on. So, I went over to their house and held her through it. I know what it feels like to want answers. I also know what it feels like to want your biological parents to love you. Even though I know her dad loved her in his own way, that still doesn't negate the fact she never felt it from him, and that abandonment she feels runs deep. I wish I could fix everything for her, take away all her pain, but instead it seems I'm just adding to it.

I'll text her, and she'll answer back, but she hasn't been going out of her way to initiate a conversation or see me like she did before. I can't say it doesn't hurt. I miss her. Every moment I'm away from her, I feel myself sinking back into the shell of a man I was before. I feel terrible about how Christmas night ended. I left her confused and embarrassed. The mixed signals coming from me haven't been fair. Of course, I wanted to finish what we started. I always want to kiss her, to hold her, to make her mine. My head and heart battle with each other constantly. If I had it to do all over again . . . I would take her to my bedroom, lay her down, and show her pleasure like she's never experienced. But right now, I just want us to go back to how things were before I messed everything up.

It's the night before our away game. We arrived in Chicago earlier this afternoon. I overheard Aspen talking with Hannah and River on the plane about checking out a little tavern tonight. The guys and I had talked about going there too, but not wanting to encroach on girls' night, I had elected to stay out of the bitter winter air and relax; maybe see if the guys wanted to hit up the hotel bar instead. As soon as I set my bag down in my room, Carter called to tell me he and Aiden were going to The Red Door Tavern tonight. It didn't take much persuasion to drag me out of my room once I found out the boys decided on going. Carter has been chasing after River for months. Leave it to my best friend to crash girls' night.

My buddies and I dash into the tavern, a hole-in-the-wall bar about thirty minutes outside of Chicago. We breathe into our hands, bouncing on the balls of our feet, trying to warm up. I can deal with cold weather, but the January air in the dead of winter in the Windy City is like a knife cutting into the bone. I take my coat off and stomp my snowy boots on the black rug just inside the massive red tavern doors.

Off-key singing rings through the bar, causing me to cringe. It must be open mic night because the guy on stage is singing a terrible rendition of Toby Keith's "I Love This Bar." I turn around and pretend I'm walking out when Carter's big ass hand grabs the collar of my shirt and drags me back.

"Oh, no can do, cowboy; you're staying here." He chuckles; a laugh spills out of me.

The guy finishes his song—thank God. We round the slender pillars, made from tree trunks, and head to the bar on the right. I rest my forearms and clasp my hands together on top of the epoxy river bar. My eyes cast a glance around the tavern, noticing the cool design and chill vibe. I don't drink the night before games, so when the bartender greets me, I order a water. Trevor, Carter, and Aiden each order a draft beer. I crane my head looking for the girls, but I can't see them in the crowd.

The bartender places our drinks in front of us. Just as I place a tip in the tip jar, piano notes pour through the speaker. The sexiest voice I've ever heard hits my ears, causing the hairs on my arms to stand on end and goosebumps to cover my entire body. My head whips around to the stage behind me so fast, I think I give myself whiplash. Aspen's fingers dance across the keys of a baby grand piano. Her upper body leans towards the microphone as she sings.

Her melodic voice is smooth—hypnotizing—and projects so much emotion. I listen to the lyrics of the song. It's as if it were written specifically for us. Memories of the past few months flash through my mind like a film on a movie reel. I become intoxicated and dizzy. My stomach dips. I can't contain my smile. She looks over the crowd to the bar; her eyes collide with mine. Though her breath hitches in surprise, she doesn't miss a note, and she doesn't look away.

"What the fuck?" Aiden says with his eyes wide open. "Holy shit!"

"Hot, can sing, and she runs a multi-billion-dollar NHL team? The woman is the whole trifecta." Carter beams next to me. "If you don't go after her, mind if I do?" He pokes.

"Yes, I fucking mind."

A laugh bursts from him. He takes a pull from his beer. "I'm just messin'. My future wife is right over there." He points his beer toward River, who is standing next to Hannah at a round high-top table, listening intently to Aspen sing.

He pats my back as he leaves to talk to her.

"Good luck," I yell over my shoulder as I push my way through the throng of people and sidle up next to the stage.

The last note rings through the speakers, and she looks over the crowd as they stand, clapping in ovation. Her southern drawl comes out when she speaks, "Thanks, y'all! I'll be here all night."

I race up the stairs, and within seconds, I'm standing in front of her. Her smile lights up her entire face. I wrap her in my arms, picking her up and twirling her around. Her giggles ring out. My forehead presses against hers. "That was incredible. You never half-ass anything, do you, Firecracker? I didn't know you could sing like that," I tell her over the crowd.

I place her feet back on the ground. "I've never heard that song before."

"It belongs to an artist from Oklahoma, Holly Beth. She's an incredible singer/songwriter. I thought her song "Trevi" just kinda . . . fit."

"Fit what?"

"Fit us." She peers up at me, her expression vulnerable.

This incredible woman never ceases to amaze me. Grabbing her hand, I lead her off the stage and towards the bar.

"What are you doing here?" She asks.

Now, I could answer her question, but we all know that I avoid topics that I don't want to talk about. The last thing I want her to know is that I've been pining over her this past week. I don't want to confuse her more than she already is, especially when I'm confused over my own feelings. So, I do what I'm notorious for; I change the subject.

"What are you drinking?" I ask her as she plops down on a bar stool. I don't let go of her hand, and I can't help but notice how perfectly it fits in mine.

"Water is fine." She smiles.

I turn to get the bartenders' attention. I'm jolted when Aspen topples into me, thus causing me to bump into Carter. His draft beer spills over the edge of his glass just as he brings it to his mouth.

"Oops! Sorry." River apologizes; she looks anything but sorry. Her eyes dance with mischief as she giggles.

"No worries, I was going to wear it anyways." Carter winks at her.

River throws one arm around Aspen in a side hug. "Tough act to follow, sister. No one will want to go up there after that. You should've followed your dream."

"Yeah? Well, starving artist doesn't really align with being a single mom."

"What is she talking about?" I ask Aspen.

She waves off my question, "Pipe dreams. Nothing really." She turns her attention to River, giving her an encouraging shove. "You should go up there!"

"Nope. I'm good." River shakes her head.

Carter leans forward and addresses River from across the bar, "Why not? You can't be as bad as the guy singing before Aspen."

"Oh, she's pretty good," Aspen chimes in. "When we were in high school, this girl owned the stage."

River takes a long pull from her beer bottle, then points it at Carter. "If you think it's that easy, why don't you go do it?" She lifts a brow.

"Maybe I will, but only if you go after me." He casually shrugs.

"Be careful what you ask for, Fight Club." She chuckles. "I'm prepared to embarrass your ass."

He tosses her a grin, "Bring it, Kitten."

Carter makes his way to the stage, stopping first to talk to the big guy managing the karaoke before taking the microphone into his hands.

He taps on the mic. "This song goes out to my girl River. She's the gorgeous blonde at the bar in the tight red dress and sexy-ass strappy heels. Kitten, give everyone a wave and show them who you are." Aspen and I burst into a fit of laughter. Patron's whistle and catcall as River rolls her eyes. She puts her arm up in the air to flash Carter a middle finger. "Total knockout, right? She has claws, but don't worry, she doesn't scratch. Well, she might; who knows? I hope she does. I like 'em feisty. Anyways, someone buy her angry ass a drink."

When the opening notes sound and Cheap Trick's "I Want You To Want Me" begins playing, I lose it. I don't understand the reason behind River not liking Carter. I haven't figured out that whole scenario. He's a genuinely good guy. The crowd sings the chorus with him, and we all join in. Aspen and I are singing at the top of our lungs and laughing at River when she crosses her arms and taps her perfectly manicured fingers.

River trots to the stage as soon as Carter finishes the song and places her lips to the mic. "Hi everyone. This song goes out to the guy who was just up here. And just so everyone is aware, I'm not his girl. This song should drive the point home." She gives a nod to the DJ, who cues up the music.

The music for Meghan Trainor's "No." plays through the speakers. River swings her hips to the chorus with her vision trained on Carter, looking him directly in the eyes.

"Oh, God. I think I'm in love," Carter says in awe, holding his hand to his chest. He continues musing to himself, "Challenge accepted, Kitten."

"Yeah, I think you accepted that challenge a long time ago." I chuckle.

Aspen pulls on Carter's sleeve. "She will realize you're one of the good ones. She's a good friend to have, if you can win her over."

That makes me curious. "What happened?"

"Let's just say a bait and switch happened." She shakes her head. "The entire situation was hard on all of us."

"Hey, Carter, remember those words you threw at me right before the first team meeting with Aspen?" I say rhetorically. "Chew on those because the same applies to you."

Aspen turns back to watch River. I study her profile, then trail my eyes down the length of her body, allowing myself to drink in her gorgeous curves. Fuck, she is the total package; her curves are in all the right places. A black dress hugs her curves perfectly, and she wears a pair of sky-high black heels with red bottoms. I'm turned the fuck on by her. She still hasn't let go of my hand as we stand to watch River sing.

After about an hour, the DJ switches from karaoke to an eclectic genre of music. We watch the girls dance together for a few songs before they drag us onto the dance floor. Song after song, we dance until exhaustion meets all of us.

Aspen and I stroll to the bar behind our friends and order water. Sweat drips down our temples. She pulls her hair up to cool off, exposing her slender neck. I can't help but want to taste her.

"Are you ready to go?" Aspen calls over the music.

I nod, turning to find Aiden and Hannah at a high-top table immersed in conversation. I tap Carter on the shoulder. "Hey, we're headed out. Can you make sure the girls get back safe?"

He nods, engrossed in River sucking her fruity drink through a straw. "Yeah, man. I got them," he says, never taking his eyes off her.

We arrive at the hotel a little after eleven. The elevator is empty and dead silent. I press the button for the twentieth floor, and she presses the one for the twenty-third. I stand on the other side of the metal box studying her, reflecting on the past five months we've known each other. Why do I keep fighting this?

Her brow furrows. "Why are you staring at me like that?"

"You're so beautiful. How can I not?" She rolls her eyes.

The tension is thick as we hold each other's gazes. She looks away briefly, then her eyes connect with mine again. She is it for me. Fuck the guilt. I know it will come back, but I'll deal with that later. Fuck the torn feelings. Right now, all I want is her. The elastic band snaps. I stride across the elevator until I'm standing directly in front of her. Reaching to the right, I press the stop button to the elevator, then lift her chin and angle her head back. Her lips part on a gasp. She looks at me expectantly as my eyes dance over her face.

I dip my head down, allowing my lips to softly dust over hers. I pull back to gauge her reaction, hesitating. I've already fucked this up once. Aspen closes the distance, brushing her pillowy lips over mine again; I slowly relax, returning the kiss. She glides her hands over my shoulders, working their way up until her delicate fingers pull on my hair, causing a moan to escape from my mouth. I tease her lips, sucking first her bottom then her top. This moment feels so right.

I break the kiss long enough to pick her up; her legs lock around my waist, and her dress bunches up around her. Our kiss becomes more frantic as we pour all of the built-up feelings we've had for months into it. She grinds her core against my cock, driving me out of my damn mind. I'm hard as hell and ready to take her to my room.

"Please," she whimpers. Not breaking from our kiss, I reach over and start the elevator back up.

We make it to my floor, and I walk her all the way down the long hallway to my room with her legs still wrapped around my waist, not giving a single fuck who sees us. I fumble for my wallet in my back pocket, not letting go of her. She grabs the wallet out of my hand, fishing out the key card while I trail kisses down her neck and collarbone. She presses it to the scanner and opens the door. Once we're in the room, I kick the door closed and saunter over to my bed, laying her down gently and nestling in between her legs.

"I want to fuck you so badly, but I'm not going to tonight." I mumble as I trace open-mouthed kisses up her neck. "What I am going to do is make you feel good," I whisper in her ear.

I pull back silently, asking for permission. When she looks at me, I can see all her emotions swirling in her eyes: desire, admiration, lust, and wariness. She gives me a small nod, and relief settles over me.

"I need words, Angel." I need her to give me clear confirmation that this is what she wants.

"Yes. Please, Cal," she moans, begging.

Thank. Fucking. God.

I slowly lift her sinful-as-fuck dress over her head but stop at her wrist. With her arms still in the dress, I twist the neckline to bind her wrist together in the tight fabric.

"You're so fucking stunning," I breathe. As I take her in, I allow my eyes to roam down to the rosy buds of her nipples resting under black lace. Fuck, she is sexy as hell. I lower my head and take one of her peaks into my mouth over the lacy fabric. She moans in response, grinding her core against me. I move over to the other one, sucking it into my mouth. Fuck, her tits are perfect. Trailing my tongue down her stomach, I suck and kiss her soft skin until I reach the edge of her sexy lace panties.

"Is this okay?" I whisper as I graze the top of the black lace with my lips.

She swallows hard and nods when I place an open-mouthed kiss right above her pubic bone. I must have been a goddamned saint in my past life to be rewarded with her sexy ass body wrapped up in lace like a present.

Hovering over her and bearing all my weight on one arm so as not to crush her, I gently move her hair out of her eyes, then suck on her bottom lip. "Look at you lying here in my bed, all stretched out with your hands bound, looking like a goddamn angel and a wet dream. I'm going to fuck your pussy with my mouth, tongue, and fingers until you come so many times you're senseless, and you can't even remember your own name." Her eyes flare with heat. Oh, kink unlocked. My girl likes dirty talk; of course she does. "Keep your hands just like that."

I dust my fingertips teasingly down her ribcage and across her abdomen, trailing down slowly until I reach her dripping wet pussy. "So damn sexy. Your cunt is so fucking wet for me right now," I murmur against her lips. As I dip a finger inside of her, she lets out a low moan. "I can't wait for you to make a mess of my face." One hit and I'll be addicted. Fuck, she's so tight. I add another finger. "I bet you taste like heaven." I kiss her deeply one more time before my lips glide down her stomach to her glistening pussy.

I breathe in her scent, and fuck if my cock isn't hard and ready to blow. I peel the sexy, black lace panties from her body and let them fall to the floor. My tongue laps her twice before she begins grinding on my face and begging for a release. When she pulls my hair, I realize she's taken her hands out of her dress. I'd like to give her a spanking for her disobedience, but I let it slide this time. Instead, I place two fingers inside her pussy and curl them upwards to hit her g-spot while my tongue laps at her clit. She writhes, and her legs begin to shake. Several curses and moans escape her lips as her clit throbs against my tongue; wave after wave, her pussy clenches and squeezes my fingers.

"That's one," I breathe a chuckle. "Next time you misbehave and untie yourself, I'm going to spank that pretty ass red, then torture your body until you're sobbing and begging for a release. I'll torture you over and over again, not letting you cum until I give you permission to."

"Fuck, Callan," she moans. "If that's punishment, I'll be sure to disobey."

Traveling back up her body, I kiss her lips, allowing her to taste herself on my tongue. Her pussy grinds against me. I rock into her, my cock straining against my pants. I want her. Fuck, I need her, but I can't. I can't make love to her. I can't give myself over to her completely.

I give her a few minutes to recover before I descend on her again, not stopping until she's incoherent and spent.

As I lay in bed with Aspen's head on my chest, hundreds of thoughts run through my mind. I look down at her. She's perfect. She's everything. I've fallen for her, completely head over heels fallen for her, but there's something I need to take care of before I can tell her exactly how she makes me feel. Tormenting guilt begins to seep back in. Fuck, I can't keep doing this to myself. I need to put this shit to rest.

Chapter Nineteen

Aspen

I lay wrapped in Cal's arms with my head on his chest. My mind is left racing. Who would've thought that Callan Miles would have such a filthy mouth? Holy shit. We haven't even had sex, and he just put some of my book boyfriends to shame. I wonder what this means for us. Are we together? Are we still just friends, or friends with benefits now?

"You know, I was thinking . . ." He trails off.

A few seconds pass, and I'm met with silence. I tilt my head up to look at his gorgeous face. Oh gosh, please don't tell me you regret this—that this was a mistake.

"Yeah? Don't waste time leaving me in suspense," I whisper.

His brows furrow. "I think . . . look, I don't know where this is going, but we've obviously crossed over from the friend zone."

He's read my mind several times in the past. It's like he has a direct line to my thoughts. A rush of electricity zings through my entire body at his words. I still don't have clarity, but at least it's something.

"Oh, is that so, Captain Obvious?" I crane my head, nipping at his bottom lip.

He rolls from his back, bracing himself on one arm while he hovers over me, then he runs his nose along my cheek. Grabbing my hair at the nape, he gently tilts my head back, trailing kisses across my collarbone and up my neck, until his lips line up with my ear.

"One day, you're going to pop off to me, and I'm going to fuck that smart ass mouth of yours to shut you up," he growls.

"W—what?" I gasp.

Who the fuck is this man? Holy fuck—that mouth! Yes, please. I volunteer; sign me up for that! I mean, if he's going to threaten me with a good time, then I'll just keep popping off. I want to make him lose his mind. I want to know what it would feel like to please him: to pull sounds from him that he's never made before, to see his muscles strain, head thrown back, to watch the look of euphoria take over his expression when I make him cum.

"You're thinking about it, aren't you?" He breaks me out of my thoughts. "You're thinking about what it would be like to be on your knees pleasing me, and I'm thinking how pretty you would look with tears streaming down your cheeks as I thrust my cock in and out of these beautiful lips." He gently pecks my lips, then pulls back and chuckles. He fucking chuckles and tosses me a wink. *Ass*.

The next few days pass in a blur. With our busy schedules, I haven't had time to think about much. But as I sit at my desk, worries begin to invade my thoughts. I haven't seen Cal since we left Chicago, and now I'm contemplating what he meant when he said we've crossed over the friend zone. Are we fuck buddies now? I mean, we haven't really slept together, but that label may still apply. Does this mean we're together?

God, can he be any more confusing? What if he regrets our intimacy? What if he decides I'm not really what he wants? What if this changes our friendship completely and I lose him? I'm driving myself insane. *Okay, Aspen, be reasonable here.* Cal's been busy: practices, interviews, and endorsement contract obligations. So, his lack of presence shouldn't worry me. When I think about our combined responsibilities, I realize this is just an irrational fear, one I really need to get over if I have any real shot at making this work with him.

I'm in the middle of working through my racing thoughts with no answer in sight when a knock sounds at my office door. I look up to see Harold, our security manager, standing in the open doorway staring at me nervously. My brows furrow in curiosity. "What's going on, Harold?"

"Miss. Taylor. I hate to bother you, but there is a gentleman here demanding to speak with you. He came by on Friday, but you had already left for Chicago. Said that you knew him, but we get a lot of that here. You know, wackos trying to get in to see the players?"

My curiosity is piqued. "Did he give you a name?" I begin to straighten up the disarray that sits atop my desk. I wasn't expecting any visitors this week.

"He said his name is . . ." Harold lifts the sticky note close to his face. "Jason Bryant."

All the blood drains from my face, and tingles shoot to my head, causing my vision to go dark. My back stiffens ramrod straight. I'm stuck in a state of shock and disbelief. A million questions and thoughts run through my mind. What the fuck is Jason doing in New York? How did he know I was in New York? How does he know where I work? He can't be here! We haven't spoken since the day he signed away his rights. What if Tucker were here? I don't want to talk to *him*. My shock turns to fear. What if I don't talk to him in this safeguarded space? What if I refuse, and he corners me when I'm out somewhere with Tucker? If that happened, how would I explain who he is to Tucker? Fear has me folding like a cheap tent. "Can you seat him in the reception area and offer him a beverage, please? Oh, and stay with him until someone comes to get him."

My trembling hands pick up my cell phone. My first instinct is to call Cal, but he's in practice, and the last thing I need right now is to have my current *whatever* he is in the same room as my son's deadbeat dad. Especially with how protective he is over Tucker. I settle for tracking down River.

River is squinting at her computer screen when I storm through her office door. "Houston, we have a problem."

She moves her mouse, clicking away. "We do! For some reason, the dpi on this logo image is set to seventy-six. It needs to be set at three hundred. I've tried like hell to convert it, but without a raw file, it's still going to be pixilated. Who does our graphics anyway? I need to give them . . ." She stops her rant when she looks up to see my worried expression. "What's wrong?"

"Jason is here."

She stops what she's doing, crosses her arms against her chest, and leans back in her office chair, causing a loud squeak to fill the room. I make a mental note to buy a new office chair. A frown puckers her lips. "Here in New York?"

I shake my head vehemently. "No. Here. In the facility. More specifically, in the reception area."

"Tha fuck?" Her eyes widen; she stands and begins to march out the door.

I place my hand on her shoulder, stopping her from stomping down there to unleash hell on him. "I'm going to meet with him, but I want you to be there, please."

"Why?" She throws her arms in the air. "You don't owe him a goddamn thing! Why not just send his ass on his merry way?"

I can see this isn't going to work; she's too close to the situation. I thought she could give me moral support to make it through this, but maybe I need someone who isn't going to shank the guy. "I know, I should. But it's better to do this here than to have him catching me off guard with Tucker present. I can just have Teagan sit in with me."

"Teagan is at lunch," she counters.

I squint my eyes at her with skepticism. "Okay then, I'll call Hannah." I pull Hannah up on my contacts.

River covers my hand and sighs. "I'll be on my best behavior. You can call them in if you want, but I'm still going to be there."

"Don't assault anyone on my premises. I can't afford a scandal right now." I direct a pointed finger her way and give her my best stern mom expression.

River turns back to her desk, locking her computer. We walk to my office in sync, where I deposit her before setting out to retrieve Jason. My heart and mind are racing, and my hands are still shaking. My emotions have been all over the place today, like a proverbial roller coaster. It's only one in the afternoon, and I'm ready to call it a day. I round the corner, finding Jason in the reception area watching this past weekend's hockey game against Chicago on the big screen.

I quickly gather myself and address him. "Jason, if you will follow me, we can talk inside my office." I give Harrold a tilt of my head towards my office, signaling him to follow.

River is standing against the wall with her arms crossed against her chest and a closed-off expression. "I would say it's good to see you, Skip, but it's really not."

I shake my head at her and direct him to have a seat. Before stepping outside my office to address Harold; I say to them, "I'll be with you in just a moment. River, try to keep your hands to yourself."

I saunter into the hallway, meeting our security guard. "If you don't mind, please stay in the conference room next door in case I need you."

"Sure thing, Miss Taylor."

I waltz back in and sit down at my desk with my hands clasped tightly in my lap. The last thing I need is for him to see that he unnerves me. Jason is seated in the chair across from my desk. His head swivels around to take in my office; then his gaze bores into me.

"What can I do for you, Jason?"

Cal

This has been a shit week. My body took a hell of a beating at our game in Chicago; practices this week have been brutal, and I still have the remnants of deep bruising on my rib cage.

Coach is standing in the middle of the locker room with a clipboard in his hand. "Alright, ladies, listen up." Coach calls out. "Johnson, good job initiating those breakaways against Chicago; I want to see more of that. This week is important. We need to lock in that dub to keep our position in the rankings. Now, I don't need to tell you how tough Colorado is. . ."

I stop listening and lose focus as my mind takes over. I begin to reel at the realization I'll be back in Colorado this week. Fuck. I hate going back to that Godforsaken place.

"Let's light 'em up this week, boys!" Coach yells out, and a chorus of chanting fills the locker room.

I hit the shower, then dress as fast as possible. As I run up the stairs to leave the facility, I catch sight of one of the security guards standing watch over the entryway to the executive offices.

"What's up, Michaelson?"

Daniel Michaelson is around my age. He was on the N.Y.P.D. but was injured in the line of duty five years ago. He is one of the best security guards we have here. I'm pretty sure as soon as Harold retires at the end of this season, Daniel will be taking over his position.

He gives me a nod in greeting. "Miss Taylor has a visitor. Harold radioed for me to guard this area to make sure no one comes down to interrupt you guys during practice."

That confuses me. What the fuck is going on, and who would be visiting that we would be concerned with? "Do you know who the visitor is?"

"No. I'm sorry, I don't, Mr. Miles. Harold didn't say." He says with a hand resting on his gun.

Now, I'm freaked the hell out. I make a mad dash down the hallway to her office, where I find River standing against the wall with her arms crossed, lips pursed, and her eyes shooting daggers at the man seated in front of Aspen's desk. I casually linger in the doorway like I belong in this meeting. I don't give a fuck who this guy is; if Harold is worried enough to call Michaelson to guard the door to the ice rink, then there is no way in hell I'm leaving Aspen in this room without me.

"So, Skip. Are you going to speak, or just sit there and look like a literal idiot?" River asks as I walk through the doorway.

Who the fuck is Skip?

Chapter Twenty

Cal

Aspen's eyes flick up to mine, and she gives me a short nod to come in—like I needed her permission at this point. Skip, whoever the fuck he is, sees her attention has been divided and turns his head to peer up at me.

He has dishwater blonde hair, brown eyes, light skin, and a medium build. Objectively, he's a good-looking dude but nothing to write home about. He goes to open his mouth, but River cuts him off by holding up her hand.

"Now, Skip." River says. "Just so you know, none of us are leaving, so whatever you have to say can be said in front of all of us."

"You know damn well that's not my name. Would you please quit calling me that?"

"You skipped out on ten years of your son's life, so it's fitting. And no, I won't," she retorts.

The puzzle pieces quickly fall into place, and my blood boils. What the hell is this guy doing here? Possessiveness like I have never felt radiates through me. Immediately, I want to pummel his face into the ground, but instead I saunter over to Aspen and give her a quick peck on the lips. "Sorry, I'm late." I look into her beautiful green eyes, and I can see fear there. "Practice went over." We haven't defined what this is between us, but for some reason I don't want this guy to know that. Let him think she and I are together.

I turn to him and hold out my hand for him to shake. "Hi, Callan Miles," I say sternly.

"Jason Bryant." He takes my hand; I squeeze harder than necessary.

Like he needs an introduction. I know exactly who he is. My question is, why the fuck is he sitting in Aspen's office? He flexes his hand once I release him. I can see some of Tuck's features in him, like the smattering of freckles and his nose maybe, but that's about as far as the resemblance goes.

He scratches the back of his neck nervously. "I . . . uh . . . I'm sorry to hear about your dad."

Silence lingers in the air for a few minutes as if he doesn't know what to say.

"I . . . I know it seems out of the blue, but . . ." He stammers again, and Aspen throws him a pointed look to spit out whatever the fuck he has to say. "I made a huge mistake when I signed over my rights. I, uh . . ." He runs a hand through his hair. "I was only eighteen, you know? And you know how my parents are. I didn't really know what to do. I was about to go to college, and I thought I was doing what was best for him."

"You mean you were doing what was best for *you*," Aspen cuts in. "How is leaving a single mom, who is still in high school, to care for a baby the best thing for him?"

"I was a selfish prick, yes. But I also feel like I wasn't mature enough to make the decision to sign my rights away. I want to make things right."

My chest radiates with pain. Tuck is *mine*. I'm the one who's been doing homework with him and picking him up from school when I'm not in practice. I'm the one who taught him hockey and makes it to his games. I'm also the one who took him to enroll in school. I have dinner with him. I celebrate holidays with him. I make time for him every fucking day, whether it's in person or a phone call, to ask him how his day went. I have been the only male present in his life. Am I being selfish? Fuck yeah, I am. I don't give a flying fuck.

This guy has been absent for over ten years, and now that Aspen has come into a windfall, he wants to show his face? Fuck no! I feel blindsided. No. I'm not Tuck's dad, but I realize I've been filling that role for the past six months.

She hums and stays silent, calculating for a few minutes before she finally speaks. "I find it very convenient you didn't come to see him in the few months you lived in the same town as us. You lived one block down the fucking road, and not once did you stop by."

"I didn't know what to say to you, Aspen."

"Pfft." Aspen shakes her head. "You know what? It really doesn't matter." She says to him.

I open my mouth to speak, but she holds up a hand. I don't have a place here, but somewhere along the way they became mine to take care of. I'm calling a spade a spade. This guy doesn't want Tuck. I know Aspen can handle herself, so I shut my mouth.

"You gave up your rights; he doesn't know you. Hell, I don't know you anymore. I'm not picking up what you're putting down."

She grabs a pen. What is she doing? Taking notes? Then she pulls a checkbook from her purse. Jason's eyes follow the checkbook, and he eyes her curiously.

"How much, Jason?"

"W-What?" He asks.

She begins to write his name on a check. He peers over her desk trying to catch a glimpse of what she is writing. "You heard me, how much? Look, we all know Tucker isn't what you really came here for, so I'll ask you one last time. How. Fucking. Much?" There is venom in her tone.

Jason averts his eyes to the window behind her before bringing them back to her. Then one by one, he looks to each of us. "Can we talk alone?"

Wrong answer. I've had enough. I slam my hand on the desk, drawing his attention to me. Aspen and River both jump in surprise. "No.

You can't." My voice booms. "There is no reality in which I would ever leave my woman alone with you, so cut the shit if you're playing fucking games. If it's money you want, just say it—name your price, and I'll take care of it myself. No questions asked. If you want a relationship with Tuck, well, we can figure that out too. But I'm warning you right now, don't you fucking dare fuck with that kid if he's not the reason you're really here."

He stares at me, probably gauging just how serious I am, but he remains mute. He doesn't realize the lengths I would go to for Aspen and Tuck. I would light a fucking match and watch the world burn to the ground around us with a smile on my face if it meant protecting them.

I turn to Aspen. "Okay, get his information. Like you said, we don't know him, and there is no way in hell I'm letting anyone we don't know come around Tuck without a background check."

I roll my lips together and address Jason in the most professional and diplomatic way possible, even though that is the furthest from how I want to behave right now. "We have a lady in public relations who has contact with a private investigator. If you truly want to know Tuck, write down your information: full name, past three addresses, social security number, date of birth—you know, all the pertinent information. The report comes back pretty quickly. It may take a couple of hours, though, so you're welcome to hang out in the game room, or you can . . ."

"We're in bankruptcy." He exasperates, putting his hands in his hair.

Aspen goes to speak, but this time, I'm the one who puts up a hand to silence her. "Are you disclosing this because it's going to show up on the background check?" It's taking all my willpower to restrain myself from obliterating this asshole. I want to be wrong about him, but I know I'm not. A person doesn't just pop up out of nowhere after ten years if there isn't money involved, especially when he knew where they were all along and had ample opportunity to make amends before now. His jaw ticks. He knows he's busted.

"Three hundred thousand will pull us out of bankruptcy," the fucker says. I want to punch him in his goddamn face for trying to use Tuck. I flick my eyes over to Aspen, and she looks just as pissed off as I feel.

"Remember, no questions asked. Put your checkbook away," I say to Aspen, even though the woman has more money than me. I'm taking care of this shit, and as a parting shot to Jason, I say, "I take care of what's fucking mine. Write down your bank details, and I'll have the funds transferred."

I pull out my phone, scroll through my contacts, and stroll over to the window in the back of her office to make the call to my financial advisor. I watch Jason as he writes down his banking information.

"There will be no coming back from this, Jason. Please don't make this choice." Her voice catches as she pleads with him. "You have no idea the abandonment Tucker will feel if he finds out about this, but I do." She pats her chest. "I know what it's like. It's bad enough that you walked away the first time, but doing this—selling him out for money . . ." She points at the paper. He sets the pen down and glances at me before directing his attention back to her as she continues, "Please. Just don't. I don't care about your financial status. If you want in his life . . . just . . ." She begins to sob. "Just say so. I won't keep him from you; I promise."

I can't stand that she is feeling this rejection all over again. I can hear the little girl in her begging for her own dad, and it's breaking my fucking heart. I go to her and wrap my arms around her as her body wracks with grief. "We can help you," I tell him over the top of her head.

"I'm sorry." He says and walks out of the door.

"River, take her. I'll be back in a few minutes."

She nods, and I release Aspen and guide her towards River. I grab the slip of paper he jotted down his information on and rush out of the office, making a beeline for the parking lot. When I get outside, Jason is approaching a parked white sedan with a rental car emblem.

"Jason!" I call out.

The car beeps as he clicks the fob, opens the door, then turns to face me.

"I have to know, is this what you really want? To walk away from your son again? She just told you we would help you get out of this financial mess. We won't hold it over your head. If you want a relationship with your son, we will help you and Tuck to navigate that."

"You and I both know I didn't come here for the kid."

I throw my arms up in the air. "What about his siblings? Don't you think he has a right to know them?"

"Siblings?" He frowns. "Those are my girlfriend's kids."

"You take care of another man's children, but not your own child?" I ponder his idiocy.

"Look man, are we going to stand here and discuss trivial shit, or are you going to help me?"

"I'll give you what you want, but you will stay away from Tucker for good. Don't come back another ten years down the road and try to start a relationship with him. This was your final chance. He's mine now. You understand?"

He shrugs.

I hear boots scuffling behind me and turn my head to find Michaelson with his arms crossed and biceps straining from his navy-blue security uniform.

"Hey, Champ." He nods to me, "Aspen sent me out here to check on things."

I turn my focus back to Jason. "I asked you a question, but maybe you didn't hear me. Do. You. Fucking. Understand. Me?"

"Yeah, I understand." He ducks down into his car.

The engine revs as he starts it; then he's reversing out of the parking lot and driving off towards the exit, leaving nothing behind but his bank information and another heartbreak for Aspen.

I dial my financial advisor.

"This is Nick."

"I need to make a three hundred-thousand-dollar transfer."

"That's a lot of money, Cal. What's it for?"

I really don't want to get into the details of Aspen's life, but this is what I've hired him for—to manage my finances, so I don't have to. I tell him the entire story, praying Aspen will be okay with it.

"You do know he will come back. People like that are like leeches. Once you give them money, they will find a reason or way to come back for more. As your advisor, I'm advising you against this."

I rub my hand down my face. "Fuck my life. Look, I don't care. I want this taken care of. It's a drop in the bucket for me. Just handle it." I rattle off the routing and account number, then hang up.

These emotions are too much for me to handle right now. I send a text to Aspen letting her know everything is taken care of and head to my car.

We leave for Colorado tomorrow, and my time there isn't going to be pleasant. It's inevitable that my past and my future are about to collide.

Chapter Twenty One

Cal

No matter how hard I try to escape the guilt, it eats away at me like acid. Even though I've taken steps to move forward, I feel stuck in a never-ending loop of confusion, remorse, guilt, and self-loathing. In the moments I'm with Aspen, everything seems fine. I seem fine. But it's when I leave her that I become conflicted and confused, and the guilt begins to gnaw at me again. No matter how hard I try, I can't seem to move on completely.

I've been avoiding Aspen for a week; since Chicago. I know she can feel the distance I've put between us. She's intuitive and can tell when something is off. If Jason hadn't shown up at the facility, I would've continued to avoid her. I was on board during the moments leading up to our time in my hotel room. One hundred percent all in. But the very next morning, when I woke up in a mass of tangled sheets with a woman other than my wife lying on my chest, panic and regret set in.

Waking up with Aspen in Chicago wasn't like the night we fell asleep in my backyard. There was no intent for more when we were lying in my lounger having a conversation. Sure, even then I wanted her, but now, I need Aspen like I need my next breath. She's the last person I ever want to hurt, and I want to move forward with her. I need to move forward with her. She breathes life into me and makes me feel. She makes me live. I can see the future with her and Tuck. For that reason, I'm here now, to talk to the woman I thought I'd spend forever with.

The snow crunches under my feet as I make my way to the very last place in the world I thought I'd ever come back to. I don't know if it's the cold wind hitting my face or the impending conversation that causes moisture to pool in my eyes.

"Hi, Baby." I squat down, dusting the snow from the top of the cold granite, running my hand over her name etched into the stone. "I'm sorry it took me so long to come see you, but I've been in a really bad place since you left me." My eyes gloss over and my nose burns. I feel the first tear fall down my cold cheek. I shudder a staggering breath as I allow our memories to play in my mind for the first time in years.

I try to gather myself so I can talk to my wife, but the air won't fill my lungs, and my body trembles. The pain takes my breath away. "You were my entire world, you know? God, I miss you so much. I remember the day we met during our freshman year in college. You remember that?" I ask, even though she can't respond. "You were standing in the middle of the campus quad, trying to juggle your coffee, books, and a map. I had never seen anyone more beautiful in my life. Then you looked up at me with those big blue eyes, and I was done for. I fell in love with you right at that exact moment. I asked you if I could help you find your class, and you told me," I pause to wipe my face, trying to collect myself. "You told me the last thing you would ever do is ask a man for directions." My shoulders shake in laughter, but the laughter quickly shifts to body-wracking sobs.

My jaw ticks back and forth. "On our wedding day, you looked me in the eyes, and you made promises to me. I never . . . I never thought you would break them, but you did, Paise. You were supposed to love, honor, and cherish me until death do us part. It wasn't supposed to be when you decided. We were supposed to grow old together. In sickness and in health. I loved you when you were sick. I know your heart was hurting, but why did you do this to us? Why did you do this to me?" I try to catch a breath, but it's like hot a branding iron is being pressed to my lungs. I struggle to make it through the one-sided conversation—sobs continuing to wrack my body. "I would have given up everything for you. I would have walked away, contract be damned, if I knew." I place a hand on my chest and rub, but it doesn't alleviate the ache. I just want the pain to go away.

I sniff and wipe my tears from my face with the back of my hand. "I spent the past four and a half years wishing I could have been enough for you to have chosen me. I have to be done with feeling sad all of the damn time. I can't live like this anymore." I place my head on my hand resting on her headstone and weep. I let the years of pain pour out of me right there. I collect my tears again with my other hand and wipe them on my jeans. "I've met someone. I'm in love with her, but I need you to be okay with me moving on. I can't move on . . ." A staggering breath escapes my lips as the tears continue to pour down my face. "I can't move on with her while thinking you're looking down on me in disappointment, thinking I've replaced you. Fuck, Paise. I can't keep hanging on to a ghost. You're not here with me. I just need a sign that it's okay to love her. Please, allow me to love her. Walking through this life by myself is so damn lonely. I need her. Please, just give me a sign—any sign—that I can start living again: no more guilt, no more regret. I need peace." Defeat engulfs me. I feel so alone and gutted—my body and mind in agony. I fall onto the cold, wet, snow-covered ground and sob. "I just need fucking peace."

I don't know how long I sit there waiting for a response that will never come; maybe it's minutes, or it could have been hours, but a hand gently falls to my shoulder. I look up to find an old man, who must be pushing late seventies, hovering over me. He's dressed in a pair of black slacks, with a grey button-up dress shirt resting under his suspenders. He's holding a bouquet in his hand. I wipe my face and try to collect myself as he gives my shoulder a tight squeeze.

Cold and wet, I rise from the ground, standing to meet his gaze. "I lost my wife twenty-three years ago to cancer," he says, releasing my shoulder. The old man takes a couple of steps to stand in front of the headstone situated next to my wife's. He squats down and places the bouquet of pink daisies on the base of the headstone. He looks up at me from where he's stationed. "It's never fair to lose someone you love. I've asked God my fair share of questions." He dusts the snow from the headstone. "But what I've learned over the years is that sometimes he doesn't answer us back the way we expect. Sometimes, the answers we seek are already right in front of us." He stands, taking a couple of steps toward me, then places his hand on my shoulder. He gives another gentle squeeze before pulling back. "We don't always understand why things happen the way they do, son. But what I've come to learn when it comes to our trauma is there's a juxtaposition—how would anyone know peace if there was no chaos?" My breath catches in my throat and my eyes well with more tears.

"You have to grab hold of what's good and concentrate on that. What's done is done. You have to keep living and know that just because our loved ones aren't physically here, it doesn't mean they aren't with us every day." He pats on my chest. "Always with us, right here. You can't live for the dead, son; you have to live for the living. Live for yourself."

I pull him into my arms. My body shakes as I cry into his shoulder, not even caring that I don't know this man. "Thank you," I say on a ragged exhale. "Thank you so much."

With a fatherly hug, he rubs my back.

I release the old man, then place a kiss to my fingers, and touch them to my wife and son's headstone—one last goodbye. "Until we meet again. Take care of my baby, Paisley. I love you both so much."

Giving the old man a handshake, I thank him again. He gives me a soft smile and pats my arm as we say goodbye. I don't know if it was Paisley or a higher power who sent him, but either way, I'm thankful because I really needed him today. As I make my way back to the airport, a sense of relief hits me. I feel lighter. For the first time in over four years, I feel free.

My phone rings as soon as I walk through my front door. It's ten o'clock at night, and I'm physically and emotionally exhausted. I ignore the call, make my way down the hall to my room, and throw my suitcase on my bed. I'm just ready to unpack and hit the sack. To my utter dismay, my phone rings again. Sighing, I take the device out of my pocket, but the biggest smile lights up my face when I see who is FaceTiming me. I click the FaceTime icon and accept the call.

"What's up, Tuck?"

"Cal! You will never guess what happened!" He says, sitting with his legs crossed in the middle of his bed, bouncing excitedly.

"What happened?" I sit down on my bed and forget about unpacking to give him my full attention.

"I scored a hat trick tonight at my game! It was so awesome." The phone scuttles as he reaches to grab something, then he comes back into view. "See! My coach signed a puck that says, 'First Hat Trick.'" He holds up the puck next to his smiling face.

"No kidding? That's awesome, Tuck! I'm going to have to take you out for ice cream to celebrate. Did you guys win?"

He frowns. "Of course we did. What kind of question is that? We won four to two."

This kid. He lights up my world. Nothing beats coming home from work and getting a call from him. "I'm so proud of you, Tuck. Is your mom around?"

He looks off to the side, frowns, then back to me. "Uh, she said she's going to bed. Anyways, I just wanted to tell you about my hat trick. Oh, and I saw your game! Ivan had a shutout against Colorado. That's amazing! I bet Rich's dad was *upset*." He laughs. "You played good too. Your slapshot was sick. Really went hard in the paint in that game."

I can't contain the laugh that bursts out of my mouth. "That I did, bud. It's hard playing against a team you used to play for. Sometimes, you just gotta show them what they're missing."

"Well, you did that. Okay, well, I have to go to bed now. I'm glad you're home. I've missed you."

"Me too, Tuck. I've missed you too."

"K. Well, 'night."

"Good night, Tuck." I hang up, tossing phone onto my pillow, and begin unpacking my suitcase.

I know Aspen well enough to know she was standing right there, and I'm sure she's figured out by now that I have been dodging her. I hate it. I hate hurting her. I know without a doubt how I feel about her, and it's time she knows it too. Once I unpack, it's a pure battle of will to stay home and not march over to her house. I'm tortured by how I've left things with her, but I'm exhausted, and it's late. I know she doesn't want to talk right now. Plus, I need to work up the courage to have the conversation we need to have.

Just as I'm about to strip down for bed, my doorbell rings repeatedly.

Chapter Twenty Two

Aspen

Aside from that god-awful day Jason came wandering into my facility and brought all of the abandonment issues to the surface, I haven't seen or heard from Cal. And as if that wasn't bad enough, he just left me there, broken into pieces in my office. He said he'd be back, but instead he texted me. I knew to trust my gut. He avoids me, then asks my son if I'm around like nothing is wrong? That's why I pretended like I was going to bed. Petty? Immature? Yeah, maybe. But now I'm thinking about him having the audacity to ask my son if I'm around when he's been the one dodging me all fucking week, and I'm riled up all over again.

I expected so much more from him than this. Beyond pissed, I put on my coat, then let River know I'm heading over to Cal's so she can keep an eye on Tucker, even though he's in bed. By the time I make it across the street, I'm livid. I ring his doorbell over and over like a complete psycho. A few seconds later his door opens.

I'm in his face. "Do I mean anything to you?" I glare at him. My heart pounds in my ears as I wait for an answer.

He doesn't say a word. He just stands there, stunned. Tears immediately well in my eyes; the pain radiating in my chest is crushing. I nod in acceptance of his silence and release a deep sigh. It hurts like hell. Stupid. Stupid. Stupid. I can't believe I came over here. What the fuck did I expect? I begin to walk away. He grabs my wrist, pulling me inside, wrapping me up into a bone-crushing hug while kicking the door closed.

"Stop it!" I yell with my face squished against his chest, trying to push him away, but he only holds me tighter. "What is it about me that makes me so damn unlovable, Cal? Please, just tell me so I can fix it," I beg in desperation.

He kisses the top of my head, squeezing me tight. Cradling my head, his fingers weaving into my hair as he takes his other hand and gently tilts my head to look at him.

"Is that what you think?" He pulls back, staring at me with glossy eyes. "You think you're unlovable?"

He dusts his soft lips across mine in a featherlike kiss. "There's nothing about you that needs fixing. It's me." He pats his chest. "I'm the one who has deep-seated issues. I'm the one who's fucked up. Not you—never you, Angel. You're fucking perfect. You're a ray of sun peeking through the clouds right after a rainstorm, promising a better day. You're a guiding light in the darkest tunnel. There's not a single thing that I don't love about you."

"So we're doing the whole 'it's not you, it's me thing'?" I swipe a tear.

"Can you come sit down so we can talk?"

I'm reluctant, but with a sigh, I hang my coat on the coat stand beside the door, then follow him through the entryway and into his massive living room. He sits down on the couch. I'm surprised when he pulls me into his lap to straddle him. One hand resting on my hip while the other holds my hand.

"I'm going to lay it all out there, so bear with me." I nod in response as tears begin to pool in his eyes. He wipes them away. "I'm so damn tired of crying, but I know it's supposed to be healing, and I want to finally heal." He gives a self-deprecating laugh before he becomes somber.

I take in his expression and find vulnerability staring straight back at me. I frown in confusion, but now I'm also worried. I keep my mouth shut and wait for him to collect his thoughts.

Cal takes a deep breath, then exhales, looking me directly in the eyes. "I've been absent in my own life for years, and I haven't wanted to connect with anyone—until you. You make me feel alive. I've spent years coasting through life without feeling anything but pain, anger, and more recently . . . guilt. For the past few months, you've made me live, but the guilt has been eating away at me for feeling the way I do about you and Tuck. My past and future were colliding, and I didn't know what to do with that. I'm sorry I've been so selfish. You've been giving me all of you, and I've been taking, and taking, and taking.

'You're like a dopamine hit; it feels so damn good to be around you, but I haven't been fair; I haven't given you anything in return. I'm sorry for that." He finishes on a whisper, then presses his lips to my temple before continuing. "I haven't been open with anyone about all the details, but I trust you. I want you to know . . . I'm about to dump a lot on you, and what I'm about to tell you isn't pretty, so I want you to be prepared, okay?" He caresses the back of my hand with his thumb, as if he is trying to comfort me. I hold his gaze and let him speak.

He releases a sigh. "My wife died, Aspen." My eyes blow wide, and a gasp of shock leaves my parted lips. "Every day that I'm with you, I feel things I've never felt before. The guilt from that eats me alive. I loved her so much; she was my wife. But with you it's . . . different. I didn't know what to do with that. When I'm around you, I forget about being sad. I get so lost in you that I forget about missing her. But when I'm away from you, the guilt for what I feel for you fucking tears me apart. Like I'm not supposed to or allowed to feel this way for you."

I sniff and wipe my face. Empathy for what he's been going through washes over me. This sweet man has been living in literal hell, and here I was pissed off because he didn't give me the attention I wanted. I cup his cheek, staring into his red-rimmed eyes. He wraps his arms around me and continues.

"I've always wanted a family," he whispers, then he clears his throat. His focus shifts to his lap like he's ashamed. "I already told you a little bit about my upbringing, but I never went into too much detail. When I was young, my mom wasn't in the best position to care for me. I spent the majority of my childhood homeless, bouncing from park benches to whatever shelter had room for us. I did that until my mom died of an overdose. I was Tuck's age."

"W—What?" My brows furrow.

"I had a rough childhood until Seattle's head hockey coach, Jeffery Miles, adopted me. I knew when I became a dad, I was going to provide an extraordinary life for my child, like Jeff did for me. I wanted to be the best dad and give my kid everything I never had. I wanted to be like my dad, Jeff."

"Do you still speak to your dad? You never mention him."

"Sometimes, but not often. I became really good at shutting people out over the past few years. Honestly, I've been scared to talk to him. I feel terrible about how I've skirted around and completely avoided him. He provided a loving and stable environment to grow up in. He's the best dad. I wanted to be the same for my child. So, when Paisley became pregnant, I was so excited—completely beside myself."

His eyes well with more tears. "Midway through Paisley's pregnancy there were complications, and our son didn't make it to full term; he was born sixteen weeks early."

I'm stunned. "Oh my gosh, Cal."

I can't even fathom what he's been going through all these years; my heart shatters for him.

He wipes my tears away, then attempts to erase his own, but they flow freely. He takes a ragged breath. "After the delivery of my son, Paisley decided she didn't want to . . . she couldn't handle it . . . she, um . . . she was diagnosed with postpartum psychosis." He struggles to get through; his jaw ticks as he tries to keep it together.

"She went back and forth from being in a catatonic state to being in a state of hysteria and mania; sometimes she was just downright delusional. She refused to name our son, refused to go to his funeral, refused to acknowledge the loss, and the weight of everything bore down on my shoulders to deal with alone. Dad tried to help as much as he could, but he lives in Seattle. Her parents are pretty much useless, so I was completely alone."

He takes another shaky breath. "I had to do everything on my own." His voice cracks.

I try to bring him comfort. I rub his back as he collects himself. I just can't imagine this nightmare. Like, how does he even function? If I lost Tucker—no. I can't even imagine the thought.

"I took care of everything. I made funeral preparations. I named him."

"What did you name him?"

He looks at me, then looks away. He takes a deep breath, and on a sob, he speaks again. "Xander. After the man who watched out for me when I lived on the streets." He begins to sob again. Deep, gut-wrenching sobs. "I haven't been able to say his name since the funeral because the loss is so painful. I didn't want to revisit it. I lost him too, you know?" His face scrunches up in pain, tears barreling down his face, as he weeps. His inhales become shorter as if he can't catch his breath. I can tell that he has been holding on to this like a ticking time bomb ready to explode, so I stay silent and let him fall apart. Holding this in as long as he has, and doing so alone, isn't healthy.

After a few minutes, he finally collects himself. "No one really thinks about the fathers when there's a miscarriage or a preterm loss. I had to deal with the loss of our baby without any real support because everyone was concentrating on Paisley, and I was okay with that at the time. I mean, my teammates were there for me, but most of them didn't know what to say or do. I watched my wife lose her mind while simultaneously trying to take care of her, the funeral arrangements, and the obligations I had with the team."

"The Colorado executives were as supportive as they could be, but I was under contract, and my time for bereavement ran out. I had just signed a three-year contract. Paisley and I were going to counseling, but it was during the busiest time in hockey season, so I could only attend a few; I was forced to be away a lot. We found a great doctor who prescribed her medication. I thought, eventually, we could make it through the loss, our broken hearts would somewhat heal, and then we could try again. After a few months of medication, she started to feel more like herself, but that's when she took a turn for the worse. She took it upon herself to stop therapy and eventually got off her medication, against her doctor's advice. I had no idea. If I had known, I would've broken that damn contract." He trails off, shaking his head.

I can feel his pain so emphatically. I wipe my tears with the back of my hand. When he begins sobbing again, I gather the sleeve of my shirt in my hand, reaching up to wipe his face. His tear-filled hazel eyes lock on mine. I can't bear it. My heart aches for him. Seeing that raw pain in his eyes undoes me, and I sob right along with him.

"I was pulled from the seventh game of the championship series. My teammate's . . ." Tears stream down his face, his body wracks with grief, struggling to let out his next words. "My teammate's wife . . . she found Paisley. She umm . . ." He gasps for a breath. I wrap my arms around him, trying to give him every bit of comfort I can. I stroke his hair while he continues. "I wasn't enough." He shakes in my arms as sobs wrack his body.

I wrap him tight in my arms until he calms down, then I hold his face in both of my hands, wiping his tears with my thumbs. "You are enough, Cal. She must have been utterly and completely broken. I can't imagine the pain either of you were going through. What she did, it wasn't your fault."

He stares at me, gauging my sincerity before he nods in acceptance. He wipes his eyes again. "I think I know that now. I went to see Paisley yesterday while I was in Colorado. I needed to sort some things out before I could move on. This sounds so stupid, but I needed permission to move on with you. I want to be with you, Aspen. I've been wanting that for a long time, but I just couldn't get out of my own way." He sniffs and wipes his face with the back of his hand again. "I think I'm ready if this is what you want. If I'm what you want."

I continue to soothe him by running my fingers through his hair while my arms encompass him. I place a gentle kiss on his lips. "I've been waiting on you, Hotshot." His body visibly relaxes. "You know, you weren't one hundred percent accurate when you said you haven't given me anything in return. You may have been holding back from telling me about your life and your past. But you've been giving Tucker and me your present. You make him happy. You make me happy. You're important to us. Maybe at one time you were coasting through life, but for the past few months, that's not what it's felt like, not to me anyway." I stroke his hair, consoling him.

Now I know why he's kept me at arm's length this whole time. Even though I'm in a somber state about the revelation of his wife and his baby, I'm glad to be the one he felt safe enough with to share his past with. He brings his hand up to my face and caresses my cheek with his thumb before he kisses me softly.

He pulls back, and I see an earnest gleam in his eyes. "Thank you for everything: for bringing me joy, for pushing me out of this godawful headspace, for forcing me to live, and for placing your trust in me, not only with your heart but also with your son's. I love him, Aspen. I love him like my own, and I would do anything in this world for him. I will *always* be here to protect him."

I look for the truth, finding it in his eyes as he regards me with so much adoration. He kisses me one more time before whispering. "You don't mean anything to me, Aspen; you mean everything. You own every piece of me. I don't want to lose you because I'm stuck in the past; I'm ready to move on. I'm ready to put all of this behind me."

I release a breath as he engulfs me in his strong arms, holding me tight. "You have such a big heart, Cal. You love hard, and there is nothing wrong with that. They will always be a part of you, and I'm not looking to replace her."

"I know, Angel. It's just been hard to comprehend that moving on doesn't mean replacing, but I get it now."

"I think I know a way we can honor her and Xander's memory if you are open to it."

With my head placed in the crook of his neck, his fingertips stroke through my hair. "I would love that actually," he finally states.

"I also think you should talk to your dad."

He plays with the ends of my hair. "Yeah. I probably should."

I don't know how long we sit wrapped in each other's arms, drawing comfort from one another as we grieve his past together. Eventually, he tips up my chin and kisses my lips. "Okay. Enough with the heavy," he says softly.

With my legs wrapped around his waist, Cal picks me up, carrying me through the living room, the entryway, and then up the stairs to his master bathroom.

"What are we doing?"

He wets a washcloth. "I'm going to wash our tears away." He begins to wipe my face. "Then I'm going to walk you back home."

Once my face is patted dry with a hand towel, he takes my chin in his hand and angles my face up towards his. He peppers light, feather-soft kisses all over my face before taking my lips in a tender kiss. Butterflies take flight in my stomach. This man is not what I ever expected. I think back to our first encounter and snort a laugh, kind of ruining the tender moment.

"What's so funny?" He muses with a smirk. "Do I amuse you?" He lifts one brow.

I shake my head, then think better of it and nod. "You keep surprising me. Gone is the brooding asshole who hit my car, and standing in front of me is this incredible man who is so tender and sweet."

Cal lays the washcloth over the laundry basket to dry. Chuckling, he strolls back to me and lifts me off the counter with such ease, then places me on my feet. "Awe, you think I'm incredible?" He smirks as he washes his face.

I roll my eyes, like he needs an ego boost. Leaning against the doorjamb with my arms folded across my chest, I watch him. "I'm sorry, did you hear me say incredible? I think you must be imagining things because I'm pretty certain I said *incorrigible*."

Cal pats his face dry with a hand towel and laughs. He sets the towel down on the counter; then suddenly, he bends down and grabs me by the waist, hoisting me over his shoulder—fireman style. He carries me into his room and plops me down in the middle of the four-poster king-sized bed that's draped with a light gray down comforter. I scamper to climb away from him, but he pulls me back to him by my ankle and descends on me with an onslaught of tickles. "What was that?" He continues to tickle my ribs. "I don't think I heard you correctly the second time."

A fit of giggles erupts out of me, and I try to fight him off, but it's no use. "Okay! Okay! You're incredible!" I wheeze between laughs. "You're Incredible! I give up! Mercy!"

He smacks my ass and drops a peck to my lips. "That's what I thought."

He moves off me and stands beside the bed, placing his phone on the charger. Still on the bed, I hop to my feet so I can tower over him. I know I'm playing with fire, but I don't care. I grab one of his pillows and toss it at him. The pillow lands a playful blow to the back of his head before falling to the floor. He turns around, tongue in cheek, as I giggle. My eyes go wide, and I squeal when he effortlessly jumps onto the bed and wraps his arm around my waist. We both tumble in a fit of laughter, but our laughter dies down as his eyes map my face. His fingers tenderly move my hair away from my eyes.

"You're so beautiful," he says, nipping my bottom lip. "And you're going to look even more beautiful when your ass is painted red with my handprint."

"Mmm. Is that so?" I sass.

"You have no idea, Angel," he breathes. "Keep testing me."

"Hmm. Do you have a kink for spanking your bosses?" I giggle.

"When we're in the bedroom, you're not my boss. I'm the boss. Do you understand?"

I don't respond until he raises an eyebrow. I nod my head, but apparently that's not good enough because he says, "Words, Aspen."

"I understand."

"Good girl." His lips skim my throat.

I think I may have a praise kink because hearing those words come from his mouth is a complete fucking turn-on.

"I'm going to tie you up." *Kiss.* "Tease." *Kiss.* "Torture." *Kiss.* "And manipulate your body until you're fucking dripping, writhing, and begging for release." His lips hover over mine. "I'll deliver pleasure so overwhelming that it's on the brink of pain. I won't be done with you until you're completely wrung out, pleading with me to stop."

I bite my lip imagining all the things he would do to me. I'm left panting, and my panties wet with desire.

He kisses my lips again, then he winks. "But, as much as I want to keep you here all night and take my time with you, I really need to walk you home." He gives my ass a gentle tap and lifts himself off me.

I'm left reeling, confused, and so fucking sexually frustrated. He's just going to work me up and send me home? What the fuck is wrong with him? He must see my frustration because as he helps me off the bed, he pulls me to him, then whispers in my ear, "It's called delayed gratification, Angel. The first time I take you to bed, it's going to be all about us. Today was hard and emotional for us both. Plus, it's after one in the morning. There's a little boy sleeping in his bed, expecting to see his mom when he wakes up."

And there it is. The reason this man completes me.

Cal walks me across the street to my house. When we reach my front door, I turn, wrap my arms around his neck, and bring his face to mine, kissing him deeply.

"Thank you for trusting me, for opening up to me, for giving me pieces of you that you've refused to give anyone else."

He kisses my forehead. "When I said that you own me, I meant every word. You own every piece of me."

I peer up at him through my lashes and whisper, "I don't want you to go. I don't want you alone tonight."

He grabs my hands from around his neck and brings them to his lips; kissing my knuckles. "I'll be okay. It's only a few hours until we both have to be at work."

I scrutinize his sincerity for a moment before nodding my head reluctantly.

He bends down, teasing my lips with his own before delivering a kiss that leaves my toes absolutely curling. "Now take your sexy ass to bed," he whispers when we break apart. Cal reaches around me, opens the door, then ushers me in. "Good night," he says before he quickly closes the door behind me.

Bossy ass.

Chapter Twenty Three

Cal

The hockey arena is a cacophony of chants and cheers, but over the noise I can still make out the clicking of sticks as the boys try to force the puck out of possession. That, along with the swishing of the skates on the ice and the clanking of the puck against the boards, are the best sounds in the world . . . well, aside from the little noises my girl made a few weeks back in Chicago. My mind is invaded by thoughts of Aspen's sweet, seductive sounds and the way she looked at me through the curtain of her long, thick lashes as I laid her on that bed in the hotel room and explored the curves of her body with my hands and mouth. *Fuck.* I need to redirect my thoughts, pronto. The last thing I need is to be standing up in a crowd of parents, cheering for Tuck's team with a raging hard-on.

I cup my hands around my mouth, "Let's go, Tuck!" I yell out, clapping as he takes possession of the puck and moves it down the left side of the ice. I take my seat next to Aspen, with her mom on her other side. Katherine listed her house with an enticing price to sell quickly. As soon as someone made an offer, she booked her flight. She flew in today and is here to surprise Tuck.

Tuck dekes, cuts, then passes to Williams, a defenseman. Williams passes the puck to Elija, the team's right winger. Elija rounds the crease but is blocked by the opposing side, who gains possession. The puck is passed back and forth until it ends up on the weak side of the opponent's defense. Zimmerman, the left winger, breaks out, then passes back to Tuck. Who knew a little league game would have me on the edge of my seat?

"I'm surprised your boy isn't a goalie," Aspen says to Ivan as he cradles his new baby girl in his arms. Aspen tosses her hand sanitizer back into her purse, then holds her arms out for Ivan to pass the baby. He carefully places Ivy into Aspen's waiting arms, and fuck me, if seeing her cradling a baby doesn't give me insight into what our future could look like. Aspen and Katherine fuss over Ivy as Aspen runs a finger along the baby's forehead, then down her cute, pert little nose. A longing creates a tightness in my chest. I want to be a family with Aspen and Tuck.

"Trust me, Ivan tried," Evie cuts in with a chuckle, pulling me from my daydream. "Elija kept skating out of the crease and into the middle of the ice to get to the puck, leaving the goal wide open. Plus, he's too aggressive to be a goalie."

My head jerks back to the ice when someone beside me gasps. "Oh, shit," Ivan curses.

My brows pull down into a tight frown of confusion. "What happened?" I ask Ivan.

He nods his head in Tuck's direction. "High-sticking. That kid jabbed Tucker in the neck," he says. *What the fuck?*

Aspen, who's still cradling Ivy in her arms, forces her attention back to the ice as Tuck grabs his neck. She passes the baby to Katherine and jumps to her feet. I do the same. She tries to shuffle around me to run down to the ice, but I intercept her, grabbing her around the waist and hauling her back to me. Aspen tries to wrestle out of my hold, but I pull her back tight against my front and speak low in her ear. "Angel, I know your momma bear instincts are kicking in right now, and you want nothing more than to run down there and check on him, but don't. He's okay; look at him." She glances down to where Tuck stands. The ref is checking him over, and Tuck nods his head.

"You've never been a ten-year-old boy. If you go down there and fuss over him, you're only going to embarrass him; his pride will be more bruised than his neck. He wants to look tough in front of his team, and he can't do that if his mommy is down there fussing over him like a little baby." Aspen turns her head to glare at me.

"Trust me." I kiss her forehead.

As Tuck shakes it off and begins skating, I guide Aspen back to her seat. The ref makes the call and sends the kid to the bin, and Tuck's team goes into a two-minute power play.

Peering around us from the other side of Evie, Carter breaks the tension. "I'm getting a drink from concession; anyone want anything?" He's asking all of us, but his eyes are trained on River.

She pulls her wallet from her purse. "Actually, a Coke would be good," River says.

She leans around us, reaching out to pass cash to Carter. He refuses her money and leaves his seat beside Evie, making his way to the concession stand.

As the game continues, I watch the puck pass back and forth behind the opponent's crease. Carter gains my attention when he comes back with two drinks and hands one to River before plopping his ass down in the seat next to her. *Oh, this should be fun.* I chuckle to myself, realizing his ploy. He obviously went to get drinks as a ruse to relocate to the seat beside River.

"I knew you would let me buy you a drink eventually." His tone is playful, and his expression mischievous.

"This was a one-off. Don't get used to it." River retorts, a waving her hand in the air. "Thanks, by the way."

The dimples that our teammates have deemed as "the panty dropper" make their appearance when he smiles, and he tosses her a wink. "You're welcome, Kitten."

River rolls her eyes and growls, "Stop calling me that."

In the years I've known Carter, he's never pursued a woman to this magnitude, though he's never had to. Women flock to him in droves. I don't know if it's the thrill of the chase or the fact that he's the most determined person I know and can't let her go. Either way, my bet is always going to be on him. Carter leans forward to focus back on the game, both elbows resting on his knees with his cup clasped in both hands.

Directing my focus back to the ice, Tuck rears back to shoot the puck. The goalie moves to the right as Tuck fakes him out and sends the puck into the left side of the goal. We all jump up at the same time, cheering loudly as the siren goes off. Tuck skates around the ice as his teammates pat him on the helmet in celebration.

The puck is back in play; Zimmerman is battling against the boards with the boy who hit Tuck. Elija skates up and checks the kid. The boy turns and bows up to him. Elija pushes him while mouthing off. They're in each other's faces. Before anyone has time to gain control of the situation, the boys are scuffling, and both fists are flying. The refs blow their whistle several times, but the boys don't stop. The linesmen break them apart and throw them both into the box for a five-minute major penalty.

Aspen leans back, glaring, and crosses her arms tight against her chest. "That's what he gets for messing with my kid."

I chuckle as River gawks at her with wide eyes.

Aspen must feel River's stare of disbelief because she turns her head in River's direction. "What?" She shrugs. "Don't look at me like that." She stretches an arm out and points toward the ice. "That boy is a bully. We've played this team once already, and he always plays dirty. What he did was dangerous, River. He deserved whatever he got. That's what enforcers do. They keep dirty players in line. He stood up for Tucker."

"He's not just a bully on the ice; he's a little prick at school too," Evie says.

River slightly rears her head back. "They're only ten!"

"Yeah, but that's hockey, River. I think that's actually the boy's favorite part of hockey. Just ask Carter." Ivan cuts in, chuckling.

Carter leans back, stretching out both legs in front of him. These seats are not the most comfortable for someone who's six foot three. He lifts one shoulder in a shrug. "It's not like I love to fight. Think of it like this: If someone went after Aspen, how would you respond? Would you let someone mess with her or put her in danger?"

"Of course not."

"Exactly. My job as an enforcer is to protect my star player from being targeted with dirty hits. That's what Elija was doing. What that kid did to Tucker was clearly intentional if what everyone's saying is true. Elija was doing his job," Carter beams at her.

"How are your teeth so perfect?" River blurts. "I mean . . . I . . . I've seen your fights. I'm just surprised you don't have any missing," she stammers.

Carter laughs and leans forward in his seat. His eyes flick back and forth between hers as he observes her. "Awe, Kitten. You actually pay attention to me?"

She lets out a snort. "Absolutely not; forget I even asked."

"To answer your question, three and a half years of braces and a life with permanent retainers, but these four . . ." He beams at her with his gleaming white teeth and taps on the four implants, ". . . are fake."

I shift my attention away from them and glance at the clock as time runs out. The game ends with a score of three to zero. We jump up, cheering for the boys as they stand in a line and slap hands with the opposing team.

As everyone collects their belongings, Katherine passes Ivy back to Ivan. "It's been a decade since I've had a baby around to cuddle."

She rubs a knuckle down Ivy's cheek, then lifts her head up to meet Ivan's eyes. "Thank you for letting me hold her. Lord only knows if this one will ever bless me with another grandbaby." She jerks her head toward Aspen.

"Mom," Aspen groans. Her cheeks flush with a pink hue as she shakes her head in embarrassment.

Katherine playfully knocks her shoulder with Aspen's. "What?" She chuckles with mischief in her eyes. "I'm just being honest. I miss having a baby to spoil."

Aspen rolls her eyes and snorts a laugh.

We walk down the stairs toward the locker room, where we're to wait outside for the kids. The double doors burst open, and a group of rambunctious preteen boys spill out. Tuck and Elija are among them, and they race to us, playfully shoving each other out of the way to gain the lead. Tuck looks up, and his face completely lights up.

"Mamaw, you're back! Are you staying this time?" He runs to her, embracing her in a big hug.

Laughter and raised voices echo around us as Tuck's teammates roughhouse and chase each other around the stands. Parents mill around talking to one another as they collect their kids.

Katherine hugs him tight. "I sure am, kiddo. You know what? I have the best idea! Maybe your mom could ride back with Cal. Think we could convince her to let us borrow her car so just the two of us can celebrate your win with some ice cream?" She winks at him.

I'm all for this plan. We had three away games last week, and I just got back last night from another one. That, combined with River moving into her own place and not being around to watch Tuck so Aspen can sneak over, has given us no alone time these past couple of weeks. Though I did sneak over late last night because I was dying to see her, I didn't stay long. Katherine is trying to use discretion around Tuck, but his eyes zero in on my fingers intertwined with his mom's, and the corners of his mouth tug into a grin. Fuck! I wasn't thinking, and clearly, she wasn't either. I don't know why she hasn't told him we're together yet.

"Is my mom your girlfriend?" He sings songs mockingly. Aspen quickly tries to pull her hand from mine, but it's already too late, and I'm not letting her go. It's apparent that he already knows or at least suspects.

I shrug. "I don't know, Tuck. I think that's up to your mom."

The ball is in her court; it's not my place to tell him we are together.

She clears her throat, and her face turns a pretty shade of pink. "Umm . . . maybe we should have this discussion at home?"

"You're holding hands, and your face is as red as a tomato." Tuck shifts his heavy equipment bag further up his shoulder. I release Aspen's hand and take it from him. "So . . . are you?" He asks again.

Aspen glances at her mom with skepticism. "Are you sure you're okay to drive in this big city without getting lost?" She asks, attempting to change the subject.

Tuck cuts in. "And I did walk in on you two kissing in the kitchen in the middle of the night."

Aspen's eyes pop wide, and her head snaps back to Tuck. "Y—you what?"

"You two were kissing by the fridge. It was gross." He dramatically shivers his body, then shoves his finger down his throat, making a gagging noise.

"You were supposed to be in bed." Aspen nibbles on her bottom lip; it's a tell that she's uncomfortable with this conversation.

Tuck lifts his left shoulder in a shrug. "Yeah? So were you." He chuckles. "I needed to use the bathroom and went to the kitchen for a drink, but after seeing you two, I wasn't sure I could keep anything down. So, I just went back to bed."

Carter's laughter rings out, amusement glittering in his eyes.

Aspen rubs the palms of her hands down her face in embarrassment. "Okay, Tucker. That's enough."

I laugh as I pull her to me. "Come here."

Aspen groans, gripping the front of my shirt in both fists; she briefly buries her face in my chest.

When she turns her head toward her mom, I release her. "Okay, so back to you taking Tucker . . . will you be okay—"

"Aspen Ryan Taylor, what do you think GPS is for?" She waves her hand around in the air. "Now you two go on. Shoo. I want to spend some quality time with my grandson."

A frown tugs at my brows as I study Katherine. I'm surprised and confused. Ryan? As in Ryan West? Aspen was named after her father? That's something I never saw coming. There is no way Katherine would have named her daughter after a man who abandoned her, or that she herself wasn't fond of. I keep that filed in the back of my mind. It's definitely a conversation worth having at another time.

Aspen hugs Katherine. "Thanks, Mom."

Her mom whispers something in her ear.

Aspen blushes again. She reaches into her purse, pulls out her keys, and places them in her mom's waiting hands.

Carter saunters over, wrapping me in a hug. The hug isn't a side hug or a handshake man hug. It's a full-on hug. "I'm so proud of you, bro," he says as he pulls back, slapping me on the shoulder.

We say our goodbyes, and I place my hand at the small of Aspen's back, guiding her to my truck. Reaching into my jeans pocket, I grab my keys, spinning them around my finger as we walk through the parking lot. The cold air hits my face as Aspen quickly wraps her coat tighter around her.

"What did your mom say that caused you to look embarrassed?" I click the fob, unlocking the truck.

"Nothing important." She reaches out and opens her door. I slam it shut. She turns to me, shocked, as I back her up against the door and cage her in, pressing my body tight against hers.

"One would think you'd know better than to open doors when I'm around. Call me old-fashioned, but that's my job, Angel."

I take her lips between mine in a sweet kiss before reaching around her and opening her door. She climbs in, and I pull the seatbelt over her, clicking it in place, and tightening the strap to make sure she's secure. Her eyes give a dramatic roll.

Gently, I take her face in my hand and turn her head toward me. "Did you just roll your eyes at me?"

Her lips slowly turn up into a mischievous grin. "And what if I did?"

"Behave." I nip her bottom lip before shutting the door.

I want to tie her down, edge her, and torment her body until she's whimpering and begging to cum. When she sasses or rolls her eyes at me, those actions make me itch to spank her ass and punish the sass right out of her until it's dripping all over my fingers . . . or my cock. I have a proclivity for kink. And the way Aspen's eyes lit up when I praised her, or the way her thighs rubbed together when I told her I wanted to spank her ass red, tells me no matter how inexperienced she may be, that she has them too.

Let's not forget about all of the smutty novels resting on Aspen's shelves . . . I mean, the girl is into some dark romance shit. I have social media too, you know—thanks to Teagan. And I now follow one person—Aspen. The shit Aspen comments on some of the posts . . . and the fact that for the past couple of weeks, I've been snagging novels from her room without her knowledge to read when I'm away lets me know she's into the same things I'm into. What? Don't judge me. I wanted to see what my girl likes. Eventually, I learned to read those books in my hotel room because sitting on an airplane next to a teammate while I'm sporting a raging hard-on is not my idea of a good time. The more books I read, the more I realize that she's been a brat and pushed my buttons on purpose. My dick hardens at the thought. I'm ready to fuck her the way she's never been fucked before. But I want our first time together to be slow and tender; ease her in a bit before I unleash.

I round the back of the truck and adjust myself in my pants before jumping in and taking her back to my place.

Chapter Twenty Four

Aspen

The truck hums to life as Cal turns the key in the ignition. He winks, throwing the truck into reverse before making his way out of the parking lot. We drive to his house in silence. Not an uncomfortable silence, but one that certainly gives me too much time to think. I wonder how this evening will play out. God, just thinking about how he had his way with me in his hotel room has my thighs rubbing together involuntarily. My fingers twine together, and my teeth nibble on my bottom lip.

I didn't want to tell him when he asked, but my mom told me not to worry about coming home tonight. She knows how our schedule has been since we've become an item. I've been waiting for what feels like forever for a night with him. God, I've missed him so freaking much.

I cast a quick glance at Cal. The sight of him makes my heart leap. I want him to finally take me to bed and do the most sinful things to my body. He would completely wreck me. If our night in Chicago is anything to go by, I will be wrecked with a fucking smile on my blissed-out face. I hope this whole delayed gratification bullshit is over with. There are just things a toy cannot do for a woman; I want to feel his hands and his lips all over me.

My mind is doused in sexual thoughts. I mean, after he just bossed me, how could it not be? Something tells me this man is a gentleman in the streets and a sadistic, kinky fuck in the sheets. When I took my hands out of the makeshift binding of my dress, he said he wanted to *spank my pretty ass red*—now that's something I can get behind. It makes me want to misbehave so he'll deliver on his promises.

You'd think, as inexperienced as I am, that I wouldn't know what I would want or like when it comes to sex, but I've read enough books to know how my body responds to certain situations. Sometimes, I think I'm a little fucked up. It's probably one of the reasons why I've never really cared to have a random hookup. I've heard River's stories, and most men she's been with were selfish and boring. She would complain about how she would have to finish the job herself. Why would I want to be with just anyone, especially someone who would leave me disappointed? That would be a waste of my time, and time is something I've never had much of.

The way Cal's hand went to my throat—both in the alley and in the elevator . . . that was hot. When I think back to that argument in the alley, if we had admitted our feelings for each other then, he could have just fucked me right there against that brick wall while he restricted my airflow. See? Never been choked out before or had sex out in the open where anyone could see, but apparently, I'd like it. Case closed; I'm fucked up. But maybe Cal is a little fucked up too.

He reaches over the console, takes my left hand, and places his lips to my knuckles. "I can feel you thinking over there. What's going on in that pretty little head of yours?"

Oh, God. Wouldn't he like to know? No one has ever been able to read me as well as he can. I'm surprised he even has to ask. I remain silent as I glance at him. A knowing smirk sports his beautiful face.

I shrug a shoulder. "Nothing really," I lie.

He hums.

What was it that he said? Oh yeah! *One day, you're going to pop off to me, and I'm going to fuck that smart ass mouth of yours to shut you up.* I wonder what scenario funneled through his mind when he said that. Did he see me lying with my head tilted back on the bed, both hands tied up and hoisted to a restraint hanging from a hook bolted to the ceiling? My legs spread and restrained with a spreader bar while he fucks my mouth until saliva and tears run down my face. Callan Miles doesn't seem like the type of man to need a map, if you know what I mean, but I wonder if my fantasies would scare him off. One night with him—one freaking night—and we didn't even have sex, yet he created a monster.

Cal parks the truck in his circular driveway, turns the truck off, and hops out. I don't wait for him to round the truck to open my door. Instead, I open my door and slide out.

He shakes his head as he fists his keys, walking to the front door. "You're pushing me to my limit, Angel."

"Maybe I'm trying to," I sass.

Oh yeah . . . by the look on his face, he knows what I'm doing. He shakes his head, laughing, as he unlocks the door and pushes it open for me to step inside. I hang up my coat and follow his stride to the living room, where he picks up a remote from an end table and presses the power button. He lowers the volume of country music to a comfortable level. It's a genre I didn't expect him to listen to, though his tastes have been pretty eclectic in the past. The volume is loud enough to still make out the music but low enough to engage in conversation. After placing the remote back on the end table, he makes his way to the kitchen.

"Are you hungry?" He asks.

"I could eat."

Rummaging through the fridge, he pulls out a couple of vegetables, a container of thawed chicken, and a bottle of wine. He takes two wine glasses out of the cabinet, then fills both glasses before handing one to me.

Clinking my glass to his, I wink, "To a kid-free night."

"To a kid-free night." Cal chuckles, taking a sip.

When he sets the glass down on the counter, his lips lift into a left-sided smirk. I know that smirk; it's a devious one. He grabs a cutting board out of the cabinet, setting it on the counter, then crosses the kitchen to the sink, where I follow. A smirk still graces his lips, and it makes me wonder what crazy thoughts are running through his head right now.

Once we've washed our hands together, he turns to grab a towel. As soon as he turns to hand me said towel, I flick the water from my hands at his face. A loud laugh escapes my lips when he grabs me by the waist and spins me around. He lowers me to my feet in front of the cutting board. "Don't think I haven't been keeping tally in my head of all the times you've been a brat. Your punishments are adding up."

"Oh, promises, promises, Hotshot. You talk a big game, but you have yet to deliver on anything you've threatened. One might think you're just talking out of your ass."

"Yeah, you won't be saying that when *your* ass is on fire, will you?"

"Mm-hmm. Do it, then talk about it," I wink.

From behind, he presses his body against mine and buries his nose in my hair. I brace my hands on the counter—my body on full alert. As he speaks low into my ear, goosebumps prickle along my skin, and a tingling sensation rushes to my head. "I would like to feed you. You're going to need all the energy you can get for what I have in store for you." His fingertips trace down my neck. "I'm going to worship every inch of your body, then make love to you nice and slow . . ." The heat from his body leaves mine, followed by a loud crack that echoes throughout the kitchen and makes me jump. *Fuck!* My ass *is* on fire, but I'm completely aroused. Again, I feel his breath on my neck, and his body presses against me. "That was just a taste of what's in store for you. Are you ready for me to deliver the punishment you've been begging for?" Sexually frustrated and aroused, I nod. His low chuckle fills my ear, "Be a good fucking girl . . . and cut those up," he whispers, kissing my cheek. *Fucking tease.*

I'm left panting as he moves away from me and sets the oven to preheat. It takes me a minute to collect myself, but I begin to cut up the broccoli and green onions *like a good fucking girl* while he seasons the chicken. Once the task is complete, I set the cutting board next to him and lean back against the counter.

"So, any word on when your homeowners will be back?" He asks as he places the chicken in a baking dish, then scrapes the vegetables from the cutting board into a bowl.

I freeze and turn to him. "Oh. Oh, God." I panic, pinching the bridge of my nose. "Fuck! I have to figure something out pretty quickly. Time just kinda snuck up on me. I only have about a month left. How did I let this slip?"

Cal adds a mixture of rice, water, cheese, and a can of cream of mushroom soup to the veggies and gives it a good stir before placing the mixture on top of the chicken. Then he tops the casserole with cheese. He looks so sexy doing such a minuscule task. This is nice—just the two of us after a crazy day, laughing, playing, and bantering while we prepare a meal as a couple.

"That tends to happen when you're as busy as we are. Any ideas floating around in that brilliant brain of yours?" He shifts his focus from me to his phone and sets a timer before sliding the device into his back pocket.

"Not yet. I guess in a worst-case scenario, we can just crash at River's apartment until we can find something."

"Or . . . and hear me out . . ." He says as we wash our hands in the sink, "You two could just stay here with me."

My head jerks back. "What? Cal, that's ridiculous. We just got together and . . ."

"And even still, I already know you're it for me. Both of you. I want you here . . . always. When I come home from away games, I want to come home to you and Tuck. I want to see his smiling face and hear about his day before he goes to bed, and then I want to climb in bed next to you every night. Is it really too soon, Aspen? We've been dancing around this relationship for months."

Jason Aldean's "You Make It Easy" plays low in the background. Cal wraps his arms around me. My hands reach up around his neck, and I play with the hair at his nape as he sways us back and forth. I can't contain the smile on my lips as I look up at this amazing man. I want to say yes so badly, but I'm scared.

His eyes hold mine hostage. "I'm fucking obsessed with you. When I'm with you, the world stops spinning, and everything just goes . .

. still. For years I've begged for peace, but I've quickly come to realize that you are my peace. You're my comfort. My silence when the world around me is too loud. Angel, you're everything." He takes my chin and brings his lips to mine. It's not a breathtaking, lip-bruising kiss, but a sweet one. "I hate every second we're apart, so please, just promise me when the time comes to hand your keys to the owner, you'll at least consider staying here."

A happy tear slips down my cheek. "I'll consider it." The words leave my lips before I've even thought about what would happen if we moved in and then he decided he didn't want us anymore. He's shown me time and time again those thoughts are completely irrational, but they're still in the back of my mind.

Cal takes both of my hands in his and removes them from his neck, kissing my knuckles before he lifts one of my arms and spins me around. I'm brought back to his chest, and we dance there in the kitchen for what seems like forever. This is a window into what my future could look like with him, what it would be like if we lived here. Going to Tucker's games, making dinner together as a family, dancing in the kitchen. I love him. I think I've always loved him even when I thought I hated him. From the moment I saw him down on the ice with my son, I've fallen so completely in love with this man.

The timer on Cal's phone rings, and he pulls it from his back pocket to silence the alarm. He pulls a bubbling casserole out of the oven, plating it up while I refill our wine.

We make our way to the table, and I take a seat next to him and dig into the casserole. When I bite into the cheesy goodness, I can't help the moan that escapes my mouth. I'm not even a fan of chicken, and this is delicious. Cal gives me a heated look, then shakes his head as if to clear his mind of whatever lust-filled thoughts I assume he just had.

We eat in silence until we're almost done, then he clears his throat. "I, um . . . I spoke with my dad earlier today."

I set down my fork, surprised that he finally adhered to my advice, "Yeah? How'd that go?" I take a sip of wine.

Cal wipes his mouth with his napkin. "Emotional. It was good to finally hear his voice. He said if we make it to the playoffs, he's going to try to fly out to watch the game, that is if his team isn't in the playoffs too. If that doesn't pan out, he'll for sure come down this summer."

"That's amazing. I'm incredibly proud of you. That must have been a tough conversation." I rub his arm, then pull my hand back.

He scratches the back of his neck. "Well, it wasn't easy. But I'm glad I did it. I've really missed him, you know? *And . . .* I told him that I can't wait for him to meet the woman who pulled me from the depths of hell."

My smile widens, but I'm still taken by surprise. "You want me to meet your dad?" I take the last bite of my meal as I gauge his sincerity.

"You still don't get it, do you?" He shakes his head in disbelief, then clears the table.

I trail behind him as he walks through the kitchen to the sink. He turns on the water as I stand beside him. I try to take the dishes from his hand so I can rinse them, but Cal bumps me out of the way with his hips, which causes a giggle to escape my lips. With the dishes rinsed, he places them into the dishwasher, dries his hands on a hand towel, then takes me by surprise when he turns around and picks me up. My legs instantly wrap around his waist, and as I cling to him, he buries his head in my neck.

"I'm yours." His low voice sends a shiver down my body. When he leans back, beautiful hazel eyes flick across my face, and butterflies erupt in my stomach. "I don't know what I have to do to prove to you that I'm not going anywhere. When are you ever going to realize that I'm a permanent fixture in your life? There is nowhere in the world that I'd rather be than right beside you. I love you, Angel."

I close the space between us and kiss him.

His lips part, and my tongue grazes his as I pour every ounce of my soul into this kiss. Cal carries me toward his bedroom but stops midway up the stairs to press me against the wall. *What is it with him and carrying me and walls? Whatever it is, it's hot as hell.* My hands are in his hair, and one of his is tangled in mine. His hips grind into me, and through our clothes, his hard length rubs against my clit. We become more frantic, and he swallows my moan by kissing me so hard that I'm sure my lips are going to be swollen and bruised. "You have no idea how long I've waited for you," he mumbles against my lips. "Now . . . lose the blouse."

Within seconds, I'm grabbing the hem, lifting the silk fabric over my head before dropping it onto the floor. I'm lifted higher, and Cal's head descends as he takes each nipple into his mouth one by one over my white lace bra. His lips return to mine. My back leaves the wall, and he carries me the rest of the way to his bedroom.

With my feet deposited back to the ground and our connection broken, I stand panting and beyond senseless. His left hand squeezes my hip, while the right one wraps around to unclasps my bra. He peels the straps from my arms. White lace falls to the ground. He lowers himself to his knees, takes off my shoes and socks, pops the button to my jeans, then glides the zipper down.

I hold onto his shoulders as he strips the denim from each leg; nipping and trailing kisses from my thighs to my ankles. My white lace panties are the last thing to glide down. With them lying on the floor next to me, his hands slide up my thighs before grabbing a hold of my hips. He breathes me in, then his tongue begins its assault on my pussy while his eyes connect with mine.

Fuck, he knows how to make me feel good. This man is a god in the bedroom. My hands pull his hair—moving him even closer—and I throw my head back. "Oh, fuck," I moan.

He pauses his onslaught, and I look down at him as his gaze peruses me. "Goddamn, you're pretty." My quaking legs part a bit to give him better access. His fingers slide inside me. "Fuck, Angel, your pussy is dripping. Is this all for me?"

"Everything's for you, Callan," I pant as his mouth returns to me.

His tongue and fingers continue to work their magic until my entire body tenses. All of the blood rushes to my head, and stars burst behind my closed eyelids. It takes a few beats to catch my breath. I peer down as he wipes my arousal from his glistening lips and chin with the back of his hand.

Cal stands, and I grab the end of his shirt, lifting it up his torso. As my knuckles skim his sides, goosebumps pebble his flesh. It's empowering to know I have that kind of effect on his body, that I can make him feel the same way that he makes me feel. He reaches behind his head and assists me by pulling off his shirt. Before I even have a chance to admire his body, he bends his head and teases my lips with his, then his tongue gently caress mine.

I rub against his hard cock through his clothes, then fumble with his belt. After unbuckling his belt, I unbutton and unzip his pants, letting them fall to the ground. He toes off his shoes and pulls off his socks, then stands upright wearing a smirk on his lips and a pair of boxer briefs. I didn't think he could be any sexier . . . that is, until he releases himself from said boxer briefs, and they hit the ground next to his jeans in a heaping pile of fabric.

Holy shit! This man is an Adonis with muscles cut from his jawline all the way down his body. Angry veins run down the length of his big, hard shaft as I allow my eyes to take him in, I'm left wondering how the hell he's going to fit. It's been years since I've been with anyone, and by the looks of things, this incredibly intoxicating man is going to rip my pussy to shreds. I take a deep breath and try to calm my nerves.

Cal has just singlehandedly turned my entire world upside down, and I want to return the favor, or at least try to, but he grabs my wrist when I reach for him.

He takes my chin in his hands, tilting my head back to look him in the eyes. "You'll spend plenty of time with that pretty little mouth wrapped around my cock, but not right now. I thought I made myself clear the first time, but I'll go ahead and reiterate what I said before. When we're in the bedroom, you're not in charge. You spend every single waking moment making enough decisions for yourself and everyone around you. When we're here, I call the shots. Do you understand?"

"Yes."

"Yes, what?" He demands.

Oh, dear lord. I didn't think it was possible for me to be even more turned on, but here I am.

I give a dramatic roll of my eyes. "Yes, I understand." I know I'm intentionally being a brat, but he doesn't know that *I know* what he wants me to call him. So, I'll sit here, play dumb, and let everything build up until he's reached his limit and delivers what I want.

He chuckles low. "Now, now. Do you really think you can get away with that? I know what you're doing, and it's not going to work. I also know a little secret about you."

A sharp breath escapes my lips; I swallow hard, then lick my lips.

He tsks, "You see, I've been doing . . . a little research. Let's call it: Callan Miles' DEFCON 1. In my research I found some interesting things about you. On shelves across the street sits a slew of books. Very dirty . . . incredibly naughty . . . and extremely smutty books, owned by none other than . . . you. So, I know that you know how to address me properly. Do you want to try that again, Angel?"

My eyes widen. I'm fucking busted. What the fuck is going on? How the hell did he get ahold of my books without me knowing? Good grief, I'm hanging on by a fucking thread here.

I nod, and I nibble on my bottom lip, knowing my cover is blown, "Yes, sir."

His hand strokes my head. "That's my good girl."

Fuck. Hearing him call me a good girl is even hotter than when he tied me up. It makes me want to be his good girl all the time. My eyes light up.

"If you don't want anyone to know your secrets, Aspen, maybe you shouldn't annotate your favorite scenes. Now, scoot up on the bed. I don't make promises I don't intend to keep."

I do as he orders, internally begging him to praise me again.

He saunters to the nightstand and grabs a condom and a bottle of lube, tosses them on the bed, then climbs up and settles between my legs.

Lifting my left foot, he kisses the top, then kisses and sucks on the pleasure points all over my body.

Expert fingers bury into my pussy, scissoring and stretching me to fit his girth as he takes a nipple into his mouth. Then his fingers make a come-hither motion that causes my back to arch. I lose my fucking mind as he bites down on my other nipple. An orgasm hits me like a tsunami. Ohmygod!

He removes his fingers and places them to my lips. "Open," he commands. "I want you to see how good you taste."

My eyes widen. Umm . . . I've never done that before.

One eyebrow raises, daring me to go against his command. Wanting his praise, I hold his wrist, open my mouth, then close my mouth around his fingers.

"Suck."

Like a needy little whore, I do exactly as I'm told—sucking those skilled fingers into my mouth, and twirling my tongue around as I wait for those words I long to hear leave his lips.

The man doesn't disappoint, "Good fucking girl," he growls before kissing me.

He releases my lips, and a serious expression crosses his face as he looks me in the eyes. "I don't want anything between us, but if you're uncomfortable with that, I'll respect your wishes."

I shake my head. "I'm on birth control, and I've seen your health report."

"Good, because I want to fill this pussy with my cum and watch it drip down these sexy ass legs."

Oh dear god. He's going to be the death of me.

Picking up the bottle of lube, he squirts a generous amount into his hand, then rubs it over his length and my pussy—even though I'm already wet. He gives his cock a few pumps, then he lines himself up with me. As the head of his dick breaches my entrance, I tense up, anticipating the pain. My lids are squeezed tight in anticipation.

"Angel, look at me." I pop open my eyes and meet his sincere gaze. "If you want me to stop, just say the word. Okay?"

I nod.

He's much bigger than any of my toys. Inch by inch, he carefully pushes in, stopping a little at a time either to tease the hell out of me or to give me time to adjust.

"That's right." He strokes my hair. "Such a good girl for me." He pulls back before slowly gliding in again, forcing himself a little deeper, "God, you feel like heaven."

Stilling his body, he kisses me until I've adjusted to him. The defined muscle of his bicep and deltoid flex as he braces his weight on one arm. He's trembling, and it's not from holding his weight; from the look in his eyes, I can tell it's from the effect I have on him. Then, as if he knows what I need, he slowly glides out before sliding back in—repeating his movements. I meet his thrusts, taking him deeper. My God, he feels incredible, but when he does this tilt thing with his hips and hits a spot deep within me—holy fuck, I don't think I'm going to last long. I've never felt so full. My fingers dig into his back. Slowly he makes love to me. My head tilts back and my spine arches.

His lips trace along my collarbone and my neck. "I feel like I've waited a lifetime for you, Aspen Taylor. It's the juxtaposition, right Angel? God, I love you so damn much."

A tear falls to my cheek from the overwhelming emotion this astonishing man stirs within me. Then, my vision darkens, my body tingles, and my pussy begins to contract around his cock as another orgasm hits me.

"Goddamn, your pussy is gripping me like a vice. I'm about to cum." He growls. He shifts his body, lifting my leg and throwing it over his shoulder, driving deeper into me. Over and over and over in rapid succession, he fucks me harder until finding his release. "Fuck, Aspen," he breathes.

Cal peers down at me and steadies himself with one arm, mindful not to crush me, and sweeps stray hairs away from my face. I lift my head to kiss him, "I love you, Callan Miles," I whisper against his lips.

Emotions swirl in the midst of his eyes before he buries his head into the crook of my neck.

Chapter Twenty Five

Cal

As the sun begins to set and my bedroom grows darker, one side of Aspen's body is shadowed, creating a silhouette. Bracing my weight on my right arm, I allow my eyes to peruse Aspen's face. God, she's fucking stunning. I remove stray hairs clinging to her forehead and cheek, committing this moment to memory. An ache resides deep within my soul as my eyes map every contour of her beautiful face. I've never felt this way in my entire life. I just want to give her everything.

Is this normal? It's as if I can't get close enough to her. Maybe that's why it's called making love, because the only way to get closer is to bury yourself deep inside that person—to connect with them in the most intimate way.

Call me a simp. Hell, call me whatever you want; I don't give a shit. This woman lying underneath me is my endgame. Right now, in this very moment, I realize hockey doesn't mean shit. There's absolutely no competition. If someone came to me and asked me to choose between the Stanley Cup and Aspen Taylor, hands down, I would choose her. Every. Single. Time. And I wouldn't bat an eye; I would have no regrets.

My priorities have quickly shifted in a short period of time. Above everything, her and Tuck's happiness is all that matters to me. How can they be happy with me if I'm not around to create memories with them? The last thing I'm going to do is let my second chance at love and a family slip through my fingers. I'm away almost as much as I'm here, and I feel certain that isn't the life I want anymore.

She lifts her head, and with a kiss, a whispered mumble graces my lips. "I love you, Callan Miles."

The affirmation nearly takes my breath away. Something about hearing those words accompanied with my full name grips my heart and tugs. I don't understand the reason, and I don't have to. That's it. I'm done for.

I exhale deeply, lifting my head. My eyes hold hers hostage. "I love you too." I place a gentle kiss on her lips. "Are you sore?"

She shakes her head in response.

With a devious smirk, I let my possessive side take over. "Oh, that's about to change. You're going to feel me for the next few days. Every time you sit, I want you to be reminded of exactly who this sweet pussy belongs to." I peck her lips.

Lifting myself off her, I sit on the edge of the bed and plant my feet on the ground. I move to the closet where an arsenal of items I've ordered for her rests. A set of leather cuffs resides in one of my drawers. I pluck them out, along with a flogger, and saunter toward her tauntingly. The flogger rests by my side in one hand; the tresses brush my leg with each step I take, and the clasped leather cuffs dangle from the fingertips of the other. She eyes me curiously.

"Stand," I command.

She scrambles off the bed—more than eager to please—and stands to her feet. My eyes travel down the length of her body. Fuck, she twists me up and turns me inside out. I allow the cuffs to fall to the floor next to our feet as I stand in front of her. "Fucking beautiful. If this becomes too much for you, let me know by using a safe word. We'll keep those safe words simple: red, if you need me to stop; yellow, if you want me to slow down; and green, if you're doing okay."

Excitement flares in her expression, but I can tell she's nervous as she nibbles her bottom lip.

I graze a knuckle down her arm, watching the goosebumps rise and pebble her skin as I circle around to stand behind her. "Do you understand?"

"Yes."

"Yes, what?"

"Yes, sir."

"Good girl." I stroke her head.

She sighs in delight at my praise. I move her hair to one side and kiss the back of her neck. Her hand reaches up, cupping the back of my head.

"Did I tell you to move your hands?"

She quickly drops her hand back to her side.

"Now, tell me, Angel . . . I want to hear it from those sexy lips: Why do you continue to be a brat for me? Rolling your eyes, opening doors, backtalking me, flicking water in my face?"

An immediate response doesn't come. I circle back around to face her, holding the flogger, so the leather tresses lightly tease and feather along her skin. Gently grabbing her chin with my thumb and forefinger, I force her attention from the floor to me and raise an eyebrow as if to ask if she really wants to continue this little game she's been playing.

She swallows hard and licks her lips. "I love to watch you lose your mind." Her eyes flick between mine, then travel down my chest. "I want you to lose control and do filthy things to me."

My dick twitches just thinking of the filthy things I'm going to do to her. "Hmmm. And what filthy things, pray tell, keep you up at night with a wet little cunt, devising your schemes? Do you want me to bind you?" My eyes trail down her torso to her glistening pussy.

"Yes."

"To blindfold you?" A mixture of our cum drips down her thighs. "To degrade you . . . to call you my whore?"

"Yes."

Fuck, that's hot.

"To edge you over and over until you're losing your mind?" I collect my cum and shove it back inside her—where it belongs, "Now, there's an idea."

She gasps as my fingers push inside her. My thumb rubs slow, tantalizing circles over her clit as my fingers move in an upward motion. I add a third finger, twisting my wrist, and changing my pace.

"Oh fuck. Oh fuck," she moans.

"Do you want me to spank your pretty ass?" My words hit exactly as I intend them to, and her body is responding beautifully.

"Y—yes, Cal, I'm . . . I'm so close."

"There you go again," I warn, "Right now I'm not your Cal; I'm your sir. Understand?"

"Yes . . ." She nods, "Yes, sir."

"You knew what you were doing to me today, yet you did it anyway, didn't you?"

She nods.

"Do you think of my hand gripping your throat—like that night in the alley?"

"Yes."

The leather cracks across her ass, and she lets out a whimpered moan as her arousal intensifies and drips down my hand.

"Y—yes, Sir."

"Do you wish I would have fucked you there in the open for everyone to see what's mine?"

Her eyes squeeze tight; short pants and whimpers leave her lips.

"You're mine; you've always been mine."

Her pussy clenches tight around my fingers. So beautiful, so fucking responsive, on the edge of release. Just as her body tenses up with an orgasm, I remove my fingers.

"No . . ." She begs, her breaths ragged. "Please . . . please . . . don't stop," she cries.

"Only good girls get to cum, Angel." I bring my fingers coated with a mix of our cum to her lips. "Lick. You already know how decadent you taste, but allow me to show you how much better you taste when your cum is mixed with mine."

Fire blazes in her eyes. She's frustrated. Good. Her hand grips my wrist, and her tongue darts past her lips. She swirls her tongue around my fingertips, then gives a few teasing licks. Fuck, this may be more torturous for me than it is for her. Pre-cum leaks from the tip of my hard dick as a vision of Aspen taking my cock between those swollen lips invades my mind.

Moving to stand behind her, I notice her taut, flawless ass. That's about to change. "Bend over and pick up the cuffs." I order.

With her bent over, her pussy is on display for me. It's taking every ounce of self-control to not fuck her hard right now in that position. Like the brat she is, she stays bent over. I run the leather tails up her back to her ass. I'm mesmerized as the strips of leather fan and glide across her tanned skin. With a flick of my wrist, the flogger snaps. She flinches, and a gasp leaves her lips. Her pussy glistens with a mix of her arousal and our cum; it begs to be fingered, fucked . . . or licked. Thinking of tasting her makes my mouth water. I strike her ass with the flogger twice more, then drop it to the floor and move to stand at the foot of the bed.

"Grab the cuffs and get on your knees."

She does as she's told . . . for once. Resting back on her heels with her head bowed, the cuffs are clasped in her grip, resting on her lap.

"Crawl to me."

Shifting to her hands and knees with the cuffs still in her clutches, she crawls to me; her big tits sway from side to side. I inhale deeply, letting the air fill my lungs. Fuck me. She takes her place at my feet, resuming her previous position. Gently, I run my hand from the top of her head to the ends of her long, silky, black hair. Emerald eyes flick to mine through a curtain of dark lashes.

I lift her chin with one knuckle and hold out my hand palm up. "Give me the cuffs, Angel."

She drops the cuffs into my palm, then holds out both wrists. I pepper both with kisses, then buckle the leather straps around each one.

"Bend over the bed; show me how wet your pussy is," I tell her.

She bends at the waist, bracing herself with her hands on the bed. The brat is gone, and in its place is a woman who's compliant and ready to do anything to please me. Her back arches as she glides her body down in a tantalizing movement until her stomach meets the bed.

"You're an eager little whore for me, aren't you?"

She's a vision, with her cheek pressed against the bed and her wrist bound above her head. My palm glides across her ass. "You practically begged for this, didn't you?"

"Yes, sir," she whispers.

I pick up the flogger, teasing her perfectly round ass with the falls. With a flick of my wrist, the whip comes down very lightly across her back. She moans and writhes in anticipation as the strands of leather slide down her spine. "I can't wait to fill you up with my cock. To feel your pussy squeeze me tight, but first, I'm going to give you what you've been begging for. Now, count."

Crack!

She hesitates, "One."

I caress her ass with my palm, soothing the sting. Alternating from the flogger to my palm, I give her ass another slap. The slap echoes around the room. A nice pink handprint is splayed across her right ass cheek.

"T—Two."

My fingers trace the lines of the handprint left behind. I strike for the third time. Her cries echo throughout the room. She's writhing and moaning, lifting her hips off the bed.

"Give me a color."

"Green," she breathes. "That's three."

If she were to say yellow, I don't think I could continue. What if she doesn't truly know her limits? Pushing her too far scares the hell out of me, but I continue to alternate back and forth between the flogger and my palm, soothing the sting of each swat. By the sixth spanking, she's panting harder; her pussy is wet with arousal, my dick is hard as fuck, and I'm ready to fill her full of my cum. "Fuck, your ass is a pretty shade of pink. Are you okay?"

"Yes . . . just please. Please . . ." She whines.

A smirk falls on my lips. "Give me a color."

"Green. Fuck, it's green. Please."

I tap my hand between each thigh. "Spread them."

The eager little minx quickly spreads her legs for me. I fuck her with my fingers until she's just on the edge, ready to tumble; I pull back. She releases a breathy whimper. Bracing herself with her hands, she glares over her shoulder in frustration.

"Fuck! Cal, please!"

I smack her ass, then bring my fingers to my lips to taste us on them. "We do taste good together, don't we?"

Falling to my knees, I spread her ass cheeks and bury my face in her cunt, lapping her up. She presses into me, the greedy little thing, and I edge her again.

"Please . . ."

"Did I break you, Angel? That seems to be the only word in your vocabulary right now."

I stand to find her sobbing. Fuck, fuck, fuck . . . I went too far.

She must feel me spiraling. "Please don't stop. I'm just . . . I'm overwhelmed."

I think she's had enough . . .

"I'm okay. Still green," she reassures me.

Standing, I allow her a few minutes to recover before finally giving her what she wants. I thrust into her. Fuck! She feels incredible. Like a goddamn silk vice wrapped around my dick. When she clinches her pussy around my cock, my eyes roll to the back of my head. I have to still myself for a second to keep from cumming too fast. Her long hair is off to one side in a tangled mess. I gather the locks, wrapping them around my palm before giving a little tug as I pound into her.

"Fuck, Cal, I'm so fucking close."

My palm strikes hard across her ass, and she cries out in response. I flip her over, so I can see her face, and shove my way back inside. Her moans and the sound of skin slapping skin echo around the room as I fuck her relentlessly. She's close; I can feel her pussy pulse, the walls of her cunt closing around my cock in a tight grip. My thumb finds her clit, and I rub tight, firm circles, bringing her closer to climax. She looks so damn good lying there, bound, her tits bouncing as I rock into her.

"Ohmyfuckinggod," she cries, her words running together.

"If that's what you want to call me, Angel, but instead of the one you worship, I'll be a god who worships you; fuck, you bring me to my goddamn knees."

"Mmmm . . . Yes . . . Fuck," she moans.

Her hips rise and meet mine thrust for thrust. Running my other hand all the way up her body, I grip her throat and take a nipple into my mouth. There are so many sensations traveling through her body right now with my thumb on her clit, my mouth on her nipple, and my hand restricting her air. I bite down, just enough to cause her nipple to sting. She screams out. That little bit of pain sets her off like a rocket. I release her throat and let her ride it out until I can't hold off any longer; she feels too damn good.

"Fuck . . . Aspen . . . Fuck." I thrust into her harder.

The way she squeezes my cock causes me to lose my goddamn mind and spill into her. I brace myself with both hands on the bed, my body hovering over hers; I give her a few more thrusts.

"You fucking wreck me," I say panting.

Her hair is a mess around her, sweat glistens on her brow, and she looks completely wrung out with her eyes half-mast, but she's never looked more perfect. The moon's light shines in from the window and casts a glow on her skin. *My Angel.* I move up her body, then unbuckle the leather restraints, rubbing and kissing each wrist as they're released. As she lays there, I brush her damp hair back from her face and kiss her lips.

"How you doing there?"

I wrap her in my arms, worried that maybe I went too far, but a smile spreads wide across her lips. "I'm fantastic. Wow, who knew it could be like that?" She muses.

I smile back. "I didn't take it too far?"

She gives me a pensive look. "God, no! You were perfect."

Her reassurance relieves my anxiety. She takes my hand and intertwines our fingers and sighs dreamily. "I didn't know that I would like it so much. I mean, obviously, I'm very well versed when it comes to kink just based on what I read. What we just did . . . was incredible. Experiencing it firsthand is entirely different than reading it. Be careful, Callan Miles; you may be creating a monster." She giggles.

"Just promise you'll use your safe word if you need to. Your pleasure means more to me than my own, and I can't stand the thought of hurting you or working you too hard because you're trying to please me. Plus, scenes are all about trust. I need to be able to trust you will tell me if it's too much, just as you need to be able to trust that I know your responses well enough to know when you've reached your limit."

She presses her lips to mine. "Promise."

I leave Aspen in a mess of blankets on the bed and move to the bathroom, where I run a bath for her. She's lying on her side, right where I left her, looking like the angel she is, and watching me through the open doorway when I return. Lifting her off of the bed bridal style, I carry her into the bathroom and set her feet to the ground.

She twists her fingers together. "Um . . . I need to use the restroom."

I chuckle, "So use it." I hold my hand out to show her where the toilet is as if she can't see it through the open doorway.

She shakes her head. "I'm not peeing while you're standing right here."

"There's a door to conceal yourself." I turn off the water to the bath and start the jets.

She stands naked in front of me, her arms crossed tight against her chest—pushing up her breast—as she stares me down. "But you'll hear me pee."

I roll my eyes. "Angel, I just had my tongue buried inches deep inside your pussy licking our cum, and you want to be shy now?"

She continues to stand unmoving and staring at me with a raised brow.

"Fine. I'll give this one to you." I put my hands up in surrender and back out of the bathroom, closing the door on my way out.

I straighten the bed, then run downstairs to grab a glass of water and an Aleve from the cabinet. After giving her time to handle her business, I tap on the door.

Her voice is muffled on the other side of the door. "You can come in now."

When I step inside the bathroom, I find her already in the tub, the high-powered jets massaging her muscles.

"God, can I just live here? I would spend hours in this tub." Her eyes widen. "I mean . . . I . . . uh . . . of course I was only joking."

I grab a washcloth out of the cabinet and turn on the faucet to wet the cloth. "Don't joke about that."

She scoots forward, and I slip in behind her; the water rises and spills over the side. Taking her chin in my hand, I carefully wipe her face, then pour body wash on the cloth. "For a split second, I was excited."

Her pink-painted toenails peek out of the water as she moves her heel to the jet. She sighs, "Since we're on the topic of places to live, I need to visit one of my father's properties up north. Think you could take me tomorrow? I don't want to go alone."

"That depends on if my boss can get me out of practice," I laugh.

“Pfft. Luke would have my head for that.”

I glide the cloth over her breast as I wash her body; the sound of water trickles from the cloth to the bathwater. “If you can wait until one o’clock, I can take you to your dad’s.”

“That should work. I’ll call Mom in the morning to see if she can pick Tucker up from school.” She leans her back against my chest. Turning her head, she places a kiss on my jaw.

Last time Aspen went to view her dad’s properties, she ended up giving one of them to River, then decided not to view the rest. I’m a bit concerned about how tomorrow will go. I want to take all of her pain away, to do this for her, but I can’t, so I guess the best I can do is be the man she needs. The supportive boyfriend who comforts her when this all becomes too much.

Chapter Twenty Six

Aspen

The jets from the bath massage my deliciously aching muscles as Cal bathes me. He worked me hard, but I could tell he was holding back. I turn around in the tub and straddle him. Running my hands through his hair, I kiss him hard and passionately. I want him again. He's going to turn me into a fiend. I didn't think sex could be this good, but I guess that's to be expected when the last time you had sex was in high school with a selfish boy.

"As much as I want to fuck you again, Angel, I think we need to give your body time to rest," he says to me as he lightly runs the cloth over my skin. "Right now, I want to take you to bed and hold you."

I stay silent, trying to devise a plan to make him fuck me again. Maybe I need to be bratty . . . no, he will see right through that. Sighing, I take the cloth from his hand. I pour his body wash on the rag, run it down his chest, over his shoulders, down his arms. My eyes trail my hand's movements. His body is completely insane, and I bask in the fact that he's mine.

Once we're both washed, he taps my leg. "Time for bed."

I lift myself to stand. He follows suit, stepping out of the tub, and grabing a towel for each of us before wrapping me in one. We both make our way to the bed, where he places two pills in the palm of my hand and hands me a glass of water. Throwing the pills back, I take a sip.

"Drink the entire thing."

I eye him as I swallow the entire contents of the glass.

"Good girl."

When he says those words to me, my entire body lights up. I guess that's what people call a praise kink. I'm here for it . . . he can call me his *good girl* all damn day, and I would never get tired of hearing it. He tosses the covers back, and I climb in.

He leans over the bed, arms locked, both fists against the mattress, his muscles flexing. A towel is tightly wrapped around his waist, hair mussed and sexy, while droplets of water rivulet down his chest and abs. Why does this feel like some form of torture? Him standing there looking like that is like dangling a cookie in front of a child and telling them they can't have it.

"I'll be right back. I need to clean everything up." He drops a kiss on my lips.

As I watch him clean the leather through the open door, my eyes become heavy. Somewhere in my subconscious, I feel the bed dip and his arms wrap around me. I stir as he buries his head into my neck.

"I love you, Aspen," he whispers.

Get in and get out. That's the mantra I repeat to myself as we take the winding road to my father's house. The National Weather Service's warning of a winter weather advisory repeats through the truck speakers.

"Maybe we should turn around and go back, do this some other time when we don't have a chance of freezing rain."

"It's just a winter weather advisory. Winter weather advisories in New York are like tornado watches in Oklahoma. Did you run to a cellar every time there was a watch, or did you go about your life?"

I mean, I guess he has a point, but still, I'm nervous. The plus side is that practice ended early because Luke had an appointment. Thank God. We were able to leave earlier than expected, which means we should be able to make it home before the storm hits.

When I heard the weather this morning, I told Cal we should just stay home, but he said we had enough time, and he was adamant that I needed to put this behind me. I guess that's what happens when your boyfriend bears witness to you having a breakdown. Yeah, that happened. Just what I needed at the time—to embarrass myself further as if I hadn't already done that enough on Christmas night. The day we all came back from my father's apartment, I couldn't hold it together. With no indication as to why my father truly left me or if he even loved me, I was a complete mess.

It's the same cycle over and over. Feelings of rejection and abandonment are buried so deep that no matter what I do, I just can't seem to move past it. My mom can say whatever she wants about them protecting me, but for some reason, I'll never believe her. Maybe I too have some deep-seated issues.

Last time I attempted something like this, I ended up a crying mess in my room, wrapped in Cal's arms. I was completely broken, and like the true friend he is, he picked up the pieces and held me together. I'll be stronger this time, I tell myself as the navigation system alerts us to take a right. Pulling up to the iron gate, I dig through my purse for the code and hand the sticky note to Cal. I take a deep, calming breath. Here we go.

He enters the four-digit code into the keypad and presses the pound key. The gate opens; its wheels squeaking as they run along the tracks. Trees in their skeletal forms line the lengthy drive as we make our way to the house. House. Ha! That's an understatement. More like a mansion. What is it with these single men living in these massive houses all alone?

Maybe I'm just used to the simplicity of living on the farm in Oklahoma. There was no reason to impress anyone because everyone lived pretty much the same way: uncomplicated. Here, in New York, it's all about who's wearing whom, your financial status, where you live, what gala you're attending; the list goes on and on—a repetition of keeping up with the Joneses. I don't want Tucker to be raised that way. I want him to be humble and kind. I don't want him to flaunt his money and status around. This isn't the life that I had planned for him, but it's one we are going to make the most of. All I can do is instill good values in him and pray they take hold.

"You doing okay there, Angel?" Cal breaks me out of my thoughts. "I sense those wheels turning."

My eyes train on him as he rounds the driveway and parks. "I'm good. Don't worry about me."

"I'll always worry about you." With our fingers interlocked, Cal places a kiss on my hand before releasing it, then he hops out of the truck.

Usually, I would mess with him, open my own door, and hop out, but today I'm not feeling so playful. Being here makes me sick with nerves, but I'm tired of procrastinating. Cal's right: the longer this lingers over my head, the longer I'll feel this anxiety, and above everything, I need closure. He rounds the front, and I wait until he opens my door.

I blow out a breath as he reaches for my hand to help me. I jump down from the passenger seat. "Okay, let's get this over with before the storm hits. The last thing I want is to be stuck here."

"If we had just taken the helicopter . . ."

"You already know I'm not touching his assets. The only reason I took over the team is because I didn't really have a choice."

I hear thunder in the distance as we approach the front door, and look up to the gloomy sky.

Cal's head tilts back as well.

I groan, "Think if we leave now, we can make it home?"

He pulls his phone out of his back pocket and clicks an app. "Um, I think we should have looked at this before we left. It wasn't supposed to start storming until late tonight, but this shows a pretty nasty storm headed this way, and it's ahead of schedule." He winces. "We need to make this quick or make peace with staying here tonight," he says.

I glare at him. This is not happening to me. "What happened to 'Winter weather advisories in New York are like tornado watches in Oklahoma . . . blah, blah, blah'?" I mock him. "Let's just go in and check it out. I am not staying in this house longer than necessary."

As we walk into the dark house, I turn around and flip the light switch on the wall right beside the door. Nothing.

"Great!" I flip it back down. "Looks like we'll need a flashlight." I reach into my back pocket for my cell.

The light from my flashlight app bounces off the walls, creating an eerie feeling. "Okay, time to explore."

Instead of heading toward the main part of the house, we take the stairs to the second floor. Cal leads the way, peering around corners as if someone is going to jump out of the shadows. I stay no more than two steps behind him. We find several guestrooms and bathrooms upstairs before trekking back down to the main floor to the great room. It's there I stand with my jaw dropped to the floor in shock. Above the mantle hangs a professional picture of Tucker and me. Pictures of both of us in different phases of our lives are strategically placed on the mantle in beautifully designed picture frames in various sizes.

My hand covers my mouth as I gasp in shock, and Cal's arms wrap around my chest from behind as he places a kiss to my temple. "I don't think he wanted this separation from you; to leave his family behind. As hard as it is to believe your mom, by the looks of this, they really were protecting you."

Remaining silent, I take in the room, then walk over to the mantle. I pick up a picture of my eight-year-old self, sitting on my paint horse in front of our old farmhouse with a broad smile lighting up my face.

"I remember this like it was yesterday. Mom had just bought Blaze . . ." I trail off, turning my head to find Cal at my side, eyeing me sympathetically.

"It wasn't Mom that bought Blaze, was it?"

He clicks the side of his mouth. "Doesn't seem like it." Cal takes the picture from my hand, changing the subject. "Look how cute you were, all snaggle-toothed."

"Har-har." I trace the intricate design of the frame. "I used to share all my secrets with him, especially about the boys I liked. We would talk for hours, or rather, I would talk, and he would listen as I rode him through the pasture and along trails behind our house. I would come home from school and hop on him bareback, and then we'd jump the fences to our neighbor's property . . ."

Cal gives me a look like he can't believe I'd actually enjoy that. "What? I'm a bit of an adrenaline junky. I like to go fast. Mom gave a couple of our barn cats to the neighbor, and that was the quickest way to visit them," I laugh.

His eyes stay trained on me, waiting for me to continue. "When Blaze would see my car coming down our gravel drive, he would run along the fence line, excited to see me. Apples were his favorite, and like clockwork, he would always stand at the fence when I parked, waiting for me to bring him a treat . . . until one day, about six years ago, he wasn't. I knew something was off when he didn't run along that fence line. My initial thought was that someone had stolen him, but that didn't make much sense. So, I went to the pasture to look for him. He had stepped into a hole and broke his leg. A wild hog was rootin' around. No matter how hard I begged, the vet said there was nothing we could do. Lost one of my best friends that day."

"Damn, Aspen."

"Yeah, farm life isn't for the faint of heart. I had to go out and find that damn hog before it created more holes or mauled one of our cows. Hunted that thing for days." I take the picture from Cal and set it back on the mantle.

Cal walks over and picks up a picture of me holding Tucker in the hospital. "You were glowing."

"I was a mess."

"No. You were beautiful." He smiles, then sets the picture back in its place.

We continue our exploration until we come to the end of the hall. I look left, and through the open door, I find an office with floor-to-ceiling windows. I step inside with Cal following behind me. To my right is a built-in bookcase containing hundreds of books. Intrigued by my father's literary interests, I bypass the executive desk—centered in the room—and move directly in front of the bookcase.

I run my fingers along the spines of the first editions: Ernest Hemingway, Charles Dickens, Oscar Wilde, Jane Austen, and F. Scott Fitzgerald all rest collectively on the oak shelves. Wow. I can't even imagine how much these are worth.

Turning around, I take in the large office. A small table with a decanter and glasses rests in a corner just inside the door. I wander over and uncap the crystal, then pour two fingers of the amber liquor into two glasses. I swirl the contents, then bring it up to my nose. Hell, I don't know what this is, but it's strong and makes me wince. Cal raises an eyebrow.

"What? Don't judge me. I need something to get me through this shit. Plus, what kind of daughter would I be if I didn't raid my dad's liquor once in my life?" I giggle.

I saunter to Cal with an outreached hand, passing his drink to him, then I take a sip of the spicy, amber liquid from my own glass and sputter. "This stuff tastes like straight shit."

He throws his head back and laughs. "Oh, Babe. You must not know what's good. This is scotch. Extremely good scotch."

Cal takes his glass and walks over to the window, resting his body against the windowsill. He observes me as I gulp down the contents of my glass and go for a second round. It's awful and burns as it travels down my esophagus to my stomach, but I really do need something to take the edge off. Sauntering back to my dad's desk with a new glass, I set it down on a coaster and sit in his office chair, spreading my hands out over the oak surface. Where to start . . . where to start. I drum my fingers against the wood.

There are seven drawers, including the top middle. Finding them unlocked, I rifle through them, discovering nothing noteworthy. My head swivels to the bookcase, and my eyes roam a row of books until they stop on the bottom shelf. My feet kick off the floor, the chair rolls backward across the wood surface, bringing me to a set of leather-bound books. When I pull one off the shelf and open it, I gasp in shock. Cal waltzes over to see what I've found. I gaze up at him, my eyes stinging behind my lids.

Using my feet, I scoot the chair forward until I'm in front of the desk, then I go through the journal. Fumbling through, I flip page after page after page. This makes absolutely no sense to me. I slam the leather journal closed, hop out of the chair, and stalk back over to the rest of the books that look like this one. I grab all the remaining bound leather books from the shelf and stack them, one on top of the other, on the desk.

My heart beats in rapid succession as I open the cover of the leather-bound journal to the page that is dated on the date of my birth. "Bingo," I whisper.

Cal stands behind me, peering over my shoulder as I read. Anxiety courses through me. I don't know what I was expecting to find here, but it wasn't this. Now, I sit in his black leather chair with his journals in my possession, or rather letters to me—and all appear to be dated throughout my life. I'm scared to read them. I consider packing them all up and taking them with me, but curiosity eats at me. I find words on the pages to be smudged—as if something was spilled. I flip through the next few pages to find the same but in different areas. After reading the first few lines of the first letter, I realize that they were written in despair and agony. The only thing spilled onto these pages were tears.

Chapter Twenty Seven

Aspen

July 24, 1997

My Dearest Aspen,

My heart is so incredibly full, but at the same time it's severely broken. Today your mother gave birth to my sweet little girl. Though I was not there to witness your birth, nor to hold you as I so desperately desired, I can tell you with one hundred percent certainty there is no greater love than what I feel for you, my darling. I'll never understand how I can love someone so deeply that I've never met nor laid eyes on. When your mother phoned to tell me about you . . . the blush on your cheeks and your head full of thick, black hair . . . I could not help but envision a smaller version of her, though your mother thinks you look like me. She said it's still too soon to tell what color your eyes are, but I wonder if you will have her brown or my green? One thing you should never doubt, my darling, is that you will always have my heart. I truly wish we didn't have to protect you this way and that I could be present, but this life will leave you to be scrutinized, and sometimes it can be dangerous. I do not want you in the public eye. One day you will understand. The pain I feel from being apart from you and your mother is crippling, but it's a decision she and I made together. I dream of a day we can meet in person, and I can only hope you will forgive me. I pray you will give me a chance to explain everything to you, maybe when you're old enough to bear the weight of what this kind of life entails . . .

Slamming the journal shut, I pinch the bridge of my nose. Deep guttural sobs wrack from the depth of my soul. This is too much; I can't read the rest of this here. Cal's strong arms come around me, and I tilt my chin up to look at him. I'm unable to mask the pain. My mother was robbed of the love of her life, and I was robbed of a father. The unfairness of the situation unsettles me. One thing is for certain from the contents of all of these journal entries: Even though my father was absent, he loved me.

I sift through the journals and pick a random one in the pile. I flip the pages to the middle of the worn book. As I read, my lips tremble, and my heart begins to ache. Tears pour down my cheeks. Reading about the heartache my father has endured has given me a different perspective. Suddenly, I'm lifted out of the chair bridal style as Cal takes my place and situates me over his lap. He holds me until my sobs taper off and I've collected myself.

I reach over and close the journal. "I think the answers to all my questions are in these journals. We need to get out of here before the storm hits. Can you help me carry these to the truck?" My voice is hoarse and broken. I extract myself from his lap, deciding to come back another day to tackle everything else.

"Sure." He places a kiss on my temple, then I hand him the stack of journals.

Even though I'm heartbroken, a sense of peace settles over me as I lock up the house and make my way to the truck. I plaster on a smile of gratitude as Cal opens my door, even though I don't feel like smiling at all. Once we're both in the truck, he takes my hand and kisses my knuckles.

"What do you need from me? What can I do?" His eyes trace my face as he holds my hand with both of his to his lips.

I exhale a long breath. "Will you stay with me?"

"I was planning on it."

Cal coasts down the drive to begin our journey back home as I reflect on my dad's words. I think back to the paparazzi surrounding us. That situation must have been so scary for Tucker. Hell, it scared the heck out of me. They still follow me around, but they don't get close anymore.

I exhale a resigned sigh as understanding washes over me. Seeing my son on the ground like that was . . . terrifying. I don't know why I've never thought to hire private security for Tucker.

I'm lost deep in thought when the tail end of Cal's truck fishtails. Grabbing ahold of the door, my heart leaps into my throat, "Oh my god!" I let out a gasp.

"You alright, Angel?"

"Yep. Just wondering who it is that can't drive for shit." I chuckle, trying to ease the tension.

Freezing rain is drizzling down on the roads, and they're becoming slick. I know it's not Cal's fault the truck skidded off to the side like that, but damn, I almost had a heart attack. He jumped off the interstate once we got closer to home. I argued with him because, duh, the state is more likely to salt the interstates than the side streets, but what do I know? I'm just a country bumpkin with little experience with how the state of New York handles the roads. I understand where he's coming from, though. He said he witnessed a terrible pileup on the highway a couple of years back and would rather us slide off the road than be smashed by several vehicles. I'm surprised he didn't just take us to a hotel for the night.

"Thirty more minutes until we're home." He grips the steering wheel tight, his knuckles turning white. We're about fifteen miles from my house, but he's driving about twenty to thirty miles an hour.

I blow out a puff of air and try to take my racing mind off of the hazardous road conditions. A lot can happen in fifteen miles with how this rain is freezing so fast. Even though he's driving like a grandpa, I'm genuinely scared.

We have snow and ice storms in Oklahoma, but they're usually mild. I can count on one hand how many times we've had a major ice storm in my twenty-seven years, and that's maybe twice. I remember a particularly bad one when trees and power lines were snapping left and right. Now, at the news of winter weather, people run to the grocery store to buy out bread and milk, leaving the shelves barren, as if the icepocalypse is bearing down on us.

I think that stems from the one and only ice storm that had us out of power for an entire week. I can't really remember how old I was; I might have been ten at the time. I woke up one morning to pouring down rain and no power. River and Marcy drove their side-by-side to our house, and we all had a weeklong slumber party. We huddled up in front of the fireplace, keeping warm, playing games, and roasting marshmallows. Mom and Marcy cooked our meals over the fire and found interesting ways to keep us entertained. It's one of my favorite memories.

"I have a question."

"Hit me with it."

"You don't have to answer this one if it's too hard."

He side-eyes me. "I'll try."

I worry my bottom lip and fiddle with the air vents to give myself something to do. "What's the one memory you don't ever want to let go of?"

"Oh, this should be fun," he laughs with a playful smile on his face.

"You totally don't have to answer," I tell him.

He shakes his head. "No, I'm game. Am I allowed to use two memories in conjunction with each other?"

"Sure," I shrug. "Why not?" I beam.

These past couple of weeks, Cal has been opening up and sharing more about his life, but I still tread carefully.

"The moment you got smart with me about knowing who I was, combined with Tuck's 'Do you know who he is? He's Callan Miles.' Now, that . . . was funny shit. I could hold on to the look on your face for the rest of my damn life."

I roll my eyes. "I shouldn't have even asked."

We slide to a stop at a stop sign, and he turns his head toward me. "I'm kidding." He sighs, "The one memory I would most hold onto is the moment Tuck stood on the ice and asked me to teach him to play hockey."

My head jerks back, and a frown tugs at my brows. "W—why? There must be better memories to choose from."

"Nope." He turns the heat up and continues ahead. "That's the one."

Well, that's unexpected. I figured there would be a memory of his late wife, and maybe there is, but he doesn't want to talk about it. "But why? I mean, it's not the most sentimental memory."

"Well, it kinda is. That was the moment everything changed for us, and that's the moment Tuck became mine."

"Tuck became yours . . ." I repeat.

"Yup." He pops the p. "That moment led me to falling in love with you."

First, he's talking about us moving in together, and now he's placing his claim on my son? What's next? Marriage and babies? This is all moving too fast. I don't even know if we are going to last. Don't get me wrong; I want us to. I love this man with my whole heart, but what if he decides to sign on with another team clear across the country?

His contract is up for renewal, and all I've heard from his agent is that they are considering their options. If he takes another contract, it's not as if I'm in a position to just up and move. I have responsibilities here: to my team and to Tucker.

"You're quiet. What's on your mind?"

Before I can answer, my phone rings. Mom's name flashes on the screen. I press the green accept button and place her on speaker. "Hi, Mom."

"Thank God. How close are you? The roads are beginning to freeze, and the news is talking about a pileup on I-278."

Cal raises an eyebrow as if to say, I told you so. "Hi Katherine. We're almost home. I'm taking it slow, but we'll be there in about five to ten minutes," he says.

"Okay, sweetheart. See y'all when ya get here. Be safe." The phone beeps three times, indicating she's disconnected the call.

"My God, you two are so country." He laughs.

God, he has a nice laugh and pretty teeth. Hockey guys aren't supposed to be model gorgeous or have pretty teeth. That thought strikes up another question.

"Why do the guys on the team call you Smiley?"

He laughs. "Well, did you ever see me smiling when you first met me?"

"No. Absolutely not."

We slide to another stop sign just outside of our estate. He turns his head and winks. "Exactly. It was Carter who started it. My last name is Miles, and usually teammates would put a y on that, but since I was a brooding asshole . . ."

"Carter named you Smiley," I finish for him. "That's clever. So if you weren't a broody ass, then they would have called you Miley?" A laugh bursts from my lips.

"Milesy, and don't you start that shit. It's already bad enough that the guys call me Smiley," He laughs.

"I like Miley better . . . Ooh, or I could just call you Cyrus."

He side-eyes me with a glare.

I throw my hands up. "What? No one would even know what's going on. I could confuse the hell out of everyone. It could be our thing."

"It will not be our thing. Hotshot is our thing." He peeks over and shakes his head. "You just wait until I get you home."

"Okaaay, Billy Ray."

He shakes his head, and we both bust up laughing as we pull up to the security booth at our estate. The security guard is absent. Cal presses a code into the keypad, and the gate opens.

We finally arrive home and burst through the door laughing. Both of us are soaked and shivering. "I'll grab us a towel. Just go to the laundry room and strip off that shirt."

"Oh good, you're both home safe." My mom comes around the corner. She lowers her voice, "Tucker is in his room. Something at school upset him, and he won't talk to me."

I run upstairs, with Cal following behind me, and open Tucker's door. "Hey, buddy."

Tucker lays on his bed tossing a hockey puck in the air before catching it. "Hi, Mom."

"Hey, Tuck." Cal walks into the room and sits in the desk chair next to Tucker's bed. "What's going on?"

"It's stupid."

I pinch my bottom lip, look to Cal, then back to Tucker. "Well, if it's so stupid, then why are you so upset?" I sit on the end of his bed; the mattress squeaks under my weight as I shift.

Tucker rolls his eyes. "You wouldn't understand."

"Okay, so you don't want to talk to me about it. I'll give you some space." I lift myself from the bed. When I make it to the door, I stop and look over. Cal hasn't moved.

He leans back and spreads out in the chair, making no attempt at following me. I leave them and walk to my master bathroom. Pulling a couple of towels out of the cabinet, I lay them on the counter. A hot shower sounds nice right about now. I strip out of my wet clothes and step into the shower. The water stings at first, but my body soon adjusts.

Grabbing my lavender wash, I scrub my body, noticing the bruising love bites Callan left behind between my legs. The small bruises on my thighs are purple and a good reminder of where he's been. A smile spreads across my face as I think back to last night. I'm deliciously sore.

I step out of the shower, dress, then make my way back to Tucker's room, where I stand outside the door, eavesdropping.

"I feel so stupid," Tucker's voice carries into the hallway along with the sound of controllers clicking. "Oh man, no, go back the other way; you can attack from the side."

"You're not stupid. You're the smartest kid I know."

"And just how many kids do you know?"

"A lot, and not a single one of them is as smart as you."

The hallway is met with silence, so I take that as my cue to move toward the room but stop when Cal begins to speak again.

"Look, Tuck." He releases a deep breath, and the game silences. "That kid's delivery could have been a lot better. Actually, it wasn't his place to say anything at all, but some kids are just assholes. My question is, does it matter? I'm right here, choosing you every single day. I do the same things with you." Tucker remains quiet.

"You don't have to answer that. I've been where you are, and I understand where you're coming from. You know, I didn't have a dad either until I was adopted."

"You were adopted?"

"Yeah." Callan's voice is hoarse and a little broken. "He's the best man I know. When I was a teenager and would see my friends with their fathers, I would get jealous that I didn't know my own. But, when I grew older, I realized that the man who adopted me chose me, and how awesome is it for someone to handpick you to be their son?"

"You would be the best dad." Tucker says. "I just wish that you dating my mom made you my dad."

My chest aches, and a tear falls down my cheek. I wipe it away with the back of my hand. Damn it! My heart breaks for my son.

Why? Why does this keep happening? This generational bondage just keeps repeating over and over, and I'm sick of it. I'm just glad Cal was able to talk him through whatever the kid said to upset him. I hear the game start back up again and decide to head downstairs to talk to my mom about the journals and give the boys time together.

I find Mom sitting at the island, her mind elsewhere, with a mug in her hand. "Hi, Mama."

She jumps, and her hand flies to her chest. "Dear lord, Aspen. You scared me half to death."

I saunter into the kitchen and pull a mug out of the cabinet, filling it with coffee. "Lost in thought?" I place the coffee pot back on the warmer and sit beside her.

"Just worried about you and Tucker. I messed everything up good. I'm truly sorry, sweetheart. I know today was hard for you. It seems like it was a hard day for Tucker too." She holds her mug in both hands, turning it this way and that.

"Well, I didn't know it at the time, but I think I've found closure where my dad is concerned. I just want it to end here in this very moment. I'm afraid I'm always going to struggle with abandonment issues, but I'm going to work on that. I think I'm going to hire a sports psychologist for the team. I'll find someone who is willing to take me on too. I also think it's time to put Tucker in counseling."

She sips her coffee, the steam rising from her mug. "You think Cal will take advantage of that opportunity?"

I shrug, "I don't know, but at least a counselor will be available if he chooses to. I shouldn't have been eavesdropping, but from what I gathered, Tuck thought by me dating Cal, it made Cal his dad. Like, where did that even come from?"

"Well." Mom moves my hair from my shoulder. "He probably has friends with step-parents. That would be my guess."

I huff a breath. "Maybe. Cal called him 'his' on the way home, and it scared me. I internally freaked out. Why do I think every man is going to walk away, Mom? It's a genuine fear of mine."

Mom stands and walks to the sink, dumps out her coffee, then washes her mug. "Why is that a bad thing? Him claiming Tucker, I mean. He has been a father figure to him for the past six months now, and he hasn't let him down yet. What makes you so sure he's going to? Those boys have a bond so deep that I can guarantee you, without a shadow of a doubt, that if something happened between you two and y'all broke up, he would continue to fill that role."

"I would," Cal's voice comes from behind me, causing our heads to turn. Fuck my life, he just heard all of that. He leans over and kisses me on the top of my head. "But nothing is going to happen, and we aren't breaking up . . . ever; not as far as I'm concerned, so you can go ahead and cast those fears aside. I love him, Angel, and I love you. I'll remind you as many times as I have to that I'm not going anywhere."

Mom winks, then sits down beside me. "See? Now, tell me how today went."

I fill her in on the journals sitting in the backseat of Cal's truck and tell her about the house. "He loved you, baby. I know you don't understand why he did . . ."

I cut her off, "Mom. I get it. I don't agree with it, but I understand it. You both did what you thought was best. I can respect that. It doesn't mean I have to like it, though, and it doesn't mean your choices didn't mess me up."

"I'm sorry," she whispers.

I need to come to terms with this. I need to move on and stop letting this hold me back. Ultimately, it is what it is, and I have to stop holding it over my mom's head. It's time to move forward and start putting that part of my life behind me.

"I know." I stand and wrap my arms around her. "I forgive you, Mom. I know you had the best of intentions at heart. I love you for that."

Tears slide down my mom's cheek. "Thank you."

I wipe her tears. "Don't cry, Mama. It's time to heal and move on. I don't know about you, but we've had a long, emotional day, so Cal and I are going to bed." I kiss her forehead then give her another hug.

"Goodnight."

"Goodnight," we both say in unison as Cal takes my hand and leads me upstairs.

Chapter Twenty Eight

Aspen

With her jaw on the floor, River sits next to me, watching Carter, who is positioned in our direct view, no less. "Oh. My. God. They do this at every game, and I've been missing it?"

I burst out laughing. "They have to stretch their hip flexors, so they don't pull something. Yes, they do this at every game, River, where have you been?" The cold air coming off the ice hits me; I shiver and huddle closer to River to steal some of her body heat.

Tilting her head to one side, she studies Carter's movements and answers, "Obviously not in the right place at the right time. Jesus. If his hips can move like that . . ." She nods toward him. "I can't even imagine what he's like . . ." She trails off.

"In bed?" I laugh, finishing for her. I cast a glance around, finding a couple sitting a few seats over and a row back. I lean in, cup River's ear, and whisper low, "I can't speak for Carter; all I know is Cal did this hip roll thing last night that had me chanting God's name like a priest at an exorcism."

"That good, huh?" She doesn't take her eyes off of Carter as he tilts and rolls his hips in a thrusting motion.

Carter changes up his routine, first stretching out one leg and then the other, before bringing them back in and moving them from side to side. And just when I think he's about to wrap up this little show of exhibitionism, he does something I would never expect: He settles into middle splits.

"Wow." River's eyes flash wide.

"Wow, is right. You have no idea. Those stretches aren't just good for the ice." I turn my body to face her. "I thought you didn't like Carter."

"I didn't." Her head swivels my way. "I don't."

"Uh-huh. Don't worry, your secret is safe with me." I giggle and toss her a wink.

Carter skates over to the glass and taps on it, attracting River's attention. "Did you like the show, Kitten? That was all for you." His voice is muffled through the plexi, but he speaks loud enough so we can understand him. He places his fist over his heart. "I'm playing this game for you, baby. See you at home."

He blows her a kiss.

She rolls her eyes.

He points at her. "Keep practicing that for later," he calls out.

River stands up and cups her hand around her mouth, "In your dreams, Fight Club," she yells.

"Uh. Want to tell me what that's all about? What's going on between you two?" I look from her back to Carter as he skates off.

"Absolutely nothing."

"Mmhmm. That didn't look like nothing."

Mom and Tucker catch my periphery when they walk down the last two steps and make their way to their seats. I usually sit in the owner's suite, but Tucker wanted to be closer to the action tonight. Mom and Tucker plop down beside me, each with a popcorn and drink in hand. "Oh good, we didn't miss anything," Mom says.

River and I look at each other; both of us bark out a laugh. Mom raises a brow. I lean over, keeping my voice low so Tucker doesn't hear me. "Carter was stretching and doing hip thrusts for River. I think they have a thing."

"We DO NOT have a thing. Like, at all. It was just entertaining." She throws her hands up in defense.

"See you at home, *Kitten*," I mock in my most masculine voice. "I'm playing this game for you, baby."

"We bumped into each other on the elevator. Thanks for the warning, by the way." She changes the subject, rolling her eyes.

"Ooh, practicing already," I tease.

"Did you know?" She leans over me and steals a handful of popcorn from Mom.

"Know what? That you have the hots for Carter, but you won't admit it? Yep, hit my radar."

"No, you idiot." She laughs. "That he lives in my building," she says, tossing a few pieces of popcorn in her mouth.

My eyes widen. "I'm sorry. What?"

"You heard me," she says with a mouthful, covering her mouth with her hand. Her eyes squint in accusation. If I knew Carter lived in her building, I would have told her. Though, I wish I could've seen her expression when she found out.

"Wow! Okay. I did not see that coming. Um. No. I didn't know that." I stumble over my words, "Why wasn't that the first thing out of your mouth today? Actually, why didn't you immediately call me? When did this happen?"

"I found out this morning."

I want to continue this conversation, but seats begin to fill around us. The players have finished their warmups and are back in the locker room until time for introductions. The atmosphere is a mixture of excitement and tension—our section overflows with spectators wearing black and red jerseys.

Die-hard fans stand to the left of us with beers in hand. All five of their faces are painted black and red. Whoops and cheers climb to a deafening decibel as the lights dim and rock music blares from the speakers surrounding the arena. Suddenly, the music stops, and the jumbotron begins to play a new hype video for The New York Blaze.

At first the video is distorted: white noise scratches and a static screen scrambles in and out with a silhouetted man. Flames ignite in the background as the person finally comes into focus. Standing with his arms crossed against his chest is a tall, intimidating man wearing an old-style white goalie mask with a thin red strip on each cheek. A black hoodie is pulled up over his head, concealing his hair. He tilts his head this way and that, tauntingly.

"You forgot your manners the last time we met. I'm here for retribution, and rest assured, you will be punished." The distorted voice says menacingly as the crowd screams. The video flips from the masked man to highlight reels before switching back to the masked man. I know it's one of my players, but with the voice changer, I can't tell which one—at least, not until the real voice for the masked man says, "Now, it's time to turn up the heat." My heart stops, and my core throbs.

Realization dawns that the fans are not the only ones he's trying to hype up, and our opponent is not the only one who he's promising punishment to—it's me. I swallow thickly. The crowd goes berserk, oblivious to his little polysemantic speech.

River bumps her shoulder against mine. "What did you think?"

My head shakes in disbelief at Cal's very public display of promising retribution for the backtalk I did last night. I school my expression and turn to her, "Holy shit, River, I'm in shock. You did that?" I yell over the chanting and cheering, pointing at the Jumbotron.

River has been stepping into a more vital marketing role here recently.

"It was a joint effort," she yells back, "That was all for you, and it was Cal's idea." She laughs. "He said you would love it."

I bet he did. She rambles on excitedly, not realizing Cal's intentions or his fucked-up type of foreplay, but I do. Holy shit.

I force my focus back in front of me. Pictures of each player are projected below onto the ice as they are announced and skate to the center of the arena. This is the last game, and if we win this, we make it into the playoffs.

Once the introductions are made, the starters line up to face off while the other players skate to the bench. The puck drops. Our opponent wins the faceoff. Their center passes the puck back to a winger. Carter is on him in a millisecond and plucks the puck from him, then makes a long pass to Cal. Cal passes to Aiden. Aiden passes it back to Cal. He passes to Carter, who shoots it right between the goalie's legs and into the goal.

Carter skates past us, blows River a kiss, pats his heart, and points to her.

"Oh my God." A girl in front of us squeals to her friend, "Did you see that?"

River rolls her eyes. "It wasn't for you, fucking puck bunny," she mumbles under her breath.

I rear my head back. "What the—? River! What has gotten into you?" I frown.

River has never been the possessive and jealous type. I have a sneaking suspicion that something is going on between those two. She's never kept secrets from me. "You gotta give me something," I say over the roaring crowd and eye her curiously.

She bursts out, "We almost kissed. Okay? God, I can't hold it in any longer." She huffs a sigh. "Actually, I almost kissed him." River palms her forehead. "God, he's just so . . . urgh . . . so persistent . . . and . . . and . . . and . . ."

"And hot?" I finish for her.

"Yes, and hot . . ." She trails off, waving her hand around, unable to form a coherent sentence. "I mean, look at him: with his sexy-ass dimples and his hot-as-sin body—"

"Okaaaay. How about we talk about this when we don't have networks, gossip rags, and fans milling around the facility?"

"Can we just not? I don't want to talk about it anymore. It almost happened, but it didn't, and it will *never* happen again. We can just forget

I even said anything." A blonde lock falls into her face. She huffs a breath of air, blowing the hair from her eyes. If she thinks I'm going to drop this, she's wrong; dead wrong.

I'm reeling even though Cal called it a long time ago. We made a bet, and that six-month mark is quickly approaching. Instead of concentrating on the game, my eyes are trained on Cal, both on and off the ice. His skates slice through the ice in graceful movements. He's hypnotizing.

Even though we gained an easy goal within seconds, the other team has held us off the rest of the time. The game is minutes away from being over; we're only up by one point. Cal skates up the center. One of the opponents tries to check him, but he ducks away, passing the puck to Trevor.

As Cal passes, another guy slashes the stick across Cal's stomach. It looks like an accident, as if the guy was just trying to reach for the puck, but a penalty is called, and we go into a power play. We're only minutes away from victory. If they can hold them off from scoring for just three more minutes, we'll have it in the bag.

Our guys move into umbrella formation, and Cal faces off again in the circle. Sticks clash as he pushes the puck to the left side to Aiden. For the next couple of minutes, the puck passes back and forth between us and the opposing team. The damn thing is moving so fast, my eyes can't stay trained on who has possession until it comes over to our side against the boards directly in front of us. Trevor and another guy are fighting for the puck against the boards, their sticks clacking as they tangle with each other. Everything happens so fast. Carter comes in to assist and checks the other player. The guy shoves Carter. Carter rears back his fist. River stands to leave. Carter suddenly drops his fist and backs away with his hands up. River sits back down.

"Um. Can anyone fill me in on what's going on?"

River shrugs. "He asked me why I wouldn't give him a chance." She points to the ice, "I told him that was why."

A frown pulls at my brows. "River, that's not fair. He's not Jax. Just because he's what you would consider to be violent on the ice doesn't mean he is like that when he is off the ice. Fighting is part of the game. You know he would never hurt you, right?"

She stands and looks down at me. "Of course, I know that . . . because I'll never give him the chance to." I watch her as she climbs the stairs.

Just as those words fly from her mouth, the game ends and the buzzer sounds. Our fans go nuts, screaming and jumping up and down. We're in the playoffs, and everyone is losing their shit. I can't even enjoy the celebration because I've just upset my best friend.

We all stand up and make our way toward the locker room entrance to wait for the players to emerge. They usually head to the gym for a postgame workout. With this win under our belt and playoff games on the horizon, I'm sure Luke will release all the guys so they can celebrate. While we wait, I chat with our fans and sign autographs. It isn't long until Luke appears from the locker room.

"Katherine?" Luke says to Mom, and her attention is immediately drawn from the conversation she's having to him.

"Excuse me," she says to the lady and takes the few steps in his direction. "Luke, it's so good to see you again."

Luke gives my mom a hug. "It's good to see you too."

Uh, what? Wait! Hold the damn phone! They have only met a couple of times, and now they are familiar enough to hug each other? I mean, my mom is a hugger, but Luke? My head volleys back and forth between them as they stare at each other, and an awkward silence lingers in the air.

I break the tension I feel coming off them in waves. "Good game tonight, Coach."

"Thanks." He clears his throat. "Have you seen Hannah around?"

I try to peek over the crowd surrounding us to look for her. "I haven't seen her. Want me to text her real fast?"

"No." He shakes his head. "That's okay. She's around here somewhere. I'll go find her." He returns his attention to my mom. "So how long are you in town?"

"Oh, I live here now." She moves her purse up on her shoulder, cuts a glance my way, then focuses back on Luke.

He raises his arm and looks at his watch. "Well, I better go find Hannah. We have dinner reservations."

"Be safe," I call out just as Mom says, "It was good to see you again, Luke," with a flirtatious smirk.

I roll my eyes. Oh, for Pete's sake. "Mom," I scold.

She playfully bumps against me and whispers. "What?" She dramatically shrugs one shoulder.

"Nothing." I shake my head, looking for Cal.

"I'm starving, Mom. Can we go now?" Tucker interrupts and pulls at my sleeve.

Mom ruffles his hair. "How about I take you? We'll grab the greasiest burger we can find on our way home while your mom finishes up here." Her eyes meet mine. "You good with that?"

"Yeah." I nod. "Thanks, Mom."

I tell them goodbye and try to call Cal but receive no answer.

I pace back and forth in front of the locker room doors. I wait . . . and I wait . . . and I wait. An hour has passed, and the players have all trickled out of the building—gone out to celebrate, no doubt. The arena is mostly empty, aside from the janitor, Aaron, who is packing up, and Liam, the Zamboni driver, who has just resurfaced the ice and is putting the machine away. I tap my foot impatiently, checking the time on my cell. I try calling Cal again to no avail. I swear to God, if he left me . . . I shake my head. He wouldn't do that. He wouldn't leave me here stranded.

All the facility lights click off, and the ambient lights kick on. My heart kicks up to hyper-speed. "Hey!" I yell, stepping out of the little alcove concealing me and back into the arena. "Hey!" I call out again, trying to garner someone's attention. My voice echoes through the empty space, but all I'm met with is silence. Fuck! What did Cal do? Go out the back? And why the fuck would he leave me here?

Pissed off, I stomp back to the locker room and sling the door open. I'm greeted with pitch black. Okay, now I'm creeped out. I blame it on all those horror movies River and I would marathon-watch as teenagers. This is exactly how they start. I shiver at the thought.

Trekking up the stairs toward the exit, I catch sight of a figure standing in the announcer's box, backlit by a glowing red light. I start to run up the steps to get their attention. I hate the dark, and knowing I'm not alone gives me a sense of security.

That is until I close the distance between us. All the blood rushes to my head, and dizziness overtakes me when I see the hockey mask tilting to one side, looking at me, as if he's the predator and I'm the prey. In the back of my mind, I know it's Callan, but the way he's staring at me unmoving is freaking me the fuck out. I walk backwards down the steps, backing away slowly.

My breaths come in rapidly as adrenaline and excitement course through my veins. He slowly stalks out of the booth and stands facing me on the steps.

"Run, Angel."

Holy fuck! I turn and run as fast as I can down the stairs and into the hallway. I bypass the locker room. That would be the first place he would look. I try to push various doors open, only to find them locked. I don't have time to fiddle with my keys. *Fucking Aaron. Goddamnit!* The gym has no door, so I can run in there. No—the space is open and offers no hiding spot. Think. Think. Think. He's going to round that corner any second. I have no choice but to dart inside the weight room. Slow, heavy footsteps echo down the hallway as they approach. My back hits the wall.

Fuck. My heart races in excitement at the thought of what he'll do to me once he catches me. The footsteps stop at the open doorway. I slap a hand over my mouth to conceal my rapid breathing.

His feet shuffle; then he continues walking down the hallway. I think I'm in the clear, so I sprint to the middle of the room, quickly turning around in a circle to look for someplace to hide. Fuck. Fuck. Fuck. Bingo. I look behind me as I head for the door to the equipment room. I don't even care that it's bathed in complete darkness at this point. I ease the door open and quickly close it behind me. Leaning back against the door, I take in ragged breaths.

I know it's just a matter of—

"You know . . ."

A gasp flies out of my mouth, and my hand soars to my chest.

"I was thinking you would play a little harder to get. You made this game entirely too easy, like herding sheep to the slaughter." Cal's hard length presses into my hip as he crowds my space. A combination of his cologne and body wash wafts in the air around me. The woodsy smell makes me delirious. An electric current shoots right through me, causing my core to throb. An aching need builds within me.

The lights flicker on, and Cal stands in only a goalie mask and worn jeans hanging low on his hips—showing off that sexy V. He grips the hair on the back of my head and tilts my head back. My eyes lock with his through his mask. "I see the way you bite your lip and how your feet rub together when something in your smutty little book turns you on. I would have never guessed that my sweet angel would have such a dark side. Masked men, Aspen?" He tsks, "You are a filthy little whore, aren't you?"

Cal removes the mask and tosses it to the ground. "I would keep it on, but I want you to witness what you do to me when I fuck this pretty little mouth." He growls, then squats down, removing my shoes and socks before peeling my jeans and panties down my legs.

His hands glide up my body as he stands. "I'm sad to see this go too, but I really want to see these gorgeous tits." He slowly removes my Blaze jersey with his name on the back and my bra. "Did it excite you to be chased by a masked man?"

"Yes," I breathe.

He teases my lips. "Did I absolve your curiosities?"

I moan in response as he takes a nipple into his wet mouth. He moves to my other breast, biting down just enough to cause a sting before soothing it with his tongue. "Did my little adrenaline junky receive her fix?"

"Cal," I moan, in desperation.

I never thought I would experience what the hype was all about, the thrill of being chased, of not knowing when he was going to pop up out of nowhere . . . of being caught, but my boyfriend seems to understand the assignment.

"On your knees. Take me out."

I do exactly as he says. I go to my knees, unbutton his pants, then take him out.

"I want these red lips wrapped around my cock. I want to feel you gag and choke until the tears are running down your gorgeous face," he demands, pulling down my bottom lip with his thumb.

"Lick," he commands.

I lick the tip of his cock; a bead of precum hits my taste buds, and I revel in the taste of him.

Cal tilts his head back and closes his eyes as I take him into my mouth. "Fuck, Angel. Your mouth is sinful."

He grabs the back of my head and forces himself deeper. My eyes close tight as I try to open my throat, but still, I gag from the obstruction.

"You can do it . . . yeah, just like that . . . you're taking my cock so well . . . don't stop."

I pull back, relaxing the back of my throat, then swirl the tip of my tongue around the head of his cock before taking him deeper. His eyes lock with mine when I look up at him. I relish in the pleasure shown on his face.

"This goddamn mouth was made for me to fuck." His hand slaps the wall, and he begins to pump into my mouth unforgivingly. I sputter and try to pull back, but he grabs the back of my head again and holds me in place. Saliva is pouring down my chin, and tears run down my cheeks.

"Touch yourself. Slip your fingers in your wet pussy and let me watch you play."

Never having someone watch me before makes me hesitant, a bit insecure, and embarrassed. I ignore his demand and brace my hand on his thigh.

"Nuh-uh. I told you to play with yourself, Angel, and that's exactly what you're going to do. Now, stick your hand between your legs and rub your clit. Make yourself cum for me, and you better do it quickly because I'm close."

I push my insecurities aside and do as I'm told. Knowing that I'm pleasing him—making him lose his mind—is such a turn-on; it doesn't take me long before I'm on the brink of tumbling over the cliff.

"You're going to swallow every last drop. Now, cum for me, Angel," he growls.

His voice tilts me over the edge. The room dims and my eyes close. Blood rushes to my head, leaving me to feel as if I'm floating, then he releases into my mouth. The taste isn't what I expect—not bad, just foreign. I do as he says and swallow, then pull back as he wipes my mouth.

"You're a fucking goddess on your knees for me." Cal strokes my hair. "This mouth is mine." His thumb brushes against my bottom lip. "And these tears are mine. The only way I ever intend to make you cry is out of pleasure or happiness. No one else is allowed to have these tears, understand?" He wipes my tears away and he lifts me up.

Cal puts himself back in his pants and strolls to the cabinet containing the hockey equipment. He reaches up and grabs a plastic tube from the top of a shelf before walking back to me. He opens the clear tube and dumps a new puck with our logo into his hand. "I'm going to fuck you against this wall, but since your cleaning service will be here in . . ." He looks at his watch. "Well, any time now . . . you have to be quiet." He places a kiss on my swollen lips. "Now, open your pretty mouth."

Chapter Twenty Nine

Cal

My woman never ceases to amaze me. Every fantasy, every fucking desire I've ever had, she fulfills them so willingly with no questions asked. With her, anything goes. Prime example: her standing here with a doe-eyed expression, waiting for direction like a good girl, while I hold a hockey puck to her lips.

"Now, open your pretty mouth."

She opens her mouth, and I place the puck between her lips. Damn, I love how submissive and compliant she is, always ready to please me. What she doesn't understand is that pleasing her pleases me. It's why I did what I did tonight: played a game of cat and mouse and stalked her through the facility in a goalie mask. I didn't take it too far; I only wanted to give her a sample to see if fear play and mask play were something she would truly like. Honestly, it would have freaked most women out, but Aspen isn't like most women. After witnessing her consistently reading books with two pages of trigger warnings, I'm finding that my girl is a little darker than most.

When she was lying on the couch with her feet propped on my lap, reading Navessa Allen's *Light's Out*, biting that deliciously plump bottom lip and rubbing her feet together as if she were trying to relieve an ache between her legs, I knew she was reading a spicy scene. A few days later, I added her novel to my collection of stolen ones from her bookshelf and devoured the pages within a couple of days. I want to know her carnal urges and peculiarities. I don't ever want Aspen to feel as if she needs to hide herself from me. Her fantasies are mine to fulfill; her kinks are mine to unlock. I want to make every single one of them a reality and watch her unfurl like a fucking flower.

With her mouth gagged, I spin her around to face the wall. Both hands slap against the black-painted surface to brace herself.

"This is going to be rough and fast. You're going to take it, and you're not going to make a fucking peep. Those sounds you make, they're mine—just like you're mine."

The chances of her being quiet are slim, but if she knows what's good for her, she'll do as I say. If her cleaning crew has made it in, the last thing I want is for them to hear her or stumble upon us fucking. My girl seems to be a bit of an exhibitionist. I know she's fantasized about being fucked in a public place, but her pussy belongs to me. No one gets to see what's mine. That's why I waited until everyone left. It's a win-win scenario.

I take myself out of my pants, then bend her over, and tease her wet slit with the head of my cock. Slowly, I slide inside her, giving her time to adjust. She moans loudly around the puck as I fill her.

"Shh," I warn her, reaching around and pinching her nipple.

I slide my hand up to grip her throat as I deliver on my promise. The sound of our bodies slapping together echoes throughout the room. She looks back at me—her teeth clenched tight around the puck, whimpering around it. Sweat streams down my abs, and I work her body hard, fucking her roughly. Knowing she's close, my fingers squeeze her throat. She loves when I restrict her airways; it makes her erupt and pool like a fucking volcano within seconds every single time. Puck still in place, she screams a muffled explosion of pleasure as she cums.

From behind the door, I hear a squeak coming from one of the cleaning carts.

I twist her hair around my hand, jerking her head back. "Behave." My movements still, and I torture her clit with my fingers. "Do you want me to stop?"

Her head shakes back and forth vigorously. I pound into her, bringing her to the brink of another orgasm, then I pull out of her. She whimpers, then spits the puck out of her mouth, gasping deeply for air. I smirk.

"Don't fucking stop," she breathily demands.

"Did I tell you to spit that out? I think it's cute that you think you're my boss right now just because we're at work. Look at you, telling me what to do, or in this case what not to do."

Knowing she likes the thrill of being caught, of being watched, I decide to give it to her with the cleaning crew on the other side of the door. I lift her against the wall; her legs cinch around my waist. I thrust into her over and over, harder and harder, bringing her right to the edge.

"Fuck, Cal," she cries out. I quickly swallow her moans, caressing my tongue with hers, then I bite her lip. She's just about to tip over when I still and empty inside her.

"Fucking asshole," she growls in frustration.

"Maybe you need to stop being a brat. We both know when I get you home . . ." I lean over and speak low in her ear. "You." My lips trail down her throat. "Will be." I lick and suck her pulse point, then trail my lips back up to her ear. "A good fucking girl for me and do what you're told." My knuckles hold her chin. "Do you want to know how I know?"

"How?" She pants.

I nip her bottom lip, then give it a suck before releasing it from my mouth. "Because you want to cum again." I swipe my thumb over her bottom lip. "And only good girls get to cum. Isn't that right, Angel?" I wink. "You are going to be a begging, blubbering mess by the time I get done with you." I take her hand. "If you want to finish what we've started, you need to get dressed. The cleaning crew will come in here any minute."

Once Aspen is dressed, I crack the door a little to look both ways. With the thrill of someone catching us, we dart out of the equipment room, run down the hallway, and into the arena like two teenagers. Not that it matters if we're caught since she owns the damn place, but if they heard her on the other side of that door, I would rather them not know who those sounds were coming from. She giggles as I chase her up the stairs and through the exit to the parking lot. I grab her by the waist from behind and swing her around. Her laughter rings into the cold night air. I place her back on her feet and slap her ass before giving her a kiss.

God, I can't wait to take her home and do unspeakable things to her.

The last few days have been complete chaos. Between work, grueling practices, Tuck's games, and Aspen helping her mom find a new home, we haven't had much time together. We're on the road for the next four days for playoff games, but the good news is Aspen, Tuck, and Katherine are traveling with the team this time. Road games are tough for me. When they're not with me, I feel like I'm losing control; sometimes I have full-blown panic attacks. Even though we won't see much of each other, at least I know they're safe, and if something were to happen, I'm close by. Laughter fills the Suburban. Tuck and Katherine are in the backseat cutting up as the hired driver takes us from the airport to the hotel.

Lost in thought, and a little nervous about tonight, I look out the window. We pass the benches I once slept on, and I quickly turn my head. I would go through everything in life a thousand times over if it led me to this remarkable woman sitting beside me, but I don't want to relive it right now and kill the excitement coursing through me.

I squeeze Aspen's hand and kiss her knuckles. "I love you."

Fuck, she's gorgeous.

"Love you too, Hotshot."

Looking back at Tuck, he gives me a silly face, and we both burst out laughing. I love that kid. I want to give him the world, to give him the life he deserves with a dad who loves him. I want more than anything to make Aspen my wife. I want to spend my life loving her, making her laugh, and proving to her that real men stay. Reaching into my jacket pocket, I wrap my fingers around the velvet box, making sure it's right where it's supposed to be for tonight. I decided this would be the best time to propose. I don't want to wait anymore, and since our families are here, I just can't think of any better time.

My phone buzzes in my pocket; I pull it out, then click the green accept button on the screen.

"Hey, Dad."

"Hi, Son. Sorry I couldn't be there to pick you up. I was tied up in coach's meetings all day. I take it you all have arrived safely."

"Yeah." My eyes lock with Aspen's. "We're here. Are we still on for dinner tonight?"

"The reservations have been made. Are you sure you're ready for this?"

"Yep." I respond, facing forward. "Never been more certain of anything in my entire life."

"Alright. I'll see you at seven."

"Can't wait. Bye, Dad."

We pull up to the hotel, exit the vehicle, and help the driver unload our luggage onto the bellman cart. The bellhop rolls our stuff inside as the SUV drives away. We're making our way into the entrance when out of nowhere the media begins to surround us. Chaos erupts as microphones are thrust in our faces and journalists begin barking out questions over each other.

"Mr. Miles, there are rumors surrounding you exploring free agency; are they true?"

"What does free agency mean for you and Miss Taylor?"

"Is it true you are leaving the New York Blaze organization?"

"Miss Taylor, were you aware that Mr. Miles has chosen not to renew his contract with your organization? What does that mean for your relationship?"

As more questions are yelled, Aspen, Tuck, and Katherine stand stunned. Aspen looks to me for answers. I avert my eyes, not wanting her to see the truth in them. Apparently, news travels fast, especially when it's leaked. Aspen's eyes widen. Tuck's head lowers in defeat. She quickly schools her expression and takes Tuck by the hand.

"No comment at this time," she says, pulling him into the lobby.

Fuck, fuck, fuck, fuck. This was not how she was supposed to find out. I was going to have a conversation with her tonight after I proposed.

"Asp—"

Aspen ignores me and walks to the front desk of the lobby with Tuck. Her mom and I trail behind her. I look at Katherine, hoping she will help me out of this mess. She shakes her head. My shoulders fall. I just want to explain myself, but Aspen was completely blindsided, and she's shutting down.

She whips around, "Is it true?" she asks with fire in her eyes.

I don't answer. I don't know the best way to. I'm just mute.

"I need an extra room if you have it, please," she says to the clerk behind the counter.

"Aspen."

She cuts me off, "Not now."

"Please, just—"

She turns around and faces me. Looking around to see if anyone is listening, she lowers her voice, "Cal, I said not now. We are going to talk about this, but it's going to be in a private setting when it's just the two of us. I need to collect my thoughts."

The clerk hands Aspen the extra room key, and she slides it over to me. "Put that in your pocket." I do as she says, slipping the plastic keycard into my pocket. After we exit the elevator, we follow several steps behind the bellhop to the room. I try to hand the keycard to her mom, thinking it's for her, but Aspen covers my hand. I frown in confusion.

"You can stay with us until the bellhop leaves; then you need to go to your own room." She whispers.

My heart sinks. Today has literally gone to shit. I wait as the bellhop places our luggage inside Aspen's suite. She walks directly to a bedroom and closes the door quietly behind her. I sigh deeply, picking up my suitcase and taking it to my new room.

Tossing the luggage onto the bed in my lonely ass hotel room, which is five floors below Aspen's, I pull up my agent's contact. The phone rings once before he answers.

"Cal?"

"It's Mr. Miles today."

He sighs on the other end. "Shit. I'm sorry, man. I left you a voicemail, but I'm guessing you didn't get it. How bad is it?"

"Bad enough your job is in jeopardy."

"It was my new personal assistant. She was in my office when I was talking to you the other day, and she must've run to the media."

"She works for you, right? So, she's obviously signed an NDA. We'll just—"

"It's a little more complicated than that."

"What do you mean?"

"I mean exactly what I said, and before you ask, no, I can't sue her."

"Why the fuck not—?" I release an exasperated breath and pinch the bridge of my nose. "For fuck's sake, Nate, please tell me when you say personal assistant, you mean the kind that actually works for you in a professional manner."

I'm met with silence. "Goddamnit, Nate!" I roar.

"I wasn't thinking, Cal. I'm sorry."

"We're going to chat about what this means for our professional relationship later. In the meantime, this is your mess to clean up, and I expect it to be squeaky fucking clean within the next two hours. I swear to God, Nate, if this fucks things up with Aspen, I will fire your ass with no hesitation. I don't care how far back our friendship goes." I click the red button.

Nate has been my agent since he took over his father's sports management firm. He was a buddy from college and referred me to his dad when I was drafted a decade ago. I still consider him a good buddy, but I have half a mind to fire his stupid ass. There's no telling how many times I've told him that one of those women would eventually cause a problem someday.

Plopping down on the bed, I rest my head back on the oversized pillows. I reach inside my jacket pocket and take out the box. My thumb flips the black velvet lid open and closed, over and over again. I'm lost in a daze thinking about how this day should have gone. Instead of a day filled with happiness and ending with a token of my promise to love Aspen and Tuck forever, my girl is hurting, and there's not a damn thing she will let me do to fix it right now.

Sitting up, I come to terms with the fact that a proposal isn't in the cards for me today. Unzipping my suitcase, I take one last look at the diamond ring before closing the box and tossing it into the side pocket of my luggage. This is so fucked. I pace back and forth in the hotel room, waiting for Aspen to show up. Surely when she said we would talk in private, she meant immediately.

As time slowly passes, I look at my watch; it's already a quarter after five, and it's time to head out to meet my dad if we are going to beat traffic, assuming they're all still going to meet my dad tonight. It's not surprising that after two rings her phone goes to voicemail. Figures she would press the fuck you button on me right now. If she thinks I'm giving up that easily, she is dead fucking wrong. I head to her hotel suite and knock. Katherine opens the door and steps into the hallway.

"Cal, right now isn't a good time."

"I need to explain," I plead.

Katherine takes my hand in both of hers. "I'm sure there's a good explanation for all of this, and she will listen. Just go to dinner with your dad and come back when she's had time to process. Okay?" She pats my cheek. "It'll all work out in the end, Sweetie; give her a little space. She's trying to navigate the emotions of being your girlfriend while being your boss and staying professional. This is a tough position for her to be in, and she needs a minute."

My head drops with my shoulders in defeat. Katherine gives me a hug, and I wrap my arms around her slender frame. She releases me, places a hand on my shoulder, and squeezes. "She loves you, Cal. She'll come around; just give her a little time."

Nodding, I turn around and head back down the hall. I pull out my phone and call my dad.

"Hi, son. Are you guys on your way?"

My heart feels like it's stuck in my throat. What do I tell him? I swallow thickly.

"Dad?" I choke out. Recovering, I mask my emotions with a cough. "I, um . . . I really wanted to see you, but can we take a rain check?"

"Is everything alright?"

"Yeah. Yeah. Everything's fine. Aspen just had something come up that she can't get out of. You know how it is."

"No. That's fine. I have some things I need to do here anyways, so that actually works out."

"Can we do lunch tomorrow?"

"Tomorrow's game day."

"Exactly. Maybe having lunch with me will soften the blow of us kicking your team's ass on your own turf." I chuckle.

"You're a mess, kid. Okay. I'll see you tomorrow. I love you, Son."

"Love you too, Dad."

I press the red dot on my screen, then text Aspen.

Me: I love you, Angel.

As I exit the hotel, I slide the phone into my back pocket. Rain pelts down in sheets, harmonizing with my mood. Stepping out from under the awning, I tilt my head back toward the sky and allow the forceful drops to pour down on me, wishing they could wash away this awful day. Minutes go by before my phone buzzes in my pocket. I duck back under the hotel awning.

Aspen: I love you too.

Drops of water litter my screen from my dripping hair while my fingers fly across the screen.

Me: Can we please talk?
Aspen: Maybe tomorrow. I'm not in a good headspace tonight.
Me: We really should talk about this now.
Aspen: I can't deal with this shit tonight.

I wait for another text to come through, watching the text bubbles dance across the screen then disappear. Fuck this shit. With my mind made up, I storm back inside the hotel.

Chapter Thirty

Aspen

I close the bedroom door behind me and sit on the bed. My head hangs in despair. Why is this happening to me? Just when I thought I could never be happier. My heart aches. Can a heart literally break? Is that even possible? This hurts so damn much. *Fuck!* I should have known getting involved with my player was a very bad move on my part, but I guess you can't help who you fall in love with.

My door flies open, causing me to jump as it slams against the wall. "Why'd you do that, Mom? Why'd you send Cal away?" Tucker cries.

"Baby, now's not the time. I just needed some time to think. You wouldn't understand." Trying to conceal my tears, I turn my head away and wipe my eyes.

"I'm. Not. A. Baby. And I understand more than you think."

I inhale deeply, letting the air fill my lungs, then I count to ten, so I don't lose my patience with Tucker's tone.

"Come sit." I pat the spot beside me.

Tucker moves to sit on the bed, peering up with a glare. What am I supposed to tell him? I don't have all the answers yet, but one thing is for certain: Cal is leaving the team. The deer-in-the-headlight expression on his face when we were confronted by the media confirmed that, not to mention the fact that when I flat-out asked him, he didn't say a fucking word.

For the life of me, I just don't understand why he would keep this from me, especially since he knows my history. The least he could've done was had a conversation with me—prepared me—so I wouldn't have been blindsided. I guess this is what happens when you get involved with your employee. The boss is always the last to find out, right? Fuck. My. Life.

I focus all my attention on Tucker, trying to keep my emotions in check in front of him. "You're right. You're not a baby, so I'm just going to shoot it to you straight. I'm certain Cal is leaving the team. I don't know what that means for our team or for our family. I can't leave the Blaze; if he chooses free agency, I'm not sure what's going to happen. We just need to expect the worst and hope for the best."

"Cal's not going anywhere." He rolls his eyes.

"Look, Tucker. I've had my fair share of experiences—"

"He's not leaving." He shakes his head emphatically.

Deciding not to argue with a ten-year-old little boy, I let it go. I probably shouldn't be telling him anything until I have all the facts anyway because all I have are speculations. I release a breath. "Come here." I hold my arms wide.

Tucker cuddles into me. "You're wrong, Momma."

"God, I hope so, Buddy." I whisper, kissing the top of his head and holding him for a bit. "You okay?" I finally ask.

"I'm fine. Just sad you made Cal leave. I think that was mean."

I don't want to patronize Tucker again by telling him he doesn't understand. Cal and I are supposed to be a team; we're supposed to discuss major decisions with each other.

Tucker jumps up. "Okay, well, I'm going to unpack my X-BOX and hop on Fortnite with Elija."

I nod, trying to keep the tears at bay in front of him. "Okay, close the door behind you, please."

The dam bursts, and the tears fall as soon as the door quietly clicks behind him. I give myself ten minutes to cry before I'm back in boss mode. My team needs me to separate my feelings. Putting my personal life aside, I grab my phone and dial Teagan.

"I was just about to call you. News about Callan just broke over here."

I climb onto the middle of the bed, sit with my legs crisscrossed, holding onto a pillow. "What are they saying?"

"Nothing definitive. Only that his contract is up and that he's decided not to renew his contract with the Blaze organization. They did mention his free agency, but T.T.S.N. is stating they don't have any confirmation, and as of right now, the rumor coming in is that he's retiring. Any idea why that might be?"

"Well, Teagan, I wish I could say that I have the answers, but I don't. All we have are rumors and speculations too. I will say, I think it's true based on his reaction today. The only thing is, I don't know if he's retiring from the league or exploring free agency."

"Have you spoken to him?"

I clear my throat. "No. I will, but I just need a minute to compartmentalize." I release an exasperated sigh. "Go ahead and put out a press release stating that anything heard up to this point is rumor and speculation and the Blaze organization doesn't have clear confirmation on neither Mr. Miles' plans for his future within our organization nor the league at this time. However, we should have more information momentarily, and at that time we will submit a formal announcement. Think that will tide them over?"

"I don't know. You of all people know they can be vultures, but I'll try."

I laugh. Boy, don't I. "Thanks, Teagan."

"You're welcome." The phone beeps, indicating she's hung up.

"So did he say if the rumors were true?" River asks me through the speaker of my phone.

"He didn't have to; his face said it all. God, River. I can't—" My heart feels like it's literally being ripped out of my chest. "I don't want to—" Breaths deep enough to fill my lungs are not coming in; I'm sure I'm having a full-on panic attack. Am I supposed to place my head between my knees,

301

or does that cause you to pass out? Though, maybe passing out wouldn't be such a bad thing right about now. At least then I would be able to escape this pain. "I can't live without him. What if he's decided to explore his free agency and he moves across the country?"

"Aspen, you need to calm down. You haven't even given him a chance to explain anything."

A chime dings through my phone and a notification pops up. "He just texted me." I sniffle.

"What'd he say?"

"Hold on . . ." I click the notification and read his last text. "He basically says that we shouldn't wait to have a conversation." I shoot off a text to him, then continue, "I don't want to talk to him yet. I'm fucking terrified of what he'll say. I want to sit here in my bubble and pretend. You know?" Standing to my feet, I take a ragged breath and pace the area in front of my bed. "Why would he ask me to move in with him if he was just going to leave, River? The thing is I wanted to say yes right then. Can you imagine if I had? God, I would have moved in just to be asked to move right back out."

A knock raps on the door, and Mom peeks her head in. "Luke and Trey are here."

Tears trail down my cheek. I swipe them away with the back of my hand. "I have to go."

"Okay, sis. Talk to Cal. Most importantly, listen to what he has to say before you pop off with that smart mouth of yours. I love you."

"Love you too." The phone beeps, letting me know she's ended the call.

Staring back at me in the full-length mirror is a very broken version of myself. How am I supposed to go out there, face these two men, and be professional? I don't think I have that in me right now. My face is red and splotchy, and I look like a goddamn raccoon. I grab my makeup wipes out of my luggage and begin to wipe the black makeup from under my eyes. It's not perfect, but I guess it will have to do.

Cal is leaving me. I know he is. The media circus outside, Luke and Trey popping in, is all the confirmation I need that I'm losing him. They're probably here to tell me that he isn't renewing his contract or that he's moving to another team across the country. I should have known this was all too good to be true. Like I've said over and over, men don't stick around for me. I shouldn't even be surprised at this point.

Taking another look in the mirror, I give myself a pep talk to stay professional and not cry. I walk out of the bedroom to greet my guest, "Sorry about that. What can I do for you two?" I try to keep my voice cheerful.

"You don't have to do that, kiddo," Luke says, wrapping his arms around me. Of course, I start crying all over again. God, I'm a mess.

Trey takes a seat. "We heard the rumors and thought we'd come by to see if Cal could fill us in on what's going on."

"He's not here." I release Luke and reach for a napkin setting on the counter. Taking a deep breath, I decide there is no better time than now to get down to business.

"I will say from the expression on Cal's face when we were bombarded by the media that we're not dealing with mere rumors here. I think it would be a good idea to start looking at possible draft picks for his position now." My bare feet pad across the carpet as I pace back and forth through the sitting area. "With us being so high in the standings, we're missing out on at least the first twenty-five picks. Look at the farm teams; see who we can bring up. We also need to look at trading up in the draft. Give someone our pick and a future first-round pick to put us higher up in the selection process. Hell, throw in a player as well; I don't care at this point. All I know is I think we're losing our best player, and I want plans: A, B, C, and D. Understood?" I lean against the window with my arms crossed, trying my hardest to stay professional.

"You got it, boss," Trey says, at the same time a loud knock sounds at the door, causing me to damn near jump out of my skin. Mom has already sent Cal away, so I don't know who in the world this could be. Slowly, I open the door before the damn thing slams against the wall. I'm immediately tossed into the air, and my stomach lands on someone's cold, wet shoulder. "Sorry, gentlemen," Cal calls out. "My woman and I have some business to take care of."

Chapter Thirty One

Aspen

"Put me down, you big lug." I pound on his back. "You're soaked."

He slaps my ass hard. Fuck, it stings like fire. "If I put you down, are you going to run back to your suite or follow me to my room?"

I hang upside down as he carries me fireman style through the hallway and into the elevator. "Please, put me down. This is making me nauseous."

He slaps my ass again. "Answer the question."

Once we're in the elevator and trapped inside, I'm finally placed back on my feet. He prowls back and forth in the small space, keeping his eyes trained on me like a caged lion as we ride down in silence. The elevator doors open, and he gently grabs my arm to usher me forward.

The couple entering the elevator as we exit gives us a curious glance as I jerk my arm out of his hold. "I can walk without assistance, you know?" I snap.

Here we are in this swanky hotel with my bare feet padding down the hallway. We stop in front of Cal's room. He swipes his keycard and holds the door open for me. I stand unmoving, scared out of my mind of what he will say once we enter that room. His hand gestures for me to enter. The room is dark, aside from a dim light that glows from the other side of the cracked bathroom door, giving us just enough light to see. With a resigned sigh, I plop down on his bed and wait for him to speak. He pulls dry clothes out of his luggage and strips out of his wet ones. His ripped muscles flex as he changes into shorts, and I have to force myself to look away. I'm too upset right now to even think about how good he looks. My stomach is in knots, and I'm losing my mind, waiting for the worst. I pick at my nail polish, wishing he would just hurry up and speak. Dressed, he leans back against the dresser, scratching the back of his neck.

"What do I have to do to gain your trust, Aspen?"

I stop picking at my nails. "What do you mean by that? I do trust you," I say, frowning in confusion.

"You trust me to walk away like everyone else. You trust that I'll abandon you and Tuck, that I'll leave you both heartbroken."

I stand and close the gap between us, so he can look me in the eyes when he breaks my heart. "Isn't that what you're doing? You're leaving us, right? Going to explore some new team?"

He sighs in exasperation and removes a strand of hair from my face. "You really think that after everything we've been through, after I've poured my soul out to you and given you my whole heart, that I would leave you? That I could leave you?"

I bury my head in his chest and cry. "They said you were exploring free agency. That means changing teams."

"I know what free agency means." He tilts my chin up. "Look at me." He thumbs my tears, wiping them away. "I love you. I am never leaving you. Now, will you please just give me the chance to explain everything?" Taking my hand in his, he leads me to the foot of the bed, sits, then pulls me down to sit in his lap. "I never had intentions of going to another team, but my plan to retire at the end of this season is a different story." He rubs slow circles on my back. "As for the rumors and the media, I was speaking to my agent, Nate, who also happens to be an old buddy from college. We were catching up, you know? Shooting the shit. I assumed he was alone when he had me on speaker. Apparently, he had a girl from one of his clubs at the office doing God knows what, and—"

I put my hand up. "What kind of club?"

Cal stares at me. I tilt my head to the side, studying him with a frown. He tilts his head back as to say, *You know what kind of club.*

Surely, he doesn't mean what I think he means. My eyes widen in disbelief. "Noooo. No way. I thought those only existed in books."

"Yes, they're very real." He chuckles. "Nate owns three of them. One in New York, one in South Florida, and another one in Las Vegas. He spends most of his evenings at the one in Las Vegas where he lives."

"Aren't they illegal?"

"No, darlin', you ain't in Oklahoma anymore," he says in the most exaggerated southern accent.

I snort a laugh. "First of all, that is not how I talk. Thank you very much. And second, that's . . . wow . . . that's actually kinda hot, if I'm being honest." I fan my face.

"Can we get back on track here? As I was saying, she heard the conversation and ran to the media."

"And there's nothing we can do about it?"

"Nate is handling it. Well, I told him to handle it, or I'm firing his ass, but since I'm leaving the league anyway, I guess that threat doesn't hold any real weight."

"Why didn't you tell me you were thinking about retiring?"

"I was going to tell you tonight when we were alone, but then the damn media ruined all my plans." Cal's fingertips feather across my skin as I stare at the different colored blue patterns of the painting hanging on the wall. "For so long, the most important thing to me was hockey. Deep down in my soul, I believed if I didn't win a Stanley Cup, then Paisley died in vain. So, I worked my ass off day in and day out to be the best hockey player in the league." He releases a deep breath. "I can't continue to put that on myself, and I don't want to. Don't get me wrong; I still love the game, but up until recently, I was obsessed with the sport." His fingers tangle with mine. "But now I have a new obsession."

"Yeah?"

"Yeah." His eyes slowly move up to meet mine. "I spent so long hiding from the world that now all I want is to be present in it, to experience everything life has to offer; I want to do that with you by my side."

I twist my lips deep in thought. "I think we need therapy."

"I think you might be right." He laughs, "Will your new sports psychologist see me after I retire?"

I lift my head and stare at him in wonder. "You would do that? You would go to therapy?"

"We're a team, Firecracker." He presses his forehead against mine. "Which means we do what's best for each other. If that means we need therapy, then we'll do it together. I'll always do what I think is best for you. That's one of the other reasons why I decided this season would be my last."

I pull back from him, running my hand down his cheek. His stubble prickles against my palm. "If we're a team, that means we can't just make life-changing decisions without talking it out first. I don't know what gave you the inclination that I'd want you to retire."

"It's not that I thought you wanted that from me; it's what I thought you needed."

"Well, I don't need that. What I want and need more than anything is a life with you." I take a deep breath, working up the courage to tell Cal something I've been keeping from him. "I haven't been one hundred percent transparent with you either." I bite my bottom lip nervously. *He needs to know, Aspen; just spit it out.* "I'm not actually the owner of the team."

Cal's brows furrow in confusion. "What do you mean?"

"Tucker actually owns the team. I have custodianship until he completes college. I've been allowing everyone to believe I'm the owner to protect him. I can't sell off the organization or walk away without it messing with someone's life. My son and my players' livelihoods are literally in the palm of my hand."

I sigh and continue. "The only person who has the authority to sell the organization for a profit is Tucker, and that's not until he's twenty-five. The will basically states: If one of us decides we don't want to run the organization between now and then, all assets of the organization will be sold, and all profits will be donated to a pre-designated charity of my father's choice. If I don't run this team for Tucker until he graduates college, he will lose his legacy and part of his inheritance, and my players will lose their jobs. Was it a manipulation tactic on my father's part? Abso-fucking-lutely. I'm always going to pick Tucker over myself, and he must have known that. I guess what I'm saying is if you're in this for good, you're going to be tied down here."

Cal doesn't think twice about what I just said. He doesn't rear back his head or make a face. He simply kisses me. "I love you." He says against my lips. "The way you put Tuck above yourself and everything else. He's very fortunate to have you as his mom."

"Yeah, well, his mom is stressed out about her son's favorite player leaving the team. I just don't know how I'm going to break the news to the poor kid that 'Callan Miles, the best center in hockey,' is retiring. Whatever will I do? You're going to break my son's little heart." I giggle as Cal tickles my side. "But in all seriousness, is there any way I can convince you not to retire? Maybe stay on the team another year . . . or two?"

"Yep." He answers too quickly.

My head jerks back. Wow, that was entirely too easy. I thought he might groan or say no.

"Blowjobs. Lots and lots of blowjobs," he deadpans.

I snort out the most unattractive laugh and smack his chest. "I'm serious."

He falls back on the bed, taking me with him, then rolls us over. "How about I agree to your terms if you agree to mine?" He runs his nose along my jaw, then whispers in my ear. "Move in with me, Angel."

A slow smile spreads across my face. "This is extortion."

He kisses his way down my stomach. "Please." He pops the button of my jeans. "Please, move in with me. Be a good girl, say yes, and I'll sign for two more years." He stands and slides my jeans down my legs.

I think he just unlocked a new kink because I'm loving a begging Callan Miles. He lifts me up and then removes my shirt. I watch as he folds the fabric. He places the makeshift blindfold over my eyes and ties it behind my head, then lays me back down.

"You drive a tough bargain, Mr. Miles," I breathe. A delicious sensation washes over me when he gently blows a trail of light air up one leg and down the other. His breath mixed with sensory deprivation is driving me insane. I'm writhing underneath him.

"You don't want to let your team down or leave your boss in a bind scrambling for a new player, do you?" I moan out as he tastes me.

He chuckles low under his breath as he moves up my body. "You brat. Your heels are pressing into the mattress, sweetheart. Your pussy is throbbing and begging to be filled. All you have to do is say one little word containing three little letters, Aspen, and I'll give this tight little pussy something to take that ache away. I'll make you cum so hard and leave you so delirious, people will think you're speaking in tongues for the next week. Say yes. Then and only then will I sign your two-year extension."

He rubs the head of his cock along my entrance, teasing me, "Please, Angel. Please. Just say yes." He pushes his length inside me in slow, tantalizing strokes. I'm tired of being afraid. It's time I took a real chance at something incredible. Something life-changing that we have decided on together.

Cal has stepped up time and time again. I want this. More than anything, I want him. There's no more room for hesitation. "Yes, I'll move in with you."

His fingertips lightly trail over my ribcage, the side of my breast, and my collarbone, leaving a trail of goosebumps along my skin. His featherlike touch slides up my neck in slow, sensual movements until he's lifting the fabric from my eyes and tossing it onto the floor.

There's so much vulnerability in his gaze that it makes my chest physically ache. "You mean that?"

"Yes," I whisper against his lips. "I love you. I want to spend my life with you. Of course, we'll move in with you." My arms wrap around him, and I cling to him like a lifeline. We take our time making love, worshiping, and unraveling each other well into the early morning hours.

Chapter Thirty Two

Cal

FOUR MONTHS LATER

Carter spots River walking out the back door with a casserole dish in her hand. Jumping up from the patio chair, he walks over to her eagerly. "Here, let me take that for you. You need anything else?"

I snort and grab a beer, popping the top. I hand it to Aspen before grabbing another one for myself.

"Dude's laying it on thick, isn't he?" Aspen mutters in that sexy-as-hell southern drawl. "By the way, you still owe me one hundred smackeroonies."

I bark out a laugh. "Smackeroonies? I'll give you some smackeroonies." Trailing my hand up her ribcage, I lean in and speak low into her ear, "Listen, Angel. I have much better ways in mind to pay you back for that little bet, and none of them involve money." I peck her lips, keeping it PG in front of our company. Her laughter trails after me as I stroll to the lounger by the pool.

If you had told me a year ago that I would be back here, in this very spot with the love of my life . . . well, I would've probably grunted and told you to fuck right off. It's crazy how life changes in the blink of an eye.

I've always thought of life as a road with a million different turns along the way. Every single decision made is a turn in the road, which is met with obstacles and more decisions. Part of me also believes in events so random and so incredibly coincidental that they couldn't possibly be anything other than fate. Sometimes, I wonder if Puck wouldn't have been in the middle of the road that day, and if I hadn't run into the back of Aspen's car, if we'd be where we are right now.

I believe every single occurrence in my life led me to this stunning woman. I would walk through the fiery depths of hell, suffer through every single heartbreak, and endure the trials and tribulations in my life one hundred times over if it led me to her. She brought me to the surface when I was drowning in grief.

We've been through four months of counseling, and though we've worked through so many of our individual traumas, we still have a way to go. Through the process, our relationship has grown so much stronger. Aspen and her therapist have been going through the journals her father left behind, and together they've been working through her abandonment. As for me, I'm learning how to communicate instead of shutting down. I'm also learning that no matter what I do, I can't control everything around me. Now, that was a hard lesson to learn.

Carter saunters up beside me. "How's the foundation coming along?"

Pulling off my ball cap, I run my fingers through my hair and slip it on backwards as I sit down in the lounger. "Man, it's fucking great." A genuine smile spreads across my face. "Aspen's made a lot of connections these past couple of months, and now everything is moving in the right direction."

In honor of Paisley and Xander, Aspen and I are building a foundation that will have free on-call grief counselors, a 24-hour crisis hotline, and support groups to assist all family members with neonatal loss. We're also working to bring awareness to postpartum psychosis, which is a rare condition outside of postpartum depression. I've been attending support groups, and I've found talking about my trauma is actually helping me heal. Healing means therapy, therapy means talking and talking means reliving those memories. One of the things I've learned this year is sometimes, you just have to face your demons. It's going to take time, but we're healing.

"I never thought I would see the day," Carter says, tipping back his bottle of beer."

"See what day?"

"The day you wouldn't be a broody asshole. You're actually smiling. You seem so happy. I figured you'd be moping for months after our loss in the playoffs . . . to Boston no less. Fuck, that hurt."

I chuckle, crossing my legs at the ankle. "Yeah, well, Sean Mac is a beast. Plus, there's more to life than hockey, you know? Even though we lost, I still feel like I've won," I say as I watch Aspen pick up the basketball that's rolled by her foot and toss it back to Tucker. "So, you think he'll fit in with the team?" I ask.

"Who? Sean Mac? Oh, hell yeah. I think we'll jive. I mean, his image could use some work, but he's a pretty good guy underneath all that superficial bullshit."

Plopping down into the chair beside mine, Carter leans back with a grin on his face as he watches River bend over to grab a beer out of the cooler.

"What the fuck are you grinning about?" I chuckle and shake my head. "If chasing River were a career, you'd make more money than you do in hockey." I remember him saying some very similar words about avoidance at my barbecue last year.

"Mark my words, bro. One day, I'm going to make that girl my bride." He tips his bottle toward me, then takes a pull from it.

"I'm not making any more bets as far as your ass is concerned." I learned my lesson on that; though I haven't paid up yet, I do intend to. I look over at my woman, catching her staring at me. *Oh, do I intend to.*

Aspen saunters over with River trailing behind her. I pull her down onto my lap. "Did you just see who my mom walked in with?" she asks.

I crane my neck trying to catch a glance. "No. Who?"

"Luke," River responds. "She's got that glow too. Her entire face is so expressive. Look, she's beaming."

Leaning over, Aspen drops a quick kiss on my lips. "I'm just glad to see her eyes shine like that," she says.

Carter laughs, "That's what sex will do for you."

Aspen's eyes nearly bug out of her head, and she visibly shakes. "Ewe. Gross. Shut up, Carter!"

"Never thought I would agree with this one." River thumbs toward Carter, "But . . . he ain't wrong, sis."

Aspen stands. "Okaaay . . . and on that note, I'm going to go say hi to the little harlot."

The late evening sun beats down on us, causing sweat to drip down my temple. Carter stands and makes his way over to the pool. I toss my phone onto the table, then sneak up behind Carter. I bend to push him in, but at the last moment, the bastard grabs me by the leg, pulling me in with him. We both fall into the cold water, laughing and splashing each other. A year ago, I would have never attempted such an act. Too caught up in my grief to have a playful bone in my body, you would have found me in a lounger brooding and mad at the world.

"Have you spoken to her about it yet?" Carter asks over the beat of the music playing in the background. His arms and legs move back and forth as he treads to keep his head above water.

I swim to the side of the pool, lifting myself out. "Nope."

"What do you think she'll say?" Carter asks, as he pulls himself out of the pool.

I peel off my shirt. Grabbing two towels from the lounger next to the pool, I toss one to Carter. "Eh, I think we're both on the same page."

His head turns, and I catch his line of sight. He looks at River with the same longing I once felt for Aspen.

Tucker bounces the basketball on the new court we've built, the sound echoing throughout the yard as he and some of the kids from the neighborhood play. I cast a glance around me, relishing in the life we're building—the found family we've created. One year later, we've come full circle.

It's well into the night when our last guest leaves. I've put everything away and cleaned up the outdoor kitchen while Aspen put Tuck to bed. I'm just about to make my way into the house when Aspen steps out onto the patio carrying an old quilt. She kisses me, lightly scratching her nails across my stomach as she saunters past, making her way onto the grass. She whips the quilt in the night air, allowing the gentle breeze to straighten it out as it falls to the ground.

"I'll be right back," I call out to her as I walk back to the house.

Running upstairs, I peek in on Tuck, finding him asleep in his room. I pad back down the stairs to the kitchen, stopping to grab a few things along the way before making my way back outside.

"Come." She pats the place next to her and lies on her back, but I make no move to sit. I just want to take in the view of this gorgeous woman for a few minutes. This is the way I found her a year ago, another turning point in our love story. Her black hair is laid out all around her on the blanket, in wild and messy waves. The baby blue sundress rides up her thigh, showing off her glowing, tanned skin as she looks up into the night sky.

I finally take a few steps into the yard. "You know . . . I was thinking."

Her head turns on the blanket to look up at me. A smile blooms across her pretty face. She giggles, "What kind of wild idea do you have up your sleeve this time? All week you've been feeding me with all your crazy plans. I have to say my favorite was . . ." She becomes distracted by the wine bottle in my hand. "Ooh, you brought the goods," she muses as I saunter closer to her.

Kneeling, I set the two glasses and the bottle of wine down on the blanket. "I was thinking . . . I want to wear yours and Tuck's last name on my jersey this season."

Aspen sits up and palms her forehead, shaking her head back and forth, laughing. "Here we go again. What is with you, Hotshot? You've been saying crazy shit all week. Why in the world would you want to wear the name *Taylor* on your jersey?"

"I don't, Angel."

Her expression is one of confusion as I reach into my pocket and pull out a diamond engagement ring. Her hand flies up to cover her beautiful, plump lips. She looks at the ring, then back at me as tears well in her eyes.

"Know why I call you Angel?" I reach over, brushing my knuckles down her soft cheek. I take her trembling left hand in mine as she shakes her head. "It's because you pulled me from the depths of hell. There I stood in front of you, a broken shell of a man, and piece by piece you mended me back together." I feel the first tear trail my cheek, then the next. I don't wipe them away because, for once, these are tears of joy, not of sadness. "I wasn't living until you breathed life back into me. I'll love you in this life, and I'll continue to love you into the next. You're my peace, my best friend, and the absolute love of my life. Will you marry me?"

"Oh my god, yes!" She cries.

"There's one more thing . . ." I say, holding her gaze. "I would like to ask Tuck if he'll allow me to adopt him . . . to become his dad."

She nods. "Yes! Yes, yes, one million times, yes." She rises up onto her knees, throwing her arms around my neck as she sobs into my shoulder. "I love you," she cries.

When she finally untangles her arms from around my neck, I slip the ring onto her finger, then gently kiss her lips.

"You know what this means, right, Hotshot?" She whispers against my lips.

"What?"

She pulls back, looking me dead in the eyes, and says, "I own you."

The End . . . well, for now.

Epilogue

River

The blinding morning sunlight pours into my apartment. I press my face further into the pillow, releasing a muffled groan. Who the hell thought it would be a good idea to live in a corner apartment surrounded by windows? Oh, yeah. That would be me. The jackhammer digging into my skull isn't helping matters at all.

My phone rings like a screeching siren. God, why do I feel so sick right now? The room spins behind my eyelids. Reaching for the irritating device, I slap the top of my nightstand until I find the menace in my grip.

"Hello?" I grumble into the phone.

"River, where the hell are you?" My mom screeches. "Aspen's been trying to call you all morning! Are you okay?"

"Yeah, Mom. I'm okay. Can you stop screaming at me? I don't feel well."

"Well, that's what you get for the stunt you pulled last night . . ." Mom yammers on. "You need to hurry your ass. It takes thirty minutes to get to the venue—"

Venue?

I crack an eye open.

This isn't my apartment.

Fuck! It's Aspen's wedding day!

I pop up, swinging my legs to the side of the bed. The room spins around me, and I have to take a deep breath to keep from getting sick. Wait! Why am I not wearing any clothes? Spotting a white T-shirt on the floor beside my foot, I bend down and pluck it off the ground.

"If you don't stop moving the bed, Kitten, I'm gonna be sick,"

I freeze. My head swings in the direction of that voice.

What the ever-loving hell is Carter Fucking Graham doing in my fucking bed?

Except, as I look around the room, I realize that he's not in my bed . . . I'm in his.

Fuck. My. Life.

WANT MORE?

RIVER AND CARTER'S STORY

COMING SOON !!!
2025

Acknowledgements

To my husband, Thad: You have always been my biggest cheerleader and supporter. The sacrifices you make to make my dreams come true do not go unnoticed. You pushed me through like you always do. Thank you for your input and advice (solicited and unsolicited). I'm sorry I couldn't work the scene in that you wanted. Maybe the next book . . . okay, it will definitely be in the next book. You deserve at least that. :~P

To my daughter, Kiley: Wow. What a wild ride, right? Thank you for listening to a million revisions and ideas. Thank you for brainstorming with me and staying on the phone for hours listening to me read sections (only the clean stuff, y'all). You have cheered me on and helped me stay the course. I could not have done this without you. I love you.

To my daughter, Lauren: Well, the book is done now, so . . .
I love you. XOXO. P.S. You're only allowed to read chapters 1-17; then you need to skip all the way to chapter 32.

To my son, JD: Thank you for being one of the most supportive people in my life. Thanks for listening to my crazy ideas and reading the one hundred revisions of chapters 1-8. I love you. P.S. The same applies to you that applies to your little sister.

To Brandy: Gosh, I don't even know where to begin. You are inspiring! Not only did you edit this entire book, (sorry if I missed something; it's not a reflection on Brandy's edits.) but you also helped me along the way to become a better writer. Thank you for always being there to answer my questions. Every step of the way, you've been cheering me on and giving me your feedback and honest opinions, all of which I value and greatly appreciate. Thank you for taking time out of your life to help me. You don't know how much you mean to me. I love you.

To Jacey: You have been on this wild ride since day one. Thank you so much for your input and advice. I appreciate you being my second set of eyes. You have been a huge motivation to my success. Thank you for spending the last week of edits grinding and making sure everything is in top shape. I love you.

To My Author Besties: M.J. Miles and H.B. Elliott, Thank you for your support. Thank you for pushing my content and helping me market the hell out of this book. I love you both.

To Erin Branscom: You took this little indie author behind your booth at a tradeshow and showed her the ropes. Without your advice, I wouldn't have even known where to begin. I'm happy to have found a new friend. Thank you!

To Julie: You are always the one person I know I can depend on to give me guidance and direction. Thank you so much. I value your friendship, and I love you.

To Brittany Rice/Leanne Blade: I truly think people are placed in our path for a reason. One thousand times thank you. You, my friend, are top tier, and I cannot believe that I'm lucky enough to work with you. Love you, friend.

And finally, THANK YOU! Thank you for being a part of the New York Blaze world. Thank you for taking the time to read my very first novel. I can't wait to introduce you to more Hockey Book Boyfriends that you will absolutely fall in love with!